THE AUTHOR IS DEAD

THE AUTHOR IS DEAD

A. CARVER

CONTENTS

A Map of Carver's Rest

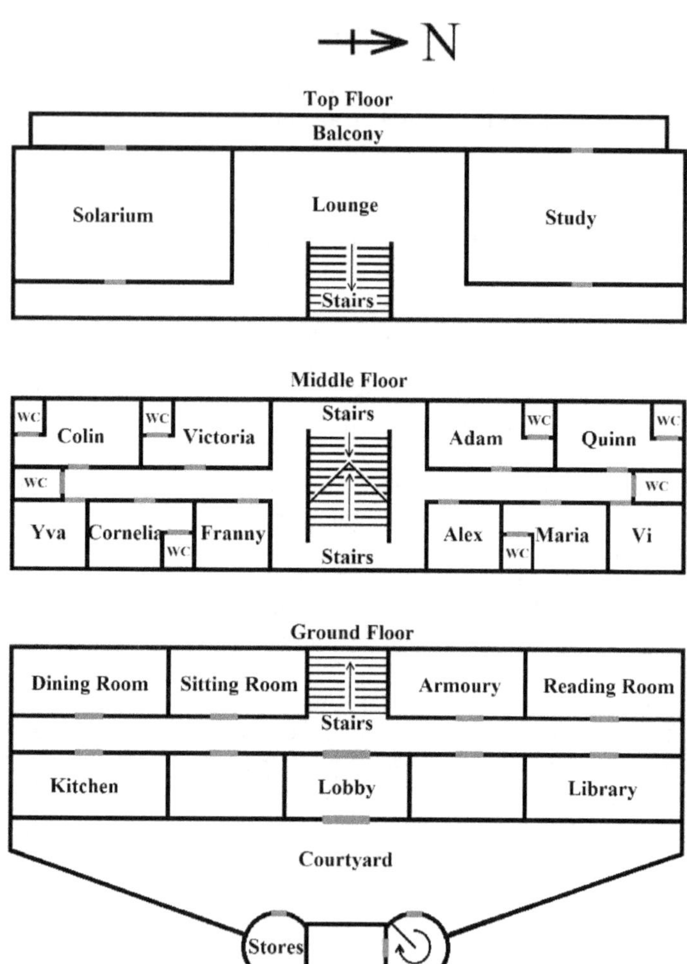

CHAPTER ONE
BETTER LATE THAN NEVER

It wasn't that she was having second thoughts about accepting the invitation. A little trepidation was natural, given the circumstances. But as the taxi crawled through benighted country lanes, sleet crawling down the windows and threatening any minute to become heaviest snow, Alex had to admit that the prospect didn't look quite so golden now as it had on a first impression.

Fretting about first impressions was an exhaustingly regular pastime for Alex Corby, one which her parents had said was just her age and later said she should have grown out of. The invitation had made a good first impression. Actual paper mail rather than e-mail – very personal, very traditional; gold edging on the envelope; an elaborate and familiar insignia embossed upon the back... The sender had stopped short of a wax seal, but it wouldn't have been out of place. But it was the prospect offered that thrilled Alex – an offline meeting of the great and good of her little corner of the Internet, from the very person whose biggest fans they were! It almost overcame Alex's conscious inferiority in that, where others were invited for their ability, or invited for their celebrity, she was invited at random, the arbitrary winner of a contest entered without any expectation of winning.

As the vehicle halted in the slush and reversed yet again in pursuit of a half-hidden turnoff, Alex resisted the urge to start biting her fingernails. Taxi etiquette forbade asking the driver if he thought they would be there soon, as it was tantamount to asking if he knew where they were, which seemed increasingly unlikely. An evening's arrival for a two-day birthday celebration at the famed Adam Carver's humble home on the remote Scottish coast promised an atmosphere of mystery and intrigue unmissable for any fan of his work – but on reflection was not the most practical proposal. Wouldn't a hotel have sufficed, she wondered, with a fancy restaurant and a function room, and, so long as she was fantasising, a steaming hot bath to soak in rather than soaking in the weather?

Though of course, if rumour was accurate, then Carver's home was no mere cottage on the cliffs, but quite a hotel in itself. Considering the man's reputation, Alex fully expected that his offer was both exciting and slightly unsettling by intention; a frisson of pleasurable fear was the finishing touch. A vast and remote country pile; great names from far and wide; meetings after dusk: Adam Carver had set his humble soirée in the unmistakeable shadow of Agatha Christie and countless other equally dead authors of sinister fare – to whom he was, of course, the living successor.

Adam Carver! He was Alex's childhood hero. Encountering his books when she was very young – too young, she once heard her parents mutter – and already more a reader than a conversationalist, she was easily hooked. The Carver formula of gothic mystery spoke to her – tales as brilliant and melodramatic as the author himself, a wild-haired figure with trademark white suit, who somehow balanced the demands of authorship with the many public appearances he charmed his way through with a perpetually ironic air. His mastery of his art and his palpable self-confidence were an inspiration, and the travails and triumphs of his heroine Sanguinaria allowed Alex to dream that there was hope even for someone as talentless and ordinary as she feared she was.

…But even she, as a fan, had to ask: What kind of man wants a birthday party like this? She was going to find out. If the taxi ever got there, of course.

Over an hour later, and over an hour late, the taxi got there. It slid to an undignified halt in what was now inarguably snow, weather which Carver could not have predicted but which would no doubt have delighted him as much as it frustrated Alex. The pale dusting on the road looked worryingly unbroken, as if nobody had driven across it all day, let alone within the hour. But the wrought-iron gates which gleamed under the headlights and the name worked elaborately into the dark metal were unmistakeable. Beyond these white-capped walls, through the pitch-blackness beyond the gates, was Alex's destination at last: Carver's Rest.

"About time!" growled the driver as he wrenched the handbrake up. He swivelled in his seat, showing Alex for only the second time a side of his head other than the stubbly back. "You paid in advance," he conceded, "so off you go. Quick as you like – I don't want to be sleeping in the car in the middle of nowhere tonight."

"Thanks," Alex said quickly, scrabbling awkwardly for the door with one hand and grabbing with the other the heavy backpack she hadn't entrusted to the boot. She was halfway out of the door and half-covered in snow before remembering one last question. "You'll be here again tomorrow, though, as agreed?" she asked, aware that it now seemed like a lot to ask.

"Yeah, yeah," muttered the driver automatically – but just as Alex was on the brink of shutting him in, he thought of a real answer, the kind of answer that strikes dread into the heart of any winter traveller. "Weather permitting."

Slush spattered Alex's shoes as the taxi skidded off into the night, leaving her quite in the dark. Carver's Rest, in addition to looking as if nobody had been there all day, looked as if it wasn't even expecting guests. There were lamps halfway up the two globe-topped gateposts, but neither was on, and the gates rattled unambiguously. There was no sign of anyone waiting nearby to escort a missing invitee. Was it possible, Alex wondered, that Adam Carver had taken out all of his guests to, say, that hotel with the fancy restaurant? No – the unmarked snow, she realised, proved that nobody else had driven or even walked down that road for at least an hour. Anyone who was on time could not have left. Could Carver, then, have chosen the occasion of his birthday to play an enormous and cruel prank on an unsuspecting fan? Alex tried not to believe this either.

Alex's had, of course, a phone in her coat pocket; but it never had any reception when she needed it, and now was one of those times. Still, it did make a working torch. If worst came to worst and there was no other way to attract attention, Alex was seriously considering climbing over the gate and begging at the front door, the alternative being to freeze and die on a lonely road at midnight. But where there is light, they say, there is hope; and on one of the gateposts was an intercom.

Alex pressed the button, and the intercom lit up. Seconds passed, and she pressed it a few more times for good measure. Snow began to seriously heap up on her hair and back. She hadn't expected to be outside. Alex considered holding her backpack overhead as an umbrella, but on reflection huddled over it instead. If her autograph-ready first editions got wet...! The intercom finally clicked into life, and a voice which could have been a woman's crackled out.

"Good grief! It's not Alex Corby at long last, is it?"

"Um, yes," Alex said – adding, inadequately, "Sorry I'm a bit late."

"*A bit...?*" the voice echoed, before saying, "Anyway, just hurry up here before you freeze! I'll open the front gate."

The intercom clicked off, and another noise stirred in the dark. Through the narrow field of light, Alex watched as the great black gates trembled in place, and then slowly drew back into the shadows, leaving only an enormous hole between the gateposts. In daylight those automated gates would have seemed nothing more than an innocent plaything of people with money to spare – but by night and dimmest light, it was more the sign of a haunted house.

Alex wondered momentarily if this was going to be a ghost story. But she was wrong. It was a detective story, of course. Led on by torchlight, Alex padded uphill through the gathering snow, and the gates drew shut behind her and locked with a clank. The mystery begins.

CHAPTER TWO
MY GIFT TO YOU

Snow drifted lazily through the phone-screen glow as Alex trudged up the drive. In the bright haze, the contours of the driveway were just about visible for now, loosely bordered by shadowy humps which might have been frozen flowerbeds and bushes, but the snow was clearly sticking and before long the road and the scrubby grass to its sides would be distinguishable only underfoot. The horizon was lost in the night, stars and moon lost in the clouds, and it was impossible to tell if Alex's destination was a few metres ahead, or a mile – for there was still not a light to be seen. It would have been considerate, Alex's increasingly jaded inner voice said, to have turned on an outside light to guide the way. She briefly considered the possibility of a power cut – for it was, after all, an isolated house in a winter storm – but no, the intercom was working. So much for that cliché. Alex smiled at herself through the cold. Carver may have been trying his best to evoke the classics with this self-indulgent celebration, but it wouldn't do to forget the boundary between fantasy and reality.

So where was Carver's Rest…?

Irritated, shivering, and acquiring an uncomfortably damp coating of snow, Alex took the liberty of pocketing her phone, plunging the area into darkness – and there was the light, too faint to compete with her torch. It was disconsolately distant, another few hundred metres by the looks of things; and outlined in a tall, curved shape, as if it was burning some way behind a window. Sluggish in the chill, Alex's brain took a moment to rationalise the picture: The light was shining through a tunnel. Apparently Carver's Rest was surrounded by some kind of wall.

Having a wall around your garden and then another wall around your house seemed like overkill. But Alex just shrugged, and took off jogging directly for the light, keen to get inside and get this trainwreck of a journey over with. The light bloomed as she approached – and yet the road seemed to stretch farther under her feet, and the light grew into a shape distorted and enormous. As she closed the gap, Alex drew slowly to a stop, and gazed upwards in awe, disbelief. The rumours were all true. Adam Carver was living the dream. Carver's Rest, his self-designed dream home, was an *actual castle.*

Adam Carver had made his fortune from building castles in the sky – or rather, by writing *Castles in the Sky*, a quartet of young adult mystery thrillers set in gothic times and within eerie castles where baffling murders occurred with probability-defying frequency. The long-awaited conclusion to the series had recently been published, to critical acclaim, astronomical sales, and (from the hardcore fans) predictable complaints that the finale wasn't a patch on the preceding volumes. And with the fortune he had made, Adam Carver had built yet another castle – a literal one.

It was no mere boundary wall between Alex and the house, but a two-storey curtain wall built from enormous blocks of stone, topped with faintly visible crenellations. Ahead of her the wall curved outwards into two hazily-defined shapes she identified as towers, forming a gatehouse standing guard over the lorry-sized tunnel passing through to the house. The light beyond the tunnel illuminated the jagged teeth of an actual metal portcullis and a pair of chains spooling out from the gatehouse to what Alex now realised was a wooden drawbridge sunk into the ground at her feet. And beneath the drawbridge – a dark chasm stretched down and arced around the walls, and from its depths whispered the echo of swirling water.

The shiver that ran through Alex's body was not from cold but awe. It was an incredible, fantastic vision – as if the words of *Castles in the Sky* had been summoned from stone. But that jaded part of her brain whispered again to her – isn't this a bit much? A bit too excessive a display of wealth, even grotesque? How on earth had he even gained planning permission?

This more practical train of thought also reminded Alex that it was still, yes, very cold and very wet and very dark. Gawking at Carver's Rest could wait until the morning, when it would actually be properly visible. She set off again, and her footsteps thudded hastily across the drawbridge and the crevasse it spanned and into the gatehouse; a welcome respite from the weather, but Alex hurried through, for the points of the portcullis menaced above and would be a rather heavier weight to bear than descending snow…

And then she was through into the courtyard, and mercifully there was proper light, furnished by a lamp hung outside the front door of Carver's Rest. The castle keep was a less authentic fusion of the medieval and the mansion, but only slightly less; a three-storey stone-built manor with gargoyle-patrolled ramparts and narrow slits for windows, and a nail-studded front door enclosed in a gothic arch. Any house was a welcome sight after coming through the snow, but Carver's Rest couldn't be called inviting as a place to live; it was more a fortress than a home, built to repel enemies rather than welcome friends. But Alex paid the gloomy surroundings little heed, with shelter, warmth, and maybe even Adam Carver in sight. She hurried past a cluster of lonely cars and up a flight of steps and was just reaching for the bell-cord, the doorbell being of course a literal one, when with a flurry of rushing snowflakes the door lurched open.

The person who met Alex at the door was not Adam Carver, who had made enough public appearances for it to be clear that he wasn't a woman. It was probably the voice on the intercom who was now dragging Alex through the open door by the shoulder and slamming it shut behind her, making sure to twist the key in the lock and throw a bolt before turning to her guest. This gave Alex time to survey her, a professional-looking woman with a large presence and constantly-moving hands; nobody Alex recognised, though that meant little.

"Fortunate for you that I suffer from insomnia," the woman said briskly. "It must have been slow going up that drive. I'm astonished you could even get your car up here."

Alex coughed slightly. "Actually, I don't have a car," she answered, glancing away. "...Or a licence."

The woman's expression softened as she visibly reassessed Alex's age. "You poor silly child," she said, and began heavy-handedly brushing snow from Alex's head and shoulders. "Have you travelled far? Try to get here on your own? Well, that's what relying on buses or trains will get you."

"Taxi," Alex corrected, stepping just out of reach. She wasn't enormously fond of being touched by random strangers. "Sorry, I didn't catch your name...?"

"Because I didn't say it, did I?" Alex's attempt at politeness slid off her. "Maria Bole, literary agent." She stuck out a hand and enfolded Alex's own in a vigorous handshake. "I've been at this game for thirty years now, and played it with Adam for half that. I negotiate contracts, go between him and his publisher when they're not happy, and stay up late for waifs and strays who everyone else has given up on."

Alex rather resented being characterised as either a waif or a stray, but it was no time to be offended; it was time to start smoothing things over. "I'm not that late, am I?" she asked, adding an artificial laugh. Maria Bole did not join in.

"Not that late…" she repeated, and shook her head. "My dear, there is being fashionably late, and there is being shockingly late. I don't care how famous you may be on the Internet, but you are nonetheless the latter. Surely you are aware that you were meant to be here a good thirteen hours ago?"

Thirteen hours ago. Alex's brain seemed to have shut down; she could not quite understand what Maria had said. Then the shame hit. "Th-thirteen?" she stammered, mortified. "The invitation said 10 at night!"

"The invitation," Maria Bole said, slowly and clearly as if she really were talking to a child, "said 10 in the *morning*."

To misread 10am as 10pm… was it possible? "No, it can't have been!" Alex bit back, and tore open her backpack. To look like a complete idiot in front of Adam Carver and everyone would be the worst-case scenario! She had brought the invitation along as proof of identity. It was somewhere between the wash bag and the change of clothes and the four *Castles in the Sky* hardbacks…

"Got it!" Alex cried, holding the buried treasure aloft. It was a little crumpled, but that was a minor concern. She struggled with the envelope and tried to ignore Maria Bole's tapping fingers. "See!" Alex exclaimed, pointing. "It says…!"

Please arrive promptly at 10am at the following address.
10am at the following address.
10am.
am.
Please arrive promptly.

The invitation had been handwritten in an overelaborate cursive style. Where the "a" and the "m" of *10am* met, there had been a curved stroke that dipped beneath the line of text. It was possible, yes, to read it as "pm". Alex hadn't even questioned it. It was Adam Carver. Of course he wanted to meet his guests at nightfall. That was the kind of man he was. And yet – now she had been told the writing said "10am," it was impossible to read otherwise!

As Alex stared, paralysed, at the treacherous invitation, Maria peered over her shoulder. "Yes, I suppose it *could* look like a 'pm,' if you squint a bit," she mused. "Careless of him. Of course, if the arrangements really were for the evening, the invitation would have said 22 o'clock. So there would be no confusion, you know."

Alex didn't hear her. It felt as if she was holding an execution notice in her hand. She felt awkward and inadequate in company at the best of times, but this proof of complete incompetence spelled the end… Maria, perhaps sensing that the error was, to the waif or stray before her, rather a big deal, switched moods again and became more conciliatory.

"Oh, cheer up. We all make mistakes, especially when we're young. And young people always think it's the end of the world," Maria chuckled nostalgically. But seeing Alex still looking mournful, she continued on this theme. "But really, it was an honest mistake. No shame in that!" she said, clapping Alex hard on the shoulder. "You know, it might even be for the best."

"How, exactly?" Alex muttered.

Maria ignored her and went on. "In fact, why don't we just keep this mix-up between ourselves?" she suggested. "You can go to bed, and in the morning we'll simply say that you were otherwise engaged and couldn't arrive until late."

Alex looked up sharply. "Really? You won't say anything about this?"

Maria smiled coyly, and put a finger to her lips. "Nothing makes people happier than a lie," she said. "Though of course, if you try to quote me on that, I'll deny it. Now, pick up that bag and I'll show you the rooms."

Maria bustled off too fast for Alex to dwell on the situation; there was barely even time for a first proper look around Carver's Rest. Unsurprisingly for the hour, it was mostly dark, with a few lamps illuminating corners of the lobby in sepia tones; but Adam Carver hadn't sacrificed comfort for his castle aesthetic, and while the room was short on windows, the floorboards were strewn with rugs and the wood-panelled walls bore intricate hangings and ornately-framed paintings, faces ashen in the night. Maria led Alex out of the creaking entryway and into an imposing hallway, vanishing into darkness off to the left and right and with a wide staircase leading upwards into further gloom. Maria made Alex feel small, but Carver's Rest made her feel like a mouse.

"There should be a spare guest room – perhaps in the north wing," Maria said, gesturing up the stairs to an unlit landing, north apparently being to the right. "Adam invited exactly enough people to fill them all. Just find the door with a key still inside, and let yourself in." Maria glanced at her watch with an absent-minded movement, and frowned deliberately. "Any questions?" she demanded.

Caught off-guard by a prompt sure to make a person's mind go blank, Alex stuttered out an "Um –"

"Good. Goodnight," Maria said abruptly, and turned and walked off. Alex blinked in surprise at her sudden departure.

"Will you still be here afterwards, or…?" Alex called pointlessly at Maria's retreating back.

"An agent's work is never done," Maria declared, not breaking her stride. "I'm sure you can take care of yourself from here." As she strode through the door to the lobby, she looked briefly at Alex over her shoulder. "Trust me," she called back. "Things will look better in the morning!"

The door banged shut behind her only just quietly enough not to be called a slam, and Alex was left adrift. The agent's overwhelming presence and sudden absence left her feeling strangely more alone than when outside in the snowstorm, and Carver's Rest in the middle of the night felt suddenly very abandoned, as if it really were the dark and empty house she had feared. She felt a little like the heroine of *Castles in the Sky* on that fateful night she went creeping through the ruined halls of Northrage Abbey… But after a few moments' adjustment, Alex was surprised to find herself actually feeling a lot better. Maybe it was thinking of her favourite books that did it, but mere moments earlier everything had seemed to be going wrong – cold, wet, late, enormously late, patronised – and yet Maria Bole had brushed it all off like the snow on Alex's head. And then she had just swept off without even giving Alex time to thank her.

But that could wait until the morning. It had been a long and stressful day, which probably explained any feelings running high. Alex's sense of embarrassment was already starting to look embarrassing in itself, a silly and childish overreaction. Disappointment – that was another matter. Alex had carelessly missed a whole day spent with Adam Carver, Maria Bole and the others, doing… whatever it was people do in company; mingling, perhaps. That was a genuine blow. But Alex could catch up tomorrow. Yes, she thought, hoisting her backpack to the top of the unnecessarily long flight of stairs, ignoring an enormous black-viewed window and a further flight of stairs above the first, and turning into the darkened north corridor. For the dead of night, things were starting to look bright.

A way down the corridor, faint light glinted on a bright metal key, the only clue to a door's presence this far into the darkness. Alex felt for the handle, twisted it, and pushed. But the door didn't budge – on either a push or a pull. Locked, then? Alex reached for the key and tried to turn it, but that too was obstructed; it clinked against the mechanism both clockwise and anticlockwise, clearly not inserted far enough into the door. But when Alex tried to push it all the way, it met an oddly soft resistance, as if something was stuffed into the keyhole on the other side. Alex took the key out and examined it, but it looked quite normal. What was going on?

This was getting ridiculous, Alex thought. She couldn't even open a door without messing it up. The thought of getting Maria to come and do it for her was dismissed instantly. The door was just stiff. The lock was just… broken, or something; no wonder nobody else had taken this room. An experimental rattle convinced Alex that the door was *meant* to push open. There was nothing else for it but to give it a good hard shove…!

Struck with Alex's full weight, the door gave way with a tearing noise – like something being ripped apart. Checking herself over, the door swinging free and banging against the adjacent wall as she did so, Alex was relieved to find that her clothes were intact. But what had torn, then? Pocketing the key, she stepped into the pitch-black room and touched the edge of the door – and recoiled. On the inside of the door was something peeling away – smooth on one side, sticky on the other. It felt for all the world like *tape*, of all things. Alex cautiously felt up and down the edge of the door, and yes, there it was – a wide strip of tape, stuck up the entire inner edge of the door, apparently even across the top and bottom, and which had been holding the door shut. Alex felt below the inner door handle, and a strip of it had been laid over and in fact *stuffed into* the lock, as well.

What *was* going on, Alex wondered again – now not just bewildered but frankly irritated. Somebody had taped the door closed and vacuum-sealed the entire room. Even the lock had been blocked from within. What kind of bizarre prank was that? After all, the only way you could accomplish it was by being inside the room…

A sudden shudder ran through Alex's frame. Of course, that was quite right – whoever had taped the door shut *had* to still be inside. Which meant that they were hiding in the dark, watching her right now! Retreating a step, Alex passed her hand across the sleek wood panelling of the left wall for a light switch, and, finding one, half-dreading what it would reveal – flipped it on.

Dim light flared in the room, and Alex faced her first encounter with true horror.

He was squatting against the far wall like a hobgoblin, legs drawn up, arms sagging between them, wrists and ankles prominently bound tight with tape. Slumped on the chest was a face Alex recognised from the back of books and the top of interviews, laughing, smiling, winking – now twisted almost beyond recognition by a thick strip of tape stretching from ear to ear and crushing the mouth, beneath terrible wide-open eyes forever frozen in disbelief. A trickle of red ran down the face like a tear, but even the hunch of the back could not hide a far larger crimson splash across his trademark white suit, at last drawing the eye to a glint of metal – a long knife, or dagger, passing between his arms and thrust deep into the chest. Balanced on his bound hands, perversely, was a rectangular parcel wrapped in gaudy paper and tied with colourful ribbon – a birthday present for a corpse.

It was Adam Carver, and he was dead.

CHAPTER THREE
THE IMPOSSIBLE ROOM

Alex fell onto the doorframe for support, legs giving way beneath her. Shock seemed to rob all sensation from her body, leaving only her eyes, full with the sight before her. Reading a few murder mysteries had been no preparation for seeing the real thing, in the flesh; there could be no preparation. Not for stumbling into a sealed room at midnight and finding the corpse of your personal hero. Every breath choked Alex as her eyes roved powerlessly over each grim detail under the low-energy light. There was no mistake. Adam Carver would never write again, never wink nor sign a book. The body moved not a twitch, the eyes did not blink, the knife was pushed so deep into the blood-soaked shirt.

It was at once a relief and a terrible effort to look away – at whatever else might lie in that room. But the room was sparsely-decorated and uncannily mundane. A low bed shrouded in patterned sheets spread flat, no space for gremlins beneath the floor-level frame; a wardrobe in the corner, doors sagging open but disclosing only a collection of wire hangers; heavy curtains open around a fixed window. Alex even risked a glance in the shadows behind the door, but there was no space between the taped-over hinges and the panelled wall for anything to be hidden in. No, there were no other ghastly shocks waiting; they had no gap or crevice in which to hide and spring. Something about this struck Alex as strangely wrong, but she was in no state to process it. Adam Carver had been murdered! In his own home! That unimaginable reality was all-consuming.

Alex had let her backpack slip to the floor. She made no effort to recover it. Somebody had to be told about this – the police called – some defence found rather than remain alone while a killer was on the hunt…!

Alex lurched away from the door, leaving it wide open, lights on, backpack in the doorway. The bag wasn't important; the books inside would never be autographed. What was important was the phone Alex was once again scrambling for, hands shaking – but she despaired anew at its zero bars of reception. Alex cursed the phone and cursed the obscurity of Carver's Rest before realising that its very remoteness surely meant it had a landline. Another reason to find another human being who knew the layout. But where was anyone to be found? Could Alex just bang on one of the other bedrooms revealed in the doorway's light until someone woke up? Slow, too slow – and besides, who knew what might be hiding in those rooms. For all she knew, the murderer might be there – or everyone might be dead in their own taped-shut tomb!

But one person was definitely alive; the one person who was still up and awake and whom she had actually met. Maria was downstairs. She had helped Alex already – and Alex had never been more in need of help. She hurried to the stairs, clutching the banister with still-weak arms, stumbled downwards…

"Maria?" called Alex, reaching the foot of the stairs, searching every dark direction. The door to the lobby remained shut, but when she pushed it open and ran in, the soft light rested on no Maria and no-one, just portraits. She retreated to the cavernous hallway, and more closed doors led off in various unknown directions. Which to choose? Which didn't threaten to reveal something worse? "Maria!" Alex called again, louder and more desperate. "I need help!"

"Excuse me?"

Alex almost didn't hear the timid voice, half-fading into the background like a squeaking floorboard. She looked back into the hallway and managed to locate the speaker at the top of the stairs, just outside the south wing; a boy with a nervous expression on his wide face, perhaps a little older than Alex, one pudgy hand clutching a mug while the other held a soft dressing gown tight.

"I was thirsty, so…" the boy attempted, trailing off as he gestured vaguely with his mug. "Is there anything I can…?" he tried again, looking uncertainly at Alex.

It may not have been the capable Maria Bole, but Alex was inordinately relieved to meet someone of similar age and even shyer temperament than herself. "Yes!" she answered, and hurried back up the stairs, feeling a little steadier. "You've got to help me," she said urgently. "Something terrible has happened. I have to call the police!"

The boy's eyes magnified. "Really? Wait, um, wait." He blinked rapidly, and his mouth searched for a shape. "What's happened?"

"It's –" Alex glanced back towards the room, a rectangle of light falling across the corridor where the door stood wide open, and wondered how much to tell him. Was it better if more people knew exactly what had happened? Or fewer? She didn't want to take a risk. "It looks like someone's committed a crime," Alex compromised. "Mr. Carver has been attacked."

"*Really?*" the boy repeated, and craned his neck to look over her shoulder. "Shouldn't we call an ambulance? Or – or try to administer first aid?"

This was getting frustrating now, Alex thought; what did it take to report a murder around here? Maybe *actually* reporting that murder instead of tip-toeing around it would be best. And then this boy, who must have been there all day with the rest of Carver's guests, would know where to find the phone, would have an idea of who to talk to at a time like this – would know what to *do*…

"Look, just – just come and see for yourself," Alex grimaced, seizing the boy by a plush-sleeved arm and pulling him towards the north wing. A few steps into the darkness and they were there already. "Prepare yourself," Alex warned him, and gestured into the doorway.

He stood on the very edge of the illuminated floor, and peered around the doorframe. He seemed to stare into the room for a long time before turning back to Alex.

"Prepare myself for, um, what?" he asked.

"*For what?*" she hissed, and stepped around him. "For –"

The rebuke died in Alex's throat as the brightly-lit room drew into view.

There was the bed in the corner, sheets smooth; the wardrobe standing open, hangers still; the window that looked out onto darkness.

There was no body in the room.

"How –" whispered Alex, stepping automatically into the room – and almost tripping over her backpack, lying in the doorway where it had been left. Alex grabbed for the door's edge to steady herself, and there was something wrong there, too; or rather, there was something no longer wrong. Alex pulled at the door and looked over the inside surface. There was no tape at all. Not even a mark from where it had been…

"I don't understand," Alex muttered, and walked unsteadily over to the spot where the corpse had been. There was no impression on the floor; no spots of blood or anything. "It was right here." She suddenly became aware of the boy hovering by the door. "It was right here!" she cried at him, pointing urgently to the unmarked carpet.

"If you say so?" His eyes darted from Alex to the corridor and back. "But, well, it doesn't look like I'm needed here, so I'll just..."

Alex didn't really hear him. There was too much else going on, too many extreme images and ideas cascading through her brain – a savage murder, a killer in the dark, inexplicable situations, confusion, terror, exhaustion – all whirling together in a roiling mixture that surged upwards from her stomach. Alex stumbled over to the boy as he tried to slip away. "Please – a bathroom –"

He took one straight look at Alex's unhealthy pallor, and with surprising efficiency swept the latecomer down to the far end of the dark corridor and into a door which Alex wouldn't otherwise have known was there. Alex had little time to appreciate the antique vibe of stone and porcelain on the way to the sink, as she was too busy being quite sick.

When the worst was over, and Alex felt up to looking in the mirror again, the boy was just about visible in the reflection; standing half over the threshold, looking respectfully away. "Thanks," she mumbled at him.

He mumbled some platitude or other in return, before adding, unnecessarily, "Are you... unwell?" Clearly understanding the absurdity of the question as spoken, he recanted instantly. "I see. So, that's why you were late..."

Alex suspected he was using "unwell" to mean "drunk," and despised how plausible an interpretation it was – but that wasn't his fault. She glanced back at him, and he gave a smile as hesitant as his words. "You're Miss – I mean, Alex Corby, aren't you?" he said. "There was a list, you see, of people who were meant to be here, and you were the only one who wasn't, so... Anyway. I'm Colin. Colin West." He went for a handshake, but his hand was still holding his mug and he only ended up slopping water onto the floor.

As Colin abandoned her to snatch up a towel and mop up, Alex sighed and attempted to rise from the sink. Greeting her in the mirror was a wearied and sickly reflection with a thousand-yard stare. Adam Carver's corpse still flickered in the back of her eyes, refusing to be forgotten. And yet there was no proof that it had ever been there at all.

Which meant that either Alex was completely insane, or that something extremely, malevolently clever was being arranged behind her back...

"Colin," Alex said, her voice ragged as she turned towards him. "I saw something in that room."

"It's been a long day, for all of us," Colin said, scrubbing away and not meeting Alex's eyes. "You're probably very tired. Maybe you just –" He gestured abstractly with a loose hand. "– thought, that you saw something? A trick of the light, or, or you were half-asleep..."

Alex stood by his side, and waited for him to notice her there. It took for him to have hung the towel back up before he did, and he leaned away like a wind-bent tree from Alex's gaze.

"I wish," Alex said. She forced him to lock eyes and take seriously what she had to say. "I really wish that you were right. But something terrible has happened – something terrible is still happening right now." Alex paused, shaking away visions of corpses in the dark, murderers in the dark. "But I'm not stupid. You don't know me. I can't prove anything and you have no reason to believe me. I don't even understand the tiniest bit of what just happened."

It was true. Alex was only just beginning to appreciate how little sense the events of the last few minutes made. But although her attempt to try and get help had been thwarted in the most absolute way possible, there was still something else she could do. "Something is going on, Colin," Alex said. "So please – be very, very careful."

Maybe he was tougher than he looked; or maybe he was better at ending conversations than he was at continuing them. Whatever the reason, Colin West for the first time met Alex's gaze and held it. "Yes," he replied. "Yes, I will."

They parted at the top of the stairs, and Alex watched Colin wander off into the darkness. Then, it was time again to confront the room. Nothing was different on the second attempt; Alex's backpack lay in the doorway still, and the light showed a room under any other circumstances innocuous. The polished wooden furnishings and panelling reflected the light and could hide nothing.

And yet in the empty spaces terror lay. There was always something behind Alex's back, vanishing when looked for, skittering away to some corner out of sight or creeping through her peripheral vision. It was all Alex could do not to remain flattened against the wall even when unpacking the few things she needed for the night – and the spot where Adam Carver's body had rested drew the eye irresistibly.

And all the time, Alex was thinking; stranded in a maze of confusion.

It was just common sense to check the entire room over for hiding-places, or even secret passages; checking for space to squeeze to one side of the bed or behind the wardrobe, pressing against every inch of the window frame, even tapping against the panelled walls for hollow spaces. There was nothing and nowhere. The room had no hiding-places. When Alex had opened that door for the first time and looked around, there was nowhere the killer could have concealed themselves within its four walls which she could not have seen.

That was simple fact, but another simple fact opposed it: The tape on the door. The seal had made the door and thus the room completely airtight; Alex went over her memory again and again, but there was no clue that it was in any way fake or imperfect. Even without tape, there was nary a gap around the door, with the doorframe overlapping on the outside and the carpet pressed against the bottom; nobody could have interfered with the tape from outside the room, and it could only have been attached from the inside. As a lock, the tape itself was overkill. All it did was prove that the killer couldn't have left the room – and yet, they must have!

And that was what really made Alex shudder; life, and death, were now imitating Carver's art. This impossible room – it was just like the books. *Castles in the Sky*'s claim to fame was its parade of ever more unfathomable locked-room mysteries: Murders where the killer had escaped from a room that was locked from the inside. They were good mysteries, too, leaving fans so thirsty for more that some had gone digging through old books from up to a hundred years ago – though all dutifully agreed that Carver's were the best. Even Alex had read a few, albeit only by authors who were still alive.

But this taped room was a locked-room nightmare with no escape, wholly insurmountable through any solution or gimmick Alex had encountered. There was nowhere to hide in the room. There was no way to leave the room. And yet the killer must have done one or the other; for when the door was opened, they were not there. There was only the murdered corpse of Adam Carver, grimly posed.

And then that, too, had vanished – spiriting away with it the tape that had held the door so securely. It hadn't even left a mark. Alex tried to measure how soon after leaving the room she had returned with Colin West; a minute, if that? Was it enough to haul a grown man's corpse to an entirely different hiding place, and to rip off every inch of tape as cleanly as if it had never been there? The killer could not have spared even a second.

Sitting on the bed, Alex put her head in her hands. It was impossible, she thought; it was unreal. It was like a supernatural mystery, only the supernatural didn't exist. Alex was tempted just to dismiss it all as a hallucination, a fantasy, a figment of an overwrought imagination; but admitting that was just admitting that she was out of her mind – though she was beginning to feel that way. Sanity demanded acting as though the murder, the mystery, had never happened. Sure, she could have rushed around banging on doors and waking everyone up to tell them what had transpired, but all that would realistically happen was that Alex would look insane and an idiot. There was nothing that could be done now until the morning; no, nothing…

While letting such thoughts spin around and around in her head, Alex had been preparing for bed – not that she expected to sleep much. Oblivion would have been welcome, though Alex feared it would not come, more even than she feared the nightmares it might bring. Approaching the bed, which might have been a tombstone for all she expected to enjoy it, Alex threw back the covers.

Beneath the duvet was the birthday present.

It was just as she remembered. Tall, rectangular, wrapped in paper decorated with a colourful swirl and held tight with narrow, bright red ribbon.

It had all been real!

The sensible thing to do, a voice spoke quietly in Alex's mind, would be to leave it right there for the police to take care of. There would be fingerprints – DNA… But Alex had never been able to resist a birthday present; and on the brink of a mystery more terrible than any she had ever read, Alex *definitely* couldn't resist a clue. With trembling fingers, she untied the knotted ribbon; unfolded the delicately-creased paper…

From the debris emerged a book; hardcover, dustjacket shiny, pages so crisply pressed they had clearly barely been opened. Moreover, it was a book Alex knew well. How could she not? An almost identical copy lay buried in her bag at that very moment. *Death in the Walls*, the cover read – and beneath it, in letters which would gradually increase in size over the course of the quartet, was a name: ADAM CARVER.

They were being mocked. Celebrating Carver's birthday and death with a copy of his own book! Scarcely believing the sight, Alex tentatively cracked it open, intent on flipping through the pages – only to halt at the very first hurdle. The title page had been vandalised. Like Alex's own edition, it bore the legend *Castles in the Sky* above the book's title, *Death in the Walls*, and below that, Adam Carver's name – but in this edition, a neat line had been drawn across that name with the fine nib of a pen, quite destroying it. And beneath the effaced name, written in outsize, swooping letters, an elaborate signature:

The Author

Alex let the book drop to the bed. Spun around, feeling a looming presence reading over her shoulder… But there was nobody in the room. Well – there was nobody Alex could *see* in the room. But to her mind rushed anew the idea of a phantom murderer who could step through a door no matter how impenetrably it was sealed!

Cursing herself and her cowardice and all murderers, Alex grabbed her pillow and duvet with one hand and her backpack with the other and made an undignified retreat from the bedroom, not even bothering to lock the door on the way out – as if it mattered. In moments she was locked instead in the bathroom, duvet and pillow laid down against the door for an additional barricade. The glaring lightbulb was her only comfort until, hours later, exhaustion dragged her to a fitful and nightmare-chased sleep.

INTRODUCTION
by the Author

Dear Reader,

Please excuse the late appearance of my introduction. Ordinarily, I would have placed it at the beginning of the book; but I was obliged to break with convention on this occasion. I hope you will understand.

The story that lies before you is a puzzle. But it is also a game – a game played between the Author and the Reader, or between you and me. If you can identify the murderer before being given the answer, you win; if I can claim my chosen victims before you solve the mystery, I win. I assure you that the game is fair play. You will have all the clues you can ask for. Should you proceed with an open mind and the spirit of investigation, solving the puzzle and claiming victory should not be beyond you.

Let the game begin.

The Author

CHAPTER FOUR
CAST OF CHARACTERS

From dreams of laughing corpses and ghosts passing through walls Alex was jolted awake by somebody hammering on the door. The terrible centrepiece to the awful night was still fresh in her mind, but it took her a few drowsy moments to understand why there was a door looming above her and what good reason somebody could have for trying to knock it down. "Is anybody even in there?" a voice called, between bouts of impatient knocking. "You've been there for ages! My room isn't ensuite either, you know!"

Not clear on how long she had slept, but quite sure that this wasn't the devilishly subtle ploy of a murderer barred by a simple bolt, Alex unlocked the door. The boy outside stopped mid-knock and mid-glower; he was perhaps a couple of years older than her, stern-faced and with similarly staid nightwear.

"Thank you," he sighed, unconvincingly grateful. "Now, can I just –"

He paused, and his eyes slowly passed down Alex's body. Beginning to feel groggily indignant, she was just building a rebuke out of her tiredness when he spoke again. "Did you..." he asked hesitantly, as if he couldn't quite believe his own words, "sleep... in the bathroom?"

Alex looked down at her feet. Oh, *right*. Her duvet was messily piled up around them. She opened her mouth to explain, but the boy pre-empted her again.

"You know what? Never mind," he said, with a world-weary air that sounded much-practised. "Don't let me disturb you; I'll just traipse around and find another bathroom..."

He stomped off down the corridor, shaking his head. Alex gave it a moment, and tried to shake the sleep from her own head, too. It didn't work very well, but it gave her a look at herself in the mirror. Bedraggled hair, deep shadows beneath her eyes, wildly rumpled pyjamas; whether in front of a stranger or only her own reflection, it didn't feel good to start the day looking like a crazy person. Alex allowed herself a minute to groan over her lot in life, then ordered herself to get her act together. One way or another, it was going to be an important day.

A. CARVER

The facilities, while rustic in appearance, were exceptional in function; Alex offered her gratitude to the late Adam Carver for his love of comfort. Washing automatically, her mind inevitably fell back on the insoluble problem of the night before – and the more she stewed on everything that had happened, the more mad she felt; not crazy this time, but *angry*. Her favourite author had been murdered; murdered brutally, and murdered showily – his death used as the medium for some clever trick of just the sort he had specialised in, with Alex as the dupe. Using a fan to beat Adam Carver at his own game was literally adding insult to injury, and Alex for one did not intend to stand for it. Now that morning had come, Adam Carver's disappearance, and his body, could not be missed for long; everything would have to come out soon. And as the sun rose on Carver's Rest and the whole cast was assembled, she, Alex Corby, would live up to the reputation of a mystery story reader and crack the case!

Which was all very well for something to stew on in the shower, but there was one big problem: She had never actually guessed anything correctly in a mystery novel. Not in Adam Carver's novels, not in any other. She preferred to coast along and let the protagonist explain everything at the denouement. But you can't rely on that method in real life. For Adam Carver's sake, it was time to wade in, be clever, and catch the killer red-handed. So what if she wasn't as brave as the girl detectives in her favourite books? This was a mystery only she could solve. Alex swore it; swore it without any idea of how she was going to make it happen, but she swore it all the same.

Alex eventually left the bathroom washed, dressed, and feeling more refreshed than she had thought possible – but still on edge. There were so many obstacles in her way, and not just an impossible crime and a missing body. Those she set on the back burner; no matter how insurmountable they seemed, they were just cheap tricks that didn't prove anything, indeed seemed almost *designed* not to prove anything. No, her target had to be the murderer rather than the method. But even without murder on the cards, Alex knew she was a fish out of water in Carver's Rest; both the guest list and the itinerary had been a closely-guarded secret. What she needed was an ally – somebody to fill her in on the suspects and possible motives. Preferably, somebody above suspicion themselves…

At the end of the avenue-wide corridor, Alex stopped by her room for as few moments as possible, just to lock up her bag and throw the duvet and pillow back. She was relieved to find no more nasty surprises waiting for her; there, too, the horrors were receding, though they had not vanished entirely. But as she passed the crack of a bedroom window, the previously pitch-black view gave her pause. Something glowed in the grey sky, but if there was sunlight, it too was shut out by the massive curtain wall that surrounded the house and dominated much of Alex's narrow window pane. Stretched beneath the shadow of the boundary wall was the courtyard – an unbroken stretch of white, crossed by neither footprint nor tyretrack, the night's heavy snowfall having covered even her own late traces. The cars, presumably belonging to Carver and the other guests, were disguised beneath sheets of snow. The angle was wrong for Alex to see the gateway in the wall, but an illuminated arch was hazily traced on the snowy ground, letting some light through from afar. She chose to take it as a good omen. Later, she would realise it was a clue.

Alex left the room, gratefully slamming the door – and beside the stairs, somebody detached themselves from the tall banisters and approached her. Alex just about recognised the boy who had tried to get into the bathroom earlier – the man? With his hair combed severely and his pyjamas traded for a professional grey suit and even a tie, it was easy to believe he was older than she had taken him for. Alex had come dressed only as herself; and for the second time in the short morning, she felt underdressed.

"Hello again," the boy greeted Alex, even though he had never said "hello" the first time. His voice pitched a little deeper, too. "I apologise if I was a little standoffish earlier. These late nights, you know."

"I understand," she replied without understanding at all, and was about to ask just why his night had been so late when he cut her off.

"Of course, since you missed yesterday, I made sure to come back to keep an eye on you," he went on, looking down at her with an expression that aimed to be paternal and protective and actually looked just arrogant. Alex was certain he hadn't been that tall earlier, and sure enough, a glance at his feet revealed a pair of well-polished shoes with extremely thick soles. "The name's Vi Malik," he continued loudly, pronouncing it like the letter. "And you must be Alex Corby. Knowing that, I couldn't abandon one of my own."

Alex tilted her head. "One of your own… whats?"

Vi smirked with the air of one about to reveal a great secret. "You see, the two of us are already acquainted," he explained. "Because you can only be the latecomer, the contest winner Alex Corby – and I am the contest's host, the one who selected you as the winner!" He swept back his hair unnecessarily. "But I don't need thanks."

Alex's eyes widened. "You're SiegeMasterV?" she asked. "Admin of Besieging Heaven?" She'd always thought the V was a Roman numeral.

SiegeMasterV's smile flickered. "I abbreviate it to SMV these days, for branding reasons," he said, lowering his voice, but Alex wasn't listening. Their online world wasn't like social media; they didn't know each other's names or ages, and now she was trying to reconcile the image of Vi Malik – in pyjamas and in a suit – with the mental image she had formed over the years of SiegeMasterV, the administrator of the fansite she spent an embarrassing amount of time on. Founded on a free web-hosting platform shortly after the publication of *Death in the Walls*, Besieging Heaven's exhaustive archiving of news, resources, and theories on *Castles in the Sky* had made it the foremost online hub for the books, easily outpacing the lacklustre official social media – and while SiegeMasterV's early efforts had been pretty amateurish, over the years he had spent a great deal of effort, and probably money, on making the place look more professional. Conspiracy theorists posited that he had been given a paid marketing position by the publishers; but Alex had never thought there was much to that, even as the site grew flashier and his articles more grovelling. Though she *did* have second thoughts when Besieging Heaven was given the right to host a members-only contest for the opportunity to meet Adam Carver in person…

Regardless, SiegeMasterV was a big name to Alex and other *Castles in the Sky* fans, and she wasn't surprised that he'd been extended a personal invitation by Adam Carver. He had done a great deal for the author… whether officially or unofficially. Ironically, this humanised Vi Malik a little. She'd spoken to him online; why was it so hard to speak to him in real life? He was just another fan like her, after all, even if he did have connections. She was impressed by his dedication, of course – but he wasn't a great talent like Carver himself. It wasn't a real job.

"Anyway," Vi interrupted Alex's reverie, "like I said, I don't need thanks."

He could dress like it was a real job, but Alex wasn't impressed by his fishing for compliments. "I guess not," she replied. "Adam Carver told you to run the contest for the members of Besieging Heaven, and you picked the winner at random, so it's almost like you had nothing to do with it."

It came out harsher than she had intended, and Vi's face fell – and Alex remembered that, whatever he was like as a person, the community he fostered had been a huge part of her life as a fan of *Castles in the Sky*. The only other person she knew who read mysteries was an elderly great-aunt who lived a long way away, and it was a joy to find people online who shared her passion, and who had become something like friends or at least acquaintances. Mindful of this, she quickly added, "But I am really grateful to you for doing such a great job on Besieging Heaven all these years!"

Vi relaxed, clearly mollified. "I do my best," he said modestly, and gestured for her to follow him down the yawning stairway.

But as they walked together, Alex found herself sighing. "It's just a shame," she said, "that the best days of Besieging Heaven are behind us. You know, what with the series being over, and people having lost patience waiting for the last book, and forums being totally old-fashioned…"

"The glory days aren't over!" Vi growled at a quite startled Alex. "We'll colonise social media and triumph even over personal timelines and character limits! And then Besieging Heaven will be the perfect official web hub for Adam Carver's new book! I'll prove it!"

Alex gasped, almost forgetting the murder in the face of book gossip. "Wait, there's a new book?"

"Of course!" Vi answered smoothly, an effect undermined as he quietly amended, "I mean, probably." Under Alex's dubious gaze, he quickly added, "Mr. Carver hinted yesterday that there would be one! That's probably what this whole party is really about. It's a big publicity stunt."

A publicity stunt? It was an intriguing idea. Not entirely for the reasons Vi proposed, though; rather, Alex was wondering how the death of the author would affect publicity for any new book he might have written. It really depended on whether it was already finished or not…

Which thought soon brought her back to the subject at hand, as they reached the bottom of the stairs and turned south down one of the long corridors that had been so dark the night before. Alex could now make out electric lights suspended in mock-chandeliers from the arched ceilings, but they had not been switched on, and so the corridor was still gloomy, choked with grey air and floating dust. Rugs muffled the sound of footsteps; doors lined the hallway, tall and shut. Adam Carver was dead. The murderer was almost certainly still there. Would they have been able to dispose of the body overnight, or…?

"Have you seen Mr. Carver this morning?" she asked innocently. "I'm looking forward to meeting him."

Vi looked around automatically, as if expecting Carver to be lurking directly behind him. "Not yet," he said. "Maybe he gets up late." Perhaps remembering his lofty persona, he added airily, "The rigours of an author's life!"

"Or maybe he's had an accident somewhere!" Alex interjected, with not entirely feigned horror. "We should look for him!"

Vi stared at her for a moment, and then a knowing smile spread across his face. "Oh, *RedRidingBlood*," he said, using to exquisitely embarrassing effect the online name she came up with when she was twelve. "I understand you perfectly. It's natural to want to go prying around the house – and fair, too, because Adam did give the rest of us the grand tour yesterday. But…" He winked, which is never as attractive in real life as people intend. "Try not to be such a fangirl, okay?"

He walked on, leaving Alex grinding her teeth and remembering why she didn't speak to SiegeMasterV much. Always so above it all… She caught up with him as he hovered near an open doorway from which could be heard clinking cutlery.

"Mrs. Carver told us she'd have breakfast ready at eight o'clock," Vi said in a low voice, checking his expensive watch. "It's nearly quarter-past… We can tell everyone I was getting you up-to-date on what you missed yesterday."

"What did I miss yesterday?" asked Alex.

"Nothing important," Vi said, avoiding her eyes. It made her worry, that tiny deceit. "Now, follow me in and I'll introduce you."

"Wait!" Alex hissed, grabbing him by the sleeve and pulling him stumbling back. "I can't just walk in there not knowing who anyone is! It's embarrassing!"

Vi tugged his arm from her grasp. "Please don't touch my suit," he said, smoothing it. "It's my only – I mean, my best." He cleared his throat. "Fine. I'll get you up-to-date on *who* you missed, then. Now, who have you met already? Did Adam let you in personally, or was it Mrs. Carver?"

"Er, Maria Bole," Alex corrected. "His agent."

"Ah, Maria." Vi smiled familiarly. "A fine woman. Hadn't heard of Besieging Heaven, but after I'd explained we had some very interesting conversations."

"Also," Alex hurried on, "I ran into a boy called Colin West? He seemed… nice."

"I'm surprised you got two words out of him. Real life is clearly not his forté," Vi replied. "Not like online. He's one of us, too – DaVinciCorpse; chief supplier of gothy fanart. His work must have caught Mr. Carver's attention."

"That was DaVinciCorpse?" Alex asked, picturing the nervous, awkward Colin West, and comparing him to the fanartist she knew, with a passion for lecturing people about artistic integrity. "I guess I was imagining someone more… intense. Or maybe with like an anime t-shirt." DaVinciCorpse's skill was unquestioned, but his style was notoriously derivative.

Vi chuckled at her portrait of the fandom's second-favourite artist. "Still, I can understand DVC's embarrassment – with the real illustrator here," he declared.

Alex's breath caught in her throat. "No way." He never came out!

"Oh, yes way," Vi smirked, "and he's everything we imagined. A man of few words, though he shared a few with me." He beckoned to Alex. "Just take a peek; he's the only man in the room – DVC excepted." They peered around the doorframe, trying not to be seen. The room was a wide one, the walls littered with sideboards and cabinets and a vast stretch of window with a curiously blank view, and dominating the centre was a kind of medieval feast, dishes and platters stacked upon a long table where high-backed chairs half-hid a yawning Colin West and four less familiar diners. Something was strange about the scene, but Alex couldn't say quite what; it might just have been sudden nerves at realising she was the youngest in the house, or it might have been that she was focussing on the man sitting facing the door, brooding superlatively with a rough-shaven head and a prominent and furrowed brow, wearing clothes which looked like they'd survived a knife attack. "That's Quinn Shillerdyce," Vi whispered.

Alex's wide eyes took in the striking profile of the illustrator. The man who had so richly furnished *Castles in the Sky* with his portrait-style art and characteristic oil-painting covers was reputed to be some sort of maverick who'd been thrown out of art school and given his big break by Carver's series, though how much of this was rumour and exaggeration nobody knew. Shillerdyce seemed to cultivate this air of mystery, or at least did little to dispel it; he apparently disliked being photographed or making public appearances, and famously released only self-portrait illustrations so stylised as to be unreadable. This was Alex's first glimpse of his real face. She was satisfied with the reality; Quinn Shillerdyce looked like her idea of an artist, the same way Adam Carver looked like her idea of an author.

Alex and Vi retreated a few steps from the door to continue discussing the other guests behind their backs. "Alright, so who are the other three at the table?" Alex asked, gesturing towards the room. "There was a woman I couldn't see very well, but she's the only one old enough to be the Mrs. Carver you mentioned."

"Right, Victoria," Vi nodded, referring to a head and a pair of hands briefly glimpsed at the head of the table. "I haven't spoken to her enough; I don't know much about her. She mentions the city a lot, so maybe she used to live or work there – and she's great at handling guests." He gazed wistfully towards the doorway. "It must be very lonely for her up here, so far from civilisation."

"Stay with me, SMV," Alex deadpanned, waving slowly in front of his eyes. "There are two other girls in there. If DaVinciCorpse is here, I'm guessing so is BardOfDeathY?"

"Yes, of course – quite right." Vi cleared his throat. "Our friend BardOfDeathY – real name Yva Dysart, pronounced with a 'why' – is the one sitting nearest Colin, with the serious features." There had indeed been such a person, a girl near Alex's age, her expression curiously blank. Her notoriety on Besieging Heaven stemmed from a parallel trade to that of DaVinciCorpse: Fanfiction to his fanart, additional stories and spin-offs for *Castles in the Sky* which were often as lengthy and convoluted as the real thing. Alex had waded through a few; they were ingenious in their trickery, but had a joyless, clinical attitude to the characters, and indeed to humanity in general – an attitude which often extended to the writer's approach to her peers. Alex, or rather RedRidingBlood, had been given a text-lashing by BardOfDeathY for no greater a crime than nicknaming her "Deathy".

Vi caught Alex's intimidated expression. "She's much more easy-going when she's not talking about her fanfiction," he murmured. "Tread carefully, though. Just occasionally you'll catch her like a knife, and you won't see it coming..." He shrugged. "Weird kid. Brilliant, though."

Alex nodded her agreement. "So, who's last?" she asked, with a glance back towards the room.

"That just leaves Franny Smythe," Vi concluded. "Better known as the creator of *Humble Mom Reviews*."

Alex frowned. The *Humble Mom Reviews* blog was a high-profile supporter of *Castles in the Sky*, and was always first to land a review copy, sometimes months before publication – which mutually did wonders for its site traffic and advertising revenue. That wasn't her issue, though. "Are we talking about the same person?" she asked, picturing the skinny young woman she had assumed was a student, with heavy-rimmed glasses and lurid hair and a phone she continually frowned at. "She doesn't look old enough to be anyone's mother."

"Oh, she's not," Vi clarified. "That's just her persona. Franny realised that her book blog would get higher circulation if she pitched it at the middle-aged housewife demographic, and she was quite right. It was very clever marketing."

Alex eyed Vi critically. His face betrayed not a hint of disapproval. "Getting on well?" she asked, sardonically.

"Very," Vi nodded enthusiastically. "We've sketched out a few cross-promotion plans, synergy with Besieging Heaven could –"

"I'll take your word for it," Alex cut him off before he could get going. "And that just leaves Adam Carver... oh, and Maria Bole; maybe she's busy again. Is that it?"

"One last guest," Vi answered, and a knowing smile flashed across his face once again. "But surely you've already guessed."

Alex had not, in fact, already guessed, and stalled with an, "If you say so...?" She had no idea why Vi was playing around, but nonetheless, she bit her lip and tried to think. If he thought the last guest was easily guessable, then obviously it was somebody obvious – somebody comparable to the status of the previous guests. They fell more or less into two categories: Professionals, and big-name fans. Alex tried to think of other professionals linked to his series, but no names sprang to mind. An editor, perhaps? No, Carver had given an interview once in which he'd boasted about not letting editors compromise his creative vision – and then when the final book had taken twice as long as the rest, everyone wondered if his publisher had frozen him out. Agent, illustrator, reviewer – that really just left the fans. Discounting herself, a mere competition winner, was there anyone comparable to a fansite admin, a fanfiction writer, and a fanartist – or linked to all three...?

"Got it!" exclaimed Alex, snapping her fingers without great effect. "You and Deathy and DVC weren't invited at random, were you? You're here because of *The Fourth Wall Crumbles*! Which means..."

The Fourth Wall Crumbles – a notorious work of fanfiction, hosted on SiegeMasterV's Besieging Heaven, written by BardOfDeathY, and illustrated by DaVinciCorpse. The story, a fandom-originated take on what the final book in the series might look like, had been wildly popular in the long absence of the real thing – and still was, in fact, for the real thing had ended up being very different to what the fans had imagined. But as much as it owed to Vi, Yva, and Colin, there was one more person without whom it could never have been written – Besieging Heaven's resident genius.

"Took you long enough," Vi sniffed, bemused. "I assumed that you knew... Corvus Crown, our great detective, is the last guest at Carver's Rest."

"How would I know? But who cares, this is great!" And it really was, because it meant she would not have to detect alone. Corvus Crown, the theory-spinner who cracked every problem with zero effort... Alex respected their mystery-solving genius almost as much as the mystery-creating genius of Adam Carver – and now that Adam Carver was dead, meeting Corvus Crown at Carver's Rest was the next best thing. In the volley of amazing names, Alex had found it all too easy not to think about that impossible crime that had vanished in the night, to ask which of these people might have done it and why – but Corvus Crown would definitely be able to figure out what had happened! "Where is he? Or she?" Alex fired at Vi. "What're they like?"

"You know what? If you don't know already, I actually think I won't spoil the surprise." Vi sidestepped the question and Alex, and suavely held out his arm to usher her in. "I'm sure CC will be down later – but in the meantime, we're the late ones. Shall we dine?"

Alex had to admit that she was, in fact, quite hungry. Yesterday's travel rations had not been especially nourishing. "I suppose," she surrendered – and though she hovered hesitantly beside Vi for a few seconds, at last she let him guide her towards the breakfast room as if it were an elegant dinner party and she was wearing a fancy dress. This is probably really sexist, she thought – but it was hard to mind Vi doing all the schmoozing for her, since he clearly relished it and she really didn't. With his help, she would slip into the crowd like a knife into butter or a spoon into jam, both of which she rather hoped would be provided – and as the group dined and mingled, she could keep asking questions.

At which point she was suddenly struck by the question she ought to have asked all along. Why was it so quiet? For all the clink of cutlery in the dining room, nobody was speaking a word.

Chapter Five
Above an Abyss

"May I present Alex Corby – or 'RedRidingBlood' to her friends," Vi announced, sweeping her into the dining room. The diners paused in their vigil-like breakfasting to greet the two of them with varying degrees of enthusiasm.

"Nice to meet you all!" Alex waved, gritting her teeth in a forced smile. It was all very well being RedRidingBlood to her friends *online*, but real life was a different matter... But Victoria was sweeping out of her seat to welcome Alex, who got her first proper look at the author's wife; a tall and heavy-set woman with a patterned shawl around her neck, rings on her fingers, and a bored expression she had dropped in an instant.

"Vi, dear, thank you for taking care of Alex for us," she said, flashing a dazzling smile at a suddenly silent Vi. "And Alex, I'm charmed to meet you at last. Welcome to Carver's Rest." Before Alex had time to resist, Victoria had drawn her away from Vi and into a hug she had no idea what to do with. "So sorry I couldn't greet you myself," she said, when they finally parted. "Adam and I had assumed you weren't coming, but Colin mentioned a little earlier that you'd arrived while we were all in bed."

Alex glanced over at Colin, who was staring fixedly at the table, and wondered what else he had mentioned. "I'm so sorry I was late," she apologised, trying not to do so too profusely. "I'm sure Maria told you, I was unavoidably detained – and then the weather..." she improvised.

"Maria hasn't told me anything – she must be sleeping in, after her own late night," Victoria shrugged, waving Alex's apologies away. "Of course, Adam is always up late, in both senses – but I can be master of ceremonies just as well as him. Take a seat, Alex. If anything has gone cold, I can take it over to the kitchen and warm it up for you."

"Come sit here, RRB," declared Yva, failing to ingratiate herself but patting a seat between herself and Colin so insistently that it was quite impossible to refuse.

In no hurry to inform Victoria Carver of her husband's bizarre and unprovable murder, Alex yielded to Yva's demand, circling around the repast laid out on the table – racks of golden toast accompanied by every spread imaginable, cereals of every conceivable flavour, stacks of bacon, piles of sausages, eggs both fried and scrambled, croissants, pancakes, waffles, blueberry muffins, various other foodstuffs that people pretend can be breakfast when they're really dessert, a few neglected grapefruit... Even half-eaten by the early birds, it was a generous offering for ten. Alex didn't even try to resist. Breakfast is the most important meal of the day, after all, and weren't many of the best detectives big eaters? Alex slotted herself in and began stockpiling the world's reserves of toast.

"Morning, Colin; morning, D – I mean, B – I mean, Y... um, good morning," Alex greeted the pair flanking her. They had all spoken online, but she wasn't close to either of them and it felt strange and awkward to meet them in real life, especially when one of them had no name she could either pronounce or say in public.

"It's pronounced 'Yva,'" Yva supplied breezily. Colin merely smiled and nodded through a bite of muffin which was largely ending up on his woollen jumper.

"It's fantastic to finally be here," Alex declared, spreading jam with a fury. If she could get a conversation going, perhaps everyone would start revealing crucial information of their own accord – or at least, that seemed to be how some fictional detectives did it. "Though of course," she gabbled, "I arrived so late that I've really no idea what 'here' is really like..."

"It's a shame you missed the tour," Franny Smythe said, a few seats down. She had a sharp knife in her hand, but she was only cutting wedges of grapefruit. "Carver certainly dreamed big."

"You won't even have seen the view, but we can change that right now," Vi, across from her, chimed in. "Simply turn around."

"Sure, okay," Alex agreed, and leaned back to see what was so compelling about the empty windows that ran the length of the room – and then she was caught in the spell of the glass, so entranced she almost tipped over.

Carver's Rest was on the coast in the most literal way possible, for beyond the window was the open sea. Unobstructed by the shape of ship or island, the serrated edges of the ocean constantly in motion stretched far into the distance until they touched the lowering clouds.

Even with the grey and snowy morning sapping colour from the world, the meeting of iron and slate was sublime.

"It's quite a sight, isn't it?" Victoria Carver smiled across the table. "Adam never settles for less than he wants. I suppose it keeps the builders and stonemasons in a job."

"Amazing," was the best Alex could come up with on the spot.

Yva nodded beside her. "Yes, it's incredible what writing popular fiction can buy you," she said, and Alex's wonder cringed away. Discussing an author's profit motive was a grave violation of fan etiquette.

"You must be very proud of your husband," Colin said to Victoria, hurriedly filling the awkward silence.

Alex missed Victoria's reply, for having stood up to get a better view of the lie of the land beneath the window – her stomach lurched unsettlingly. She had expected a balcony, a walkway, perhaps a narrow strip of garden, and a winding staircase down to a private beach – but there were only black and brutal rocks and surging spray. Though it was a castle from the front, it seemed that, from the back, Carver's Rest was one of those fate-tempting modernist masterpieces that actually overhung the cliff edge, leaving only the floor of the dining room between Alex and a hundred metres of empty air...

She backed away and sat down quickly. "I didn't really see the house properly in the dark last night," she said, catching her breath. "I could hear there was a moat, but I didn't think it was the sea."

"Crazy, isn't it?" offered Franny. "Apparently, this is technically an island. The drawbridge is the only way in or out, and all other ways are practically insurmountable."

"Sounds secure," Alex nodded. So the house was even defended like a castle... The options for sneaking in uninvited seemed limited, but she had no idea if that was significant or not. "Maybe dangerously secure," she suggested. "What if there was, say, an accident up here?"

"There is a fence around the moat, if that's what you're asking," Victoria said quickly, seeming to miss Alex's point.

"Yes, you couldn't have fallen in, nobody could," Vi backed her up. "It's all for show, of course."

"But what a show!" Yva exclaimed. "A castle on an island in the middle of nowhere! It's completely unrealistic." This, Alex gathered, was high praise.

On her other side, Colin smiled tentatively at Alex as he dissected another muffin. "It's a bit like we're all characters in a classic mystery novel."

"Oh, and which classic mystery novels had both a castle *and* an island?" Yva suddenly fired at him. It was the sort of terse reply BardOfDeathY often gave online, and in real life it was horribly jeering... Colin's face reddened and his chin receded into his jumper, where he mumbled something inaudible. "Don't even think about saying *The Famous Five*," Yva continued, and Alex thought she had better change the subject.

"Are there any pictures of the seaward side of the house?" she asked – wondering if there were any architectural illusions in the building's layout, the sort of gimmick that tricked her all the time in *Castles in the Sky*. "It doesn't look like there's a good angle to see it from."

"You'll find some aerial photographs hung up in the lobby," Victoria said. She closed her eyes for a moment, as if in memory of a headache. "I insisted. Adam wants a painting, but only if it's painted from life – and only the shipping lanes have the luxury of that view. He's talking about hiring a boat, but there aren't any port towns for miles..."

"The island projects out past the adjacent cliffs, so it's quite isolated," Vi explained. "And the house is flush with the cliffs on three sides. You see it from the front, or not at all. Adam will show you when he comes down."

The clinking of cutlery and glasses was the only reply the table gave him. Alex looked around, and everyone was suddenly avoiding each other's eyes, avoiding each other's words, continuing to eat their breakfast with what now struck Alex as an unnaturally measured pace, stringing out each mouthful – doing anything, now, but talk...

It seemed as if Alex's strategy was paying off, sort of. The mood had shifted for the better when she had arrived, but now it was threatening to shift back to silence. The conversation had gone somewhere that nobody wanted it to go. And yet she could not think *why*. As far as she knew, the only person who knew that Adam Carver would never come down to breakfast was herself – herself, plus the murderer.

"Taking his time, isn't he?" Colin broke the silence at last, a faint quaver to his voice. "Adam Carver."

"And when we're all so keen to see him, too," Vi added. It seemed like a perfectly reasonable remark to Alex, but for some reason, there was no bright chorus of enthusiasm – not even from herself, though of course, she knew that they would never see him again. So what did the others know?

"I presume our host does intend to descend at some point, if only for breakfast," Franny said – adding, with worryingly little irony, "He can't simply avoid us until we leave."

"The way the roads are," Alex cut in – for all that she didn't understand the gist of the discussion, she could keep it going until she did! – "there's no guarantee that any of us will be leaving today at all. The snow was really coming down when I got here."

Yva laughed, harsh and abrupt. "A castle, an island, and now a snowbound manor?" she said. "I take it back; this really *is* a closed-circle mystery setting. There's no escape."

"Y!" Vi's severe expression was the same he had worn when Alex first met him. "Don't say ominous things in front of your hostess."

"Oh, sorry," Yva said, without missing a beat and without actually looking at Victoria.

Alex had almost forgotten that Victoria Carver and Quinn Shillerdyce, the two real adults of the party, were even still in the room; they seemed to have been trying quietly to blend into the background, just another portrait or piece of furniture. But now Victoria smiled, perhaps as falsely as Yva. "You needn't feel too sorry," she replied, with a narrow smile. "I'm sure Adam would be flattered."

"Um, well, anyway," Colin's hesitant voice came to fill the gap, "we will see Mr. Carver today, won't we?" He looked deferentially at Victoria Carver. "I mean, we still have a lot to say. Not to say that he owes us anything, but it would be, appreciated…"

Alex knew this was, of course, impossible – but so long as nobody else knew it, she had a role to play. "Why wouldn't we see him today?" she asked, provocatively. She looked around, finding, as expected, very few eyes willing to meet hers. "Beside his birthday, we're here to celebrate his work, right?" she went on. "I haven't even been introduced to him yet."

"There's no reason at all," Victoria answered stiffly. "Of course Adam will see you all today. He could be down any minute. But you must understand that I'm not privy to all of my husband's plans and surprises."

"So you're saying that Mr. Carver hasn't shown his face this morning because he's planning a surprise," Franny elaborated – and then continued, as if testing Victoria Carver, "He won't, for instance, suddenly fall ill and become unable to see anyone…"

As Victoria's eyes widened in surprise, Alex felt another piece of the jigsaw fall into place – and the picture was starting to look like a motive for murder. Something must have happened the previous day that had made the other fans extremely suspicious of Adam Carver. Because of this, they thought Carver was trying to avoid them – and were trying to extort a guarantee that he would not, or wouldn't be allowed to, so that they could confront him. And to read his intentions, they were going through the person who should know him best – his wife.

"My husband was perfectly fine the last time I saw him," Victoria emphasised; she was giving very little away. Either she was as out of the loop as Alex, or more likely, she was trying to keep up appearances.

"It's good to hear that he's perfectly fine," Colin said, addressing his remarks to nobody in particular, staring at the wall. But just as Alex was dismissing what looked like another sycophantic remark, he followed up with a remarkable shot across the bow: "We haven't seen Mr. Carver since yesterday evening, so we wouldn't know – but you would, Victoria, of course."

For just a fraction of a second, his eyes darted over to Alex – and with a jolt she realised what he was implying. Colin was clearly more perceptive than he let on. Alex herself had told him that the author had been attacked – and had then vanished from where she had left him. Colin was playing off her version of events against Victoria Carver's – for of course, assuming that all was well between the Carvers, you would expect that they would see each other as soon as they awoke. What Colin had learnt from Alex made it quite unlikely that Adam Carver was indeed perfectly fine; Victoria Carver should have seen him since then, so what was her story?

Alex leaned forward to get a clear view of Victoria's face as she answered. If Victoria Carver claimed to have seen her husband this morning, Alex was the only person who could know that that was a lie…!

Victoria Carver closed her eyes for a long moment, her brow faintly furrowed, as if in deep thought. Then, at last, she spoke.

"Why don't I go and fetch him right now?" she offered, and the taut atmosphere began to unwind. "That will satisfy everyone, won't it?" She rose from her seat, and with deliberate, unhurried grace, glided to the doorway. "I will return with my husband, and you can clear everything up between you," she said. "I will be back shortly."

And then she was gone, her shawl fluttering behind her, but Alex was still watching the space where she had been. Victoria Carver hadn't resolved her and Colin's problem. But she had resolved the stalemate. Alex found that her fingers were trembling a little around her toast; she didn't even know how long she'd been holding it, but if it hadn't been cold before, it was now. When Victoria Carver came back, whatever she told them, the situation would change dramatically.

But in the meantime… Alex hurriedly looked around at her peers. She knew many of them online. But in real life, in that room, she felt like she didn't know anything at all.

"So what's going on?" she asked, to the room at large. Quinn Shillerdyce was clearly trying to stay way out of it, arms crossed and eyes staring fiercely away from the table. That made it easier to speak as if he wasn't there at all. "Is there a problem with Mr. Carver?"

Vi spoke quickly. "It's nothing you need to worry about, RedRidingBlood."

"Well excuse me if that's not good enough!" she cried – louder than she'd meant to, but being sidelined *hurt*. These were people she had known for years, sort of. Even if their friendship was that bit more remote, separated by computer screens and many miles of space, they should all at least have been allies. Admittedly, she was keeping a secret of her own – but she wasn't parading it in front of them; when nobody would believe her, she didn't have a choice. But they had all chosen to shut her out rather than let her in. "Why do you think Adam Carver would avoid you?" she asked, looking from face to face. "Why do you think there's a mystery?"

"It's not exactly a mystery," Yva said.

"And, well, it's not as if it's just Adam Carver who's not here!" Colin burst in urgently. "Corvus Crown and Ms. Bole aren't here either. So maybe there's nothing untoward…"

"It's funny you should mention Maria Bole," Franny said.

She said it, and then said nothing immediately afterwards, so everyone's attention was drawn to her and left hanging. She savoured it as she savoured a slice of grapefruit. "Because of course," she said at last, "everything we've said about Adam Carver applies just as well to her."

A curious silence fell, and Alex watched as a myriad expressions passed over the faces of Vi, Colin, and even the distant Quinn Shillerdyce. Alex didn't understand it. It was almost as if Franny was suggesting –

"Interesting," Yva said, her bland smile dissolving into a more calculating expression. "Of course, I can vouch for Corvus Crown. I brought CC breakfast in bed myself, so there's no mystery there."

Alex's jaw dropped. That wasn't normal, right? Serving someone breakfast in bed while you were both guests at someone else's house? Alex recalled that BardOfDeathY and Corvus Crown were *friends*, but it sounded like there was more to it than that.

"When you bring up Maria Bole, though, it's a different story," Yva continued, and Alex shelved the thought. "Adam Carver and his female agent are mysteriously absent after an overnight party…" A nasty grin flashed onto her face. "What could the explanation be, I wonder?"

Because Alex's jaw had already dropped, she couldn't hope to hide a gasp. The idea was scandalous, and entirely malicious. Were Y and Humble Mom really suggesting that Adam Carver was conducting a – a *liaison*? Right under his own roof, right in front of his own guests, right in front of his own wife? It was scarcely conceivable. But what Alex found even more incredible was that it was Carver's own fans giving every impression of dragging their hero's reputation into the mud – the ones who, as she saw it, should instead be defending him.

And beyond even that – while several of them were trying to slander him, one of them had gone so far as to murder him.

What had he *done*?

"An intriguing suggestion," Vi murmured, and Alex stared at him aghast. "Most intriguing. I'm sure we can use that. But if it were true…"

"Which hardly matters," Franny remarked.

"*But if it were true*," Vi continued, emphatically – "what would happen now?"

"It would depend on Victoria Carver," Yva answered; while in thought, her face was blank as a mannequin. "I don't know."

"That's easy, though," Franny said. "Isn't it obvious she's trying to save face? I'd bet a lot she'll come back saying she couldn't find her husband at all. That will give us no choice but to accept the super special secret surprise explanation."

"But it won't disprove our version of events, either," Vi pointed out. "In fact, nothing can." A self-satisfied smile spread across his face. "This might just be our trump card."

The sound of footsteps in the corridor outside brought the discussion to a halt. They held their breath – even Alex, despite what she knew, silently trying to count how many pairs of footsteps there were.

Victoria Carver re-entered the room. She was alone.

"You'll have to excuse me," she said, and Alex wondered if this was what they had all been waiting for. She had an expression on her face that didn't quite fit – an expression of uneasy confusion… "The fact is," Victoria said, "I can't find my husband anywhere."

"*Really*," Yva said, and she couldn't help a wide, cruel smile spreading across her face. "You couldn't find him…"

"…Anywhere?" finished Franny; politely, pleasantly, utterly falsely. "What do you mean by 'anywhere'?"

Victoria gave a dazed shake of her head, hair spilling across her face. With the tall doorframe yawning above her, standing before the long table like the heroine Sanguinaria facing the court of the Obscurati, she looked suddenly tired and small. "He's not in his study," she explained. "He's not in his room or ensuite, either. I don't understand…"

A triumphant glance flashed between Franny, Yva, and Vi. "Would it help if we " Franny began – but was stopped by a sudden glare from Vi.

"I'm sure he'll turn up soon enough," Vi announced – and his voice was all conciliation, all charm. "But he wouldn't want us to sit here all day waiting for him. We should find some way of keeping busy." With his most ingratiating smile and a single raised eyebrow, he turned his gaze on Alex. "In the meantime, why don't we give Alex the grand tour?" he asked, as if it had only just occurred to him. "She missed being shown around yesterday, but Carver's Rest is a wonderful house. So why don't we give her our own tour?"

"What a wonderful idea!" Yva exclaimed, her exuberant glee alarmingly abrupt. Quite suddenly she turned and clasped Alex's hands. "We can't possibly let you miss out, Alex! I know you'd just love to see every inch of this place!"

It was a transparent ploy – not least since Franny had clearly intended to offer the group as a search party for Adam Carver in his own house. But under this guise, Victoria Carver couldn't possibly refuse, and for that matter, neither could Alex. For she was convinced that, somewhere in the building, the truth had to be lurking.

"Oh, thank you! What a great idea!" she enthused, though Yva's tight and lingering grip was kind of creeping her out. "That would be – like a dream come true!" Laying it on a bit thick there, Alex – but there was no backing down now. Given an opportunity to investigate Carver's Rest, she could investigate with the best of them! Literally!

"Well – yes, of course," Victoria said, clearly caught off-guard by the change of tack. Perhaps she put it down to teenage mood swings, or perhaps, as suggested by her next remark, "How can I refuse?" she saw through everything. "But Alex – haven't you finished your breakfast?" she asked.

Alex looked down at her plate. Devastatingly tempting remnants of jammy toast still remained – and she hadn't even started on the waffles …

"I can warm those up for you," Victoria offered with a trill. Oh, she was *good*.

"I'm not hungry anymore," Alex said, through gritted teeth.

Victoria sighed. "Then I'd be more than happy to show you around properly, with your friends," she said – and then, brightening up, added, "and if you still need something to do, you can help me clean up after breakfast."

Her arch expression wrung reluctant assents from all present. Even Quinn Shillerdyce nodded, sour-faced.

"Then, shall we be off?" she said, and the room echoed with the grinding of chairs pushed back. "Since there's daylight enough, we'll begin outdoors. You can't even have had your proper first sight of Carver's Rest, Alex, with how late you must have arrived, so if you can bear the cold for a minute we'll just step outside –"

"That might be tricky," growled an unfamiliar voice.

Alex stared down the table in surprise. Quinn Shillerdyce had not risen from his seat, but had at last turned his eyes on Alex and the other guests, glowering at them intensely.

"I'm sorry, Quinn?" Victoria spoke up; "Why might we find it difficult?" She cocked her head. "Because of the snow?"

Quinn Shillerdyce shook his head. "Because of the tape," he said. "The front door's been completely sealed up with tape."

Chapter Six
Traitor's Gate

Because all eyes were turned on Quinn Shillerdyce, he must have been the only one who saw the look of astonishment on Alex's face – astonishment and terror. Everyone else would merely be baffled, and with good reason; in any other context, taping shut your host's front door would be a bizarre prank to pull. But Alex knew there was an alternative explanation; and that was why her immediate response to Quinn Shillerdyce's announcement, the first thought in her head, was:

The murderer wasn't finished...!

"Sorry, Mr. Shillerdyce, but could you just repeat that for me?" Vi's voice reached her ears. "The front door has been taped shut...?"

"It's simple enough," Quinn gruffly replied. "Someone's taken a roll of tape and stuck strips clear across the gaps between door and frame. Gone over the bolt and keyhole, too – with the key in it, even. What they call a hermetic seal; nothing can get through, no matter how tiny."

Alex could picture it already; the huge door of solid wood, banded with nail-studded metal bars, now incongruously joined to its gothic stone arch with long strips of cheap-looking tape. But what did it mean? Adam Carver's tomb had been sealed up from the inside to guarantee the impossibility of the murderer's escape. But if the house had likewise been sealed up from the inside, what was that supposed to suggest? There were ten – no, there should be nine living people inside the house, any one of whom could have taped the door shut. It wasn't exactly impossible...

"I think we had better take a look at this," Yva declared. "We were going there anyway. Come on."

She strode out of the room without hesitation, the others following her in a straggling, baffled line. Alex hurried forward to join Yva at the front, matching her long strides. Yva's expression was serious, determined; there was no trace of the confusion that had spread across their companions' faces, and Alex wondered if her own face too was noticeably less puzzled than the rest. Did Yva also know something about what was going on?

Carver's Rest was a large house, but it was a short walk. The lobby was a straight shot down the nave-like corridor and a turn at the bottom of the stairs. The door to the lobby was shut, but as Yva shoved it open – Quinn must have closed it, but it didn't occur to Alex then to wonder why – Alex saw the great front door immediately, just as she had imagined. Wide strips of tape had sealed the gap between door and frame at the sides and below, so not even a thread or a speck of dust could pass from outside to inside. The heavy bolt Maria had thrown shut the previous night was similarly coated, sealing the bolt in the doorframe; and a pointed, protruding bulge below the bolt had to be the keyhole, where tape had clearly been wound around the key itself to hold it in place.

Alex had been waiting for it all to go wrong, but she hadn't seen this coming at all. The killer's next move – motive as unfathomable as ever, but the same bizarre modus operandi. …Or was it the same? There was some faint difference bothering her; something to do with the kind of tape. But she had no time to consider the significance of this difference. Victoria had erupted.

"*What* do you call this?!" she exclaimed, pointing accusatorily and furiously at the tape. "What is this supposed to be?"

"Someone's strange idea of a joke," muttered Franny; Alex saw Vi hovering at her elbow, Colin at the hall door, but Quinn Shillerdyce did not appear to have followed. "It's weird, but only a mild inconvenience," Franny went on, and reached towards the tape. "Easy enough to –"

"Don't touch that!" snapped Victoria – and, curiously, Yva. "A 'mild' inconvenience?" Victoria fumed, stepping between Franny and the door. "Who do you think pays to have that door polished, that stone cleaned? Removing this tape will leave a hideous mark!"

Something clicked in Alex's mind. *That* was the difference. The wide, brown tape used on the front door was parcel tape, the sort used to seal up heavy cardboard boxes – but the tape used on her bedroom door last night was that thinner, papery stuff used in decorating; masking tape, was it called? The sort that was specifically made to be easily removed without leaving marks…

"How inconsiderate!" Vi cried. "I assure you, Mrs. Carver, no member of Besieging Heaven would ever –"

"Well, *somebody* put it here," Yva threw in.

"Somebody inside the house," Franny observed. "You couldn't stick that on from the outside, or get through the door once it was there."

"Oh, I think I know who did it," Victoria said, with a vengeful grimace across the room.

"What about why?" Yva was studying the seal now, running her eyes over every inch of it. "Is this what people do for fun? I don't get it."

"Yeah, it's not exactly trapping us in here," Franny agreed. "No offence, Mrs. Carver, but when we want to leave, that tape is coming right off."

Colin slid into view. "I don't suppose there's any other way out of the house?"

"You know full well there isn't," snapped Victoria. "The front windows don't open, and even if they did they're too narrow to step through because of the castle design. And the back and side windows, and the balcony, they're no way out – unless you intend to abseil down the cliffs or climb over the roof…"

These words reminded Alex of her own curiosity about the ocean-facing walls of Carver's Rest, and a quick scan around the room revealed a tall frame hung in a corner containing the photos Victoria had mentioned. Walking over, she saw that they were indeed of Carver's Rest from above; and even in distant and slightly blurry form it was a startling sight. Having arrived in snowbound night, Carver's Rest, to Alex, barely looked like anything – but the photographs were breathtaking. Beyond the narrow drive she had walked up – flanked by extensive grounds which in the season the photograph had been taken apparently held interleaving flowerbeds, copses of trees, and even the beginnings of a hedge maze – there was a narrow pillar of an island, its flat top dominated by the unmistakeable shape of a modern castle. Perched on a craggy precipice, below which foaming waves leapt over jagged rocks, the castle was fortified on the landward side with a curving multi-storey barricade of stone which would by no means have been out of place in medieval times; a heavy wooden drawbridge, moored by chains emerging from the gatehouse, was indeed the only way in or out. Enclosing the outer edges of the cobbled courtyard out front were lower boundary walls which ran flush up against the cliffs and looked out north and south to the open sea. And occupying the bulk of the island, its walls dominating the north and south cliffs and actually overhanging on the west, was the house of Carver's Rest itself – a three-story edifice topped by a broad peaked roof lined with stone crenellations. The seaward face of the house was far friendlier than its narrow-eyed and brutish front; a long balcony running across the length of the top floor, and numerous angled bay windows and broad planes of unbroken glass, seemed designed to get as much out of the evening sun as the east got little of the dawn, with its tiny windows that looked out only on walls.

Adjacent to the photographs was just such a window – one of a pair of slit-shaped panes on either side of the front door, and Alex decided to check through that, too, in case anything had changed outside. Like the window in her room, it was a fixed window, set full into the wall with no way of opening short of breaking it. Outside she could see the smooth white surface of the courtyard, clean as an untyped page, and beyond it, the round towers of the gatehouse and the walls they separated. And between those towers… Alex squinted, and wiped the window with her sleeve as it fogged under her breath. In the gateway itself – was that what she thought it was? Because if so, something was badly wrong.

"We might really end up abseiling down the cliffs at this rate," she said aloud.

"I'm sorry?" Victoria's voice spoke up from behind her, with a tone of "What *now*?"

"The drawbridge is up," Alex said, reporting clearly what she saw. "And I think the portcullis is down, too." She tried again to squint at the strange object she had seen, but her mind just wouldn't resolve it into any familiar shape. "And there's something hung in the middle, I think?"

"I see it," Yva's voice called, from the other window. "Somebody really doesn't want us getting out."

"The drawbridge and portcullis have the simplest controls imaginable. They're only an obstacle from the outside," Victoria insisted. "They aren't meant to be *serious*. Alex, you never said that Adam had closed up behind you."

"He didn't," Alex replied, and turned away from the confusing sight and towards the confused and as yet unknowing widow. "And I'm sure the drawbridge was open earlier."

"How did someone get through the front door to close up?" Colin asked.

"Obviously the door must have been taped shut after that," Vi pointed out.

"This trip just keeps on getting weirder," Franny muttered. "So what – somebody's set up a bunch of obstacles to stop people from getting *into* the house?"

"Or to prove that nobody could have gotten out," murmured Alex, thinking back to the taped tomb of Adam Carver. Was the seal on the front door intended to prove something similar? Was the person who placed that tape now, however impossibly, on the *outside*...? "I think we need to go out there," Alex said, turning to Victoria. It was time to be decisive – and this time, with witnesses.

Victoria Carver hesitated, and looked at each of the curious faces around her. Her hands toyed absently with her shawl, winding it tighter and tighter around finger and neck.

"Do whatever you like," she burst out, frustration buzzing in her voice, and stormed off.

They silently watched her go, just as silently consenting to wait until the echo of her footsteps had faded away and she was definitely out of earshot.

"Do you think she's gone to find Mr. Carver?" Colin asked quietly.

Franny snorted. "I think she's gone to find some polish," she said.

"While she's gone, hurry and get this tape off," Yva ordered, pointing at the door. "Something very strange is going on here, and I intend to get to the bottom of it."

Alex felt a flash of annoyance at that protagonist-like statement, but she took a more practical lead and began unpeeling the tape, Colin following her a moment later. She was, after all, quite on Yva's side – more so than Yva could know. More than merely strange, what was going on was sinister, and as each strip of tape tore away beneath Alex's fingernails to leave rough and sticky marks on the surface below, she felt a gathering chest-tightening tension, a growing dread, of what they might find outside once the door was unsealed. What weird proof of the murderer's power of sliding through walls was waiting for them, out there in the untrodden snow?

Such questions quite distracted Alex from the fact that nobody else was bothering to help her and Colin, until at last there were only the two of them with a bundle of scrunched-up tape at their feet and a full set of sticky fingers. "Thanks, guys," she said, looking from Yva, Franny and Vi to her own damaged nails.

"You're welcome," Yva replied, and she reached past Alex and Colin to force the bolt back and twist the old key in the lock. "Now, let's see what surprise Mr. Carver has waiting for us, shall we?" she grinned, and heaved the door open.

Cold air rushed in like menace, and in moments the underdressed Alex felt herself quite chilled – whether from cold or from terrible anticipation, she couldn't be sure. Beyond the door, there was an unbroken, untouched field of pale snow like another wall between Carver's Rest and the gatehouse. Yva stepped into it without hesitation, white up to her ankles, and Franny and Vi pushed through behind her and even Colin followed, flashing an anxious look at Alex, who had been shoved aside and so found herself last in the queue. She had *wanted* to be first. At least the four sets of footprints in front of her had carved a path through the snow, and Alex was just about to add her own prints to the procession when something stopped her.

It was a hand on her shoulder.

It was a long, narrow hand, flesh shrunken almost into the bone, like a skeleton's claw. And with the hand came a dry and piercing voice that stunned Alex like sudden torchlight in the dark.

"I see I've arrived just in time."

Alex's head whirled around to look at the arm and body that held the hand, at the head that held the voice. The body was tall and straight as the dark cane held in a second pale and bony hand, clad in a black dress fit for a funeral, a gleaming brooch of arcane design its only flash of colour. The head above the dress was hooded with silver hair, and seemed fleshless without being skinless, dark-rimmed sockets glinted merciless eyes. Her bearing was something like a cruel headmistress, or a witch from a fairy tale; her appearance might make small children cry just from looking at her, as indeed Alex once had many years before.

For this woman was not unknown to Alex, who was stunned not by terror but wholly unanticipated recognition.

"Great-Aunt Cornelia?!" she gasped, astonished – and then reeled anew as her mind unfolded a second revelation. "Wait, are *you* –"

The genius renowned on Besieging Heaven as the prophet of *Castles in the Sky*, about whose real life nothing was known but whose word was as law to countless adherents – a legendary theorist who had solved the central mystery of *Hand at the Threshold* from only its synopsis, who had deduced the entire plot of *A Coffin Nail Creaks* from a pre-release preview chapter – whose oracular vision of the final volume had been outlined only to BardOfDeathY and DaVinciCorpse, and realised as the infamous fan-novel *The Fourth Wall Crumbles* – second only in Alex's esteem to Adam Carver, the enigmatic online persona known only as…

"Corvus Crown, yes," Alex's great-aunt, Cornelia Crow, nodded. "Do keep up, Alex. We have far more important things to worry about."

Across the snow, a scream broke out.

Alex tore her eyes away from Cornelia, and in a trice the pair were setting out into the road of slush left by those now gathered around the portcullis – gathered recoiling from horror. And as Alex hastened towards them with breath escaping in misty bursts, soon outpacing the old lady, an appalling scene came gradually into focus.

The drawbridge was indeed up, blocking all light and exit from the gateway of Carver's Rest; scarcely less effectual was the grille of the portcullis, sunk into the sheltered ground beneath the gatehouse. But snow had fallen there, sliding from the drawbridge as it rose – and not just snow. Blood, too, had flowed; a pool of it, a cascade running down the portcullis bars, frosting over in the icy morning but impossible to mistake or disguise.

Between the raised drawbridge and the lowered portcullis was a space perhaps two or three feet wide, inaccessible with both sides closed but safe, in theory, in case of accidents. But the person trapped in that space had come there by no accident, but by deliberate, premeditated cruelty. There was no mistaking the grim intent of whoever had manacled each wrist in a padlocked loop of chain, suspending their victim from the upper corners of the drawbridge and trapping immovably a person whose snow-capped and bloodied scalp bore the mark of violence and whose eyes were wide with desperate fear but whose mouth was stopped beneath a roughly-spread layer of tape.

But it was not from here that the blood flowed. The fatal blow was far more terrible, for death had come as a sword, cutting down through the ribcage and finishing its journey thrust into the chest almost to the hilt, the blade having been passed through one of the holes in the portcullis and its outsize crossguard held fast in place with a mass of winding strips of tape.

Incongruous in that nightmare scene was an object the same crimson as the pool by which it lay – a half-unwrapped present, tight folds of paper coming unfurled, long loose ribbon draped through the blood. Peeking out was the image of a painted face, crying out in all the horror that Alex herself now felt, and above that face were the edges of a few boldly-printed letters. Alex did not need to unwrap the gift to know what it was; she would recognise the iconic cover of *Hand at the Threshold* anywhere. A book in bloodied paper and soiled ribbon was the murderer's epitaph for Maria Bole.

RULES
for the Author

Dear Reader,

Permit me, if you will, a further interruption, that I might expand on my remarks concerning fair play. Perhaps you are unfamiliar with the rules under which we play the game of murder. It would be unfair of me, would it not, to claim to act honestly, if I was doing so under rules of my own devising and of which you had no knowledge?

As an inheritor of the great tradition of murder, I am obliged to honour those rules laid down by my predecessors. Most are, of course, unwritten, but a few are set down in black and white, and none are more infamous than the Ten Commandments of the late Ronald A. Knox. Some cynics say he never truly intended his rules to be taken seriously, let alone worshipped – but I will guarantee my sincerity. Let us carve this Decalogue of Monsignor Knox in stone.

I.   The murderer must be introduced in the first half of the story.
II. The murder must be neither committed nor solved by magic.
III. There must be no more than one secret passage.
IV. The murder method must not require long scientific explanations.
V. There must be no stereotypes among the cast.
VI. The murder must not be solved by accident, luck, or intuition.
VII.The detective must not be the murderer.
VIII.The reader must be made aware of all clues to the mystery.
IX. The reader's co-detective must not be too intelligent.
X. There must be no identical siblings or duplicates without clues.

I have modernised the commandments as a courtesy, but I am not bound to disclose the extent to which each is relevant. That is for the reader to determine.

Shall we continue?

The Author

<h1 style="text-align:center">CHAPTER SEVEN</h1>

CHAPTER SEVEN
THE THEORIST

Alex was never quite certain who had screamed, but she almost wished it had been herself, as if by screaming the fear away she could compose herself all the more rapidly. At least she had been prepared for such a gruesome scene by her own encounter of the previous night; her companions had no such experience to brace them, and could only stand aghast, vapour pouring from their open mouths.

Yva alone was studying the scene with unflinching eyes. Colin did flinch and turned away, where he set widening eyes on Alex and Cornelia. "You mustn't look!" he exclaimed, waving wildly at them, but it was a bit late for such noble sentiments.

Vi's composure seemed completely broken, and he kept on tearing himself away only to glance back again and again as if the grisly spectacle might have vanished in the interim. "This isn't happening, this isn't happening," he was muttering to himself, very far in that moment from the SiegeMasterV Alex knew. "It's got to be a trick, it's got to be special effects or a waxwork or something. It's all a publicity stunt, this is all for show...!"

"Pull yourself together," Franny snapped at him, though she too was breathing raggedly. "This is real – insanely real... What has that lunatic Carver brought us here for?"

Alex could only wonder. She had already seen the worst, and was fighting to arrange her mind around this new twist in the murderer's scheme.

Adam Carver had merely been the first victim. Maria Bole was next, and the elaborately bizarre crime scene surely proved that she had not been chosen on the spur of the moment. But why Maria? Just as it was becoming clear that Adam Carver had sinned somehow, why had his agent also fallen victim to a killer's rampage?

"I'm not – I, I can't look at this anymore," Colin was stuttering wildly – and in a sudden burst of movement he fled, wet snow flying around his feet as he hurtled headlong back towards the open door.

Franny watched him go. "You know something? He's got the right idea," she said, and started walking back to the house herself, legs trembling as they longed to run. "I'm going to call the police," she called to them. "You know the clichés – *don't touch anything...*"

She crossed paths with Cornelia Crow as she went. Alex's great-aunt had paused, and as if already bored with murder was looking back at the house, the edifice of stone with its narrow, siege-ready windows and crenellated roof. Alex wondered what she was seeing.

Vi's groans drew her back. "They're right to run. Why am I still standing here?" he asked, and she did not know what to tell him. "It's unbelievable. Someone dragging Maria out here and killing her while we were just sitting there eating breakfast…"

"What an absurd suggestion."

Cornelia had spoken. She was now staring silently at the corpse, studying it not with horror or anger but more as if troubled by a convoluted problem – though all other eyes had turned to her, some bewildered, some frankly curious. To the others, she wasn't Alex's great-aunt; she was the detective.

"Don't give up on rational thought just because you're scared," she ordered, without turning away from the body. "This is the time when you need it most. Now, tell me: Were there any marks in the snow before you all ran over here?"

"No," Alex replied quickly. Cornelia was cool under pressure – perhaps even cold – but she was right to be, Alex thought; they all needed to be. "There were no footprints at all, it was completely untouched."

Yva nodded affirmatively. "I checked through the window and was first out the door," she said. "There were no prints or any other marks."

A grim smile crossed Cornelia's face. "I thought not," she said. "And I've been enjoying the view from my bedroom for some little while, so take my word for it, there's been no fresh snow to fill in any prints made this morning."

"But then –" Vi's head seemed to lurch backwards. "If Maria and her killer couldn't have left the house, that makes the murder completely impossible!"

There was a word which felt all too familiar – but Cornelia had let out a tut of disgust. "What did I just tell you about being rational?" she barked. "If nobody has been out here since it stopped snowing, which *must* have been before dawn, then all of this was set up overnight – when nobody was likely to catch the murderer in the act."

She made it all sound so simple – and, Alex supposed, it *was* simple; an obvious deduction, really. But in the heat of the moment, it was all too easy to leap to the wrong conclusions – and stay there. Alex looked at her great-aunt with newfound respect. Great-Aunt Cornelia, to her, had always been just a remote and extremely elderly relative who lived on her own among piles of yellowing books. And yet that same old lady was not only *online*, she was also Corvus Crown, a big-name fan who saw things in books that Alex never could – and who was now surveying the scene of an actual crime with characteristic cool head and logic. Alex would never have imagined the two to have anything to do with each other; and yet, it now seemed so natural. Somehow, Cornelia Crow was exactly what she had imagined Corvus Crown to be like.

Vi, meanwhile, was looking slightly shamefaced. "Yes – that makes complete sense, of course," he was muttering. "I suppose I had *Castles in the Sky* on the brain." He let out a nervous, false laugh. "I almost thought something impossible and fantastic had happened, just like in the books."

Cornelia shrugged her bony shoulders. "Of course you did. There's a good reason for that."

"Stress?" suggested Alex.

"What? Oh, there's that," Cornelia answered, glancing at her. "But also, the murder can't have been committed more than an hour ago."

Only the sound of swirling wind and the low roar of waves disturbed the silence that fell. Alex watched as Vi's mouth opened and closed emptily, like a fish stranded in its bowl; her own thoughts went numb. How could Cornelia know that? How could she know, and yet how could it be done?

But wait – Alex could answer one of those questions…!

"The drawbridge was down!" she remembered. "When I looked out of my window before breakfast, there was light coming through the gateway. If Maria had already been chained to the drawbridge – and that sword was jammed into the portcullis – it would have stabbed her when the drawbridge was raised, while we were having breakfast…"

"So…" Vi began, and a ghastly pallor returned to his face, "we could have saved her? If we'd only known earlier that she was there?"

"You know, that's interesting about the drawbridge," Cornelia Crow said.

She didn't look bothered by the thought that Maria could have been saved, Alex noticed; no, she was just faintly satisfied on an intellectual level. The chill Alex felt out in the snow was nothing compared to the coldness in the old lady's heart. Perhaps she wasn't only being rational…

"I thought that was probably the case," she was going on, "but remember, I was eating breakfast in bed all this time, and my narrow window reveals precious little. I could only deduce the state of the drawbridge, so it's useful that you confirmed it."

She had only *deduced* the state of the drawbridge? From what, Alex wondered? She cast her eyes around, trying to look at the scene from the eyes of Great-Aunt Cornelia – no, Corvus Crown, theorist extraordinaire. But there was only the once-trackless snow, which pointed to the opposite conclusion, and the savaged body of Maria Bole. However – there being a dead body present didn't seem to trouble Cornelia at all, so perhaps there was a clue there.

Suppressing her revulsion, Alex tried to look at the corpse, take in every horrid detail. Even the bleeding wound, and the widening pool it fed; even the blade of the sword, where a red line was still running, and glistening beads of crimson still dropping below.

"She's still bleeding," Alex realised. "And the blood hasn't frozen. I don't know how it works, but maybe that shows she might not have been dead for long …"

Vi spluttered with astonishment. "What are you saying, RedRidingBlood? How can you be so *clinical* at a time like this?" he burst out. "It's not – *normal*!"

"Siege – Vi, who cares about what's *normal*!" Alex snapped back. His words had stung – but not just because she disagreed. Cornelia Crow might have been clinical, but Alex didn't think of herself the same way. It wasn't that she didn't care. She was doing this *because* she cared. "Don't you see," she told him, "that for Maria's sake, we have to find out what happened…"

Cornelia ignored this exchange, and turned slightly. A half-lidded eye rested on Yva Dysart. Of course – Corvus Crown and BardOfDeathY were friends of a sort. "A second opinion, Yva?" Cornelia asked. "You've been awfully quiet."

"Just relishing the sound of you in action, CC," Yva said, stepping forward with a clinical smile of her own. BardOfDeathY, Alex thought, maybe *really* didn't care.

Yva gestured towards the body, which she had been studying for some time. "With the caveat declared that none of us are trained medical professionals," she began seriously, "and with the low temperature interfering with the rate of cooling... I would agree she's been dead no longer than an hour. Not by my well-researched understanding of the process."

Alex stared at her in amazement. BardOfDeathY was seriously a budding forensic scientist? That was absurdly convenient – perhaps even suspiciously so. Or had she picked up this knowledge solely to write better fanfiction?

"Good," Cornelia, to whom the question didn't matter, nodded thoughtfully; "very good." Alex wouldn't have put it like that, but it was all information. "Of course, the police could do a better job, but they aren't here now, and we don't know when they will be. For the time being, it's best if we can make a preliminary investigation of our own. You do understand why this is important, don't you, Vi?"

"Well, yes, I see your point," Vi mumbled, straightening his cuffs. "Maybe it is correct – proper. They'll thank us for it." He paused, and his professional demeanour, so lately regained, wavered once again. "But didn't you just prove that this really *was* impossible?"

Alex's eyes widened; she'd gotten so caught up in the detail that she'd forgotten why it was important. The unbroken snow proved that nobody had left the house since dawn. But it was also proved that Maria had definitely been murdered since then. The two facts flatly contradicted each other, but they were both completely true!

"Didn't I tell you there was a reason you thought this had been an impossible crime?" Cornelia asked, leaning on her cane with both hands. Alex, who was watching her attentively, could not miss a faint glint in her eye, a faint twist to the corner of her mouth.

Uneasily, she realised that Great-Aunt Cornelia might actually be *enjoying* this. "You weren't aware of it consciously," Cornelia had continued, "but your brain knew the body was quite fresh, even though another fact contradicted it. If you want to get anywhere you'll have to learn to draw out those unconscious observations, and make them conscious."

Alex spoke up. "But then how do we make the facts fit together?" Impossible was still impossible!

"Elementary," smirked Yva. "We get more facts."

"So instead of standing around in the cold all day," Cornelia Crow said commandingly, "let's go and get them."

And leaning on her cane, she struck out across the untouched snow with a hobbling gait. Her destination was a low door nearby, set into the base of the nearest tower. Vi's eyes followed Cornelia, and he suddenly seemed to understand something.

"Of course, the gatehouse controls!" he exclaimed. "This explains everything!"

Alex flashed him an oblivious look. Once again, she was out of the loop. "This doesn't explain anything to me," she admitted, as the trio of herself, Vi, and Yva followed Cornelia the short distance across the snow. "What's in the towers?"

"On the opposite side, nothing but a storeroom," Yva explained, pointing to the second tower and its own small door. "But in this one, there's a staircase leading up to a room above the drawbridge and the portcullis – you know what, let's call them the gates, it's shorter. Anyway, that's where the controls for the gates are; Carver showed us them yesterday and even demonstrated how they work."

"And that resolves the problem!" Vi cried, shaking with excitement. "The murder was committed by taping that sword into the portcullis and then raising the drawbridge with Maria on it, pulling her into the sword – right? It had to be set up at night, but once everything was arranged, the murderer never had to set foot in the snow again – they just had to wait in the gatehouse to raise the drawbridge!"

"But if they did that," Alex pointed out, glancing nervously at the tower, "wouldn't that mean that the murderer is *still in there*?" Something else struck her as she thought about this theory. "But no, that's impossible..."

A clattering sound interrupted her. Cornelia had pushed open the tower door, which evidently was neither locked nor sealed with tape or any other obstacle. She looked back at them over her shoulder. "What are the three of you waiting for?" she called, tetchily.

"Nothing important," Yva replied, and strolled over to join her. "There's nothing to fear," she remarked to Alex and Vi as she went. "If the murderer was capable of just killing a person right in front of him, he wouldn't have killed Maria in such a roundabout way, would he?"

"Him? He?" Alex repeated, to no answer. Did BardOfDeathY have a suspect in mind? But there was a much more difficult problem for her to worry about, a problem the other three seemed to have forgotten – one which did away with the threat of a murderer lurking in the gatehouse, but replaced it once again with the menace of the impossible. For if Maria's murderer had hidden in the gatehouse all night, *how could they have taped shut the front door of Carver's Rest from inside?*

There was no time to think about it. Already Cornelia was vanishing up a narrow set of spiral stairs, and Yva was stepping into the tower to join her – whether from a wish to bravely back her up, or at least be seen as no less cowardly than a frail old lady. Alex hurried after her, not wanting to be again at the back of a queue – but in the event she managed to catch something that Cornelia and Yva didn't. Just as she was about to step into the dark and claustrophobic tower, she heard a noise behind her back – a kind of click, or snap. A familiar noise. She glanced behind…

Vi was hanging back, looking directly at the body on the portcullis – or perhaps not so directly. Rather, he was looking through something he held in his hand. It was his phone, and as Alex watched, with yet another *snap*, he tapped the screen and took a picture of the corpse.

Alex must have made some slight noise or croak, as Vi started and turned quickly from his corpse photography. He could not miss the revulsion on Alex's face. "Don't get the wrong idea," he said hurriedly. "Like Corvus said, this is for the police – in case anything gets moved later."

"…Right," Alex replied, turning her back on him with some trepidation. It was a good explanation, of course. It might even have been a true one. But she could not suppress her initial impression that Vi was some kind of ghoulish necrophiliac. The real-life SiegeMasterV was proving to be kind of a letdown… Shuddering, she hurried into the tower, Vi at her back.

The air was cold but no icy wind blew within the tower. The spiral stair was coiled tight, so Alex could see only the odd glimpse of Yva Dysart's boots stamping up ahead of her, and no sign of her great-aunt farther around the circle. She found herself biting her lip in fear of what might be at the top, for just as it was impossible for the killer to be waiting there, it seemed equally impossible for them to be anywhere else. The killer could not have crossed the snow. The killer could not have crossed the tape. The killer could not be anywhere…

And then they were there. The stairs terminated in a tiny round chamber into which Cornelia, Yva, Alex and Vi crammed themselves. The gatehouse was before them – and yet it remained off-limits; for there was no means now of entering it.

The gatehouse, which was really too fancy a name for the small room above the gates and between the two flanking towers, was a rectangular chamber with a few slit-like windows and no entrance but from a doorway beside the tower stair – and at that moment there was indeed no entrance. A gate of vertical metal bars separated the stairwell from the gatehouse, hinged on one edge and bolted on the other – which was the problem. Somebody had covered the bulky bolt apparatus over and over in many layers of parcel tape, a thick brown bundle that quite obscured the original fastening and made it impossible to move – for it had, of course, been taped shut in the locked position. Cementing the impression of impenetrability was the presence of, set atop the taped bolt, a slender lit candle. The candle now was burning low, torrents of melted wax dribbling over the brown tape.

"Pure showmanship," Cornelia said dismissively, warming her fingers on the candle. "It hardly stops anyone from manipulating the controls if they really want to. It doesn't even stop us looking in."

This was quite true. The gaps between the bars were not wide enough to pass even an arm through, but they were enough to see all the way around the gatehouse, even into the shallow corners immediately left and right of the door. The room was essentially empty, and freezingly so, for quite beside the unglazed windows there was along the floor a slit-shaped shaft through which the portcullis would pass when raised, and a pair of holes in the outside wall through which the drawbridge was drawn up or down. Through the shaft and the holes ran two pairs of narrow but strong-looking chains, presumably fastened to those gates, and each pair was linked to one of two chunky winch systems dominating the room, comprising long chain-wound cylinders terminating in a single substantial-looking metal box which presumably housed a motor. Evidently this did the job of raising and lowering the gates so the Carvers did not have to perform the manual labour themselves – and not just the Carvers, for the murderer's touch was evident in a further trio of candles smouldering atop the motor casing, burnt down about as much as the one on the lock. Finally, wires clipped to the seams of the floor joined the motor to a pair of narrow metal levers on the far wall with plates on either side of them reading "DRAWBRIDGE" and "PORTCULLIS." Both levers were pointing diagonally down, a plaque beneath them reading "CLOSED," but had they been inclined upwards they would have instead indicated a sign reading "OPEN."

Vi was staring avidly at the candles. "Those candles prove that someone was here at night – but how did they get out?" he asked, wildly. "Those windows and the portcullis drop are too narrow for a human to fit through." Suddenly he slammed a fist into the palm of his hand. "I've got it! They must have been hiding behind the door at the bottom of the stairs so they could slip past us –"

"I checked, there was no space behind the door for anyone to hide in," Yva replied tonelessly. "You can look for yourself when we go back."

Cornelia had bent down to scrutinise the bundle of tape, and was muttering indistinctly to herself. "End of the tape… yes, here, our side and pointing upwards… just as I suspected." She straightened up slowly, and turned back to the group. "The killer having been out here all night is not an option," Cornelia said. "They must have returned to the house before the snow stopped, so that their tracks would be erased. From that mess around the front door, I take it you all know why."

"Because the door was taped shut on the inside," Alex pointed out at last, and an interested smile spread across Cornelia's face. "The killer had to have been inside the house to do that," Alex continued, "and couldn't have left afterwards."

"Not the same way, anyway," Yva added.

"But then how could they have tripped the switch and killed Maria?" Vi insisted. "It's *impossible –*"

"You poor child," Cornelia interrupted, looking down at Vi with pitying, patronising eyes. "I almost don't want to disillusion you. Seeing your wonder at this seemingly impossible feat takes me back to my childhood."

Vi twisted his head. "Excuse me, but, 'seemingly'?"

Yva was now wearing a pitying look that imitated Cornelia's perfectly, to Alex's irritation. Who was the great-niece here? "The fact is, SMV," Yva said, even copying Cornelia's tone, "this kind of trick is old hat to old hands at impossible crimes like us. We must have seen it countless times. Somebody is murdered on the other side of a stretch of snow, or sand, or mud or whatever, which not a footprint has crossed…"

"Adam Carver did that one, of course," Alex interrupted. Volume Two, *Hand at the Threshold*; nobody could have crossed the unmarked snow to the infamous leaning turret, and yet a murder without a murderer had occurred inside. At this, of all times, a fan could hardly forget the book's eerily prescient twists and turns.

"Yes, yes, give me *some* credit," Vi retorted. "I've read *Castles in the Sky*, obviously, and other mysteries besides. But that kind of thing only happens –"

"In fiction, yes," Yva replied, as Cornelia rolled her eyes. "CC's recommended me countless impossible crime books for my own research – but she's read them all." Yva's own eyes were aglow with something scarily akin to worship. "CC knows literally every trick in the book."

And, as if on cue, Cornelia Crow made a dramatic flourish with her cane, struck it against the floor, and began to speak.

"I am the ultimate armchair detective, solving the cases that can only be solved from an armchair – ones in books," she announced, with sudden enthusiasm. "You children with your eleventh-hand copies and shiny reissues don't know you're born. *I* bought them all when they were first published. The Golden Age of Mystery? I was there! I was alive at the same time as all the greatest mystery authors you've never heard of, I've been reading murder mysteries for longer than your three lives put together, so believe me, I know this funny business inside out."

It was probably an impressive speech, to the right kind of fan; and Alex was impressed. Such a history of cracking mysteries, and such a legacy – it gave Alex a surge of confidence that they could unravel this conundrum, like a rallying cry to an army... even if her own favourite authors were more recent. They were all alive – save for one recent exception.

"I see," Vi said at last, nodding at Cornelia Crow. "So... you're sort of like Miss Marple."

Cornelia glowered frostily at him.

"...Jessica Fletcher?" he tried again.

She sighed, and rolled her eyes. "I suppose Nancy Drew is out of the question," she muttered.

"*I'm* like Jessica Fletcher," Yva interrupted.

"*Anyway*," Alex cut in, "there's something more important we should be talking about right now, remember? The murders?"

Cornelia raised an eyebrow at "murders," plural – but she didn't press the point, not then. Instead she cleared her throat as noisily as she was able, which was unflatteringly feebly. "Oh, yes – unmarked snow, or near offer," she recalled. "Trivial, on its own merits. Either it wasn't really unmarked, or there was another way entirely – or the murderer never crossed it at all."

"And it's frankly obvious how this one was done," Yva broke in. "It was string, wasn't it? That's how half of all impossible crimes are done! While it was still snowing last night, the killer tied a loop of string to the drawbridge switch, ran the string all the way down the staircase and through the tower door, back across the snow –"

She stopped suddenly. A blank, uncomprehending expression began to spread across her face.

"Seen the wrinkle, have you, Yva?" grinned Cornelia. "It was a good try. But if that front door was completely sealed up with tape – and you'll have checked that it was, I'm sure – then there'd be no pulling any string under it."

"Mr. Shillerdyce was the one who told us about the tape," remembered Alex. "He must have seen it before he came to breakfast."

"He was there even before me and DaVinciCorpse," Yva mumbled to herself, "so that makes it before my estimated time of death…"

Cornelia nodded at them, and continued. "Going through the windows is out of the question, too, since none of the windows at the front of the house even open – and I already looked back, just in case, and none of them are broken, either." A sardonic quirk turned her lips. "No shortcut solutions here."

"Wait, I have an idea," Vi interrupted, his eyes shining. "Carver's Rest was inspired by the castles from *Castles in the Sky*, right? Then wouldn't the front door be a red herring, because the house is riddled with secret passa–"

Cornelia held up a hand in front of his face. "Let me stop you there, SiegeMasterV," she said. "Don't even finish that sentence. I refuse to countenance the use of a secret passage as a solution to an impossible crime. It's an unwritten rule."

"Technically, the *written* rules allow for one secret passage," Yva nitpicked. "Though I agree –"

"You don't mean Knox's so-called rules – or was that one of Van Dine's?" Cornelia said, curling her lip as Alex wondered what they were talking about. "Please. Those *guidelines* are just so many ways of saying 'write well and don't cheat the reader' – and a secret passage is a cheat. I refuse to acknowledge any." She scowled into the gatehouse. "Not unless I see one with my own eyes."

"Well, anyway –" Yva was gaining her second wind. "A string could've been pulled through the windows at the *back* of the house! The killer could have gone out on the top-floor balcony last night, tied one end of their string to a rock, thrown it clear over the roof, picked it up at the front of the house and looped that end around the switch, and then pulled it from the far side of the house sometime this morning. You can see that, if the switch was in the 'open' position, you could use string to pull it down and then the loop would just slide right off –"

Alex cleared her throat, and Yva paused. Alex had been half-hoping not to be noticed; she had seen the way BardOfDeathY dealt with her detractors, but all the same, this brute-force solution was so dubious that she had to speak up. "I'm really sorry, but isn't this… a bit silly?" she suggested, nervously. "You'd need so much string, and going around all these angles and corners – I'm not sure it'd work at all, especially not without leaving marks somewhere."

"Now that I think about it," Vi added, backing her up, "we were nearly all right in front of each other over breakfast, weren't we?" He looked around. "Who'd have had the opportunity to sneak off and reel in a hundred metres of string? It would be too obvious."

Of course, Alex thought, there *were* a couple of people who did not have a complete alibi for breakfast; just two, in fact. Cornelia Crow herself – who she had no intention of accusing – and, more interestingly, Victoria Carver… But SMV was right. It would have been too obvious. If you ignored the impossible window-dressing and reduced it to a question of pure timing, there were too few suspects; the murderer would have made it too easy. Would the person clever enough to have conjured up Adam Carver's impossible room really have overlooked such a fact? And after all, Alex reflected – it wasn't as if she even *believed* Yva's explanation.

"Well, none of that disproves my theory," Yva retorted. "Just because it's awkward doesn't mean it didn't happen. In fact, because this is real life and not an elegant work of fiction, it's *more* likely to happen." She paused – but it seemed it was chiefly a pause for effect, as a self-satisfied smirk was spilling across her face. "And in any case, having solved the *how*dunnit, I can confidently declare *who*dunnit, too."

Alex's jaw dropped. That was *fast*. BardOfDeathY wasn't even much of a theorist, yet here she was, cracking the case before even Corvus Crown. Why couldn't RedRidingBlood turn out to be the smart one? She had vowed to solve the case, yet she was being outcompeted by people with only half as much information.

"Really?" Cornelia was asking Yva, looking impressed. "Nicely-done, my dear. I would be rather interested to hear what evidence you have that I've overlooked."

Alex thought she detected a slightly equivocal note in that last statement, as if Cornelia was not actually at all confident that she *had* missed anything – but Yva didn't notice. "Allow me to explain," she began –

"Hold it, Y," Vi instructed, drawing himself up in his characteristic way. "Perhaps you haven't noticed, being so carried away in your theories, but we're still virtually outdoors in the icy cold." That explained why he had his hands stuffed in his pockets. "I'm sure your theory will be just as good inside. But think of Alex here. Have a heart."

Alex rolled her eyes – but it *was* very cold, now that he mentioned it, and she really wasn't dressed for the weather. Going back inside didn't sound bad at all. She just didn't want it to with Vi's hand on her shoulder again. Cornelia's eye seemed to catch her shivering, and the old lady announced, "Indeed, we may as well return to the house. We've seen all there is to see here."

"Me first!" interrupted Yva, barging past Vi and rattling down the stairs. Vi gestured grandly for Cornelia to go first, and she responded by glaring at him and pointing down in turn. He took the hint and went first – and the moment his back was turned, Alex was startled to find Cornelia's piercing eyes meeting her own. Alex couldn't help but take a step back as her great-aunt leaned slowly close to her.

"I don't want to cause a panic at this stage," the old lady murmured, "but did you notice the state of the wires?"

Alex hadn't, and she hadn't even time to think about what she hadn't when Yva's voice suddenly echoed up the staircase. "Stop. What are you doing there?"

Cornelia scowled over her shoulder, and in a black rustle she and her cane were gone, their three footsteps tapping down the stairs as fast as she could manage. Alex was about to join her, but – those wires… She stepped over to the doorway and peered through the bars, eyes rapidly seeking out the trailing wires between motors and levers –

And she saw it. One of the wires – the one controlling the portcullis – had had a section of a few inches in the middle cleanly cut out and removed.

That was all she had time for. Alex was already ripping herself away and hurtling down the stairs even as she processed it, and the conclusion was indeed frightening enough to flee from. The portcullis was effectively jammed, and they were trapped in Carver's Rest.

Although the moments seemed drawn-out, it was probably not so many seconds after Yva had spoken that Alex reached the bottom of the staircase, finding Cornelia still negotiating the final steps. Alex craned to see over her shoulder; the angles were terrible, but she could just about make out Yva staring in the direction of the body… And then they were emerging into the snow, and Alex could look herself – and she was startled not to see the body at all. It was half-concealed by a white bedsheet or tablecloth that was being tucked into the portcullis by none other than Colin West, who was straining not to brush against the bloodied sword handle.

Fortunately, the time it took for Cornelia and Alex to reach him was also the time it took for him to sputter out an explanation. "It seemed… disrespectful?" he suggested, gesturing to what was still visible of the ghastly scene. "It's what you do with, you know, bodies, so…"

As he stretched the sheet the rest of the way across the portcullis, squashing his feet into the rungs of the grating to avoid bloodying his shoes, the last glance of Maria's petrified face before it was hidden away reminded Alex of just what was at stake. She couldn't begrudge Yva her evident brilliance, of course; that was childish. This wasn't about who could get to the truth first. This was about getting to the truth *at all*, before somebody else died horribly.

Yva's expression, meanwhile, was rearranging into a façade of merciful benevolence. "Yes, of course. Well done, Colin."

Colin hopped down with surprising grace and looked bashfully at his feet – and noticed something there.

"Um," he spoke up, and gestured into the red snow. "What do you want to do about…"

The cold blood spreading at the foot of the drawbridge had reached the shiny wrapping of the gift left near Maria's body. Among the folds of paper and loose loops of ribbon, the cover of *Hand at the Threshold* was still visible.

"You're right. It could be a clue," Alex cut in quickly. "I know we're not meant to touch anything, but we shouldn't let the evidence get damaged either."

Yva was humming indecisively, but Cornelia stepped in to take charge. "I'll take responsibility," she said, a pair of dark silk gloves suddenly on her fingers. "I'll handle it as little as possible, in case of fingerprints – though what premeditated murderer would leave them these days I can't imagine."

"I'll just take a few pictures for posterity," Vi said, and quickly bent down to the book to snap a few close-ups. This took long enough for Cornelia's knees to finally bend, where she gently brushed aside the wrapping paper and lifted up the book, pausing only briefly to frown at a black tail-end of ribbon.

"A little battered," she said, turning over the book and flipping through a few pages in the middle. "But it seems like a perfectly ordinary copy of *Castles in the Sky* Volume Two."

"The blood didn't leak into the back pages, did it?" Colin cringed. "It would be horrible if –"

But Alex was already speaking over him. "Look at the title page," she interrupted, before her mind had time to point out how suspicious this would sound, and Cornelia frowned strangely at Alex before obeying. Everyone around Cornelia craned their heads to see what she would find there – everyone if they had only left space for Colin; and, as Alex suspected and half-dreaded, the name of the author had been obliterated and replaced by a signature in florid handwriting.

"*The Author*," Yva read out, as if the rest of them were illiterate, and a serene smile spread across her face. "I knew it. The smoking gun."

"Oh, so that's your theory, is it?" Cornelia asked, with irritating obliquity. "A bit obvious, don't you think? But let's settle this inside; Alex, you also have something to tell us."

"That's right," Alex nodded, but said no more as they marched through the trampled avenue of snow, Cornelia's fingers tight as a vice on the book. There would be no proving now that the snow between themselves and the body had been unbroken when they had opened the door. But did the snow really matter, Alex wondered? The first murder, as only she and the murderer knew, had been committed the night before, when the snow had only really begun in earnest. The murders were surely planned in advance, judging from their complexity; so the murderer could not have anticipated the state of the snow. Did that prove, as Great-Aunt Cornelia had suggested, that the murderer had indeed never crossed the snow at all, had never needed to? That the unbroken snow was perhaps not a challenge to the detectives, but a clue?

They still had to wait for Yva before they could return to the house, as at the last shivering minute she suddenly had an idea, and ran around the pale mounds of cars sweeping snow from the windows and peeking underneath to deconfirm clever hiding-places. But eventually they slammed the door on the snowy outdoors, locking it tight, for all that seemed to matter to the murderer.

"Just hold on one second," Alex told the others, and then it was her turn to run off as the others were stamping snow from their shoes. Victoria Carver would complain about her treading wet footprints everywhere, but that was the least of their problems. She couldn't produce the *first* body, but she could at least prove that something really had happened last night – something that was connected to the *second* body…

Inside Alex's room, nothing was changed, to her relief. The first birthday present was still where she had left it, and she stuffed it into her emptied backpack, wrapping paper and all; this, she thought grimly, would certainly grab their attention. Nobody had followed her; the corridors were wide and empty as an abandoned building, the windows grey as walls. It wasn't a good place to be alone. She ran back as she ran there, only now feeling eyes on her back.

As usually happened, though, when Alex thought she might this time be the centre of attention, she was wrong again. As she hurried down the stairs she found instead that everyone was gathered around Franny Smythe, who had apparently popped up the moment her back was turned. "…and as we know, the whole place is a black spot," Franny was saying, as Alex drew up.

"What's going on?" she asked, since apparently nobody ever noticed her except when she didn't want them to.

Franny jumped and looked around. "Oh, it's only you," she said, grimacing. It seemed she was more alarmed than she wanted to let on. "We've been cut off, that's what's going on."

"The phone and, and even the wireless router and everything – they've been stolen," Colin volunteered, with panicky eyes.

"Unplugged straight from the wall," Franny picked up from him. "I went and checked with Mrs. Carver, and there's no other landline or wifi source – and like I was saying, there's no mobile reception here either."

"The murderer's trying to isolate us from the outside world," Yva said, eyes shining with a terrible energy. "It's *just* like the books…"

"Did either of you tell Mrs. Carver about the murder?" Cornelia interrupted sharply, eyes on Colin and Franny.

"Er – I…" Colin stammered.

"Yeah, he did; she knew by the time I got to her," Franny filled in. "She seemed stunned, but she gave me straight answers, at least."

Fear twisted Alex's heart again, and her hand began to feel sweaty on the book. "So does this mean," she said quietly, "that the murderer's still not finished?"

"Absolutely," Cornelia Crow said, and she had her eyes on the backpack on Alex's shoulder. "It's no good just barring the exit if the police can simply helicopter in. Cutting off communication is more reliable for the murderer's purposes than just preventing us from leaving."

"I don't see how we're prevented from leaving," Franny frowned. "We just open the drawbridge and portcullis and drive out. Unless you're saying the controls have been sabotaged or anything?"

Cornelia scowled. Alex guessed she hadn't wanted to reveal this so soon. "That is correct," she admitted. "The portcullis switch cannot be used. Of course, we are now all calm and collected enough to accept this news with equanimity."

"Hold on, you mean we're trapped here?" Vi broke in, his equanimity now needing no more than a light tap to crumble. "With a murderer on the loose?"

"Of course, we were effectively imprisoned even minus the sabotage," Cornelia continued, paying him no mind. "To get out, we would have had to cut through the tape sealing off the gatehouse controls; would have to cut the tape holding the sword to the portcullis; would really have to cart Maria out of the way too, and that might take bolt cutters. Well, you can try if you want; repairing the electrics can't be much more additional work, it's really just the murderer's finishing touch. ...However." She looked slyly around the listeners. "That on its own is only hard labour. But who here would be keen to admit to the police that they had destroyed half the evidence?"

A sharp intake of breath passed through the circle. Cornelia had been one step ahead, Alex realised. Alex herself wouldn't have looked at the impediments to exiting as anything but a brute-force problem – one that at worst might be a time sink, for a group chiefly comprising a bunch of teenagers who didn't look as though they exercised much. But what Great-Aunt Cornelia was proposing was that whoever thought they should go ahead regardless, destroying the crime scene and leaving most of the evidence unusable, had a high chance of being the murderer...

Franny looked uneasy, but undeterred. "I see what you're saying," she began, "but what exactly are you proposing? That we just sit around here and wait to be murdered?"

"Wait, maybe," Cornelia replied. "I'm sure several of you must have families who are expecting you, and who might be worried when not even a call comes through; they might get in touch with the police if we are found to be cut off. Sooner still, I'm sure I'm not the only one who hired a taxi to get here and home again, and if the weather gets no worse they should be showing their faces early this afternoon. We just have to hold the fort until then and ask for help through the intercom."

Everyone except Alex, who shortly followed suit, looked towards a small electronic panel next to the front door. That must have been where Maria had summoned her on the previous night. If Maria hadn't stayed up so late for her, perhaps she wouldn't have died, Alex thought – but then she held the thought. Why *had* Maria been up so late, again? Alex vaguely recalled her giving several different explanations...

"What if –" Vi started, but Cornelia had anticipated him.

"If somebody were to sabotage the intercom later, then that would be a waste of time as we can still shout and throw messages through the windows in the gatehouse," Cornelia forestalled him. "But if you're that concerned, you'd be better off working out some other method of crossing the wall. There are bound to be some ladders or rope around here. Whether that's faster than getting the gates working I couldn't say – but it leaves the police a better chance of proving who the murderer is."

"I was waiting for that," Yva said excitedly. She had listened very patiently, but now her enthusiasm seemed to be getting the better of her again. "The police *might* be able to prove who the murderer is, sure – but why wait for them when we can crack the case and capture the murderer ourselves?" She was, Alex saw, shaking with excitement. "If we do that, we can tamper with the evidence as much as we want!"

"Oh for crying out loud," sighed Franny, and gave Yva an exasperated look. "This isn't some book in which plucky kids outsmart a bunch of adults and finger the most unlikely person as the killer. This is real life. Leave it to the professionals!"

"Too late for that," Yva shot back. "I already know who the murderer is!"

Colin gasped. "You do?"

"Of course. Isn't it obvious?" she smirked. "The killer is Adam Carver!"

CHAPTER NINE
THE AUTHOR IS THE CULPRIT

Alex put her head in her hands. This was exactly the theory she had been afraid of – the wrong one. The one that turned the wronged and tragic victim she admired into a brutal killer. And she couldn't even prove it was wrong!

But she *could* prove it was incomplete.

"Just – just stop right there for a moment, Yva," she broke in, hesitantly. "Just hold it for a second... Wait."

A crowd of eyes fell on Alex expectantly; never a situation she liked to happen. It made her feel tense and sweaty and lost for words. So, wordlessly, she dropped her backpack and pulled out the birthday present, and all eyes fell on that instead, and became astonished.

All save a single pair.

"Ah, the first one. I did wonder," Cornelia said, giving every impression of having known exactly what was going to happen. "I'll be taking a look at that, Alex. Now, let me see…" Alex relinquished the book to Cornelia's gloved hand. The old lady opened it instantly to the title page, and nodded. "Just like the second," she muttered. "Only six people here – I wonder if we've already reached a full complement…?"

Yva seemed to have quite lost her appetite for theories, and looked furious. "Where did you get this book?" she demanded, poking Alex hard in the chest. "What have you been up to?"

"Oh!" Colin gasped, his wide eyes on Alex. "Then last night, you were telling the truth!"

"You too?!" Yva glared at him. "Why am I always the last to know everything?"

Cornelia sighed loudly. "Don't exaggerate, Yva," she chided. "Just let Alex get on and tell her story."

"*Thank you,*" Alex said, with some relief. It would be hard enough to say what she had to say without being constantly heckled. She took a deep breath, and spoke the four words that changed everything.

"Adam Carver is dead."

And she explained everything that had happened to her the previous night.

"...so basically, although I can't prove it, Adam Carver can't be the killer because he's already dead," Alex finished at last.

Not surprisingly, nobody seemed to know how to react; especially without a corpse, Alex's story had a nightmarish air of unreality. But one person knew exactly how they wanted to react.

"*Most* intriguing," Cornelia said, and her eyes were shining. "When I saw all that tape beside the front door, I had my hopes, but this is really exceeding them!"

"But what were you *thinking*, RedRidingBlood?!" Vi exploded. "Why didn't you raise the alarm? Call the police?!"

"Because I didn't want to look completely insane!" she threw back at him. "Look what happened when I *did* try to raise the alarm! The body vanished, the tape vanished – it was like magic, and I didn't know what else would happen that would make me look deluded! What if I'd called the police and just had to sit there while everyone stared and the police searched and found nothing and decided Mr. Carver had just gone for a walk or something?" Alex ran her hands through her hair as scenarios no less dreadful for having been avoided rioted through her mind. "They might even think *I'd* done it, and hidden the body, and just wanted attention or something! I went through this over and over all night, wondering if I'd done the right thing, and what I should do next –"

"Well, *I* think you did the right thing," Colin offered, tentatively. "I'm sure I'd have done just the same –"

"But why didn't you at least tell CC?!" Yva trampled over his kind intentions. "She could've put me onto this and we'd have this case wrapped up by now!"

"Because I didn't know she was here!" Alex shot back. "I didn't even know who Corvus Crown *was* until we met just now!"

"What, really?" Yva's energy seemed to vanish, and she responded with flat surprise. "Ha. I suppose I'm *not* always the last to know everything."

"That makes more sense now. I had assumed you knew all about Corvus Crown," Vi admitted. "Adam Carver read your name from the guest list yesterday, and she told us right away that you were her great-niece."

Alex looked over at her great-aunt with some resentment. Yva's quip about not, after all, being the last to know everything had stung.

Guest list secrecy and online privacy were important, yes, but had she really wanted to, Cornelia Crow could have telephoned her Carver-fan great-niece days ago to share the opportunity she'd been given; could have identified herself as Corvus Crown *years* ago. Alex had even been the one who recommended the series to Cornelia Crow in the first place! She had been visiting her great-aunt with her parents just after the series had gotten going, reading *Death in the Walls*, and had remarked to her mystery-loving relative that it seemed like her sort of thing…

Cornelia shrugged, as if it was no big deal. "How tiresome that we couldn't have cleared this up sooner," she said. "But I had no evidence that you were quite so devoted a fan as to be a fellow member of Besieging Heaven. Well, I only meet you and your mother and the rest of the family once a year, and alas, they never talk about books." Alex just never talked. Her extended family included nobody anywhere near her own age. "I'm so glad I worked out this Internet business, you know," Cornelia continued, smiling nostalgically now, her eyes closed. "It is so difficult to find anyone else to read mysteries with, especially when it comes to the really great authors – which is to say, the dead ones. How fitting that Adam Carver has now joined their ranks!"

"Oh good, it's stopped being boring," Yva said, with stunningly open rudeness. "Time to talk about my theory again."

Much eye-rolling ensued.

"Oh yes, your wrong theory about Adam Carver being the murderer," Franny sneered first. "So much for that."

"Actually, yes, so much for it!" Yva retorted, unfazed. "Late though it may be, I'm very grateful for Alex's witness statement. The rest of you may be too slow to see it, but actually it confirms my theory!"

If Yva thought that being a detective was all about making people's jaws drop, she had that part down pat. Alex, stunned to silence, turned instinctively to Cornelia Crow – and saw that she had merely raised a single eyebrow. Alex wished she had her great-aunt's composure in the face of absurdity. How did Adam Carver's death *prove* that he was the murderer? How could it?

Yva gave every impression of a person trying and failing to hide their relish at being the centre of attention, and, after swaggering to the centre of the room, bowed theatrically. "Thank you for your silence," she smirked. "It's a bit early, but you can consider this the denouement. Now, I shall explain it all." Folding her hands behind her back, she began to strut about the room like a fictional detective as she spoke. "I'll return to Alex's problem in a moment, but let me begin with the second murder, which, being the first I knew about, I solved first…"

Alex rubbed her aching forehead, and wondered why her great-aunt was apparently friends with such an insufferably smug person. Of course, she supposed, many fictional detectives *were* insufferably smug, but being a detective didn't make them any more tolerable. And she wasn't yet ready to accept that Yva was a detective at all – save perhaps in her own imagination.

"Franny and Colin weren't present for the full discussion, but suffice to say, Maria's murderer was obliged to flip the switch for the drawbridge from across an unmarked expanse of snow and within a house entirely sealed up on the nearest side," Yva explained, accompanied by a series of airy gestures. "A simple problem; it was immediately obvious that the switch could easily be operated remotely, by means of a length of string run underneath the tower doors and across the courtyard and roof of the house to the rear windows. But the question of who was responsible appeared to be impossible to demonstrate." She paused, and smiled complacently. "…For a few seconds, at least."

A disgusted groan was the only reaction this gloating got from Alex. Yva ignored it, and turned her back on her audience – only to immediately swivel dramatically to face them. "But consider this!" she cried. "Who has been mysteriously absent all morning – and who has an office at the rear of the house with a top-floor balcony which would be perfect for accessing the roof? Adam Carver!"

The thrust of Yva's theory dawned upon Alex, and she tried to dissect it while ignoring Cornelia's cackling. Alex's observations were all that proved both Adam Carver's death and the time period within which Maria might have been murdered; and although Alex knew that her observations were entirely correct, Yva clearly intended to discredit her in some way that made absolutely everybody a suspect. However, with Adam Carver dead, and his body missing, it was impossible for him to have any kind of alibi –

so it was easy to nominate him as the culprit for anything you liked. This held true even if Yva's theory about the ridiculously long piece of string proved false; so long as Mr. Carver's body remained hidden, Yva had a foolproof accusation which nobody could disprove. Could a lazy solution like that really be the correct one?

Alex shook her head. In reality, of course, Adam Carver was the *only* one with an unshakeable alibi, no matter when or how Maria Bole was really murdered: He was already dead while Maria was still walking around quite alive. There was no case for a timing trick; Alex had walked across the open drawbridge and through the raised portcullis minutes before, spoken to Maria Bole almost *moments* before finding Adam Carver's body. Would Yva propose that Maria was murdered by some bizarre trap of Carver's which could have been triggered both remotely and post-mortem? Or…

Yva was still yammering away without giving anyone a chance to work things out for themselves. "Adam Carver: He was the only one with complete freedom of movement over the breakfast period," she was droning unbelievably on. "Victoria Carver could not have known she would be given an opportunity to leave the table, and Corvus Crown is clearly too infirm to manage the previous night's heavy lifting."

"I would have preferred 'intellectual,'" Cornelia muttered.

Yva wasn't listening. "So Adam Carver is the only possible suspect. From this deduction, we can move on to explain the first murder – apparently that of Carver himself," she continued, and Alex started to pay particular attention. "A seemingly insuperable conundrum, as Alex Corby presents it – a perfect imitation of a perfect locked-room mystery…"

"Imitation?" Alex couldn't help from interrupting. That unbeatable, airtight locked room was what she called an *imitation?* "You mean, it was some kind of copycat crime?"

Vi tutted in disapproval. "Y, is this fiction we're talking about again?"

"I'll field this one, Yva," Cornelia interrupted. She drew herself up to her not unimpressive full height, as if preparing to teach a class on the subject, which in fact she attempted to do. "All of us who have read Adam Carver's work," she began, with academic delivery, "must know something of the locked-room mystery – an impossible crime, for which the Golden Age produced countless solutions. If I may briefly refer to Dr. Fell's excellent lecture on the subject –"

"Is this really important?" interrupted Franny. "None of us are detectives. This is juvenile!"

"Franny has a point," Vi conceded, in following. "This isn't the time to talk about books. Maybe if you could skip the background?"

Cornelia and Yva gave the pair a pair of exceedingly ugly looks. Alex felt uncomfortably stuck between the two sides. This wasn't a book club or a discussion on Besieging Heaven, it was true; two people had really been murdered. All the same, the form the murderer's actions had taken could be no coincidence in Adam Carver's house; it was as if a great stack of golden-paged mysteries was casting its long shadow over this case like a pointing finger.

"Fine," Cornelia conceded, after grumbling away in an undertone. "The abbreviated version, then: Alex's taped room – and the entire house, if the murderer inside couldn't touch the murder scene outside – are perfect locked rooms, ones no murderer could ever escape from; sealed from the inside without even a molecule of open space leading outside."

This was fair so far, Alex thought. There had been no gap or wrinkle in the tape on the front door of the house through which even a particle of dust could be introduced – sure, the house was presumably ventilated, but that didn't count. And there were no grounds on which to believe the tape sealing her own room shut had been any different, and nothing suspicious or questionable about its appearance once the door had been opened – unfortunately.

"Furthermore," Cornelia Crow went on, "tape is in and of itself not a new device. Carr and Rawson both wrote taped rooms; even challenged each other to do it, actually…"

"So the solution's already out there?" interrupted Franny, who looked around the group with a smile of relief. "That's great! We can just take it from them!"

But Cornelia was clearing her throat noisily even before Franny was done. "Excuse me," she growled, "but I don't think I had finished speaking. Regarding this copycat idea in particular – point one, the fact is no murderer worth their salt would steal their solution from a book. Poor form, dreadfully poor form."

Alex was not convinced that a murderer would care – and she wasn't sure she liked the way this was going. If Adam Carver's murder was a copycat crime, Alex wondered what kind of lunatic would kill a mystery author with a method out of a mystery book; it was so hideously ironic as to be inhuman. But Cornelia was so certain it hadn't been done. "…How many ways can there be of escaping from a room taped shut from the inside?" she asked, nervously.

"To a creative mind," Cornelia answered, ominously, "there could be any number." She paused before continuing, ruminating on some unknown thought of authors long-dead. "For my second point – well, it would be dishonourable to give away the solution to a mystery. But speaking solely of the taped-room solutions I personally am aware of, I don't believe any could have been used here at Carver's Rest."

Thunder and lightning might as well have crashed at that moment, and stormclouds hurled down rain. Alex couldn't imagine even *one* explanation for this most impossible of situations. And yet here they were, half a century from Cornelia's Golden Age, and the ingenuity of some murderous intelligence had added to the record.

And yet, all through Cornelia's explanation, Yva Dysart was smiling.

"There's no need to panic," she declared, though nobody had gone that far. "The brilliant mind responsible for *The Fourth Wall Crumbles* has already cracked the case. I admit I'm not as familiar with this form of problem as Corvus Crown is, but I don't need to be, because I have already deduced a solution just now. From a statement of the premises alone, the truth can be found. Indeed, any of you might have done the same, had you not abandoned rational thought at the mere mention of that great scarecrow, the 'impossible crime'."

"Yva, you're clearly enjoying yourself, but could you please get on with it?" Vi demanded, wearily. "This isn't a game. You do understand that two people have been murdered here, don't you?"

Yva only smiled complacently. "Other people may understand this 'fact', but I understand only what logic tells me," she replied, debuting yet another infuriating potential catchphrase. "But since you insist, I'll be brief. Consider the following: I have already shown that the second murder can only have been committed by Adam Carver. The corollary, and the solution to the first murder, is self-explanatory: *Adam Carver is not dead!*"

If she didn't have their full attention before, she did now – for all except Alex, who had seen it coming. Yes, she could see Yva's logic, and couldn't deny that it was an elegant explanation. But she had to deny the facts Yva was assuming. For not only had the would-be detective submitted a mockery of a solution for the second murder, it seemed she was waving away the first murder entirely!

"Yva, what exactly are you saying here?" Alex spoke up. She gave the fanfiction writer her most withering look, the one she had only ever used in her head rather than risking it on real people. "I know what I saw. Do you think I hallucinated it or something?"

"I believe in the truth of your *impressions*, RedRidingBlood," Yva insisted, unconvincingly. "I completely believe that you saw something which *looked* like what you claim to have seen. But by your own admission, the light was dim; you did not examine the body. Your immediate assumption was that Adam Carver was dead – and your mind has reinforced that impression in your memories. Probably you genuinely believe he did not even blink, or breathe."

"He *didn't*," Alex said.

"How well could you have seen if he did?" Yva scoffed. "Could you possibly have told the difference between Adam Carver's corpse – and Adam Carver made up to look like a corpse, with red paint on his shirt and half a knife strapped to his chest, and tape positioned halfway around each wrist and ankle so that it appeared to be joined in the middle?"

Alex opened her mouth to reply… and she could not. Yva, much though she hated to admit it, had actually managed to make her feel uncertain. Not uncertain, as she had once so hoped to believe, that she really had hallucinated the awful sight of the author's dead body, but uncertain that she could not have been somehow tricked. Could Yva be right? Could Adam Carver have been living and breathing even then, his eyes moving and blinking, his chest rising and falling, his nostrils flaring for breath?

No – no, Alex did not think so; could not think so, no matter how easy it would make her life. She trusted her first impressions. She didn't think Carver could have sat so still, stared without blinking, used trick tape around his wrists and ankles; didn't think he could have been anything but dead. But all she had were those first impressions; she had no proof. And without proof, she had no counter-argument.

"I'll lay out how the whole trick was done," Yva was explaining to the now-rapt listeners. "For whatever reason, Adam Carver wanted Maria Bole dead – and once it became clear that one of his guests would be a particularly late arrival, he immediately conceived of a plan to remove himself from suspicion. Before retiring to his study that evening, he cleared the stage by encouraging his guests to observe a de facto curfew while privately requesting Maria Bole to stay up to receive his final guest. Once alone, he improvised an apparent fatal stabbing by breaking the blade of one of his collection of old daggers and securing it around his chest with tape – using the same tape to create an apparently continuous loop around his wrists and ankles which was in fact severed in the middle, allowing him to move and walk freely."

Alex risked a glance around. Cornelia Crow was watching Yva with an intent but unsettled look, like someone who wasn't sure if they had locked the house after they left; Franny and Vi had equally uneasy expressions, torn between not taking Yva seriously and yet seeing that a perfect solution was being handed to them. Colin just looked completely overwhelmed.

It was an unconvincing argument. But it was the only one possible!

"With all the guests having chosen a room and retired to bed, Carver identified the one unoccupied room that Alex could select," Yva continued. "Letting himself in, he sealed the door shut from the inside with tape, turned the light out, and slumped against the far wall to wait. And once Alex had eventually entered the room, seen his sham corpse, and fled, he immediately sprang into action – abandoning the 'birthday present', tearing the seal of tape free from the doorframe, and slipping away to his study or some other hideaway. Once the coast was clear, he then got on with the business of setting up Maria's murder whilst everyone else was asleep. That having been committed, Carver is now either lurking somewhere in Carver's Rest, waiting for an opportunity to commit his next atrocity, or has already parachuted down to a hidden motorboat at the foot of the cliffs to make his escape."

With a flourish to demonstrate that she had concluded her theory, Yva bowed once again, evidently expecting applause. She held the bow for a long time before straightening her back. "Any questions?" she asked, possibly rhetorically.

"I have one," Cornelia said. "Why did he need to tape the bedroom door shut? Wouldn't the plan have worked just as well, or even better, without an impossible contrivance?"

"Pride," Yva answered immediately. "Likewise the reason he's leaving autographed books scattered about. He couldn't help but advertise his ingenuity one last time before fleeing the country."

"And the motive?" Franny asked, surprising Alex with a relevant murder mystery question. "Carver's rich and popular and lives in a dream home he designed himself. Why would he throw it all in the trash just to kill someone in a weirdly public way, when he could've crept up on her in an alley or something?"

"*Motive*," sneered Yva, with palpable contempt. "Motives don't matter in murder mysteries. You only ever find them out after the criminal's been caught, and it's usually something you couldn't possibly have anticipated. I'm not required to explain why Carver did it; I just need to show that only he could have done it, and I have. The end."

She glared around, challenging anyone to argue back – and Alex did *so* want to argue back; argue back against the theory which dismissed her own experiences as hollow lies, her own hero as a hollow man. But when even *motive* was out of the picture, when she couldn't just say "Adam Carver wouldn't do that!", how could she find the words? She just couldn't.

As it happened, however, somebody else could.

"A-are you sure?"

Alex looked with amazement at Colin West, who hadn't spoken in so long that she had almost forgotten he was there. He must have been saving himself, his threadbare confidence, for when he really needed it. Yva glanced at him out of the corner of her eye without bothering to turn and face him.

"Is Mr. Carver really the only person who could have done it?" Colin enquired, very tentatively. "I mean, it's very clever, your idea

– and so is Mr. Carver. But what if there's another answer – an even cleverer one…"

"Oh *really*?" Yva rounded on him with a too-wide smile. "So what's your explanation, then? What's your explanation as to how Carver was murdered in a room sealed from the inside with tape and nowhere to hide?"

Colin cringed before her, and his eyes darted everywhere as Alex held her breath for him. "…A ghost?" he guessed at last.

Alex had the good grace to feel guilty for laughing. It wasn't clear that anyone else did.

"Really, now, Colin, that is very droll," Cornelia spoke through a smile, taking the floor while Yva was incapacitated with hilarity. "But there are too few supernatural trappings here for even mystery novel characters to be so gullible." Colin's lip quivered, and Alex was just about to say something when Cornelia finally pulled herself together and addressed the assembled. "I think that's quite enough time spent standing around arguing and getting nothing done," she said, with all the authority of the only real adult in the room. "Solving the murder doesn't get us out of Carver's Rest, and we really should be devoting some time to that. Now, does anyone here not care about the mystery?"

Colin put up his hand tentatively. Franny followed suit.

"Good. Two people with nothing to do with each other," Cornelia said. "I want the pair of you to dig out Victoria Carver and work on a way past the walls. It's probably best not to be explicit about her husband being either a murderer or their victim, so make sure to handle the situation delicately."

The prospect of handling anything delicately appeared to quite terrify Colin, but Franny nodded firmly. "Good to see people are finally talking sense," she said, and turned and went, Colin stumbling over his feet to keep up.

"Now I need another two people with nothing to do with each other to do some investigating for me," Cornelia continued, and pointed her cane at Yva and Vi. "You two will do."

Yva nodded. "You're right. It's probably safe to assume that me and SMV aren't accomplices."

"And if you think we should be keeping an eye on each other," Vi surmised, "I'm mature enough not to take that personally. So, we're searching for clues?"

"No, you're following instructions," Cornelia corrected. "I have a plan for you two, and it involves nipping your own secret passage theory in the bud, and saving the police some time later, too. Here, take this."

She tossed him a shining object. He fumbled the catch.

"You too, Alex," Cornelia said, and Alex saw that her great-aunt had given Vi a bedroom key. Yva stretched out a hand for Alex's. Alex gave hers to Vi, too. "The whole place is full of wood panelling, so it would be perfectly easy to conceal a secret passage," Cornelia was explaining. "I want you to go over Alex's bedroom, and the rest for good measure, and give them the works: Tap on the walls for echoes, poke at panels – take the wood panelling clean off the wall, if you can. And if you see Quinn Shillerdyce, rope him in to take care of the heavy lifting."

"Ackroyd," saluted Yva, who seemed rather pleased with the whole arrangement. "We'll start by going around getting everyone's room keys."

"What about Maria's, though?" Vi queried. "Or Carver's?"

"Not an issue," Yva breezed. "I know how to pick locks."

"You probably shouldn't mention that in public," Alex suggested. "Or to the police."

"Pick locks only as a last resort," Cornelia ordered her. "You know the police will examine the interior of locks to see if they've been picked, and you don't want to disguise any sign of the killer having done the same thing. For the same reason, make sure you put on some gloves before you go through Maria's jacket for her bedroom key."

"What?!" exclaimed Vi and Alex together, Yva echoing them a little too slowly.

Cornelia gave them a stern look. "We can't give the murderer an opening here," she said fiercely. "They almost certainly plan to strike again, and since contacting the police is out of the question, we're not in a position to just all stare at each other in a room until help arrives. Whether it's to stop the murders or just explain them, we have to do this ourselves." Her expression then softened a little

– just a little. "Now, what are you still standing around for?" she asked. "There's a murder to solve, and the only ones who can solve it are we mystery fans. Chop chop!"

She banged her cane on the floor twice, and if Vi didn't oblige her by jumping to attention, Yva did, hurrying Vi through the front door and slamming it behind her. It swept the room with a rush of cold air that lingered, floating free around a silent Alex Corby and Cornelia Crow.

Now that it was just the two of them, things were different. The seconds passed, and felt like minutes, and still not a word was spoken between them. Alex looked at Cornelia, now, and Cornelia looked back. There was a meaning in her eyes which Alex couldn't quite read, but could certainly assume, because she felt it herself, too.

She was disappointed.

Alex was at last alone with Corvus Crown. She was at last alone with the only Adam Carver fan she had ever known in real life, and found that she knew her even less than she thought. Even sharing the room with Cornelia Crow, she felt lonely. Lonely in a house of death where her experiences were being dismissed and her own relative thought her so useless as to give all the jobs to everyone else.

"Yes, you're right," Cornelia suddenly said, and Alex jumped. "There's nothing we need to say to each other. We have work to do too, of course. Now pack these books away and come along."

"W – what?" Alex stuttered, as the old lady thrust the two giftwrapped books into her arms and began to walk away. "You mean – you're giving me a job?"

Crow-like, Great-Aunt Cornelia half-turned to her. "Silly girl. What were you thinking?" she asked. "You have the most important job of all. You're helping me to solve the case."

CHAPTER TEN
THE ASSISTANT

The tapping of Cornelia's cane echoed through the corridors of Carver's Rest, accompanied by two pairs of footsteps. Alex could keep pace with Cornelia's walking, but she was lagging behind Cornelia's thinking. Being promoted to co-detective was more than she had hoped for, if a slight climbdown from her original ambitions, but the turnaround from being seemingly nowhere in the great Corvus Crown's estimation was so fast.

"So – where are we going, then, and what are we doing?" Alex asked, as she walked unsteadily alongside someone whose destination she couldn't guess. She didn't know quite how to relate to Great-Aunt Cornelia, but she knew what she should say to Corvus Crown. "I'm grateful – I mean, I'm happy to help, but – how?"

Cornelia halted at the foot of the stairs, throwing Alex off-balance. The old lady angled her head at Alex once again.

"I need an assistant," Cornelia Crow said. "I won't say a Watson, as it's a terrible cliché and the poor man's reputation has been rather dragged through the mud, but..."

"But basically, you mean a Watson," Alex finished. She needed a less clever person.

"I need a second pair of eyes, a second pair of ears, and a second brain to think with," Cornelia replied dispassionately, "and a reliable one, too. I know I can trust myself, and I'd trust you before anyone else in this house. Not much could slip past both of us."

Cornelia had spoken without emotion, but her words gave Alex a feeling of pride mingled uncomfortably with doubt. Alex thought back to her readings and rereadings of *Castles in the Sky*. On second reading, and third, and, yes, fourth, it turned out that actually quite a lot had slipped past her. It begged a question. "Why me?"

"Chiefly nepotism," Cornelia admitted, which was a blow. "But the luxury of being a relative means I can be confident that you have absolutely nothing to do with what is going on here, which is more than I can say for any of the others. Besides," she continued, "you're a reader, aren't you? You must have solved a few mysteries in your time."

"Um," Alex said. Why, she asked herself, did she have to have second thoughts on someone else's behalf about her own reliability? "I... know the theory."

Cornelia looked down at her, and raised an eyebrow. "Well, it's a start, I suppose," she muttered to herself.

Alex racked her brains for a better argument in her favour, before Cornelia could turn and call for someone else. Self-promotion never came easily to her. Yet this time there was indeed an argument within easy reach.

"And," she said abruptly, feeling she was interrupting a thought if not a statement – "I really want to solve this mystery."

This clearly intrigued Cornelia. She gave Alex both eyes this time. "Why?" she threw at Alex.

"Because it's wrong!" Alex found herself saying, and was surprised by how forcefully she said it. "The murderer's arrogance, the way they use people..."

You didn't need to know who, how, or why to see the cruelty of it all.

It had the desired effect. Alex didn't know what Corvus Crown's criteria for an assistant were, but a slow smile was spreading across her great-aunt's face. "You'll do," she said, and, looking pleased, she began to move.

"But – !" Alex, no, don't ruin it – but rising grinning into her mind was an uncomfortable image of the detective's closer acquaintance. "What about Y? Yva?"

"Yva," Cornelia repeated, and she smiled indulgently. "A hardworking and amiable girl, but –"

Behind, they heard a great door open and close, and footsteps. It was telling that Cornelia fell into silence when Yva herself, Vi trailing at her heels, marched through the hallway across from them; Vi gave a polite nod, but Yva was so set on her purpose that she didn't notice her friend or even the nod as she and Vi vanished upstairs. She was wearing gloves, and they didn't look clean...

Cornelia gave their footsteps time to disappear as they had appeared, before continuing in a lower voice. "A hard-working and amiable girl," she murmured, "but I know what she is. Nobody can gamble on trusting her." Without pausing to explain, she continued straight on to the next question. "And, to return to your original question – if you want to know where we're going and what we're doing, why don't you tell me? Work it out."

Was this a lesson in detection? Alex thought through a couple of obvious options. "We're *not* asking for alibis," she said, with some confidence.

Cornelia gave a small nod. "Indeed," she replied. "Nobody will have an alibi for anything that happened last night, since we know nothing about when either of the murders were arranged save that everyone would have been either in bed or nearly there."

"And for Maria's murder," Alex picked up, "if the murderer even needed to be on the scene, we already know where everyone was and who has an alibi or doesn't. Me, Vi – probably everyone in the breakfast room is ruled out, except for Victoria who left for a while, and…"

"And I, who was not there," Cornelia agreed, stating what Alex had left unstated. "And I suppose we must add Adam Carver, who, dead or not, is unaccounted for. Do you understand yet why he had to vanish, Alex?"

"Erm –" Alex was caught off-guard without a theory. "To… buy time to kill Maria?" she attempted – quickly adding, "And to provide another suspect?"

"A good start – but more importantly, it allowed the murderer to remove the tape," Cornelia said – and, before Alex could riddle out how that worked, her great-aunt had gone on to say, "Oh, and there's one more person who could have killed Maria."

"Um…" Alex rattled through all the suspects in her head. Cornelia gave her a significant look.

"It's you," she said – and turned away to hobble down the corridor, without waiting for Alex to reel her mind in.

Alex was stuck there, in fear of what Cornelia had meant. Was Alex herself a suspect? Of course, *she* knew she was innocent, but could other people think her guilty? She looked back on the morning, what would be different if she *was* guilty – and then she saw it, the danger factor. The only person who claimed that the drawbridge could not have been raised until seven people had joined the breakfast table was herself. If she had lied, then she had no alibi…

But on a moment's reflection, there was light. There was still the evidence of the taped front door – and that came from Quinn Shillerdyce, who had clearly arrived at breakfast some time before Alex. If the door had already been sealed when she woke up, there was no way she could have triggered the drawbridge afterwards. The fact that nobody else could have done it wasn't much comfort, but it was something, at least. Blinking back to reality, Alex saw that Cornelia had gained a little distance on her; she ran to catch up –

When Cornelia spun around and gestured for silence. Alex stumbled to a halt, unconsciously expecting a lecture on running in the corridors, and when one was not forthcoming she listened to the silence instead. At first, it was as if a cloak had fallen across Carver's Rest, muffling the castle – no footsteps, no voices, no rattling objects, everything mummified in the stillness of a crypt. But from out of the walls, faint sounds crept into Alex's ear, one by one – a faint rush that might have been wind or crashing waves; strange knockings from somewhere above her; and, nearest of all, there were indeed voices…

Cornelia gestured to a nearby door, and raised her eyebrows at Alex. Alex let even her mind fall silent, the better to hear, and then nodded. The voices were behind there.

Cornelia approached the door, but Alex held her a moment. "What are we going to do?" she hissed. It felt uncomfortable, having been silent and heard quiet voices nearby, to raise her own voice.

Cornelia raised her eyebrows again. "Listen in, of course," she murmured – and then she stepped up to the door, and quite casually tilted her head to lay an ear against it. After a moment's hesitation, Alex joined her. In a murder mystery, it's not rude to eavesdrop.

Alex didn't know who she expected to be speaking privately in a room together. But she certainly didn't expect it to be this pair. It was the two illustrators – Quinn Shillerdyce and Colin West.

"A-and … death in the … your thoughts, do you recognise …"

"Need a better method … people are a problem … knack for …"

Colin's voice was as low and halting as usual. Quinn was louder, but gruffer. Between the two of them, and with the door also between them and the eavesdroppers, it was suitably difficult to make out what was being said beyond the customary snatches and fragments. Alex pressed her head even harder to the door, as if it would make any difference.

"… work to be done – experiment, develop … Should seriously consider … vouch for you …"

"Then … really think, that I …"

"… if you want others to believe … But yes, you can … Now, if you'll excuse me –"

Cornelia slid away from the door in a single stride. Alex, not quite so prepared, was still stumbling away as the door was yanked open. Towering over her, Quinn Shillerdyce stood with one long-fingered hand on the doorknob and the other curled into a fist, and his brow furrowed into a glare that showed he knew exactly what Alex had just been doing. She took another step back. In that atmosphere, he suddenly seemed like a very unwise person to annoy.

"Ah, Mr. Shillerdyce, I was hoping we might find you," Cornelia smoothly inserted; she was, Alex noticed, almost as tall as he was. "I would appreciate a quick word, and upstairs Yva and Vi will want to take a look at your room…"

"Well, they can find me there," he replied brusquely, and pushed his way past. Alex and Cornelia watched him stomp away down the hall, less vast just for having him in it, before there were just his heavy footsteps on the stairs.

It was almost a surprise to turn back to the doorway and find Colin West hovering in a spacious sitting room, between the tall seats casting long shadows and alternate windows casting stained-glass patterns, adjusting his sleeve with one hand while the other nervously pressed a large black folder to his chest. Cornelia frowned at him.

"Mere minutes, Colin, and you've already abandoned Franny?" she seethed. "Nobody should be left alone in this house right now!"

"I, I left her with Victoria – with Mrs. Carver," he stammered, looking terrified. He hugged the folder to his chest even tighter. "But Mr. Shillerdyce was there, and…"

Cornelia's expression softened; or at least, grew less hard. "I suppose that's alright," she conceded. "You may take us to them, if you please."

He delivered an obedient flurry of nods, and then trotted off nervily up the hallway. Their destination turned out to be just the opposite side of the stairs, a door left ajar which he nonetheless knocked on before leading Alex and Cornelia in. As always at the seaward side of the house, Alex's eyes were drawn and dazzled by the tall, wide windows that looked out on the sea and the distant horizon, a great expanse of jagged ripples reaching out to infinity. But then she looked around the room itself, where artificial light gleamed off countless metal surfaces, and the sea and the sky seemed to close on in her like walls as the situation grew much, much more dangerous.

Of course Adam Carver had an armoury full of medieval weapons. How could he not? Alex had wondered, perhaps subconsciously, where the murderer had gotten a sword and dagger from, having not taken Yva's ridiculous allusion to a "collection of old daggers" seriously; but the fact was that the killer had no shortage of material. A glass-topped case in the centre of the room was almost full of weird old blades, some with elaborate carved hilts and curving edges, others little more than spikes with handles – but those were nothing when the walls bore aloft an eclectic variety of swords, axes, spears, and other exotic weapons Alex couldn't put a name to, plus one conspicuous empty space which presented thin air. A bow and a quiver's worth of arrows hung on one wall in an elaborate arrangement; a further case displayed a set of maces and spike-covered flails. Deadliest of all, lurking like a great shadow in a corner, was a hive-shaped structure of metal, a man-sized sarcophagus on which a dead-eyed mask stared – an actual iron maiden!

Cornelia caught Alex's eye. "Yes, there's a reason nobody ever asked where the weapons came from," she said. "That was never a mystery."

Colin, meanwhile, had rejoined Franny and Victoria Carver, who were standing across the room inspecting the weaponry. "Ah, Colin," Victoria said, bestowing on him a tired smile. "How did it go?"

"Erm," Colin replied, and glanced back at Alex and Cornelia.

"Good morning," Cornelia said, gliding across the room towards them. "Taking inventory, I see."

"Just started," Franny nodded, tapping notes into her phone. "In case of surprises… and because there might be tools we could use; something we can make into a grappling hook, for instance."

"I'm afraid I don't keep too close a track of my husband's acquisitions," Victoria confessed. "But there's plenty of spare chain in the tower storeroom, if that's of any use; ladders, too, though none tall enough to scale the walls. You'll have to improvise."

"If they haven't been gotten rid of like the phone," Franny grimaced. The half-light caught the lines on her face and seemed to bleach her garish hair grey, so she looked much older. "It's not difficult for things to go missing in this house; you can see the spaces where the broadsword and dagger were stolen."

She gestured to the empty spaces where there was only nothing to be seen, but Alex glanced sidelong at the iron maiden instead. She didn't like to look at it; there was something about that empty-eyed mask, so wrongly human, that made her feel unwell. But since they were talking about things going missing, and one of those things was both man-sized and man-shaped...

"I don't suppose," Alex began, taking a few steps towards the iron maiden. There was a slight indent in the front which one could use to –

Alex swung the front of the iron maiden open and jumped back in a single move. A hollow space bristling with long spikes groaned open, with just enough room inside for a person to stand safely until the hatch, itself lined with dagger-like points, was shut – at which point they would be riddled with wounds. Not revealed was the corpse of Adam Carver, or anyone else for that matter.

"Yeah, we thought of that already," Franny nodded, as Alex only half-disappointedly swung the door shut. She wouldn't have liked what she imagined she might have found, but at least it would have been progress. "Overall this room is pretty open. Not many hiding-places," she continued. "I'm thinking we might just barricade ourselves in here for the duration."

"Tell me more," Cornelia said – and as she did so, Alex felt a spidery hand give her a shove in the square of the back. She was being pushed towards Colin West... Alex glanced at her great-aunt, but she acted as if she hadn't noticed the glance, so Alex pretended not to have glanced at all and instead took a few steps over to join

Colin, who had fallen back to the maces. Cornelia was soon in full flow with Victoria and Franny, expertly giving them every opportunity to talk about themselves, so Alex guessed it was her job to pump Colin for information. She gave it her best shot.

"Hello," she said.

Colin gave her a weak smile.

This was harder than she thought. Alex flipped through her memories for any involving DaVinciCorpse or even Colin, searching for any common reference points she could lean on, anything at all. Art? Alex couldn't draw to save her life. Copyright and ownership? DaVinciCorpse had started signing and watermarking all his work and justifying it at length, but RedRidingBlood had tended to tune out...

But of course – on Besieging Heaven, they all had one common reference point.

"You mentioned classic mystery novels earlier," she said. "Are there any authors as good as Adam Carver?"

Colin's face seemed to lift in an instant, like an inflating balloon. "A-as good as Adam Carver?" he stuttered. "I don't know if I should say. There are one or two really great authors who can give you more of the same – ah, but, if it's only *as good as*..." He looked over Alex's shoulder, and then, suddenly looking very guilty, lowered his voice. "I don't know if you can really be better than something you're just trying to imitate," he whispered. "Carver's good, but – I don't know if he's really *great*..."

Alex was taken aback. How could he say that, as a fan? Adam Carver *was* great. "That's like blasphemy," she said, maybe a little petulantly. "Saying that on Besieging Heaven would probably get you killed." It was then that she remembered the stakes. "...That was a really bad choice of words, I'm sorry."

Colin looked awkwardly away, and Alex looked down. Full marks for killing the conversation. She let her eyes rest on the maces, which themselves rested snugly and neatly in soft, cushioned spaces beneath the glass. The handles were all more or less the same, but one was topped with a spiked ball, another with a series of protruding fins, while a third resembled an ornate sceptre; others, the flails, separated the handle and club element and linked them with a length of chain.

So many ways to kill someone... And yet, didn't both Carver and Maria have slight head wounds? Had one of these maces been used after all – but only to stun, while blades had struck the killing blows? Alex didn't understand. Why couldn't the murderer have been content simply with knocking them down? Why tie them up, why subject Maria to a terrible death trap? Did it make it easier to kill them – or was it the murderer's sheer malice?

Alex's distracted musings were disturbed by Colin himself, who gestured uneasily at the cabinet of clubs. "Do you think," he volunteered, "one of these, was –"

"Yeah," Alex nodded. "Used by the murderer to attack their victims... They might have put it back so it wouldn't be found on them." The thought of lugging one of those deadly weapons around, though, suddenly seemed only dubiously practical. "How heavy do you think these are?" she asked. "Can we get in? I mean, if the murderer did..."

"Oh, Mr. Carver showed them off yesterday. It's easy," Colin hastened to answer. "The house is so secure that he wasn't worried about thieves. You just..." He scrabbled at the edge of the glass lid until his fingers found purchase, and then he simply lifted it up, exposing the maces to the open air.

Alex glanced over her shoulder. Victoria and Franny were facing away, chattering to Cornelia about barricades and climbing ropes. "Do you think it would be okay if we just... tried one?" she whispered to Colin. "There's no blood on any of these, the murderer would have wiped it, so there'll be no fingerprints..."

Colin shot his own nervous look at the three women nearby. "Okay, I'll try it," he said in a low voice, and stretched out a free hand. He wavered over various of the weapons before at last choosing the smallest, a kind of club for short-range battering, which he gradually lifted without great effort. "It's not too heavy," he murmured, hefting it. "At this size, you could probably tuck it up your sleeve without anyone noticing."

Alex hesitated over her next statement, but at last decided to give it a shot. "Are you suggesting," she quipped, "that a woman could have committed this crime?"

The pair snickered as quietly as they could. The old Besieging Heaven in-jokes were the best.

"Yes, obviously," Colin said at last, looking for once almost at ease. "I mean – no offence, but – do you want to...?"

"Oh, sure!" she answered, holding out her hands with what she hoped was not ghoulish eagerness. Could she handle a murder weapon as well as a murderer's calling card? It was all part of the investigation, which for the most fleeting moment seemed quite like fun.

Colin dropped the mace into her outstretched hands, and darn it, it was heavier than she expected. *"Heck!"* she muttered, with commendable politeness given the circumstances, as the mace tumbled from her palms and as if pulled by a magnet plunged straight down onto Colin's foot.

To his credit, Colin did not cry out, but his arms and legs tensed to ruler-straightness and his round face hissed like a pinpricked balloon. The black folder he had been holding tumbled to the floor, spilling a sheaf of papers.

"What are you two playing at?" a voice called, and Alex saw Cornelia, Victoria, and Franny staring at them disapprovingly. "Young people today, I ask you," Cornelia muttered, and then they returned to their conversation and Colin slowly retrieved the mace from where it was embedded into his shoe.

"No harm done," he said, very quietly, as he deposited the mace back in the case.

"I am *so* sorry!" Alex squeaked, aghast. "Let me help you with your papers –"

"No, it's alright –" he hurried out, and then they were both on the floor gathering together stray sheets of heavy, textured paper. Alex couldn't help looking. It was only human.

The papers were drawings – page after page of turrets silhouetted against a full moon, or gatehouses yawning like ferocious jaws, or ruins collapsing under ivies and lichens. Or the gruesomely slaughtered dead...

Alex stared at the sheets she had in hand, her atonement quite forgotten. "I've seen some of these," she said, her mind leafing back through page after page on the forums of Besieging Heaven. "This is your fanart."

"My portfolio," Colin corrected, tugging the sheets from Alex's hands. "Or, um, the originals, yes, of the ones online..."

"They're good," she said. "I mean, you knew that, but still."

"Well." There was the faintest hint of pride in his voice. "Not everyone likes them. Or, not everything…"

"Were they what you were showing to Quinn Shillerdyce just now?" Alex asked, realising that that of course must be it. "Getting a professional's opinion?" She tried not to make assumptions.

"I, asked him if he would take a look at them yesterday, so I guess that, um, he did…" Colin's stammer output ratcheted up as he touched on a subject near to his heart. "And he got back to me just now, he was with Victoria when me and Miss, um, Franny found her, and he asked for a word…" There was just one picture left which he had yet to file away. "And he said the same things everyone says."

Alex leaned forwards to see the picture. It was a drawing of Sanguinaria, the protagonist of *Castles in the Sky*, radiant in the elaborate wedding dress imposed upon her by the man forcing her into marriage, sublime in her misery as the cruel shadow of the diabolical Count Udolfo clawed across the wall. Her veil was thrown back, and her face, which the text described as the most beautiful in Europe…

…was a kind of inverted triangle, sporting two lines for a nose and one for a mouth, dominated by an enormous pair of glassy orbs dotted with light spots and layered with countless concentric circles. At worst, she looked like an alien. At best, she looked like anime. And always, she looked exactly like every single other character born from the artist's pencil.

Colin West could not draw faces.

Conscious of Alex looking, Colin flushed deep red and stuffed the sketch away into his folder – even though exactly the same image had been online in one of his many art threads for some years now. But criticism is never quite the same thing in person, and Alex tried to step around it delicately.

"There have got to be ways around that, though?" she suggested. "If not practice makes perfect, then – then there'll always be a need for background artists, and maybe costume designers…"

She trailed off, seeing Colin not looking any happier about it. He met her eye, and tried to smile, but his heart wasn't in it. You always know.

"Thank you," he offered, "but that's just not quite good enough... *I'm* not quite good enough. I just want to, you know, have a thing, that I'm really good at. Something I can put my name to. It doesn't have to be art. Like when Y and CC were writing *The Fourth Wall Crumbles*, I suggested some, um, embellishments, to the plot – but Yva only accepted if they would make better illustrations... and if I didn't put people in them." He gazed mournfully at his portfolio, and sighed, long and low. "It's difficult to give up on your dreams."

Colin's voice cracked on an emotion that felt almost as bad for his listener. This was all getting a bit intense for Alex. She never knew the right thing to say to other people's feelings, and not knowing made her horribly anxious. "There's still art college!" she hazarded, wildly.

"That's what Mr. Shillerdyce said," Colin nodded. "But I don't know... Everyone else would be so much younger..."

Alex was thrown by that line. "Um, what?" was all she could come back with. "But aren't you only like... our age, on Besieging Heaven? A teenager?" Colin didn't reply. Ages weren't generally disclosed on Besieging Heaven, but of course everyone made assumptions. Alex squinted, and tried to gauge just how old Colin really was. "Are you... nineteen...?" she guessed, without any confidence in the ceiling she had set.

"Um," Colin echoed, and glanced away. "I mean. Give or take, a... a decade."

"Come along now, Alex!" a familiar voice mercifully called. Cornelia had chosen the perfect time to interrupt, just as Alex had no idea how to continue. Colin West was an actual, proper adult? And she'd been talking to him like he was just another person her own age? Online, especially on the anonymous Besieging Heaven, that was inevitable and you tried to avoid thinking about it; but in real life it made her feel weird, weird in a way that didn't quite apply to the both aged and related Cornelia Crow. Not looking at Colin – Mr. West? – she hurried back to Cornelia, who was standing by the door with Victoria Carver.

"We're finished here, for now," Cornelia said to Alex. "Victoria has given me some very interesting information which we need to verify. Yva's string theory might be out of the window, as it were. You two stay together," she broke off, instructing Colin and Franny.

"Got it," Franny said. Colin stared at his shoes.

"There's just one last thing," Cornelia went on, and addressed herself to Franny. "I have to say, I'm surprised you didn't have any theories on the murders," she said. "I gather mystery novels are becoming quite popular again among young people, and as a reviewer you must surely have read countless of them."

Franny waggled her hand sideways in the universally-recognised symbol for "Eh." "Read a lot, yeah," she conceded, "but I don't have time to *think* about them, let alone read any of the classics you've been going on about. It's just a job these days." She seemed to remember something, and she let out a short laugh. "With the tiny deadline they gave me, I didn't have time to read the last *Castles in the Sky* at all!"

If she expected this anecdote to be received with genial chuckles, she was wholly mistaken. Alex's jaw dropped, and she heard Colin let out a loud gasp. There was no sign of any good impression from Cornelia or Victoria, either.

"You... never read..." Cornelia repeated slowly, as if she couldn't quite believe it, "*Conspiracies of the Obscure Tribunal*? Never read the last volume?"

"But..." Alex stammered, "you reviewed it. The publishers pushed your five-star review everywhere! There was a quote from your site printed on the *back cover*!"

"I had my assistant write something up," Franny shrugged. "Janey. Nice girl. Mostly does the paperwork, but I had her skim the book and my old reviews and throw together something convincing. She's getting rather good at it." She looked at the astonished faces surrounding her as if seeing them for the first time, and at last realised she had misjudged the situation. "Look, it was only the last book in a series," she retorted. "You can assume it's just more of the same. And it's the publishers' fault for rushing to print and giving me such a slim deadline!"

The jury grew no more sympathetic. The momentary stillness was broken only by Cornelia slowly shaking her head. "That," she said icily, "is unforgiveable, for a fan."

Franny's lip twisted. "I was never a fan," she said, but Cornelia had already turned her back and was sweeping Alex out of the room as if away from a bad influence, and Colin West and Franny Smythe and the arsenal of murder became just another exhibit in the museum of disillusionment Alex had encountered in Carver's Rest.

CHAPTER ELEVEN
AND OTHER CRIMES

Alex, Cornelia Crow, and Victoria Carver strode away through the too-silent, too-dingy corridors, and for all she felt like a trespasser in those empty halls with all their gloom and unseen menace, Alex was still glad to be away from the armoury.

"Well, that was awkward," she said, with feeling; she had no idea what she would say to either Colin or Franny when next they met. Her companions' silence suggested they agreed, so Alex changed the subject and spoke only to Cornelia, who was setting the pace despite being older than her two companions combined. "You mentioned that Yva's theory, about using string to trigger the gates, was out of the picture?"

Cornelia nodded. "Tell her what you told me," she instructed Victoria.

Victoria, whose floating shawl tickled Alex's forehead as they walked, complied with a surprising lack of ill-grace. "You understand, don't you, that none of the windows on the landward side of the house open?" she explained, and Alex nodded. "Well, the windows on the seaward side are different. They open – but only with a key, and I made sure to lock up before the guests arrived. Just to be on the safe side."

"And that key?" prompted Cornelia.

"I was getting to that," replied Victoria, just shortly enough to show that there was considerable pressure packed behind her cool demeanour. "The window locks, and also the balcony lock, have only the one key for the entire house. Without it, they're just another set of fixed windows." They reached the stairs, and she gestured upwards and to the south. "And as I'll show you, I've been keeping the key locked up in my jewellery box, so nobody should have been able to play around with the windows either yesterday or today."

That would figure, Alex thought, as they climbed the stairs three abreast. Yva's theory was that the murderer had tied string to the drawbridge lever, and run it all the way across the courtyard and over the roof of the house to a back window, where they could pull it at their leisure – murdering Maria Bole without needing to be anywhere near her. But if the windows had all been locked, and the key unavailable, that trick would no longer be viable.

Alex was, for a moment, glad to have one of Yva's bad theories ruled out – but then she remembered the corollary of this information, which was that Carver's Rest, or rather the entire outside world, had been a true locked room at the time of Maria's murder… making the crime impossible. The best you could say was that this narrowed things down.

Still, though. "Play around with the windows" – that was a rather mild way for Victoria to put it, Alex thought. They were talking about a murder trap that had killed a person just outside Victoria's front door, and her husband was very suspiciously missing. Was Victoria Carver being a little too casual?

"How much," Alex began, and Cornelia raised her eyebrows in surprise, "have Franny and Colin told you about what's going on…?"

Victoria's expression had been calm enough, only occasionally showing signs of strain, but after Alex's question it shifted – becoming rigid and drawn, too clearly just a mask. "They made certain intimations about my husband," she recited, almost through gritted teeth. "Intimations which I absolutely do not acknowledge."

Denial. That was one of the five stages of grief, wasn't it? But denial would do nobody any good in this situation. "He is missing, though…" Alex ventured.

"He could be anywhere, for any reason," Victoria snapped, not meeting Alex's eyes. "He could have been moving about the house and we've just happened to miss each other. Or he could have left on an emergency errand."

"Now, this is what I fail to understand," Cornelia interjected. "Why are you bothering to make excuses for him? A man who brought his friends and followers into his home and threatened –"

"Here we are!" announced Victoria, just on the brink of Cornelia letting slip some extremely interesting information. But Cornelia wouldn't meet Alex's eyes either, and so Alex sighed and shelved it and took stock of their current location – a door on the opposite wall and opposite wing to Alex's, though the two wings looked identical apart from being reversed left-to-right. The door had a lock like Alex's own, but Victoria simply turned the handle and pushed it open. "Now," she declared, "I'll guarantee you that the windows have not been tampered wi…"

She trailed off as she gazed into the bedroom, leaving Alex and Cornelia to peer around her. Victoria's bedroom was, in complete contrast to the guest rooms, as sleek and modern as the seaward face of the house. The low, wide furnishings were in pale pastel shades, while heavy rugs were thrown across a parquet floor. A vast mirror occupied almost an entire wall, reflecting an equally vast adjacent window and another two walls where the traditional square-panelled surfaces of all the other rooms had been replaced by panels in abstract patterns, hung with photographs with heavy white borders, a calendar of city skylines with scratchy notes against the dates, and a numberless silver clock with both fingers about three-quarters around. The décor was in startling contrast to Adam Carver's tastes, and it occurred to Alex with a jolt that Mr. and Mrs. Carver had been sleeping in separate rooms. The bed at least looked slept in, but only by one person.

The main event, though, was not the Carvers' married life. Rather, it was the smashed and splintered fragments of wood that lay among a heap of jewellery on the dressing-table.

"My jewellery box!" Victoria gasped, and with her shawl flying behind her she swooped upon the deconstructed box and started sifting through the wreckage. "If anything's missing, I'm calling the police – !"

"I was given to understand that the telephone had been removed," Cornelia said, coolly stepping across the threshold to join Victoria. Alex followed after a moment's hesitation, wondering if it was really her place, and then shut the door behind her so she could claim to be thinking of Victoria's privacy. She was momentarily distracted on noticing that the left-opening door had concealed a short corridor on the left wall, only as long as it was wide, with a further door opening towards the back of the house. Alex snuck a glance at Victoria and found her still absorbed in her jewels, so she took an opportunity to open the mysterious door a fraction; but it revealed only a narrow bathroom running alongside the bedroom, likewise terminating in a window out onto the open sea.

Although there was really no "only" about it. So Vi hadn't simply been rambling when he'd woken Alex up that morning –

there really *were* ensuite bathrooms! Why couldn't her room have had one of those instead of her favourite author's murdered body?

"Thank goodness," Alex heard Victoria sigh with relief, and she quickly rejoined them. "Nothing's missing." Victoria had arranged the sifted jewels and wooden shards into separate piles, which she was frowning at with a curious expression. "So why…?"

"I don't see a key in there," Cornelia interrupted.

Alex's breath caught in her throat. So the window key really *was* missing!

Victoria's eyes had widened to an almost unhealthy degree, and she stared at the debris with something like astonishment. "But that's impossible – ridiculous!" she gasped. "I checked in here while I was looking for Adam, and the box was untouched!"

"Really?" asked Cornelia, drawing out the question as her eyes shone eagerly. "How very interesting…!"

"While you were checking earlier –" Alex began, and cast her mind back. It was immediately after Victoria had returned that Quinn Shillerdyce had told them about the tape on the front door, and from there Alex, Vi, Yva, Colin, Franny and Victoria herself had gone to investigate, none of them separating until after Alex had noticed the raised drawbridge. So if the key *had* been stolen to open a window and pull on Yva's hypothetical string, not one of those six could have done it – and the timing would have been inhumanly tight for Quinn. Who did that leave… Alex started in surprise. Only Cornelia!

Cornelia Crow did not catch Alex's stunned expression; she was too absorbed in Victoria. "Just to be clear, you insist that this is true, correct?" she asked. "I'm a little out of the loop, but Yva filled me in on the details while my great-niece stepped away earlier – and it seems that you went looking for your husband while everyone else was eating breakfast, setting eyes on the intact box as you did so, and when you returned then everyone went to the front door and observed that it had been taped shut and the drawbridge raised. So *before* the drawbridge was found to be up, the only people who could have broken that box were, so far as you're concerned, either Quinn Shillerdyce, or me."

Victoria looked shaken; Alex was, too. She hadn't expected her great-aunt to just come out with it. "I – I imagine so," Victoria stumbled. "But of course I'm not accusing –"

"Furthermore," Cornelia went calmly on, "as I was descending to the ground floor this morning, I actually *met* Quinn Shillerdyce coming up the stairs, and we exchanged pleasantries for a minute or so; during which he told me that I must have just missed you wandering around and that the front door had been taped shut – news so intriguing I managed to prevail on him to take my breakfast tray away for me. Now, I'm not going to timetable it, but considering how things were moving downstairs, I would imagine this more or less rules out either of us as the thief – assuming that the theft took place *before* the drawbridge was raised."

Fresh evidence! Alex turned it around and around in her mind like a precious stone. Cornelia didn't intend to timetable it, but somebody should. So Victoria had returned to the breakfast table, and within perhaps two minutes, Quinn had told them about the front door and they had all decamped in that direction. If Quinn had met Cornelia coming down the stairs, he must have turned away from the group just as they were entering the lobby. Add a few minutes for Quinn and Cornelia to talk while everyone else was discussing the state of the front door downstairs, and it all seemed to balance out. Their window of opportunity to smash that box and go string-pulling was closing tight. Cornelia might still have done it had she wasted not a second after Victoria had abandoned her search, and Quinn might have done it had he too wasted not a second and had already stolen and used the key, started going downstairs, and faked coming back up when he heard Cornelia coming... but neither version of events seemed practical. Which meant that nobody could have been the thief –

"Which means that only one person could have been the thief," Cornelia announced, as if she had read Alex's mind.

"But there's nobody left," Victoria replied, nonplussed, but at least Alex hadn't had to say it. "Unless you mean Adam –"

Cornelia sighed dramatically. "I mean *you*, dear," she said to Victoria.

Victoria drew in a shuddering breath, like a victim's last gasp, or perhaps more like someone deathly insulted – and Alex was once again hurrying to catch up. Just when would Victoria have had chance to break the jewellery box…? Wait, no, it was easy. It was *her* box in *her* room, and nobody else had laid eyes on it. Victoria could have smashed the box anytime!

"Don't be absurd," Victoria finally retorted, rewinding her shawl tighter around her neck. "Why would I smash my own jewellery box? I have the only key to it. I could open it anytime I wanted."

"To disguise the fact that you'd done just that, of course," Cornelia replied, as if it was the simplest thing in the world.

"Where is the key to the box, then?" Alex broke in, desperate to ask something important – and an idea had occurred to her with Cornelia's last words.

Victoria dipped a hand into one of her pockets, and it resurfaced with a tiny key that looked as if it might have fitted a music box. "Here," she said, slamming it down beside the ruined box. "The only time it leaves my pocket is to go into my handbag whenever I go out, or on top of the box itself at night."

That was just what Alex wanted to hear. "Could anyone have snuck in here at night and taken it?" she suggested. "I noticed that your room wasn't locked –"

"It's not locked in the daytime because all of my real valuables are – *were* – in this jewellery box," Victoria answered, pointing at the wreckage. "Any theft by a guest would be obvious, so why worry about it? But at night, of course my door is locked."

"Do you leave the key in the door?" asked Cornelia, who had been watching Alex appraisingly.

"…Naturally," Victoria replied, cautiously.

"I'll check under the door," Alex said, anticipating what she was sure her great-aunt would say next, and indeed Cornelia smiled at her with an approval that felt better than she had expected. She was catching up.

"Allow me to explain," Cornelia's voice croaked, while Alex dropped to the ground, squinting at the gap between the bedroom door and the floor beneath. "Alex is proposing, I believe, that the destruction of the jewellery box was a blind, disguising the fact that the window key had *already* been stolen…"

Alex nodded to herself. It was invigorating, being ahead of the game for a change.

"Now, I noticed that this house uses those good old-fashioned locks where the keyholes run right through the door," Cornelia continued. "Consider the following: At night you lock your door, leave the key in it, and on top of the jewellery box you place its own key. Then you fall asleep. Well, what if somebody were to come along and use that old Enid Blyton favourite, where they pass a sheet of paper beneath the door, use something narrow to poke the key out of the lock, and it falls onto the paper and they pull it back under the door? They then unlock your room from the outside, sneak in, raid the jewellery box and take the window key, and leave everything as they found it – replacing the door key back on the interior of the door and turning it from the outside using our old friend, string."

"It won't work," Alex called out.

She could almost hear Cornelia frown. "Excuse me?"

"It won't work," Alex repeated reluctantly, as she stood up and brushed herself down. "There's not enough of a gap under the door, because the carpet meets it. You might get paper or string through there, but not the key…"

"Hmm." Cornelia frowned. "A pity. Well, I suppose there are always long-nose pliers to turn the key from the outside…"

Victoria put her foot down. The process was literal, but the noise was muffled by a conveniently-placed rug. "This is ridiculous," she snapped. "I would not sleep through somebody breaking into my room!" She cast an angry look upon the ruined box. "And I'm tired of these games."

"So you'll accept this conclusion, then?" Cornelia asked, almost casually. "That the only person who could have broken this box before the drawbridge was raised is you?"

"And I'll ask again – why would I break my own jewellery box?" Victoria demanded, becoming almost furiously exasperated. "That box was beautiful!"

"I don't suppose it was an antique, though, was it?" asked Cornelia – and there was something strange in the way she said it, a hint at something Alex didn't understand. "I'm sure the Carver millions would run to another. You might even already have a spare…"

Victoria let out an exaggerated tut of disgust – but she didn't seem quite so angry anymore. "The *Carver* millions," she mimicked. "I'll let the two of you in on a little secret that Adam doesn't like to bring up." Her expression grew ever so slightly self-satisfied. "The simple fact is that my parents made an absolute *fortune* in their lifetimes. And when my father died some years ago, long before *Castles in the Sky*, I inherited with my brother and became very wealthy." Her face was more than just slightly self-satisfied now. "My husband's hints last night about me playing fast and loose with the purse strings were just his idea of a joke. The so-called Carver millions are almost entirely mine."

"What?" gasped Alex. Alright, that bit about Carver slandering his wife to her face was very interesting indeed, but first things first: "But *Castles in the Sky* was a smash hit! Everyone said it made loads of money!"

Victoria Carver gave Alex a look which was trying hard not to be patronising, and failing. "Please," she said. "Everybody knows that authorship doesn't pay."

"It's sad but true," Cornelia nodded mournfully. "*Castles in the Sky* was popular, yes, but as I recall, Adam Carver's earliest books were his second job while he was working in a funeral parlour."

A nostalgic smile passed, now, across Victoria Carver's lips. "You certainly know his biography," she said, and her anger seemed to evaporate. "That was where we met, at my father's funeral. He was so kind."

Alex cleared her throat, reluctant to interrupt but with too pressing a question to leave out. "So..." she began, wondering how least rudely to ask, "does this mean that Carver's Rest was actually built with your money, and not Adam Carver's?"

Victoria looked away for a second before answering with a nod. Maybe it *was* rude, then, and Alex hesitated before embarking on the question she had to ask next.

"If that's the case," she said, "then... why did you go along with it?" She threw her arms wide. "All this, this castle... Why did you let him build it?"

Victoria blinked at Alex in what looked very much like bewilderment, as if it was a question that shouldn't even need asking. "Because I love him," she said simply.

"Oh!" Alex had to turn away to hide her blush of embarrassment. She really hadn't been expecting sentiment.

Perhaps, of course, it was because the evidence suggested the Carvers' marriage was not a happy one. They slept in separate rooms. Adam Carver had apparently accused his wife of spending all his money. And Victoria Carver's room was so different in décor to the rest of the house that it was hard to imagine she was completely happy in Carver's Rest. But nonetheless, she stayed there. So maybe the dissatisfaction had been on the other side…

"I suppose it's easy to forget love in a mystery story," Cornelia commented aside to Alex. "Non-deranged love, at least."

A soft laugh sang from Victoria. The change in subject had done wonders for her mood. "That reminds me of something Adam said once," she said, looking nostalgic. "He said that some people thought romance wasn't allowed in a mystery story – no, he said there was even a rule against it."

"Ah, I believe that's right," Cornelia nodded. "One of Van Dine's, I think." She sniffed. "Stuffy old stick-in-the-mud. It has to be a good *story* as well as a good mystery."

"I don't think I remember many happy couples in the mystery stories I've read, though," Alex pointed out.

"It is true that the healthiest relationships in mystery fiction tend not to get going before the epilogue," Cornelia conceded. "Heaven help them if they come back for the sequel. Although I suppose it worked out well enough for Tommy and Tuppence."

Alex was suddenly delighted – "I've actually heard of them!"

"Well, they are creations of the Queen of Crime," Cornelia said, shrugging bonily. "There's no such thing as an obscure Christie novel. Perhaps you should read *Partners in Crime*; I think it would suit your tastes."

Victoria suddenly let out a small gasp. "Partners in crime – that might have been it!" she said, and suddenly they were plunged back into the maze of deductions. "If two people were working together, maybe they could have broken into my jewellery box and lied for each other." Victoria's eyes narrowed at Cornelia. "Like you and Quinn. If the two of you were accomplices –"

"Accomplices are a cheap device to make things easy for the author," Cornelia growled, with sudden ire. "Of course the killer can get away with anything if they have a sufficient number of people willing to lie for them! If you'll forgive me for saying so, my dear, that was the biggest weakness of your husband's *Conspiracies of the Obscure Tribunal*."

"*Conspiracies of the Obscure Tribunal* is selling very well," Victoria said, her expression rigid. "I'm sure the conclusion must have met the public's expectations."

Alex couldn't resist risking her own opinion on that statement. "Um, it's kind of a bit more controversial than that," she admitted. "With all respect to your husband, not many people were happy with the solution to all the mysteries being that everyone was just lying to Sanguinaria…"

"Well," Victoria scowled. "That's none of my concern." She turned to the window, gazing out on the sunless sky. "He had to explain things somehow."

"And so do we," Alex said, looking once more at the shattered jewellery box. "We wanted to see if someone had the window key before Maria's murder; but everyone's been ruled out. And if it was taken *after* the murder, you could argue for nearly anyone to have done it."

"Victoria and Quinn never left the house," Cornelia muttered, checking them off on her fingers. "Colin and Franny went back and ran around on their own for a while. Alex, you went off on your own upstairs to retrieve that book – surely not time enough, but any accusation against me or Quinn would be valid for you as well. Yva and Vi should have been together, but if they were out of each other's sight for any span of time…"

"So basically, probably any of us could have done it," Alex sighed. "I thought the broken box might be a clue, but it doesn't help at all."

"It *is* a clue. Don't lose sight of the real question," Cornelia snapped. "The motive for stealing the key before Maria died was theoretically to cause her death, correct? So then, for what reason would anyone need to steal the key *afterwards*…"

"I'll leave you to it," Victoria said abruptly. "I should be keeping an eye on Colin and Franny, making sure they don't do anything dangerous."

Cornelia waved a hand airily. "Well, thank you for your assistance. Don't let us keep you."

They stared at each other, quite motionless, until Victoria made a terse gesture towards the door. "If you wouldn't mind...?"

"Oh, right...!" It *was* Victoria's bedroom. Alex fumbled her way out, Cornelia taking her time behind, and they once again emerged into the south wing's avenue of doors. The door slammed behind them, and they turned to see Victoria making to walk away. But then she paused – glanced at them critically – and turned back to the door, withdrawing a further key from a hidden pocket as she did so.

Cornelia stretched out a wavering palm. "Ah, now, Yva and Vi will need that key..."

"Then they can come and ask me for it," Victoria said firmly, as the lock clicked behind her hand. Alex and Cornelia's eyes followed the room key back into her pocket, and then followed Victoria herself as she bustled down the hallway, disappearing momentarily around the open landing before reappearing between the banisters as a torso, then a head, then just a pair of eyes peering suspiciously at them, and lastly just the sound of fading footsteps.

And then Alex and Cornelia were alone.

"Well," Cornelia said at last, tapping her cane thoughtfully upon the floor. "That was rather productive, though admittedly not in the way I'd imagined. Intriguing, don't you think? Now," she continued, squinting around the shadowy corridor, "shall we acquire Yva and Vi? They should be somewhere up here, and I'd like very much to know how they're getting on..."

"Wait," Alex interrupted, before Cornelia could tap her way away. "There's something we need to talk about first."

Cornelia's narrow eyebrows rose, which was the only way to get a good look at her deep-sunken eyes. "Really?" she asked. "Can't it wait?"

"Not after what I heard in there," Alex demanded. "Great-Aunt Cornelia, I'm tired of being out of the loop. It's time someone told me what Adam Carver did last night to make everyone hate him!"

CHAPTER TWELVE
STAINED IMAGE

Within the walls of Carver's Rest, that grey light, half-light, light without sunlight fluttered faintly at the slit-like windows and could not be let through. At sunset the grand windows at the rear of the house might be set ablaze, but for much of the day there was only the false brassy glare of lightbulbs in their countless ornate fittings; and in winter that was all day. A face seen through that jaundiced haze was so, so easy to distrust.

"Admirable curiosity," Cornelia Crow said, her hooded eyes now only suggesting a gaze. "Why don't we discuss this somewhere a little more private?"

Alex felt suddenly very conscious of the dryness of her lips, and had to resist the urge to lick them. "Why not here?" she asked.

A deceitful smile twitched on Cornelia's mouth. Alex didn't know who it was deceiving. "Because certain people don't want you to find out about this," she said, "and so I don't care for them to learn how you *did* find out."

Why did people sometimes feel like a question without an answer? Just when Alex was really starting to feel at ease working with her strange old detective great-aunt, a secret had slipped between them, and now Alex didn't understand anything again. It didn't help that Cornelia Crow made a habit of being so darn cryptic.

But at the same time, Alex wondered, wasn't there something reassuring about that? Cornelia was an old lady whose monotonous retirement apparently consisted almost entirely of reading mystery stories. She was probably absolutely relishing the opportunity to be genuinely cryptic about something important. Just like Yva Dysart, and, Alex admitted, just like herself…

…Cornelia Crow probably wanted to be a detective.

Well, of course she did. She could hardly be the killer, could she? She was about eighty years old, minimum, Alex reasoned. For her to murder anybody was out of the question. She might have been waiting a lifetime to catch a murderer, though. Cornelia Crow was trustworthy. Probably. It wasn't a detective's deduction; it wasn't completely reliable and unassailable. But it was plausible, and almost all the time, that has to be good enough.

"Alright," Alex sighed. "Lead the way."

Cornelia's smile grew almost imperceptibly wider. She beckoned with a wizened finger, and then turned and hobbled away towards the descending staircase, Alex in her wake.

Victoria Carver had already vanished; Carver's Rest was silent and no-one was to be seen. That was what was wrong with the house. It was always too quiet, too empty. It absorbed noise and kept it inside the walls. That might be good for an author's tranquillity, but in a house of murder it felt dangerous, like a threat might be waiting behind every door and corner, or perhaps worse, might already have been there and struck. If, Alex thought, a murder was being committed at that moment, behind a door that had been shut, in a room that had been locked – how would she know? As they turned from the stair and passed the closed door of the armoury, Alex fought off dark suspicions.

Cornelia walked to the end of the corridor and pushed open a door on the dark side of the house, and Alex saw why she might feel comfortable in this room. It was a library, of quite generous proportions, shelves and spines of leather or card disguising the wood panels of the walls, bookcases tall enough that even a tall person would need a footstool or an even taller friend to reach the top shelves. A further corridor of cases crossed the middle of the room, cutting out what meagre light crept through the arrowslit windows, so the room was divided into a dark half and a darker half. Cornelia led Alex into the former, and Alex could not help darting a glance through the window. But outside were only snow and walls, the shape of the towers hiding the portcullis and its shrouded victim.

Cornelia, meanwhile, had paused at a glass case, this one containing not weapons but half a dozen or so books of which Alex was familiar with exactly four. But she knew well the name that appeared on all of the covers – the name of a now-dead author. Cornelia laid a gloved hand over the first of the books in the case, and tapped her fingers upon it.

"Ah, *The Stained Glass Murders*," she said, with a smile that might have been sincere or mocking. "Adam Carver's first book. Not a great seller, not a great story, not a book even many *Castles in the Sky* devotees have bothered seeking out – though of course, I made it my business to do so. It's actually not unlike *Conspiracies of the Obscure Tribunal*, you know; all lies and unreliable witnesses. I wonder if Carver was revisiting a few of his old ideas, almost rewriting his own amateurish beginnings."

Alex spared a moment for the duplicates of the two books found at the crime scenes. "You were about to tell me what everyone invited here suddenly had against Adam Carver?" she reminded Cornelia.

"You mean, apart from having let us all down with such a disappointing conclusion?" Cornelia asked, sardonically. She swept her hand across the case, past Carver's early work and the four instalments of *Castles in the Sky*. "I suppose that getting a bad ending isn't a motive for murder, though some of us may have argued otherwise at the time. But if Carver actually *wanted* to aggravate the fanbase, well, he certainly hadn't finished, and his actions yesterday prove it. Adam Carver tempted fate last night, and all too successfully. He gave everyone in this house a motive for murder!"

Cornelia Crow delivered this line with the sort of force reserved for the cliffhanger at the end of a chapter, but it didn't have quite the same effect in real life as it would on a page. Alex was shocked, yes – but it was only the most toxic of her guesses.

"Okay, that's the headline," Alex said, looking to the door of the library to be sure that it was shut. "But what did he actually *do*, specifically?"

Cornelia looked a little put out, perhaps having hoped for a more extravagant reaction. But she quickly recovered. "Let me start at the beginning," she said, as if she wanted to put the task off yet further. "Dinner was over; a winter night was setting in. The nine of us – Yva, Vi, Colin and Franny, and myself, Quinn, Maria Bole and the two Carvers – retired to the sitting room you saw earlier; and we each settled onto a settee, or footstool, or a lovely old spindly-legged chair with cushions where it mattered and twisted bands of wood where it was just for show – and we let the great man talk. But as the hour grew late, and heads grew hazier, and drink after drink had lubricated Carver's ceaseless voicebox, what began as a typically unrevealing question-and-answer session interspersed with a few recycled anecdotes gradually descended into monopolised braggadocio – and then..." She lowered her already croaky voice to almost a whisper, forcing Alex to lean in close... "Became a personal rant."

The scene was woven in Alex's mind as Cornelia spun it. That oppressive lamplight, which unlike fire gave no relief through flickering or dying into embers – the guests, with no clue how to escape with decorum – and the author, dominating the stage from the centre, his savage wit springing to first one victim and then another like bolts of lightning.

"It was his wife he turned on first," Cornelia murmured. "It had grown uncomfortable enough in there already, but that almost lulled us into a false sense of security, for it might simply have been ironic banter of the sort some couples share. But the way Victoria went still as ice, glass forever halfway to her lips as her husband announced that she was frittering away his money and he was considering divorce – well, I'm sure we all realised soon enough that something quite unforgiveable was occurring before our very eyes. And then, of course, it was Maria Bole's turn, charged with bungling his contracts to skim the profits off for herself; Carver intimated that he would soon be dropping her like a stone. Quinn Shillerdyce was next, framed as a hack who didn't understand the books and was given too much credit, and who Carver never intended to work with again..."

"That's *insane*," Alex breathed. This made the social errors she fretted over every day seem as trivial as people always claimed. "Maybe literally insane?" she went on, trying to find excuses. "To burn all his bridges like that with the people he owed so much, we owed so much – was he that drunk?"

"Not enough to make him do or say anything he didn't mean," Cornelia claimed. "But even I was surprised, I admit – actually shocked, for still I could scarcely believe he would turn his ire on the fans themselves, who had brought him his fame and fortune. And yet..."

"He didn't!" Alex gasped.

"He did," Cornelia said, with no softening of the blow. "Franny Smythe got her review copies off the back of a lorry and he'd see her in court. Vi, Yva, Colin – nothing but intellectual property pirates whose work he would have scoured from the net. I also was insulted, but we needn't –"

"What did he say?" interrupted Alex, the question spilling out even as she realised Cornelia was trying not to relive the attack.

A fierce scowl twisted Cornelia's face into nothing but wrinkles and creases, like an expression imagined in gnarled bark. "A past-my-prime dreamer whose wrong predictions about other people's books proved I hadn't the talent to write my own," she muttered, glowering at the case of Carver's books as if she could melt them by simply looking.

It hurt. Other people's embarrassment had always been Alex's own, and the humiliation of having Carver himself be so rude to Cornelia's face, even if he was doing it to everyone, felt unbearable even at second hand. Alex couldn't even feel relieved at having missed it. "I am so sorry," she said, as if anything that had happened was her fault. "I can't believe he could have said those things to such amazing people. I didn't deserve not to be there; I can't believe I was such an idiot as to get the time wrong, when we should have been united –"

"Please. There's no need for you to feel survivor's guilt over this," Cornelia said – and just as Alex was about to thank her for the comforting gesture, she continued, "since after all – ah, that is, er, never mind."

Alex slowly raised her eyes to meet Cornelia's gaze. Cornelia tried to avert her own gaze instead.

"Mr. Carver said something about me too, didn't he," Alex said. It wasn't a question.

"Well, it's quite immaterial," Cornelia hurried out. "You weren't there, after all, so it's no motive for you…"

Why, Alex thought, did she have to feel guilty about everything. Guilt for being late to something she wanted and guilt for having missed what she didn't want, guilt for not being insulted and guilt for simply not hearing it… "Just tell me," she said, and braced herself for her favourite author to slap her in the face.

Cornelia stared fixedly over Alex's shoulder, and quoted. "'A no-talent nobody who couldn't even up turn up on time.'"

They were just words. Just words, from a man who was dead and who seemed more and more to have had it coming; words from a man Alex Corby never knew. But Alex had always felt she knew him through his work, and in her imagination; without knowing him, she still felt that his opinion mattered. His words cut to the heart.

Alex wasn't the kind of fan who showed her appreciation through creating something of her own, the way Yva and Colin did; not the kind who rallied other fans, like Vi, or tried to get inside the author's head, like Cornelia. She simply enjoyed reading the books and reading about the books, immersing herself in someone else's world. There was nothing anyone could call arrogant or self-aggrandising in that kind of fandom. Who would take such a fan's unconditional love and throw it back in their face like that?

Adam Carver had truly died for her.

"I think," Alex said – she wouldn't cry, crying was too good for the dead author – "that Adam Carver wasn't as great a person as I imagined."

"They rarely are," Cornelia nodded. "They say not to speak ill of the dead, but you're not obliged. I say this as one who has known many now dead." She stared towards the window, where a body hung just out of sight. "You get used to it, and one day you find you aren't sentimental at all about those gone."

Alex, blinking hard, said, "I don't know if I want to go that far." Maybe she would, one day – when, like Cornelia Crow, she was eighty-whatever and had lived a lifetime of other people's deaths. But maybe she didn't have to walk that road, either. She wasn't Cornelia Crow, and her life didn't have to be like Cornelia Crow's. She knew little about her great-aunt; didn't know what disappointments she had had in her life, or what coldness she had always carried with her.

Alex took a deep breath, only slightly ragged, and composed herself. "So much for avenging Adam Carver," she said, ruefully. "I wanted to do this for him."

"I say," interrupted Cornelia, "you're not giving up at this stage, are you? Just because of a typical unsympathetic victim?"

"Oh, I'm not giving up," Alex rushed to answer. "I'm not going to stop trying to solve the murders." Even as she said it, she was realising how obvious that was, that feeling. "I'm just... not doing this for Adam Carver anymore."

"Oh?" Cornelia's interest seemed piqued. "For the pure intellectual challenge of it, then?" she suggested. "Or because you can't stand to see a mystery go unsolved?"

"Not for those, either," Alex replied. She didn't think she could be that detached – though maybe Cornelia could. "Is that why you're doing this? Being a detective?"

"Hmm. Partly." Cornelia's lips grew thin, and she cast a look out into the snowy world beyond the dark. "You mustn't get the wrong idea. I'm not a hero with a good heart. I don't have a particular passion for the law or justice. I'm just an old lady who values the truth, that's all." She glanced back, and raised an eyebrow at Alex. "You?"

She hadn't thought yet quite how to match words to what she felt; to the reason why solving the mystery was still something she wanted to do. "I don't know if I'd call it justice," she confessed. "I just don't like the thought of someone causing such pain to show how clever they are."

Cornelia didn't answer, and Alex was a little surprised to find the old lady staring at her with obvious interest. "An intriguing interpretation of the murderer's motive," she remarked. "I take it you're a believer in the psychological approach to detection."

"Um, again, I don't know if I want to go that far," Alex said, a little nervously. "That's just the vibe I get from all this. I mean, the killer didn't *need* to set up those weird impossible crime things – so it must only have been because they *wanted* to."

"Just so. Everyone was in bed, or at least in their bedrooms, save the victims," Cornelia agreed. Alex began to feel comfortable again; forget the way people have disappointed you, and focus on the facts… "After he'd finished sticking the knife into his audience," Cornelia went on, "Carver said he was sick of the lot of us and he was going up to his study to write. It was around nine o'clock by then, so at Victoria Carver's encouraging and with a tacit agreement never to speak of what had happened, we each retired to our own rooms."

"But Maria didn't retire," Alex said.

Cornelia frowned at nothing. "My apologies. I really didn't think you were coming at all, if you hadn't arrived yet. I thought that was a shame."

"No, I don't mean that you should have waited up for me," Alex corrected her. It didn't seem the sort of thing Cornelia Crow would have done anyway. "I mean it's important that Maria stayed up – to past eleven, even, whcn I got in. Because she gave me about three different reasons why; she couldn't sleep, she was staying up for me just in case, she still had work to do…"

"*Really*," Cornelia grinned. "Now that is definitely a clue. There are plenty of reasons why someone might have killed Adam Carver, but no sign of the same for Maria Bole. I had been wondering if she had seen something she shouldn't have, but from what you've told me, and from the fact that the murderer is likely to strike again, I wonder if there isn't more to it."

"What if *she* was the murderer, though?" Alex asked. "And then was murdered in turn – or even committed suicide…"

Cornelia considered this. "The latter would certainly resolve the problem of the gatehouse," she said. "I can even see how she might have done it. I say, there's a point – an identical motion…"

Her speech degenerated into low mumblings Alex could not make out, while she stared at the case of Carver's books with eyes which seemed to tremble slightly in their sockets – or perhaps were making ever so tiny movements, scanning something Alex could not see.

"What is it?" Alex pressed her. "*Was* it suicide? Have you cracked the case?"

"What? Oh, of course not," Cornelia said, jerking from her reverie as if from sleep. "Suicide? Don't be silly. As I said, the murderer is likely to strike again, and they can't do that if they're dead. And you'd know why I think that, if you only thought about it yourself."

Alex thought about it herself, and knew. "It's the books, isn't it," she said, gesturing to the two books the murderer had left behind at the crime scenes. "If the murderer planned to leave volumes of *Castles in the Sky* at each of their crime scenes, it makes sense that they intend to use all four." A creeping shiver stroked her spine. She hadn't wanted to think about it, but of course it was obvious that the killer had four murders planned.

"Just so. That's why I've been trying to keep people together as we investigate, so the murderer doesn't have the freedom to act unobserved," Cornelia replied. "Although, you know, unless the murderer is incompetent, they must have anticipated..." She trailed off again, eyes far away. It was getting a little bit irritating.

"Great-Aunt Cornelia," Alex said, more forcefully. "Do you have a theory about what's going on? Some idea of who the murderer is – or how they did it, since you seem to be the expert?"

"I have some thoughts," Cornelia admitted – only grudgingly. "But it would be best if I kept them to myself for the moment."

For somebody encouraging others to do all the thinking and investigating, it was frustrating that Cornelia wouldn't even throw them a bone. Unusual, too. "Corvus Crown was never so shy with their theories," Alex pointed out.

"Corvus Crown didn't have to worry about her theories affecting the plot," Cornelia snapped. "Online, discussing *Castles in the Sky*, it didn't matter if any of us were right or wrong – but in real life, the slightest mistake might lead the murderer to do something drastic, or bias others away from the true explanation forever. All I can do is lead people in what I hope to be the right direction." Her bellicose expression suggested that being cryptic might not be so fun as Alex had imagined – but her face and tone softened suddenly. "Speaking of which – Alex, dear, *you're* young."

"Um, that's right," Alex said. It wasn't hard to be, in such company.

"Most people think about the whodunnit aspect when it comes to mysteries; myself, I prefer the howdunnit," Cornelia said, her train of thought not obvious to Alex. "But of course, one can't neglect the whydunnit, either – not just the motive for the crimes, but the motive for the way the crimes were carried out." She had that lecturer's air again, that schoolteacher's air, and it had been drilled into Alex to feel quite anxious whenever someone looked down their nose at her with that bearing. "Like a book, a crime will inevitably show its author's unique style. You've shown an interest in this side of things, Alex," Cornelia continued, ominously. "As a young and sensitive person, why don't you give me your impressions of the whydunnit?" Alex took it as an order. "What is your psychological reading of the crimes?"

"Uh, ummm..." Nothing was more likely to make Alex's mind go blank than a direct question. "Well, like I said, both the crimes were impossible, apparently, even though the murderer could just have killed Adam and Maria last night with nobody around to stop them. So the way things were set up was to show off." She thought a bit harder. "And maybe that wasn't just for our benefit. Maria was left alive for ages, basically bound and gagged. And Adam Carver was also tied up and gagged before he was killed. But Carver's body was just meant to sit in my room until I came in, so there was no need to keep him tied up; and the murderer had to have knocked him out to tie him up, so why not kill him then?" The conclusion wasn't difficult to come to. "The murderer also wanted to show off to their victims," Alex declared.

"Good…" Cornelia nodded encouragingly.

"The victims couldn't appreciate the impossible crimes, though," Alex went on, having hit her stride. "So there must be another reason the murderer wanted to keep them alive for a while. Maybe so they could say something to Adam and Maria about their motive. Maybe…" It wasn't exactly professional psychology, but it would fit! "Maybe the murderer was someone who felt powerless because of Adam and Maria," she concluded. "Like they felt they'd been gagged and couldn't do or even say anything. So they wanted Adam and Maria to feel the same way before they died."

It took a moment for Alex to realise why this theory felt so strange. But it was as if, suddenly, the murderer had become the victim.

"Excellent. A very promising analysis," Cornelia acknowledged, with a smile that gave Alex a confusing swell of pride. "For my part, I'll restrict myself to saying that, though the murderer could have tied their victims up with rope and gagged them with cloth, tape is not only very practical but doubled as a gimmick for impossible crimes. In fact, I wouldn't be surprised if the murderer used tape to secure their victims precisely because they'd already decided to use it in their locked-room illusions."

"The murderer does seem to have a theme," Alex accepted. "Maybe they were responding to those other tape mysteries you mentioned."

"I don't doubt it," Cornelia murmured. "Just another way of showing off how clever they were, since the old solutions won't work." She straightened up suddenly, as if having come to a decision. "Well, speaking of solutions which won't work, we're overdue for that chat with Yva and Vi. We've left them alone for too long."

Alex's her heart sank a little deeper as she remembered what Yva and Vi had been tasked with doing. Was crossing off more false solutions getting them any closer to the true ones? "You're right," she sighed. "The two of them should have disproved that secret passage by now…"

Chapter Thirteen
Fencing

"Hello, you two. Done anything useful yet?" was how Cornelia greeted Yva Dysart and Vi Malik, as she and Alex walked into the north wing bedroom where they were searching for secret passages; Alex herself squeezed in a small "Hi." Cornelia seemed in high spirits, despite, and hopefully not because of, the prospect of more murders; maybe she felt the investigation was going well. Alex couldn't say she felt the same, so she said nothing, and looked around at the carnage wrought by Yva and Vi.

The bedroom the four of them were standing in was next-door to Alex's, distinguishable in daylight as the middle of the three along the landward side of the north wing. Unlike Victoria Carver's room, this was clearly another guest room and was furnished identically to Alex's own, with the exception of a striped suitcase that stood near the door, and also all the furnishings having been shoved away from the walls – but the latter was Yva and Vi's doing. It wasn't just the furnishings which were off the walls, though. Alex had expected to see the pair with ears pressed to the panelling, tapping away for any sound of an echo; instead, a toolbox lay split open in the middle of the room, and they were using screwdrivers to literally unfasten the wood panels from the walls themselves. One slice of wall lay already exposed, nothing but smooth dry stonework, while its corresponding section of panelling, ceiling-high and wide as a door, was leaning against the adjacent wall beside.

Okay, Cornelia *had* told them to try taking the panels off the walls, but Alex hadn't really taken that idea seriously. She hoped Victoria Carver wouldn't find out about this.

Yva had straightened up as Cornelia walked in, and Alex almost expected her to salute. "More than half of the guest bedrooms have been thoroughly checked for secret passages, with none discovered!" she announced. "As soon as we're finished in this room, we'll be making another trip to gather keys before we can move onto the rest."

Alex opened her mouth to ask whose room they were standing in, and then stopped. It was probably possible to deduce whose room it was – and if so, she should do so. It would be good practice… and would make her look cleverer next to Cornelia and Yva. So. It was a guest room, which ruled out Adam and Victoria, whose room Alex had seen already anyway. More than half of the guest rooms had been checked, with this room probably representing the "more" – so out of eight total, since Alex knew there had been only just enough to go around, this was probably the fifth room to be checked. Yva and Vi had started off with keys for their own two rooms, and also Alex and Cornelia's, which would have made up the first four; they must have picked up a fifth key after that, and if they would then need to scrounge for multiple more keys then this probably wasn't Franny or Colin's room, as those two had been together or nearby and would have given their keys together. Quinn Shillerdyce had effectively refused to help when Alex had last seen him, so it probably wasn't his room. Which left…

Alex's eyes shot to the bed. It hadn't been slept in. That should have been her first clue, and its meaning was obvious: This was Maria Bole's room!

An involuntary shudder rattled her spine. Of course, it was silly to feel frightened. Maria had clearly spent barely seconds in this room, with no evidence that she had done anything there besides dropping off her suitcase. But still, there was something uncanny about that room, as if the shadow of death had passed across it…

These thoughts passed rapidly across Alex's brain, lasting only long enough for Vi to stand up from where he was unscrewing the bottom corner of a panel, discreetly brushing dust from his legs. He had taken off his suit jacket and tie, which were carefully folded on the bed. "We might have done more," he scowled at Yva, "if you didn't insist on checking everything I've investigated before we move on."

"Of course I have to check your work," Yva said, tilting her head as if totally nonplussed. "You might be the murderer, after all, hiding evidence behind my back."

"You know the same applies in reverse, don't you?" Vi sniped.

Yva rolled her eyes. "Don't be ridiculous. I *know* I'm not the murderer."

"But *I* don't know that," he retorted.

"What does that matter?" she replied.

"Anyway!" Alex introduced herself between the two of them. BardOfDeathY could argue all day, and literally often had. "Have you looked at the floors and ceilings as well?"

"The ceilings are bare plaster," Vi answered, gesturing upwards. "No cracks or seams. If there was a secret passage in any of the ceilings, the murderer would have had to plaster over it again from the wrong side, which is even sillier than taping a door shut from the wrong side. It's the same with the carpets; they're firmly glued down with the edges running under the panelling. Any tampering would be obvious, and we've found no evidence of it."

Alex looked around the room. "And are the walls in all the bedrooms like this?"

"So far," Yva said, tapping the bare stone. "Identical wood panels screwed straight onto the stone inner wall. Nothing suspicious about the screwholes, either; I've poked into them with a pencil, and there's no secret button or anything. Nor do they go straight through to the opposite wall in the next room, in case you were thinking that."

A couple of screws lay on the bedside table; they were a good couple of centimetres long. "The walls must be pretty thick," Alex noted.

"We took measurements, and once you add on the panels there must be around half a foot of wall between each room," Vi told her. "Once you throw in the thickness of the doors and also the carpet, the rooms are basically soundproof so long as the door is closed."

"Hmm." Alex thought back to what was only just the previous day. "No wonder nobody woke up even with me running around last night."

Vi's face took on that faintly arrogant expression it held when he knew something his audience didn't. "Funny you should mention that," he said. "I did hear a loud noise late last night – very late; I was staying up to work on something and lost track of the time."

Yva looked at him with sudden interest. "Something did wake me up in the middle of the night," she said. "I don't know what – I just suddenly jerked awake." Her eyes narrowed. "It must have been the portcullis," she said.

Vi snapped his fingers. "Of course. It sounded different from up in the gatehouse, when Carver demonstrated it, but it was just the same sort of sound."

Yva was frowning still. "How annoying. If I'd known there was going to be a murder, I could have gone out and caught the killer red-handed."

That was indeed regrettable, but Alex could not regret it; she had heard nothing. "When was this?" she asked.

"Past midnight," Vi answered promptly. "Probably more like one o'clock. I don't remember the exact time, just that I was surprised it had gotten that late."

Alex frowned thoughtfully. "That's weird," she said. "I'm sure it took me hours to get to sleep, but I don't remember hearing any loud noise like that. After everything else, it would've scared the heck out of me." She paused, trying to account for the discrepancy. "Are your rooms near each other?"

"Opposite ends of the house," Yva answered. "I have the southmost room in the south wing, with Cornelia next up and Franny past her, all on the landward side; in the north wing, it's you, Maria, and then Vi at the top. For completeness's sake, on the seaward side Colin and Victoria Carver have the south wing rooms, then Adam Carver and Quinn Shillerdyce in the north wing."

"Did you hear anything, Great-Aunt Cornelia?" asked Alex, realising that her relative had been strangely silent during this conversation. Indeed, Cornelia didn't even seem to be listening; she was frowning fiercely at the gap in the panelling. "Great-Aunt Cornelia?"

"Hmm?" Cornelia started, as if she had been fast asleep herself. "Oh, excuse me. Just thinking, you know."

"Did you by any chance hear a loud noise like the murderer dropping the portcullis late last night at one o'clock?" Yva asked her.

"Ah, yes," the old lady answered, after a moment's thought. "I was enjoying the opportunity to read in peace – a translated Paul Halter – but then I couldn't fall asleep for trying to solve it. I *thought* the sound might have been the portcullis, but I was so absorbed that I only felt irritated at being disturbed."

Alex's confusion lasted a few moments more; and then her eyes fell on the curtains standing open at the window. Of course – she had slept in a bathroom, whilst the other three had rooms with windows on the portcullis side; no wonder she hadn't heard anything. She wasn't sure if she was more annoyed now at having missed a clue, or at feeling the same way about it as Yva.

Cornelia, however, had segued to another matter entirely. "Never mind all that. Vi, Yva, have the two of you separated at any time since you left us?"

It was a vital question, and Alex devoted her attention to it, missing entirely the still more vital clue in the previous discussion. If Vi and Yva *had* separated, either of them might have tampered with the evidence, risked being murdered, even murdered someone else who Alex and Cornelia didn't yet know about... or, more pertinently, stolen the window key. But there was no way they had been so foolish, of course. Had they?

"Not really," said Vi, at the same time that Yva said "Yes."

Cornelia threw up her arms in disgust. Alex felt like putting her head in her hands.

"No, no, wait, it's not like that!" Vi cried, waving his hands desperately. "I – I needed the bathroom, alright? I'm only human."

Cornelia sniffed disapprovingly. "Nobody ever uses the facilities in a detective novel."

"Or most other novels, actually," Alex couldn't resist adding.

"Well, I'm sure that's very convenient for all those fictional characters," Vi grumbled. "But it's not like we were *really* separated. We came up with a system."

"Basically, Vi locked the door of the bedroom and took the key with him into the ensuite so I couldn't get out," Yva explained. "This was in Cornelia's room, by the way – the mirror image of this one."

Alex turned in surprise. As in Victoria Carver's room, though with the door opening rightwards in this north wing, there was a half-hidden square nook which evidently opened into a small bathroom running parallel with the south wall of the room.

"Did *everyone* have an ensuite bathroom except me?" she asked. "Oh, and Vi."

"And me, and Franny," Yva finished. "Only the seaward rooms, and the middle landward room in each wing, get one; it's consistent." She seemed to puff outwards a little, like a baby bird in need of attention. "First-come first-served, so I nabbed one early and then traded it with Cornelia so she wouldn't have to share with the scum."

"Quite the little charmer, aren't you?" Cornelia crooned to Yva's insufferably slappable face. Alex pouted, and tried to think of a way to bring her down a peg. And succeeded.

"So you locked Yva in the room and used the ensuite?" Alex loudly asked Vi. "But didn't we learn earlier that Yva can pick locks?"

There was a moment's silence as this sank in.

"Well, yes," Yva admitted. "But I didn't, so there's no point in thinking about this any further."

"Hold on, hold on," Vi interrupted. "When I left the ensuite afterwards, I unlocked the bedroom door myself, so it was still locked. Or can you relock doors with lockpicks?"

"No," Yva answered.

Cornelia glared at her. "*Yes.*"

It was a guilty pleasure seeing Yva squirm. "Well, yes, you can, but you're forgetting something," she answered, with a great deal of stalling. "I… I don't have my lockpicks with me, so I couldn't have gotten out of the room!"

"Hold *on*…" Vi interrupted again. "When we were checking *your* room, didn't you go rummaging around in your suitcase? If you didn't have any lockpicks before, you could have gotten them then."

"I didn't bring them!" she yelled, well over the brink of losing her temper.

Alex found herself grinning. So *this* was what it felt like to be a detective cornering a suspect. "Then why did you tell us all earlier that you could pick the locks on people's rooms if we couldn't find their keys?" she cried, with an attempt at a dramatic flourish which didn't quite come off, but who cares, it *felt* good…!

"You can't prove I have lockpicks on me!" Yva exploded. "You can't prove I brought them and you can't prove I used them and you can't prove I have them! What are you going to do, strip-search me? Go on, get on with it, do it!"

Vi averted his eyes at this point, but thankfully there was someone in the room who Yva actually listened to. "Do simmer down, Yva. You're embarrassing yourself," ordered Cornelia.

"Nobody is going to perform a body-search on you. We can't prove that you have access to lockpicks, but we can't disprove it, either, because you could have hidden them somewhere. Let's just call it a draw, and let it go rather than throwing this childish tantrum."

Yva lapsed into a sulky silence, but there was an ominous expression beneath her brow; if looks could kill, her eyes would have incinerated the room in an instant. "Fine," she muttered – but with unnatural rapidity, she instantly recovered her pride and tossed out, "Besides, I went to the bathroom right afterwards, so the same applies to Vi."

Vi sighed wearily. "If that's how you want it, then alright, I'll concede that I can't prove that I can't pick locks." His eyes narrowed. "Though actually, you had another opportunity to get out while you claimed you went to the bathroom, of course."

Alex didn't see it. "How so?" Could Yva have escaped an ensuite by walking through the walls…?

"She insisted on using a real bathroom," Vi answered. "She left the room with the keys and locked the door behind her, leaving me locked in."

Alex groaned internally. Did he seriously think it was a good idea to take his eyes off Yva twice in a row? If any murders had occurred since last they looked, the evidence would really be stacking up against her. "Well, I'm not sure why we were arguing about lockpicks, then," she sighed, "since Yva had *another* even easier opportunity to escape. And we shouldn't really just assume that Vi can pick locks, either."

"He wouldn't have to," claimed Cornelia. "In fact, there's an even easier way to get past a locked door, and anyone can do it."

And there it was. Another patented Cornelia Crow head-turning pronouncement, making her the centre of attention once again.

"Ah, I get it," Yva said, and she too was back to her old smirk. "Of course, it takes longer than people think to pick a lock, so it's not like I'd've had that much time out of the picture. But if it's not a case of unlocking the door at all…"

"…Then what, exactly?" Vi continued, when she didn't. "You've been doing this for hours. Would you stop being unnecessarily cryptic just to get us to ask 'what?' and make you feel clever?"

Cornelia interceded in another burgeoning argument. "Neither of you would have had to unlock the door at all," Cornelia picked up, "if you had blocked up the bolthole so it wouldn't lock in the first place."

Alex felt halfway between being bewildered and amazed at the array of tricks Cornelia had picked up from a lifetime's worth of mystery novels. Just how many ways were there of getting around a locked door?

"It's an old trick, of course," Cornelia went on. "Slip something between the bolt and the bolthole so the lock won't engage properly. Once you were in the room, either of you could have jammed some tissue paper, chewing gum, anything like that into the bolthole so that the lock couldn't lock when the key was turned. This one probably works better if Vi is the culprit, actually; by going to the bathroom first, there's a psychological suggestion to Yva that it's safe for her to avail herself of the same opportunity."

Vi shook his head wearily. "I'm not even sure that that method would work in real life."

Unusually, Yva too had let out a snort of derision at Cornelia's idea. "Please," she drawled. "Nobody could possibly manipulate me psychologically. The other way around is another matter."

Alex tried not to rise to the bait. "Arguments aside – worst-case scenario, either of the two of you could have left the room almost instantly while the other was in the bathroom," she summarised, with a sigh.

"A most unfortunate state of affairs," Cornelia said, shaking her own head. "Well, we can only hope that neither would have had long enough to have actually done anything and gotten back in time not to be missed." She looked between Vi and Yva with an almost pleading expression. "Last resort – I don't suppose either of you timed how long the other was in the bathroom…?"

Vi inhaled sharply. "I absolutely refuse to dignify that question with a response," he said, although Alex thought that was totally a response.

"I timed him. He took too long," Yva said, with absolutely no trace of shame.

Vi went quite red. "That is an unbelievable invasion of privacy! And it doesn't even matter, because only you could have left the room while I was in the ensuite."

"Oh yeah?" she retorted, childishly. "Well, I've just thought of something else. When you went to the bathroom, I was working on the far wall and not facing the doors. If you really *had* wanted to get out of the room, then instead of going to the bathroom, you could have just pretended to lock the door to the room, then pretended to lock the door to the bathroom, and then just slipped out behind my back!"

Vi gasped. "That – that," he spluttered, "is absolutely ridiculous! I refuse to dignify that with a response either!"

Alex found herself getting genuinely angry on Vi's behalf now. The poor guy was obviously completely innocent, and after all he'd done for this fandom, here was Yva simply slandering him as a ruthless murderer rather than a perfectly harmless web admin. She had to step in!

"Would you really have let him get away with sneaking out if you went so far as to time him while he was in the bathroom?" she demanded of Yva. Take *that*!

Yva just sneered. "Prove it."

She didn't even care!

It was really just as well that Cornelia chose that moment to step in, emitting a bird-like rasp as she cleared her throat. "Settle down, children, settle down," she said, as if she was corralling a bunch of infants in a nursery; Alex begrudgingly admitted that that was probably exactly how Cornelia regarded the situation. "I can see that we have reached another impasse here. Vi, Yva, thanks to your united cleverness and stupidity, we have successfully established that either of you could have left the room on two separate occasions," she recounted, with a world-weary roll of her sunken eyes. "You managed to avoid being murdered, at least, so that's something, but if we later discover Quinn Shillerdyce lying slain in a locked room then I shall really be rather upset with the two of you." She leaned on her cane as she fixed them both with a fierce glare. "I suppose the only respite is that it's unlikely either of you would have had time to do anything important."

"But not impossible," Alex said, glaring at Yva only. "Has anyone actually been keeping track of time?"

"Timetable mysteries are boring," Yva said.

"And human perception of time is so subjective as to be fairly useless in matters like this," Cornelia added. "Either of them could have done as much as murdering someone and as little as stealing the window key."

Yva looked up sharply. "What's that?"

Ah, that was true. They had still disproven *one* of Yva's dumb theories that day. "Oh, nothing," Alex said lightly – and just as Yva's frown deepened, added, "just that your theory about Maria's murder is wrong – unless Mrs. Carver is both clever enough to commit an impossible crime and stupid enough to give herself away." She paused for effect. "Or unless either Quinn or Cornelia are ninjas."

Alex went on to explain all that had occurred since they parted. Yva's reaction was disappointingly underwhelming. She literally shrugged it off. "That's fine. I've been working on another theory anyway."

"As have I," Cornelia announced, as Alex wondered if there was nothing which would not bounce off Yva Dysart. "No giveaways until we've cornered the culprit, agreed?"

"Agreed," Yva grinned, and she and Cornelia clasped hands in a firm handshake as Alex scowled on. She really needed to get cracking and start coming up with some theories of her own.

And suddenly she knew how to start. After all, there was more than one way of thinking about a murder mystery…

"Okay, I'll accept that either of you could have left the room," she said, facing Vi and Yva. "But even if you had the same opportunities, there's another way of distinguishing who might have used them – and that's motive."

The howdunnit really wasn't her area of expertise. She hadn't read a million old books containing all manner of devious tricks, and it sounded as though the murderer had come up with some new ones anyway. But Cornelia had shown her that there was also the *why*dunnit – and that seemed the surest way of solving the *who*dunnit, too.

"You've tried to keep this from me, but I happen to know that Adam Carver threatened the two of you last night, among others," she continued. "Don't ask me how I know; it only matters that I do."

"Cornelia probably just told you," Yva said.

Vi nodded. "I agree. I hoped she wouldn't, but there it is."

Cornelia raised her eyes heavenwards. "I can neither confirm nor deny…"

"*Anyway*," Alex said forcefully, determined to take charge of this line of questioning, "it seems that Mr. Carver thought that Besieging Heaven and all its fanwork was just violating his copyright, so he would have us taken down." She put on a Cornelia-esque air as she looked from Vi to Yva. "I'm sure that disturbed you a great deal. I know it disturbs me. It might even be a motive for murder. What were you going to do about it?"

"I stayed up until two in the morning composing a ten-point business plan to convince him that Besieging Heaven was a net positive to his profit margin and that there were even greater gains to be made through synergising our output," Vi declared.

"I was going to let him get away with it," Yva said.

Maybe she thought all publicity was good publicity, but Yva's attention-catching technique tended to work for only the wrong reasons. "You were *what?*" echoed Alex and Vi.

Her mouth twisted. "Besieging Heaven is just a fansite, and my fanfiction is just fanfiction," Yva grinned, with corrosive cynicism. "It's not *art*. It's practice – a portfolio, if you like. Even if it was taken offline, I can still print copies from my computer. So losing Besieging Heaven was irrelevant. What really mattered was that Carver had played right into my hands that night – giving me the opportunity to show my work to someone who *really* mattered."

Cornelia shimmered into view. "You mean Maria Bole," she said.

Yva nodded enthusiastically. "Carver had just told Maria that she wasn't getting any more business from him," she explained. "Losing him would leave quite a gap in her list – and that meant she needed a replacement. If I showed her that I could mimic Carver perfectly and substitute work of a similar style, I'd be practically guaranteed a book deal!" She was trembling with barely-suppressed glee. "Adam Carver was doing me a favour!"

Alex absolutely despised Yva's faithlessness to her community and even to her own art. …But she had to admit that she saw where Yva was coming from. And more than that –

"So what you're saying is," Alex said slowly, "that not only did you have no motive to kill Adam Carver – you actually had a motive *not* to kill Maria Bole."

"That's right!" Yva cackled. "Everything went perfectly! I couldn't have asked for better!" But then, like a centuries-eroded wall, her face fell – not into dismay, but grey apathy. "But then someone came along and killed them both. Oh well. Maybe I can pitch to whoever takes Maria's job."

Alex accepted it; it was, all things considered, a pretty strong motive not to kill – an *anti*-motive. If Yva had motive to kill Adam Carver but anti-motive to kill Maria, you could still argue that Maria might have witnessed some aspect of her crime and had to be polished off as well – but Adam Carver was barely even a factor. Even if you questioned whether Yva's feelings were sincere – and let's face it, you would probably be right to – then her facts checked out; her anti-motive was both logical and reasonable.

But so far as facts were concerned, there was still Vi to consider.

"Vi," Alex requested, as politely as she could manage, "could you show us this business plan, please? Just to check that – uh, that it, um…" She hadn't needed to say that second part, it was fine as it was, retreat, retreat!

"Just to check that it exists?" Vi finished for her, raising an eyebrow in a way that made her uncomfortable. "Of course I will; I'm not offended."

"Unlike whenever *I* accuse you of something," Yva cut in, but they ignored her.

"My tablet's buried in my luggage," Vi continued, "so I'll be a minute or two. Sit tight, ladies."

He slipped out of the door, pulling it to with one hand, and vanished leftwards. The soundproofed walls soon ate his jogging footfalls.

Yva gave it just long enough for him to be out of earshot before speaking. "You do realise that, even if he committed the murders, he still had all night to throw something together," she pointed out.

"I do, in fact, realise that," retorted Alex. "But we can also make sure his business plan is realistic; something that makes sense on its own and not just as an anti-motive."

"Huh. Good answer," Yva admitted. "That's not to say that it's even possible to manufacture a good business plan for this situation, though."

"It may be impossible to distinguish the real thing from an excuse cooked up for an anti-motive," Cornelia said. "I doubt he'd have been foolish enough not to prepare such an excuse, even if he really was the murderer, so probably this demonstration will prove nothing. Still, it's worth a look, if only to satisfy one's curiosity."

A minute passed without anything happening at all. Vi was clearly still wrestling with his luggage. Cornelia stared at the door. Yva made herself busy removing more of the wall, making an ambiguous gesture for Alex to come over and help. Alex wandered away to take a glance at the ensuite bathroom. It was extremely similar to Victoria Carver's, but lacking a window, and reversed left-to-right just as the whole north wing appeared to mirror the south. Somewhat smaller than the corridor-end bathrooms, its narrow walls nonetheless narrowly fitted all modern conveniences; a shower cubicle, a cistern, tiles on every surface. The cistern was the old-fashioned sort, supported near the ceiling with the flush operated by a chain – but apparently this was not fancy enough for Adam Carver, and so the lower end of the chain was tethered to a heavy-looking figurine of a raven placed upon a shelf, presumably in reference to the corvid which pecked out Brother Ambrose's eyes in *Hand at the Threshold*. The figurine was positioned pretty close to the side of the shelf, Alex noticed; half-overhanging the edge. It wouldn't take much for it to fall off, where its weight would flush the toilet and probably terrify some poor person in the middle of the night who had been nowhere near it.

Wait a minute…

Alex, in the very act of stepping away, found her eyes unaccountably fixed upon that grim-faced raven, its round dark eye gleaming enigmatically. There was something familiar about this scenario; some eerie, devastating similarity.

"*Great-Aunt*," Alex began, emphatic to the point of urgency –

The bedroom door smashed into the wall beside her with the force of a bullet, missing her by a breath. True urgency was pictured before her now, wheezing its lungs out in the doorway, in the dishevelled and wild-eyed form of Vi Malik.

"Come quick!" he choked. "I think there's been another murder!"

Chapter Fourteen
Victimised – and Victim

No sooner had Vi spoken than he had pushed off from the doorframe and gone running back down the hall again – Yva was throwing herself over the bed to follow him, letting a sheet of wood panelling crash to the floor behind her – Alex, after a moment to recover herself, followed. She leapt out into the corridor, Cornelia straggling behind.

Footfalls thudded down the passage away from her, and Alex just caught a glimpse of Vi swinging himself around the landing by the banisters, Yva metres behind. The crime scene must have lain beyond the stairs.

Wait. From how Yva had laid it out, shouldn't Vi's bedroom have been in the *opposite* direction?

There was no time to think about it. Vi's footsteps were already rattling even down the stairs, and she didn't need Great-Aunt Cornelia shoving her in the back and hissing "Go! I can catch up!" to send her racing after them, though that was what she got regardless. Alex tore down the hall and caught up with Yva sooner than she'd expected, the two of them pounding down the stairs without looking at their feet, running on pure instinct where if they thought for a second about not moving automatically they would surely stumble and fall. But Vi was running faster still, taking the steps three at a time.

"Vi, what are we *doing* down here?!" Alex called.

He didn't face her as he stormed downwards. "I'm only human!" came his desperate voice. "I thought I'd check on Victoria while I was out of the room! But the door wouldn't open…"

"Good grief." Yva's strained mutter reached Alex's ears, and for once she found herself agreeing. Endangering himself was one thing; embarrassing himself quite another. But still, if he had found a room that shouldn't have been sealed –

Vi leapt the last few steps into the gaping hallway and sprang leftwards and out of sight. With a jolt, Alex realised he was heading in the direction of the armoury.

Victoria, Colin, Franny – was it one of them…?

She and Yva reached the corner and spun on the spot. Vi was standing just in front of the door to the armoury, the door Alex had seen closed when last she had passed. He had his phone out for some reason, pointed forwards –

"Wait!" Alex cried – but her voice was almost immediately lost in the crash of wood as Vi hurled himself against the door and through it, tumbling into the room. In moments, Alex and Yva were staring through the doorway after him.

The inner edge of the door was lined with tape, half-unpeeled where it had once been stuck to the surrounding frame, leaving long marks along the doorframe and floorboards. It was the hallmark of the murderer, just as Alex had seen on the door of her bedroom and the front door of Carver's Rest. But even more had been deployed to swathe the figure lying prone against the weapon cabinets in the centre of the room, Vi kneeling beside her.

It was Victoria Carver, wrists and ankles bound and mouth covered with wide strips of tape, with something that looked very much like her own shawl wound around her head.

Alex gasped at the sight, but the girl beside her seemed strangely unimpressed. "What the hell is this," Yva said flatly. "She's not dead."

Alex did a double-take. How could she not be –

But it was true. There was no sign of a lethal wound anywhere on Victoria's body, or even much of a wound at all, just a faint red stain near the crown of her head – and as Vi awkwardly slid her blindfold away, revealing a flushed and terrified face, Victoria Carver blinked and sobbed and did other things which corpses are rarely reported as doing.

The murderer had struck once again in a room sealed from the inside with tape. But they hadn't finished the job. Alex stepped into the room and swept her eyes around, but there was no sign of any other body – not Colin's, not Franny's. Victoria had been seemingly alone in the room.

Hobbling footsteps and wheezing breath behind her heralded the late arrival of Cornelia Crow. She barged right past Yva and stood in the doorway, arms folded on her cane, drawing in deep breaths as she looked around. Her keen eyes gradually receded into shadow as her brow descended into a frown. "What is this supposed to be?"

she asked, irritably. "When there's someone still alive in the room who could have locked the door, it's not a locked-room mystery."

"That's what I want to know!" Yva exclaimed. "Granted, I don't see a roll of tape anywhere, so at least *one* thing left the room…"

Vi, meanwhile, had finally freed Victoria's mouth from the tape that sealed it. "Fear not; you are safe now," he cried, inflating his chest, his voice at its deepest. For just a moment he reminded Alex of the chivalrous Fitzlathom, who was forever trying to rescue Sanguinaria from evil aristocrats and bandits. It was deeply embarrassing.

"Get these off me – do something useful with one of those knives…" Victoria Carver was recovering quickly. She had clearly had a dreadful shock, but already she was sitting up quite of her own accord, gesturing to the cabinet of daggers with her taped-up wrists. Vi obediently went scrambling around the glass case, fingers prying for an opening.

"Vi, what exactly is your explanation for this?" Cornelia enquired, leaning vulturishly towards him. "We send you next-door to fetch a tablet, and you come back jabbering about a non-existent murder on another floor entirely?"

"I – I thought I would ask Victoria for her room key," Vi stuttered, as his hand hovered jerkily above the knives in the cabinet. "The first door I came to wouldn't open, and when I looked underneath on a hunch, I saw it had been blocked up by something… I ran back for help immediately." Even before he had grabbed the most harmless-looking of the remaining blades, taking it carefully to the tape that held Victoria's wrists and ankles together, Alex had an uneasy sense that there were fewer daggers than she remembered…

"Maybe you beat the killer to it?" Yva wondered, looking again at the taped edges of the door.

The debate faded into the background for Alex. She alone had been searching further through the room. She alone had set eyes on something nobody else had yet noticed. Something which guaranteed the murderer's recent presence, just as surely as the tape that had sealed the door.

Hulking in the shadows, silent and imposing, was the iron maiden. Its dead mask of a face gazed with empty and passionless eyes from above its massive body, a barrel of iron with a studded lid that would hinge open like a coffin. But somebody had dressed the iron maiden for a party. Partway down its sloping sides were several loops of ribbon drawn taut around the structure, fastening at the front around a rectangular package in coloured paper.

The iron maiden had been sealed shut, wrapped up like a birthday present along with the murderer's third gift.

One by one the others noticed that Alex was no longer at their side. She was across the room, and with slow steps now, with resignation, they moved to join her – the freed Victoria Carver with a dazed and unsteady gait. They gazed upon the ghastly birthday present in silence, and could not doubt what they were about to find.

One of the three people not among them was inside this iron coffin.

They had *not* beaten the killer to it.

"What is that?" murmured Victoria, blinking over and over at the present as if it remained stubbornly out of focus. "What is going on here?"

"Better take it off," Cornelia muttered to Alex. "I'll take responsibility. Best we know what we're dealing with…"

With a deep breath, Alex stepped forward; tugged on the present. It was stuck fast; she could see that the ribbons crossed around it, knotted on both sides to hold its wrappings tightly shut, before a separate few wide loops had been thrown over the head of the iron maiden and settled tight over its widest point. Like the cover of an unread book, the knot on the front of the package was an invitation. Alex tugged at a trailing end, and the whole arrangement collapsed into a heap of gift wrap and stray ribbon lying loose around the base of the iron maiden, the cover of a much-read book revealed in the paper folds.

A Coffin Nail Creaks – the third volume of Adam Carver's great series.

For the second time that day, Alex reached out for the door of the iron maiden. Without the ribbon to hold it fast, that lid-like door could be neither locked nor fastened; it would move all too easily when pulled. Her hand shaking almost beyond use, Alex managed to grasp the edge – and with a single swift motion wrenched it open, leaping back in fear of who-knows-what.

Spikes sprang into view as the door swung back, lining the inside of the infernal device like a magic trick gone wrong – and with them, gasps of horror.

Staring back at the onlookers was an upright figure thrice taped, once around the ankles, once around the wrists, and once around the mouth, and as if in mimicry of the maiden this person's empty eyes saw nothing. For just a moment the figure remained quite still, as if they were merely an extension of the sarcophagus, a statue – and then, whether because some fine balance inside the iron maiden had been disturbed by Alex's action, he slowly toppled forwards, seeming to sink gently through the air before slamming into the floor, exposing a fatal wound as he settled for good.

It was Colin West, and he had a knife in his back.

METHODS
of the Author

Dear Reader,

My game is the locked-room mystery, nothing more and nothing less. But this is no harsh confinement; rather, a deep chest. The locked room need not be literally locked, or even in the strictest sense a room; it need only be sealed by an ordinary bolt, an untrodden surface, even the gaze of a witness – or, indeed, strips of tape.

Fortunately for you, in all locked-room mysteries there are only three possible deceptions: The murder, the lock, and the room. These are the three keys handed down by my late predecessors, John Dickson Carr and Clayton Rawson, who knew locked rooms inside-out: Three classes of locked room, and three only. Perhaps their three keys will unlock this mystery.

Class A: No murderer was in the locked room when the victim died, but the room was caused to appear as if they must have been present. Perhaps death was not effected in the way it seemed, or perhaps it was not even murder – so long as the lock was genuine, and the murderer left before the death or was never there at all.

Class B: The murderer was in the locked room and departed, and the lock was caused to appear to have been fastened from within. The lock may have been interfered with by any number of gimmicks, or been itself an illusion – so long as the murderer did indeed leave the room after the crime, and the lock is a mere ruse.

Class C: The murderer committed their crime within the locked room, but did not leave, remaining hidden and escaping only after the room was broken open. Thus the only deception is the murderer's apparent absence.

As to what class my own taped rooms fall into? The answer, once my work is complete, will be all three.

Now, I must interrupt you no more.

The Author

Chapter Fifteen
The Least Likely Victim

Of the five living people in the room, four had faced the murdered dead before; in Alex's case, twice. It would be wrong to say they were unmoved – that they did not feel fear of the murderer, pity for the victim, anger at the injustice of it – but if their reactions were muted by comparison, it was because they had been prepared. They had seen worse.

Victoria Carver, on the other hand, went to pieces.

"Is this – that looks –" she stammered, eyes wide and round as a globe. "Colin, are you alright? Say something!" Before anyone could stop her she was on her knees and her hands were in the wound, at the very point where dagger entered flesh.

"I say, get your hands off that!" Cornelia snapped, but it was too late; Victoria's hands had already come away covered with congealing blood.

"No, no no no no no!" she screamed; "This isn't happening, this isn't real!" – and she threw herself backwards across the floor and scrabbled feverishly away, leaving bloody prints in her wake –

"Oh, for pity's sake," muttered Yva, all pretence of pity utterly abandoned.

It was obviously time for a more sympathetic voice to prevail. "Vi, you should take Mrs. Carver away from here," Alex said quickly, with a deliberate frown at Yva Dysart. "Get her, um, a drink, and cleaned up."

Vi looked only too happy to oblige – both for Victoria Carver's sake, and so he too would no more have to stare at the corpse of Colin West. He quickly interposed between Victoria and the late Colin and, muttering softly to her, hauled his hostess to her feet and ushered her away, her bloodied hands held out at arm's length like the undead of an old horror film.

Yva watched them out of the room, and then breathed out all in a rush, as if a great weight had been lifted from her back. "What a relief," she said. "I guess Vi *is* good for something, after all. With that racket gone, we can concentrate on investigating."

"You really are completely the worst, do you know that?" Alex asked, fixing Yva with a glare which she hoped would make most people feel ashamed.

Yva just laughed. "Your standards are hilarious," she sneered. "Wanting a liability out of the way is worse than being a murderer?"

"Do I have to put you two in a nursery?" Cornelia scowled, hammering her cane on the floor like a gavel. "We are all on the same side here! Cease this juvenile bickering. We have work to do."

Alex felt a jab of shame. Cornelia was right, of course. Purely statistically, Yva probably wasn't a murderer, and they were all here to capture the person who was. There was no right time to turn on each other with pointless insults. Begrudgingly, she muttered, "Sorry, Yva."

"Huh? Oh, sure, fine," Yva frowned, letting the apology drop as if she didn't know how it worked. "What have we got here, anyway?"

Alex's heart sank as she dwelled upon the reality of what they had discovered. Once again, it wasn't just any old murder. It was murder by a ghost who turned invisible in plain sight and stepped through walls as if they weren't there. In other words... "It's another locked-room murder – a taped-room murder," she said, looking at the pattern of tape around the half-open door with a kind of despair. "The murderer killed Colin and stuffed him in the iron maiden. They tied up Victoria Carver so she couldn't see or hear what was going on or even move. They taped over every crack around the edge of the door so there was no gap between it and the wall – and then they just left anyway!" The tape around the door had also sealed away all her ideas and thoughts on how to solve the crime. Being unable to think of anything felt the same as not thinking at all. "It's impossible," she groaned.

A tap on her head not quite hard enough to hurt broke her out of her stupor. "You must never come to that conclusion," Cornelia ordered, withdrawing her cane. "If it happened, it was possible. It just seems otherwise because you don't understand everything yet."

Alex sighed. She knew that, and she said so. "But I don't know just what it is that I don't understand. So that makes it *feel* impossible."

The armoury door had been taped shut from the inside, yet the murderer must have been outside of it. The front door of Carver's Rest had been taped shut from the inside, yet the murderer must have been outside of it. Alex's bedroom door had been taped shut from the inside, yet the murderer must have been outside of it. What was it that she had failed to understand?

Cornelia tapped her long fingers on the head of her cane, and nodded to herself. "Let me give you a clue, then," she said, and Alex remembered that she, at least, seemed to understand everything. "Just on first impressions, far from being impossible, there are actually three people who could have committed this crime…"

She grinned as Alex's face screwed up in confusion. "Mull that one over, why don't you – and in the meantime, let's all thoroughly search this room, and eliminate any cheap tricks. Yva, please take charge of the body."

"My pleasure," Yva said, as she surveyed the latest murder victim with eyes that might have been coldly professional or just ghoulish.

"Wait, hold on," interrupted Alex, arresting Yva on her way to the body. "Shouldn't we be leaving this to the police and, you know, not touching anything?"

"I'm only going to touch it a *little*," Yva said, shrugging her off.

Cornelia patted Alex's shoulder. "We appear to be trapped in a house with a serial murderer," she pointed out. "It's reasonable to take some liberties to protect ourselves." Which Alex thought sounded rational enough, until her great-aunt's eyes misted over. "And besides…"

"…haven't you always dreamed of this day?" Yva finished, as with a grin she bent over the corpse.

The former Colin West had settled slightly on his side, thanks to the bound wrists roughly taped together in front of him. With his legs taped together likewise, his bulky form looked something like a clubbed seal, an impression reinforced by a graze on his forehead at the hairline. It was a pathetic sight, one which Alex could scarcely bear to look at, and so she followed Cornelia's lead and looked for clues instead.

"Looks like he got whacked as well," Yva muttered behind her, testing for temperature and rigor mortis and other clues Alex had read about in books. "Fairly superficial head wound, so the murderer had to act fast afterwards." It was awfully hard to concentrate with the running commentary, Alex thought, as she surveyed the rear wall and checked that all the windows were locked – which they were, of course, and sealed tight, not that there was anywhere to go but the vertiginous abyss over the sea. She glanced over her shoulder to find Yva peering closer at the wound than Alex would have. "Standard blunt instrument – probably the same as Maria. Any sign of a weapon?"

Alex looked back at the museum of death. "Plenty," she replied, but the case full of maces was just a few steps away, so she looked it over. And, sure enough…

"One of the maces is gone," she reported. "Small enough to hide and hold one-handed. Anyone could have used it." Alex chose not to mention that this mace just happened to have her and Colin West's fingerprints on it. After all, it was immaterial; Colin had been murdered, and she had been with Cornelia since leaving him and Franny in the armoury. And where *was* Franny, anyway…?

Cornelia, peering around the weapon cases across the room, sighed. "Troubling," she said. "If the murderer held onto it, they surely intend to use it again. The same goes for this roll of tape I can't find anywhere – the murderer isn't just conjuring tape up from out of thin air, after all. Although there are some curious adhesive markings on the side of this cabinet where some strips of tape appear to have been left and then *removed…* Well, regardless, it just supports our theory of the crimes."

"Colin's death doesn't," Alex pointed out. "I can't imagine he'd hurt a fly."

"Nor even say boo to a goose," Cornelia murmured. "Yes, it is hard to imagine him ever making anyone feel powerless. But people are full of surprises, you know."

"Speaking of people who aren't surprising at all," Yva sighed, standing up and brushing her hands, "my well-researched though technically unqualified inspection of the body tells me that Colin would have died instantly with a knife in him that deep. Upward strike towards the heart, or at least towards some major arteries; probably a right-handed blow, but that's meaningless, as anyone can use the wrong hand. Definitely within the hour, maybe even sooner. Any idea who the last person to see him alive was?"

Alex fielded this one. "We'll need to have a word with Victoria, obviously," she answered, "and track down Franny Smythe, too. She should have been with him, as agreed earlier."

"She earns herself a promotion to top suspect," Yva nodded. "As such, she probably has an unbreakable alibi, or it would be too easy. Anyone else?"

"Well," Cornelia coughed awkwardly. "Besides Franny and probably Victoria – the last people to see Colin alive would, in fact, be us. Alex and I left him in here not an hour ago." She grinned at Yva. "Perhaps I should have mentioned that before you started your examination."

Yva grinned back. "Keeping me in practice? Or testing whether I would lie?" Alex got the impression that she would have been much more annoyed if anyone but Cornelia had wasted her time this way, but apparently that wasn't a problem: "I'd have checked him over anyway, of course. It's interesting work, and beats waiting for the police." She clapped her hands, as if calling for attention. "Since I've put the time in now, are there any further questions?"

Alex looked from the body of Colin West to the iron coffin he had been stuffed in. Bloody trails ran down the rear wall to pool grotesquely in the bottom, depth unclear. Lazily, a single droplet crept its way along the length of one of the many spikes, and vibrated torturously before falling at last into that pit of blood. And therein lay the problem.

"Why hasn't he been – well, spiked?" Alex asked, gesturing to illustrate the point. "Colin isn't, I mean, *wasn't* small. How did he fit in there without being punctured all over? The murderer could have just killed him that way."

Cornelia and Yva blinked at her. Their nonplussed expressions suggested that they either hadn't heard, or that she had just said something extremely stupid.

"Um," she mumbled, going red. "I mean, that is the whole point of an iron maiden, right?"

Cornelia took a deep breath. "No," she answered, shortly. "In fairness, that is exactly what you *are* meant to think, and as such it's worth examining. But no."

"No?" Alex repeated. Did she have to be wrong about everything? "Then... what? Are they meant to be like a magic trick?"

"That's actually not far off," Yva said, sounding insultingly surprised. "Iron maidens are just for show. They aren't real torture instruments, they were made up later on; if you actually tried to kill someone in an iron maiden, it would probably break." She contemplated the hoax device with an inquisitive gaze. "Colin really was stuffed in there, though, and it didn't break the maiden or him. So there *is* a magic trick."

"Like when magicians put swords through their assistants. Yes, that had occurred to me, too," Cornelia nodded.

"We're not back on secret passages, are we?" Alex asked.

"I should hope not!" Cornelia said emphatically. But she still approached the iron maiden. "I don't think it's important – and yet there must be some trick..."

Lifting her stick, she began rapping at any unbloodied parts of the iron maiden's interior – the front receiving only a few superficial taps, the sides and back taking a more vigorous hammering...

"Ah, this is more like it," she said, jabbing away at an outstretched spike. The needle-like point seemed to twist to one side as she battered away. "Now, I wonder." She angled her cane across the iron maiden's hatch, resting at the very tip of a spike. "Alex, please close that door slowly, would you?"

Alex's fingerprints were already on the door, so it would do no harm. Stepping respectfully around the late lamented Colin, she gently pushed the door of the iron maiden until it closed on Cornelia's walking stick, and as she did so, she noticed that the cane seemed to push deeper into the interior...

"Got it," Cornelia said, looking pleased with herself. She withdrew the cane. "There's a mechanical link of some sort between the hinges and the spikes. As the door closes, the spikes fold away. You couldn't kill anyone by putting them in here; most people would find it quite roomy."

That was intriguing information, certainly – but was it actually helpful? "It's strange that the murderer only used the iron maiden to hide Colin, not kill him," Alex pointed out. "I wonder who could have known about this. Maybe someone familiar with –"

"Who cares?" Yva interrupted. "Anyone with a brain could have suspected it, so it's irrelevant."

Saying that was one thing, but it wasn't as if *Alex* had suspected anything – and indeed the whole discussion proved that Adam Carver had not revealed the secret of the iron maiden to his guests the previous day. Perhaps anyone could have walked in and tested the efficacy of the iron maiden, so it was no proof that the murderer was intimately acquainted with the Carver household – but if they *were*, did that suggest the murderer was motivated by something deeper than Carver's threats of the previous night? And if not, what had the murderer been imagining would happen when they hauled Colin West's body into the iron maiden?

Colin West's murder seemed to make less and less sense. Why murder him at all? Unless the murderer's targets were never or at least no longer being chosen due to a personal grudge. But if the victims were arbitrary, could you still apply any logical reasoning to the situation? …It was worth a shot.

"I have an idea of what might have happened," Alex put forward, tentatively. "Not *how* it happened, but why."

Cornelia looked at her with appraising anticipation. Even Yva had the decency to look intrigued. "Go on," Great-Aunt Cornelia nodded.

"Victoria seems like she would be a more obvious target for the murderer," Alex ventured. "Like Maria Bole, she's an adult closely associated with Adam Carver and *Castles in the Sky*. It's weird that the murderer would kill Colin and let Victoria live – but maybe the murderer didn't have that choice at the time. Maybe it was just Colin in here when the murderer came."

"Because the two of us had taken Victoria Carver away to consider the question of the window key," Cornelia nodded.

"Right," Alex agreed. "The murderer is kind of theming the murders around the books. Maybe they've already killed their main targets, if they ever had any, and now it's more important to just commit a couple more impossible crimes, with any victim they find available."

"Kind of like a serial killer," Yva interrupted. "Serial killer mysteries were popular once, although it's best when it's a normal murder plan disguised as a serial killing."

"Well, maybe," Alex said, flustered; she already didn't like this explanation and moved quickly onto what she felt more certain of. "The point is, Victoria was out of the room, and for whatever reason, Franny was too – I don't want to say she's the murderer when we just don't know what her story is right now. Colin was alone. The murderer walked in, and did their usual thing – attacked him, tied him up, and killed him. Put him in the iron maiden." She paused. "But the door wasn't taped shut yet. And then Victoria Carver came back...

"She can't have seen who the murderer was. If she had, she would definitely be dead. Maybe the murderer heard her coming and hid. Then they jumped out, attacked her, and tied her up; blindfolded her with her own shawl. But the murderer couldn't kill her, as they'd already *used up* their third murder on Colin West. Killing Victoria would upset their pattern. So all they could do was take her out of action, make sure she had no way of knowing what had happened in the room, and then... left. Somehow." She stopped, and looked between them for any sign of their feelings. "That's it," she clarified.

"Oh. Well, adequate," Yva said, which was the nicest thing she'd said to Alex in a while. "Unsatisfying, but it makes sense."

"Yes, I think the gist of it is correct," Cornelia agreed. "It's not the whole story, but it's a good working start. Of course, there are other interpretations."

"There certainly are," Yva said, and like a raincloud approaching a parade, her worst smile spread ominously across her face. "In fact, I have one for you right now – about how the most obvious suspect committed her evil crimes..."

"Oh no you don't!"

A pinpoint yell pierced the atmosphere like a bullet. Vi Malik was fuming in the doorway, and it seemed he was developing a penchant for dramatic entrances.

"What are you –" Yva began, but Vi was raging over, still ranting.

"I won't let you say it!" he roared. "I won't let you tarnish an innocent woman's good name!"

"What are you –" Alex also tried to get out, but someone more experienced at confrontation spoke over her.

"Vi, are you capable of listening to instructions at all?" Cornelia snapped. "You do understand that I grouped people together to make it more difficult for the murderer, don't you? Where's Victoria?"

"Quinn turned up, so I left them to check on you! And found you conspiring to pin the blame on our hostess!" he screamed.

"Victoria?!" Alex gasped, and her eyes went wide. "I see –"

"Victoria didn't do it! I refuse to hear of it!" he ranted. "Look, I've read murder mysteries too, alright?! I know that people can tie themselves up! I know that anyone who survives a murder attempt is usually guilty! I know that anyone left alive in a locked room is probably the killer! But you can't apply murder mystery logic to real life!"

"It's all the same logic, moron," Yva retorted. "And get over her, she's like twice your age."

Alex had tried with the utmost politeness to ignore it, but Vi's white-knight act had gone publicly cringeworthy. The best thing would be to change the subject as quickly as possible. "Yeah, um, Vi, nobody ever mentioned Victoria…"

"You were about to!" Vi cried, jabbing a finger in Yva's face. "Don't you have any consideration for people's feelings?!"

"No," she said, as if there were nothing wrong with that. "And you're still wrong. I wasn't talking about Victoria Carver."

His mouth opened, but no words came out; just an empty breath as his body stopped like a statue, or like someone stranded on breaking ice. Alex turned away; even in books, she could never stand seeing people embarrassed. He must have been under far greater tension than he had ever let on, to misstep so humiliatingly.

The only person who had put forward the Victoria theory, in the end, was Vi himself. Worse still, it *worked*. It would have been possible for her to murder Colin the way he had implied, by sealing up the room and staying there and just tying herself up. She was probably one of Cornelia's three suspects; in fact, Alex began to think, she might be more than that. At least one other murder, and even the motive –

"Let's quickly move on," Cornelia said, careful and calm, as if stepping around a very fragile object. "Who was your most obvious suspect, Yva? Franny, I presume?"

"Not even," Yva said, and she found her smirk again as she pointed. "You are the culprit, Alex Corby!"

Chapter Sixteen
Avenging Angel

The wheel of accusation had spun around and around, careening through the ghastly morning at Carver's Rest, and at last its pointing finger had landed on Alex. Perhaps it was only fair, or even inevitable, that as the pool of suspects shrank then eventually everyone would be considered. But that didn't stop Alex from being jolted by a terrible fear – the fear that, in this house where the murderer's actions were impossible, a rational explanation might be contrived which pointed to entirely the wrong person...

She wasn't used to standing up for herself. She wasn't used to defending herself. She wasn't used to problems that couldn't be solved by running away and burying herself in a book in the peace and quiet of her room. Why hadn't she ever learned better? She needed it now!

Yva, meanwhile, was contemplating Alex's expression with easy satisfaction. "A guilty conscience betrays itself," she said, shaking her head in a manner which she might have stolen from a TV show. "That's the look of a criminal who never expected to be caught out in their guilt. They speak of it in countless mystery novels."

"No they don't," scoffed Cornelia, regarding Yva with a look which was, at last, not merely indulgent. Instead, she looked quite annoyed. "I say, Yva. Is this tosh something which you actually, truly believe?"

"Of course," she said, shrugging insouciantly. "Why would I say it if I didn't mean it?"

Cornelia scowled at her. "To get back at someone whose theories cornered you earlier?"

"Yes, I'm disappointed in you, Y," Vi tutted, shaking his head. "RedRidingBlood is just a helpless girl. She couldn't possibly kill anyone."

"I could have lived without the 'helpless,'" Alex felt pushed to say. Being patronised was differently unbearable to being accused of multiple murders. But she had to answer that accusation, too, so she steeled herself. "And Yva," she went on, switching targets, "before you say anything, you should know that I haven't left Cornelia's company since the two of us last saw Colin."

"Don't think I haven't thought of that," Yva grinned. "This time, I've thought of everything. That's how I *know* you're the culprit."

Cornelia let out her deepest sigh, tapping her cane on the floor irritably. "Alex wasn't even here for Carver's little scene yesterday," she said. "What motive could she possibly have for murdering strangers as soon as she walked through the door?"

"Right, the motive." Yva nodded thoughtfully. "I got some ill-founded complaints for not including a motive with my last theory, so I made sure to abduce one this time. Prepare yourself, Corby, for I am about to expose the secret underlying your heinous crimes." She paused, and looked Alex dead in the eye. "It was Carver's inheritance money you were after, so you removed him and anyone else he might have named in his will!" she declared. "You are Adam Carver's secret child!"

Cornelia put a hand over her face. Vi's expression fluttered from bewildered to incredulous. And Alex was overcome with an almost irresistible urge to giggle. Was that seriously it?

"Nothing to say for yourself?" Yva quipped, attempting to raise a single eyebrow and quickly abandoning the effort. "Then I'll move on, and break down your clever murder plot, death by death...

"First, the murder of Adam Carver in a room entirely sealed from the inside with tape." Yva began to prowl about, apparently so she could swivel around dramatically at key moments. "However!" she cried, doing just that. "The moment she ran to report the crime, both the body and the tape conveniently disappeared. In short, Alex Corby is the only witness to this crime. The conclusion is obvious. This impossible crime truly was impossible – and therefore, it did not happen! Alex Corby made it all up!"

"Not that old canard," Cornelia muttered under her breath. "No better than the *Castles in the Sky* unreliable narrator hypothesis..."

It wasn't a theory she could directly disprove, Alex thought. But she felt she was starting to get a grasp of Yva's way of thinking. "This is exactly like your theory about Adam Carver being secretly alive," she pointed out. "You couldn't figure it out, so you just dismissed the problem!"

"Question," Vi prompted, having regained enough cool to make a play for being the voice of reason. "In this theory, what really did happen to Adam Carver?"

Yva handwaved the question away. "It hardly matters. She killed him somehow, and then hid the body somewhere – or maybe just tossed it into the sea. Whatever she did, she had no shortage of time, her pretended near-midnight arrival being wholly unsubstantiated."

Alex had to think about that one. Right, Maria Bole was dead, which meant that there was nobody to testify that she really did arrive so late at night. So long as it was after the guests had dispersed, she could easily have arrived sooner and there would be nobody to say. In Yva's version of events, she had all the time in the world...

"Second murder!" Yva announced. "On arriving, Alex Corby asked Maria Bole to wait for her downstairs to discuss some private matter. In the meantime, she killed Adam Carver and collected the materials she needed for her next slaughter. Then she lured Maria Bole out to the gates, knocked her down, and set her up in position – having been informed long in advance by Adam Carver, her father, of just how the drawbridge and portcullis functioned."

Par for the course, Alex thought. There was nothing there that anyone else couldn't have done. But that wasn't the main event. "And then I killed Maria from the wrong side of a taped-shut door by...?" she asked.

"Simple. It wasn't taped shut at the time," Yva said. "That night, you attached a loop of string to the drawbridge lever and trailed it right up to the front door. In the morning, you snuck down, opened the door, and pulled the string to trigger the gates and kill Maria. Then you reeled the string in, shut the door, and taped it over."

And here was where the cavalry arrived.

"I'm afraid you've overlooked a clue there, my dear girl," Cornelia Crow said, and Yva flinched as if stung. "The small matter of Quinn Shillerdyce having observed the taped door before he ever arrived at breakfast...? If Alex was obliged to precede *him*, her actions would be at dangerous risk of putting the time of death earlier than you yourself announced; and thus none of those breakfast alibis would have appeared at all."

Alex beamed at her great-aunt. Partnership! She had never known how good it felt.

A flash of anger lit up Yva's face. "Illustrators," she muttered, like a profanity. "Always imposing their own interpretations on a text…" She attempted, with difficulty, to compose herself. "Alright, how about this?" she offered. "Quinn never *re*-observed the taped door. What happened was that Alex put a placeholder seal on the door using mark-free masking tape, which Quinn then saw; and in the morning, once breakfast had already begun, she slipped down, removed her original seal and pulled the string, then retaped the door with parcel tape and flushed the masking tape down a toilet somewhere…"

"No. Excuse me, Y, but no," Vi intruded. His voice held firm as he spoke. "I woke Alex up this morning, made myself look respectable, and then waited for her at the top of the stairs. She appeared from the direction of her bedroom, clearly refreshed. It's simply impossible for her to do everything she needed in that interval. Not without it *still* putting the time of death earlier than the breakfast estimate."

That was more the kind of help Alex would actually have asked him for, and she gave Vi too a grateful smile for it – while Yva let slip an ugly glower which spoke volumes… Yet even that was gone in moments.

"Alright, alright, I knew all that was a possibility – so I prepared a *backup theory*," she said smoothly. "Corby activated the gates using a self-destroying machine which burned up or melted, leaving behind no evidence. I am not obliged to describe this machine!"

Just trying to find words to articulate how stupid this theory was took Alex long enough for Vi to get in first with, "That is the most ridiculous thing I have ever heard."

"You can't just invent a theory where the only evidence is that there is no evidence!" Alex spluttered out at last. "You could just make up something like that for every murder. Maybe Adam Carver was stabbed by a machine! Maybe Colin West was thrown in the iron maiden by a machine! Maybe the murderer is an ice robot!"

"Yva, dear," Cornelia said, with a pained sigh, "forgive me, but while I know you've read a lot of impossible crime novels, have you ever actually *solved* one? Even an easy one? I've recommended you several which can be solved, as you said earlier, 'from a statement of the premises alone…'"

"Shut up, shut up!" Yva snarled at them all. Their criticism was finally getting through. "There is no evidence that Carver and

DVC's murders depended on a purely mechanical trigger! Maria's did, so the automatic murder theory is valid! Next murder, Colin West!"

"This is the one whcrc I was with Cornelia the whole time," Alex reminded them. "Even up to the last time I was in a room with Colin, she was right there."

"I will verify that statement," Cornelia announced. "Excepting the race to the armoury, Alex has always been in the same room as me since everyone separated to investigate the murders."

"I accept that statement," Yva conceded, a little unhappily. "Of course, witness statements and opinions are not reliable evidence. A more cynical person than me would argue that you could just be covering for your relative, but I will accept it this time." She met Cornelia's glare with a triumphant grin. "Therefore, Colin West was stabbed while you were in the room, before your very eyes!"

"These same eyes which I am rolling right now?" Cornelia asked.

This latest theory made so little sense that Alex found herself strangely intrigued. "So, how is that meant to work?" she asked. "When Great-Aunt Cornelia and I left the room, with Victoria Carver, Colin wasn't dead. And Franny was still here! So how did it get from there to Colin being dead in an iron maiden tied shut with ribbon, without me being here?"

"I'm glad you asked me that," Yva replied, with a devilish gleam in her eye, "though *you* won't be. To explain, let me take us back to last night…"

Her voice rose, and grew strangely calm. A faraway look came into her eyes. The trance of the storyteller was upon her. This was Yva's world.

"Corby and Colin have both acknowledged their first meeting last night," Yva began. "She stumbled on him fresh from 'discovering' Carver's murder – or rather, fresh from waiting for some dupe to leave their room to become her witless witness. But the killer saw another quality in Colin West which suited her evil aims. Consider the scene: A darkened corridor, choked by a prevailing miasma of fear; a breathless, panicking waif, and an overweight, geeky virgin; into his ear she whispers such heart-throbbing blandishments as 'The murderer could be anywhere; please protect me, Colin…!'" She shook her head with slow, mockruefulness. "It was simplicity itself for this heartless harlot to seduce him."

Speechless and thoughtless. Alex's jaw simply dropped, and stayed down for the count.

"So, not content with slandering my niece, Alex's mother, with your hidden-child theory, you're also slandering my great-niece directly," Cornelia remarked coldly. "Why not go for the full set, Yva? Who did *I* seduce?"

Vi was shaking his own head, in genuine ruefulness. "This is fanfiction, Yva," he scolded. "Worse yet, it's real-person fanfiction – the lowest form of all fanfic."

"It's completely true and undeniable," replied Yva.

It was completely false and very deniable. "I've never seduced anyone in my life!" Alex protested – and nor, she admitted to herself, was she likely to any time soon. Her romantic entanglements extended only so far as two first and only dates, neither at her own invitation, comprising one largely silent engagement with a boy from her class and one disastrous attempt with an older girl. After those, Alex had shelved the idea of romance for the foreseeable future. "Also, why am I supposed to have done this again?" she pointed out, changing the subject. "How does this get me into two places at once?"

"That's the beauty of this theory. You could indeed be in two places at once – with Colin standing in for you," Yva elaborated. "All you had to do was use your wiles to entice him into a suicide pact –"

Alex groaned. "This is exactly what people criticise your fics for!" she said exasperatedly. "People are not that shallow, they just don't work that way –"

"You'd already hidden a knife on your person" – Yva raised her voice to drown Alex out – "and while nobody was looking you stabbed Colin in the back, neglecting to push the knife in far enough to kill –"

"She's not a surgeon!" exclaimed Vi.

"Ah, but Colin was pretty fat," Yva pointed out.

Cornelia shrugged. "Point to Yva."

"He wasn't *fat*, Great-Aunt Cornelia, it's just – you're kind of really really thin by comparison, so –"

Yva concluded by just talking over all interruptions until she was done. "You assured Colin that Victoria was the murderer and convinced him to save everyone by killing her, after which he would kill himself to escape the law and you would join him in death soon after. He shooed Franny away somehow and hid behind the door of the armoury, capturing Victoria upon her return. But he failed to find within himself the courage to kill – so instead he decided to present himself as Victoria's final victim, creating a locked room to prove that nobody else was involved in his death and then shutting himself in the iron maiden, the narrow confines of which pushed the knife all the way into his heart. As for the ribbon tying the iron maiden shut, since Alex Corby was the first to notice it then it follows that she was the one to attach it, looping it over the iron maiden while everyone was distracted by Victoria." Finished at last, Yva took in a deep breath, and then bowed low. "Possible, provable, perfect."

"Poppycock," sneered Cornelia. "If this is the net you're casting to catch my great-niece, it's full of holes."

"Most nets are," responded Yva.

"Not impossible crime nets. If you want to capture the killer in this kind of mystery, you need to trap them in a watertight globe as impenetrable as their locked-room scenario."

"Um, yes," Alex sort-of agreed with the involved metaphor. "If this theory is supposed to intimidate me, it kind of completely failed. You basically didn't bother explaining either of the first two murders, and your explanation of this third murder was that I did barely any of it and wasn't even really the killer." She shrugged right in Yva's scowling face. "I won't pretend to understand what happened here, but I don't think just ignoring the problems is the answer."

Yva listened to this speech with a look which grew uglier and uglier. "Everyone's a critic," she muttered. "Everyone, especially those people without any talent of their own. Like all critics, you just have an inferiority complex because you know you're not good enough to stand on my level. This is destructive criticism. You just want to take me down to make yourself feel better about being uncreative."

"Whereas your own judgment is entirely unbiased and completely unrelated to Alex's accusations against you, I suppose," Vi said, shaking his head. "Such double-standards are frowned upon at Besieging Heaven, Y."

"Call it whatever you like," Yva retorted. "But without an answer of your own, you have no grounds on which to take down other people's answers."

A narrow smile spread across Cornelia's face. "I can give you a better explanation for how this murder was committed using an entirely different culprit."

That put a stop to the argument, as Alex and Vi and even Yva looked up at Cornelia with genuine interest. Corvus Crown, now Cornelia Crow, had long been their acknowledged expert on mysteries; and she had consistently offered the best approach to dealing with the impossible puzzles of Carver's Rest, though so far she had played her cards close to her chest.

Could it be that she had the solution? How many solutions could there be to a locked-room mystery, after all?

"Well?" prompted Vi, eagerness restrained but not subdued. "Don't keep us in suspense. Who's your culprit?"

"As you wish," she said, and pointed casually. "It's you, Vi."

Alex and Yva's eyes turned once again to the sputtering and incredulous Vi Malik, his voice jumping pitches as he yelped, "M-me?!"

And Alex started to see. Started to see how a theory for Colin's murder with Vi as the culprit might have worked!

"The room was never sealed…" she breathed.

"In one," Cornelia announced, nodding at her. "I was a little behind the rest of you, but from what I could tell, neither you nor Yva had time to check that the door really was sealed up as Vi claimed. We've established that Vi conceivably had opportunity to commit this murder; I won't venture a guess at the motive – something sordid, I'm sure – but after setting everything up inside the room, he could have taped the door shut from the inside, wrenched it open to leave, and then simply shut it normally behind him – and only acted out charging through it and breaking the seal. After all, did anyone actually hear the noise of tape ripping away from the doorframe…?"

"I didn't," Yva butted in.

"Nor me," Alex said, casting an uneasy gaze upon Vi, "but we should have, as I definitely heard it when I broke the seal on my room."

"N-now hold on!" cried Vi, his voice trembling. "That's just because you weren't close enough! *I* heard the tape rip – in fact…" He started fumbling around in his pocket, his shaking fingers slowing him down. "I can prove it!" he cried, brandishing his phone.

Cornelia slowly cocked her head, her expression nonplussed. But Alex gasped. "No way, Vi. You *weren't* recording again…"

"No better time to," declared Vi, recovering his easy smile. "Wherever possible we should be backing up our experiences with hard evidence, so we can guarantee our reliability when the police arrive. Naturally I switched my phone on and started recording as I approached the room. Just watch…"

He swiped at the screen for a few moments, and then flipped the phone to face them. On the door-shaped screen, another door was visible.

Vi had clearly turned on the camera at the last moment. No sooner had the door to the armoury swum into focus than it zoomed towards the camera at top speed. With a crash – and, yes, an audible ripping of tape – the door was flung away, and the blurry armoury appeared as if to someone not wearing their glasses, the camera settling on a figure writhing on the floor…

And then, darkness. The video was mere seconds long. But it showed all it needed to. Vi Malik's story was guaranteed.

…Wasn't it? Or was it? Casting her own mind back to the breaking of the seal, Alex felt an ice-cold stillness spread across her body. Something was wrong. Something was really, hugely wrong. Something which meant that Vi might actually be –

"Huh. Seems watertight," Yva was saying, scrutinising the screen. "I should've thought of that. Nice reporting, SMV."

"It's not reporting," Alex interrupted. "It's not reporting at all. It's a lie!"

Her quiet voice nonetheless drew everybody's attention, which was then deflected straight back to Vi. "I – don't know what you mean?" he squealed.

No. Surely not. Surely it couldn't be SiegeMasterV. And yet –

"Vi, as we got to the door, I called out to you," Alex said, trying to meet his eyes. "I called out, 'Wait!' right as you went through the door. It should have been on that video." She seized him by the arm as his eyes swam away. "Why is my voice not on the video, Vi?!"

Silence fell upon the room – a cold, tense silence, like a droplet waiting to descend from the tip of an icicle…

"Well, well, well," at last Yva murmured, looking upon Vi with surprise and something disturbingly like admiration. "I never thought you had the guts or the wits."

"I can explain!" Vi burst out in a squeaky yell. "I can explain everything! It's just an unfortunate coincidence, but –"

"Oh, but this had better be good," Cornelia said, her hand gripping her cane tight enough to shake. "I confess that, when I proposed this theory, I really didn't expect any actual evidence to back it up – but if the recording was faked somehow…"

"He could have had the roll of tape with him," Alex broke in. "When he recorded, he had his phone in one hand, the roll of tape in the other, the end in his teeth – and as he broke through the door he pulled the tape to make the right noise –"

"It's not faked! It's completely real!" exclaimed Vi – and then his voice dropped, and his eyes scuttled away. "It was just… recorded a little earlier than I let on, that's all."

"It was *what?!*" Alex cried.

Vi tried to hold onto a shaky smile, and made calming gestures for his own benefit. "Now, look," he said, his authoritative tone cracking. "I only made a slight omission in my story before. When I said that I went downstairs to see Victoria, and found the door closed and blocked, and rushed upstairs for help… Maybe I didn't rush upstairs immediately. Maybe I actually broke in first."

"You idiot," said Yva flatly.

"I didn't know what I'd find!" Vi cried. "The murderer could have been killing his victim at that moment! I might have been able to save someone! So I turned on my camera and burst through the door straight away." He took a deep breath. "But you saw what I found. There was no murderer in there – just Victoria, tied up so tightly she couldn't even see or hear. And then I thought, wait: That means there's no witnesses to what just happened. Nobody, not even

Victoria, can prove that I'm not the murderer. Even the video could have been faked the way Alex just said. So, I…" He hesitated on the last part, clearly in great shame. "I turned off the camera, shut the door behind me, and ran upstairs to get you all, so I could fake breaking open the door in front of some actual witnesses and hope that nobody noticed the discrepancies."

His story ended lamely, and he seemed to droop like a sad dog. And he dropped in Alex's estimation, too. She was almost ashamed of him. He had lied to them, and to save himself, he had abandoned if only briefly the very damsel in distress he seemed to have been searching for. But that was better than being a murderer, at least – if she accepted his story.

Yes, it was credible. It was believable. But was it *true*? Or was the very credibility of his story just another trap?

"Nothing you've just told us disproves my theory," Cornelia declared sternly. "There is no evidence to prove that your story is the truth. But." She held up a finger as Vi made to interrupt. "It doesn't explain how you could have committed either of the first two murders. So for now you're on probation, my boy. You'd better make sure you're not alone from now on, as you badly need an alibi if another murder occurs."

"Might be too late for that," said a voice they had not heard in too long, and all four of them turned towards the door.

Standing in the doorway, a bandage-headed Victoria Carver leaning tiredly on the doorframe behind him, was Quinn Shillerdyce.

"I say, you've been elusive," Cornelia said, frowning at the illustrator. "Where have you been?"

He ignored her, however, and strode across the room – strode past her. But his pace slowed, and finally drew to a complete stop, as he approached the body of Colin West…

"Damn," he muttered, and with a violent movement twisted himself away. He stormed over to the windows, his hands moving to claw across his bare skull. "Damn, damn, damn – it was all real! Damn it, it was *real!*"

"What are you talking about?" demanded Yva. "Yes, it's real, great job, we established that hours ago. Where have *you* been?"

But Cornelia's eyes were alive as if with fire. "Ah… So we're finally coming to it, then."

"Yes, I suppose we are," sighed Victoria Carver, walking unsteadily to the centre of the room, resting one arm atop a clear case of weapons. "There's no point in playing along now."

"Playing along?" repeated Alex, remembering something Victoria Carver had said earlier – and as a sneaking suspicion crept through her mind, she breathed, "Oh no…"

"Up 'til now the pair of us thought these murders were staged," growled Quinn Shillerdyce. "Because that's what they were supposed to be! Adam Carver told me last night he would fake his own death as a publicity stunt!"

CHAPTER SEVENTEEN
THE WILFULLY IGNORANT

"I knew it!" screamed Yva. "I knew it I knew it I knew it! I knew Carver's death was just a bluff –"

"Simmer *down*, Yva," Cornelia instructed, tapping the girl on the head with her cane. "I believe these two have a story to tell, and I strongly suspect it may not be quite what you're imagining."

Alex could forgive Yva this time for letting her ideas run away with her; she was experiencing the same feeling, lining up points of suspicion and knocking them down with this new revelation. She *knew* it had been out-of-character for Carver to savage his own friends and fans – had known from the start that everything about the whole get-together had felt like nothing more than the set-up for one of Carver's mysteries –

"Aye. I'll give you the run-down, as it happened to me," Quinn Shillerdyce grunted, still looking determinedly away from the corpse in the room. "Wasn't like I was in on it from the start. I only found out yesterday night. That kicking Carver gave us… Ugly. Beneath him. Certainly beneath me. So after brooding over it for a while, I took myself up to his study to give him a piece of my mind."

"What time was this?" prompted Cornelia.

Quinn shrugged unhelpfully. "I didn't look. Within an hour, at least. Point is, I went there. Knew where to go as it'd been part of the tour, of course. Met no-one on the way. Hammered on the door of his study and went right in. And there he was, sitting behind his desk looking… I don't know. Flustered, maybe; like he'd been interrupted. Piece of paper in front of him, but I didn't care about that. I went to march right up to him and ask where he got off." Quinn's furrowed brow dug deeper into his face as he looked fixedly at the sky. "Didn't get there, though, because he went all weird. Held up a finger – politely, like he just wanted me to wait. Crept over to the door and twisted the latch, locking us in. And then, with a grin on his face, he started to talk…

"Turned out I'd just about played into his hands. Dragging us over the coals like that – all an act. He wanted us to be mad as hell, but he especially wanted someone to be mad enough to come and find him like I did. Because the whole damned business was just to stage a murder as a big stunt – or a game, he said. The idea was that tomorrow morning he'd be found 'dead,' in his study, and everyone would have to go chasing around figuring out whodunnit. And whoever'd pigeonholed him like I did would have to play the role of the murderer…"

Yva clapped her hands together. "Oh, I see. So this is your excuse for why you've been behaving so suspiciously all day."

"You're damn right it is," Quinn shot back. "All morning I haven't had a clue what's going on! Carver didn't give me any instructions 'cept to be as shady as possible, said he'd prepare clues, and then shoved me right out of his room again before I could tell him what a lousy idea it was. So here's me, playing along with all this kiddy rubbish which I assume is part of his game. Go creeping about before breakfast and find the front door taped shut – I figure I'm meant to have done that, so I keep schtum for as long as possible. Victoria tells us she couldn't find Carver even after checking his study – he, or I suppose I, must've changed plans. I'm trying to talk to Colin about the portfolio he showed me when he tells me Maria Bole has been murdered – which I don't take seriously, because if anyone else had been let in on the game it would have been her, so sure, that was me as well. How, or why, I couldn't imagine, but what I could do was keep to myself so no-one knew where I was, wander off on my own, and generally be so damn useless that now I really *do* look like the murderer!" He had gotten angrier and angrier as he had rambled on, furiously rubbing his nails into his scalp. "Damn it, Carver, what the hell's going on?! This was meant to be just a stupid joke!"

"It seems likely," Cornelia informed him, "that somebody else anticipated Mr. Carver's plans. Somebody who took a rather dimmer view of last night's events."

Somebody, Alex thought, who was probably not Quinn Shillerdyce, unless his whole story was simply a bluff of epic proportions. It was a good story – one which redeemed Adam Carver just a little, though Alex found herself surprisingly uninterested in this fact – but it didn't appear to materially alter the circumstances of the murders; not unless there was something important that she was missing. But there was one person who could shed more light on this murky business… "You must have known about this, Mrs. Carver?" Alex asked. It was time to play detective.

Victoria Carver gave a start, as if shocked awake. "What?" she said faintly. "Oh; yes, that's right. Of course I knew about my husband's game. I thought it perhaps a little excessive… but, well, he convinced me."

"And did anyone else know what was really going on?" Alex persisted.

Did Victoria hesitate for just a fraction of a second? "No," she said. "No, not unless anyone guessed what we were up to."

"Guilty as charged," Cornelia said breezily. "Carver's outburst was just too convenient, and your and Quinn's reactions to the murders were just too blasé."

Alex wasn't even mad anymore about being left out of this loop. There would always be another loop which only Cornelia was in – and anyway, she had half-suspected this herself; had seen the clues, just not put them together…

"Well, excepting people who only suspected," Victoria continued, "it was just me and Adam. We planned everything about the celebration together – well, he planned it, I carried it out, buying things in, writing the invitations and so on…"

A burning enquiry struck Alex, one which potentially allowed them to get help and therefore would inevitably be thwarted. "What about removing the telephone and router?" she asked. "Was that part of the game?"

"Yes," Victoria said slowly, "but – my husband did that, that's the one thing he did. I suppose he might have needed them, but I don't know where they are now."

"In the sea, I expect," volunteered Yva.

"I expect so," Victoria sighed.

"What about the guest list?" Alex resumed. She had a problem with Mrs. Carver's previous statement. "If that was the only thing Mr. Carver prepared, hiding the phones, then were you the one to decide who to invite?" She glanced at Vi. "Who set up the Besieging Heaven competition with you?"

Vi frowned. "The marketing team with the publishers. They said they had a spare invite set aside for an ordinary fan, but whose decision that was –"

"Oh, I –" Victoria interrupted. "I – don't know a great deal about my husband's fans, so I asked Maria who would be deserving."

Cornelia narrowed her eyes at this. "Hmmm," she said, noncommittally. "While we're at it, Victoria, I don't believe we've asked for your account of what happened in this room when you were taken captive. I'm aware this must be difficult for you, but before we get blown off-course again then perhaps you could recount how you came to be tied up alone with a dead body in the room…?"

"Please!" Vi butted predictably in. "She's had a very traumatic experience! You have no right –"

"It's alright; you have every right to ask," Victoria said, heedless of Vi's righteous bluster. "Not that there's much to explain, I'm afraid." She closed her eyes, breathing deeply. "Let me see… I had just left the two of you, Cornelia and Alex, outside my room, and returned to the armoury where Colin and Franny should have been waiting. But when I got there, the door was pulled to, and behind it the room was empty." Her eyes flicked momentarily in the direction of the iron maiden, and she shuddered. "Or at least, it *looked* empty."

"Was the iron maiden tied shut at that time?" Yva broke in.

"What?" asked Victoria, startled. "I – I suppose I didn't really notice. Perhaps it wasn't…?"

Yva directed a significant look at Alex. Alex sighed. "Please continue, Mrs. Carver," she said.

Victoria nodded, and did so. "It's around this point that things start to get foggy," she explained. "I know I stood inside the doorway for a few moments, wondering where those two could have gotten to and what I should do. At last I turned to leave – and then, yes, it's coming back to me." She looked over to the doorway. "I heard a footstep behind me, in the room, and then – pain…"

She gestured loosely to the bandages that circled around her forehead, securing a soft pad to an area near the back of her skull. "Are my bandages holding up okay, Victoria?" Vi intruded. "Can I adjust them for you?"

This time she just ignored him, much like everyone else. "I suppose whoever it was must have been hiding behind the door, and when I turned around, they attacked."

As Victoria spoke, Alex looked over to the door. It didn't open against an adjacent wall, like the one in her room, so there was more than enough space for a person to hide behind it if you didn't push it all the way back, which most people wouldn't. And from that position, you could probably watch what a person was doing through the gap in the hinge. "I don't know how long I was out cold for," Victoria was continuing.

"Probably not long," Cornelia chipped in. "It's not like the films. You were likely only unconscious for a few minutes, if that."

"Yes, that fits," Victoria nodded slowly. "When I came to, I didn't understand what was happening. I couldn't see or hear anything, and my body was being moved… It took me a few minutes to realise that my eyes and ears still worked, they'd just been covered; by the time I understood that, my wrists and ankles had been tied, too. I could barely move – and my head hurt, hurt more when I tried to move, so I just lay still. But the more I remembered, the more I remained still out of fear. Something horrible had really been happening, and whoever had me at their mercy was probably a murderer."

"So you definitely couldn't see or hear at all?" prompted Vi. "You don't have any clue who it was that captured you?"

She shook her head, wincing slightly as she did so. "All I could feel were the vibrations of their feet on the floor. After they'd tied me up, those vibrations kept on knocking their way around the room – I can't say exactly where or what they did, just that they kept on moving for what felt like minutes… Eventually they just stopped dead. That was even more frightening – that I couldn't even tell where they were any more. I was terrified that the person was still watching me, standing over me, looking for any movement, anything I might do – so I just played dead, tried to breathe as slowly as possible, did anything I could to avoid attention from anyone who might be looking… Until at last someone thundered over and started to untie me."

"Anyone would have done the same," Vi said, with attempted modesty.

"Even then, I was scared that it was the murderer again," Victoria said, and Vi's face fell. "But that's all. The murderer – they were so careful. I couldn't possibly tell what had happened. And because of that, I realised that I didn't understand anything. Lying there, helpless, it gradually became clear to me that everything I'd been told this morning was real."

Yva looked from Victoria to Quinn with what looked very much like contempt. "And neither of you used your brains and thought for a fraction of a second that maybe something had gone wrong?" she asked, bludgeoningly.

"Why would we?" demanded Victoria, breathlessly. "Things like this just don't *happen*! As I understand it, the murders aren't even *possible*! And there's still no proof of what happened to my husband."

"No proof of Maria's death either, that I ever saw," Quinn interrupted. "There's a sheet over the portcullis; can't see a thing. Figured maybe it was a waxwork under there at the most."

Cornelia turned back to him. "And how was this game supposed to end?" she enquired.

Quinn snorted. "Easy. Once you'd all figured out it was me, or by midday if nobody twigged, Carver would pop up and turn out to be alive after all. He was going to explain how this was all a big gimmick to advertise his new book, which I guess was about more or less the same thing."

"How could anyone guess it was you, though?" Yva pointed out. "There *were* no clues. I'd have seen them."

"The murderer must have struck very soon after Quinn left," murmured Cornelia.

"Hang on," Alex said, a problem occurring to her. "Whoever went to Mr. Carver's study to confront him would be his pick for the murderer, right? But what if nobody came?"

"Eh…" Quinn shrugged, and looked over at Victoria. She grew a little paler.

"He said –" She swallowed uncomfortably. "He said, in that case, it would be a suicide."

"*Hmmm*," Yva pronounced, in echo of Cornelia. She clearly wasn't ruling anything out yet. Alex didn't see how suicide applied, though. As she saw it, none of the victims could have killed themselves. How could Carver have spirited himself away from the room? How could Maria have taped the front door on the inside yet ended up on the outside? And how could Colin have tied the iron maiden shut? Granted, by the same reasonable logic, nobody else could have committed the murders either. They were still impossible crimes...

"So." A voice interrupted her reverie; it was Quinn, scratching his bald head. "Looks like I've been far out of the loop. Anyone want to explain to me just what *is* going on?"

"I don't think any of us really understand what's going on," Alex admitted. Victoria nodded sadly.

"I know what it seems like to me," Vi spoke up. "Adam Carver's prank went too far – and he died for nothing."

"Perhaps," Cornelia said. Alex saw that she had picked up the third birthday present – *A Coffin Nail Creaks*. The third volume of *Castles in the Sky* for the third murder. Was there another out there, waiting for them?

That thought shocked Alex bolt upright. There was something they had forgotten – something they had just shrugged off in the midst of these revelations of the past. Something which promised a revelation of the future!

"Mr. Shillerdyce!" she exclaimed, staring at him so hard he seemed strangely nervous. "What did you mean, when you walked in? You said, 'might be too late for that,' just as we were talking about if another murder happened."

His eyes widened. "Damn! I forgot!" He struck himself in the head again and again in a rage – "It's why I came down here, and I let it slip my mind. Idiot!"

"Out with it, man!" ordered Cornelia. "There'll be time for self-recrimination later!"

Quinn paced a few steps under five pairs of eyes, giving every impression that coming out with it was the last thing he wanted to do. At last he turned back to them, his own eyes on the floor as if in shame. "I'd locked myself in my room for a while," he muttered. "Long enough. Thought I'd better get back to skulking around in odd places, acting suspicious... See if I could get my hands on Carver, too, wherever he was hiding. So I went up to the top floor. Well, he wasn't in his study, so I figured I'd take a glance in the only other room up there – the solarium..."

"And?" pressed Yva, when he fell silent. "What did you see in there?"

"I couldn't see anything in there," he growled. "That was the problem. I couldn't even get in. The door wouldn't budge, but on instinct I bent down and looked underneath… The gap was wide enough to see it had been sealed up on the other side with a big strip of tape."

CHAPTER EIGHTEEN
FEARED TO TREAD

Alex had yet to visit the uppermost floor of Carver's Rest; amid the maelstrom of mystery and murder, exploring Adam Carver's fantasy castle had fallen back in her priorities. All she had seen of the top floor was the freestanding staircase leading up to it, suspended in the air above its ground floor twin. She crept up that staircase now, the others surrounding her, barely daring to disturb the scene and yet all too aware that the lurking danger had probably already swept away, even as its presence seemed to threaten around every corner. They had already discovered some small and hours-old stains on the floors which could pass for spilt tea, but which they all knew were blood.

Alex felt little doubt as to what they would find within the sealed solarium. The precise form it would take was unknown, but there could be no question of the end result. It had been far too long since anybody had last seen Franny Smythe; and the last person seen with her was now dead. Of course, from another perspective those were strong grounds to consider her the murderer – but with everyone else accounted for and another taped room having appeared, there was no hope that the murderer had not yet struck a fourth time.

Quinn, the tallest and in all likelihood the strongest, or at the very least the person who had been nominated to go first *just in case*, crouched on the stairs just below the floor level of the top storey, and raised his head ever so slowly and slightly to the bars of the banisters. "Clear," he whispered, and he and the five others hurried to the top of the stairs and spread out to face in all directions, like police chasing down a criminal. Alex felt a strange solidarity among the six of them – despite the unspoken fear that one of them was a serial murderer. Perhaps it was the impossible nature of the crimes that made it easy to pretend, even as accusations based in twisted logic and tortured reasoning were thrown about, that the murderer had come and gone like an evil spirit.

Rationally, they knew that the murderer was among them. Yet they peered around every corner for a demon with a knife.

The stairs opened out into a wide landing that stretched to the rear of the house, an open-plan lounge of sofas and soft furnishings reclining beside tall windows and a wide pair of doors that must have led out onto the much-rumoured balcony. On a sunny day it would be a glorious spot, but in winter's gloom it was cobwebbed with shadows. Overlooking the stairs were a pair of corridors that ran across the front of the house, narrow windows shedding little light on whatever rooms occupied the north and south wings.

"Is there anything else up here?" Alex whispered. "Besides the solarium, and Adam Carver's study?"

"That's all," replied Cornelia. Her voice was low, but not lowered, and she didn't look afraid, only infected by the tension that gripped them all. "This floor is smaller, with just a single room on either side of the stairs. Large rooms, though."

"They were meant to be personal retreats for me and Adam," Victoria threw in. "My solarium" – she gestured left of the stairs, south – "I use as a gym, owing to a, ah, genetic predisposition; and Adam's study" – gesturing right and north – "is his writing room and research library, so he can immerse himself in his work in perfect seclusion."

"Let's take a look at this sealed door, then," Cornelia said, and set off in the direction of the solarium. Alex and the others trailed after her, almost single-file in the narrow corridor with its prison-like slits of windows revealing only slivers of a grey and walled-off world. With only one door in the entire corridor, their destination wasn't hard to find. The door itself looked quite normal, and there was no lock upon it.

Cornelia grasped the handle, twisted, and pushed. The door gave just a fraction, but would not open.

"There's something holding it shut, certainly," she muttered. "I don't want to push too hard; we should preserve this seal if possible. Any of you can test it, if you like."

Yva did. She gave the door an experimental shove, not much more than if she'd been trying to open a normal door, but if it budged it barely did so. Alex tried it, too. "It's heavy," she murmured, to nobody in particular. "This feels harder to open than my bedroom was, when –" She checked herself, seeing Victoria Carver standing beside her, and let her sentence stay unfinished.

"You had better verify Quinn's observations about the tape under the door, too, since these sealed rooms have a habit of disappearing," Cornelia reminded them. "I would, but these old bones... I say, don't crowd, there's not much light." Everyone else took turns peering beneath the solarium door, Vi snapping pictures as they did so. The gap between door and floor was comparatively wide, and it was just about possible to make out a curve of tape pushed into the space, stuck on either side. So far as the other edges were concerned, the doorframe overlapped the door at the top and unhinged side and left no gap to see through, and the space between door and hinges was too narrow to make out anything.

"It's airtight," Alex concluded. "I mean, figuratively, but probably literally too. It's not just one person's word, like my room and the armoury; we can all say that this door is taped up on the other side."

"Even so, we need to get in there," Vi frowned. "We can't say for sure that it's too late."

Alex sighed, looking back at the door. "But there's no other way in…"

"That's where your limited experience is wrong," Yva said, with her increasingly familiar know-it-all tone. "This may be the only entrance *inside* the house, but just because a wall is on the outside doesn't mean it can't have a door in it."

"Right, the balcony," Quinn nodded. Of course! Alex had seen on the photo of the house that it ran the entire length of the top floor. It made total sense for it to open into all three areas of the floor, so conceivably they could get into the solarium from there. But…

"Didn't you say earlier that the window key is also the balcony key?" Alex asked Victoria. "With the key missing, I don't see how we can get out, or back in, short of breaking a whole window."

Cornelia clucked her tongue. "That's an inconvenience," she said. "But needs must. Yva, Quinn, go and dig out some hammers."

"Wait!" Victoria interrupted, just as Yva was moving away. "Wait. That… won't be necessary."

With five pairs of eyes upon her, a complicated expression appeared on Victoria's face. She had no more words, but slowly reached into her pocket and drew out, pinched between two fingers as if it was disgusting to her, a small, flat key.

"*Really?*" whispered Alex, exasperated by this development. "Don't tell me that's the window key – not after we had that big argument about it…"

Cornelia's eyes were glittering with a keen satisfaction. "So your jewellery box being broken *was* all part of the game; I did wonder."

But Victoria shook her head. "You're wrong," she replied. "That *was* real. I didn't expect the key to be stolen, and I don't know who did it." She paused. "Any more than I know who gave it back to me."

Yva rolled her eyes. "Oh, come on."

"It's the truth!" Victoria insisted. "After I had been blindfolded and tied up, while the murderer was still stamping around… I felt them come close, and while I was paralysed with fear, they quickly stuffed something into my pocket." She let her gaze rest on the tiny key in total perplexity. "Why did he give it to me? With everything else, I forgot until I'd left the room…"

"Can anyone verify this?" interrupted Alex.

"I saw her take it out of her pocket," Quinn volunteered. "In the kitchen, right after Malik left."

"So basically, nobody can verify that you didn't just give it to her," Yva said.

An ugly look grasped Quinn's face, but he managed to restrain himself. "Aye, I suppose that's right, yes," he said, controlling himself with evident strain. "If that's what you want to believe, me and her could still be lying to you."

That was a new wrinkle, Alex thought. The idea had come up earlier, but if the murderer had an accomplice, a partner in crime, wouldn't it be easier for them to get away with the murders? …On reflection, though, it only really assisted with the second murder, if they went along with Yva's theory about the gates being triggered with an absurdly long piece of string – and Alex had had enough of Yva's theories. Adding in a second person only made the remaining murders even more difficult to explain. No matter how many people you have on your side, you can't put tape on the wrong side of a door.

"Either way, it's impossible to tell," Alex concluded.

Vi cocked his head at her. "I'm sorry? What's impossible to tell?"

"Never mind," Cornelia said, hushing him; she, at least, seemed to have followed Alex's train of thought. "We have business to attend to, remember? Let's head out onto that balcony."

She made shooing gestures to Victoria Carver, who got the hint and led the way back down the corridor. Passing around the staircase, Victoria started to advance on the balcony doors opposite.

"Ah. An indulgence, if I may," Cornelia called, and the procession stopped. She cast a significant look down the opposite corridor. "At this juncture, it's about time we took a look inside your husband's study, don't you think? We can get to the balcony through there just as well as we can here, so we may as well kill two birds with one stone."

Victoria wavered. "I suppose we could," she said, reluctantly. "Although it might be locked…"

"You told us at breakfast that you'd looked for him in there," Cornelia reminded her. "In fact, you expected to find his supposed 'corpse' in there, too, didn't you? Why would it be locked now?"

Victoria nodded slowly. "Yes; I suppose you're right." She started moving towards the north corridor, noticeably more slowly than before. It was almost as if she was afraid of something.

Not that somebody cared. "Hurry it up," Yva said impatiently, shoving forward in the queue. "Remember, Franny could be being murdered in that solarium right now! We have to save her!"

"Honestly, girl! You're like a child in a sweetshop," Cornelia grumbled, but as Yva jostled past it was clear her words had had the desired effect; Victoria increased her pace, and threw herself at the study door like someone forced to dive into the cold ocean.

Inside the study –

Was nothing in particular. No corpses or tape or any other grisly relics, at least not in plain sight. Adam Carver's study was, in fact, a surprisingly ordinary room, remarkable only for its scale. It was something like a house in miniature, with Carver's desk and chair facing outwards from the side wall, a pair of comfortable armchairs drawn up in front of some bookcases opposite, even a minibar in the corner. Wide windows stretching the length of the far wall let in little light on this miserable day, a fixed skylight alleviating the gloom scarcely more – but in brighter seasons they would have beamed on oversized framed prints of various Carver book covers, from *The Stained Glass Murders* to *Castles in the Sky*, and photographs of himself receiving various literary awards and laughing with other celebrity authors. The study could be said to mix business and pleasure – but not family; Alex didn't see a single picture of anyone besides Carver himself.

"There's nothing here," Victoria said, sighing with what sounded like relief.

"Well, it was worth a look," Cornelia said, but maybe she hadn't really looked yet. There was nothing *on* the desk aside from a simple lamp, but you could hide anything *behind* it, after all. Alex caught her great-aunt's eye, and she promptly hobbled over; the others were approaching the balcony door, but Alex let Cornelia squint at the darkness behind the desk before switching on the lamp. "I say! It really *was* worth a look."

"What is it?" Yva asked eagerly, but Alex wasn't in a hurry to say. Carver's writing chair and the rug beneath it were matted with dark brown stains, standing out harshly under the yellow lamplight. The stains were about where you would expect them to be if a person sitting in the chair had been stabbed in the chest.

"It's blood – old blood," Cornelia said, as the others gathered around. Vi promptly slid himself in Victoria's way, clearly understanding what this meant. "I'm sorry, Victoria," Cornelia sighed, straightening up, "but I'm afraid the pretence is all over. It certainly wasn't Maria or Colin who bled out here, nor even Franny; this has been here for hours."

Victoria went white as a sheet, her own blood draining away as efficiently as it had from the person who had died in that chair. "You're lying," she said, shakily; her voice and hands trembling. "It's not really there. It's not real. O-or it's from another person we don't know about. It's not – !"

"That's right, that's right," Vi said soothingly, drawing her away from the desk, and this time she did not resist. "You can't believe anything you didn't see with your own eyes. Mr. Carver probably faked those stains with paint as part of the game…"

Yva watched them go with a strangely knotted face. "Who does she think she's fooling?" she asked Cornelia and Alex. "Acting like someone in a soap opera. I don't get it."

"She's in denial about the murder of a husband she loves," hissed Alex, low so Victoria would not hear. "Of course she's upset!"

Yva gave Alex a pitying look. "Please. Only fictional characters feel anything that deeply."

Cornelia's cane rapped on the table. "Let's not push the issue for now," she said. "Remember what we came here for." She cleared her throat, drifting away from the desk. "Mrs. Carver, the balcony, if you would? No guest has any business barring themselves in a room in your house, you understand."

Victoria had just settled into one of the armchairs, but jumped at the sound of her name. Vi shot a fierce look at Cornelia, but frankly Victoria looked to be in a state where she would jump at the turn of a page. "Oh yes," she muttered, absently. "The solarium, of course. You know, I'll wager that's where Adam's hiding. Let's –"

She swayed on her feet, and at that moment Quinn suddenly appeared from the direction of the minibar bearing a small glass of brown liquid, which he thrust into her hand. Without hesitation, she downed the whole glass. "*Ugh*," she declared, with feeling, and dropped the glass back into Quinn's hand without looking at him. "Let's get this over with."

Alex felt Cornelia's nudge in her ribs. "It's that old trick of bringing someone around with a swig of brandy!" the old lady whispered excitedly. "Even *I* thought they only did that in books."

"Please don't you lose focus too," Alex muttered, as they congregated around the balcony door. A tall window of glass with a heavy frame, it looked and presumably functioned identically to the balcony door in the lounge area; it bore a long handle with a keyhole in the shaft, and when Victoria inserted the key she made a simple quarter-turn sideways and then turned the handle also a quarter to the side, and the whole door hinged open.

It felt as if the very waves had risen up to fling themselves into Carver's Rest, so harsh was the cold streaming in and shaking the pictures on the walls. The snowy courtyard hours earlier had been cold enough – but here at the back of the house they were fully exposed to the blast of the ocean wind, roaring across the countless miles of churning sea that stretched unmarked by boat or island beneath the grey sky it reflected. It was a bad place to suffer from a fear of heights. But it was also a bad place to be a detective.

"What the –" Quinn started, and Alex knew why. There seemed to be no way a person could have left the solarium by the balcony, either.

The problem of the courtyard had returned with a vengeance. Outside each door and end to end and up to the clean rails of the ornate black railing, the entire surface of the stone balcony was coated in a smooth and unbroken layer of snow.

No snow had fallen since dawn.

"That settles it," Vi spoke up. "Nobody could have come along the balcony without leaving footprints. Whoever taped up the room must still be in there." As if to settle the point, he raised his phone and snapped a picture of the full length of the balcony, snow untouched.

Cornelia glanced sidelong at Alex and Yva with a patronising expression. "One pities them sometimes, doesn't one?" she said.

"What's your point? He's right," Quinn frowned. "The only ways out are the door and the balcony, but the one's taped up from the inside and we can see the other hasn't been trodden."

"The killer could already have slipped out behind our backs, though," Alex suggested. "Just removed the tape from the door and walked right out of it." She paused. "That doesn't seem like the murderer's style, though. They don't leave problems with obvious explanations."

"Why are we wasting time on a problem that doesn't exist?" snapped Victoria. "The men are right. Nobody can have left my solarium without leaving a trace, so let's catch either them or the trace."

She put a hand on the windswept railing and stepped out onto the balcony, flinching as the snow rose to touch her ankle. But she was on a mission, and in a moment was striding ahead with the others following shivering, a single file of traffic destroying the evidence of the untouched balcony as they went.

"The balcony was out of the question anyway," Vi muttered to Alex. "Victoria has had the key since the third murder, and the doors out from the study and lounge were clearly locked."

They were passing the central doorway into the lounge area as he spoke, and Alex saw that he was quite correct; the handle was definitely in the closed position. She gave it an experimental tug as she walked past, but it was firmly locked. Even if the murderer could have hovered above the snow, they had no unlocked doors available to re-enter the house.

"You can't unlock these from the outside, either," Alex observed, speaking with difficulty through chattering teeth; the outside handles didn't even have keyholes. "The murderer would have had to unlock the doors they needed ahead of time."

"That's by design," Victoria's voice filtered through the wind. "If somebody locked the door from the outside and then dropped the key off the balcony, they'd be trapped. So the locks are all on the inside, all three."

"If the one into the solarium is locked, that's the last nail in the coffin," Quinn said, in a curiously prophetic turn of phrase.

Victoria had reached the windows of the solarium, and stopped. Leaned in close to the first window, forming a seal with her hands to blot out reflections.

And recoiled with a scream.

Instantly the five guests surrounded her, but it was too late – they were all too late, far too late. The murderer had indeed come and gone like an evil spirit, leaving behind not a trace of themselves, only of their cruel actions.

Beyond the glass was a room half-filled with sofas and chairs that faced the window and the anticipated light, the other half filled with gym equipment and exercise machines of various descriptions – yoga mats, a treadmill, a robust set of pull-up bars and other such modern torture devices. It was nothing Alex imagined you wouldn't see in a perfectly normal gym not situated in a vanity castle on the edge of the world. Nothing except for the dead.

Slung over the top of the pull-up bars was a narrow length of silvery chain. One end descended straight, in a rigid, taut line, where it terminated shortly in a loop around a neck. A body hung limply down from the neck, wrists behind its back, feet well off the ground, while above the neck was a choked-blue face with eyes bulging behind a pair of dislodged glasses and strands of bloodstained bright hair. While she was only missing there had been hope, but now she was found, and Franny Smythe was dead.

The other end of the chain ran equally taut into the shadows beyond, and found its anchor in the frame of a door which had been made into a wall, wide strips of tape forming a square around its edges and patching door and frame together without a gap. But the chain was not tied to the door handle. It was wrapped around the dead arm of a man.

Victoria Carver had not screamed for Franny. She had screamed for the man with the wild hair and the white suit turned red, mouth and wrists and ankles taped, sitting with his back against the taped door and a gift in colourful paper balanced on his hands.

The corpse of Adam Carver had returned from the unknown, and killed Franny Smythe in a room from which there was no escape.

Chapter Nineteen
Crime of a Revenant

"Well, this is a headscratcher," Yva remarked, as Vi and Quinn led away a distraught Victoria Carver. "So, how did you do it?"

Alex took her eyes off the terrible sight within the windows, and found that Yva was looking at her. "Do what?"

Yva sighed. *"Get out of the room,"* she said, with the emphasis of one who thought it was obvious. "I've already brought the other murders to your door, so you might as well confess to this one. It would be a shame if nobody ever knew how clever you'd been."

"Oh, give it up, Yva!" Alex scowled, turning away in disgust. "Great-Aunt Cornelia? Can you see…" She paused, considering how to word her question. "Anything I can't?"

Cornelia had stalked on farther through the snow, hers the only footprints leading to the door of the tomb. Alex feared that her question had been lost to the wind, or drowned out by the mystery expert's intense mental focus; Cornelia clearly wasn't listening as she cautiously stretched out a hand – let it hover over the handle of the door, as if she feared it might burn her –

The handle rattled in her fingers, and her face seemed to fall for a moment. "Naturally, it couldn't be that easy," Cornelia mumbled.

"Oh, are we going in?" asked Yva, eagerly. "Wait there and don't do anything while I get a paperweight or one of those maces to smash in the window." She turned on her heel and ran off, snow splashing around her boots.

Alex looked back at Cornelia. "Weren't we trying earlier *not* to disturb the crime scenes, like Maria's? This looks like a perfect locked room, so shouldn't we preserve the evidence?"

"Oh, we went past that point long ago," Cornelia said dismissively, peering intently through the balcony door. She shivered and hunched her shoulders up against the cold, looking even more bird-like than usual; as if relishing what she saw.

Though the two corpses in the room made her shudder, Alex tried to conduct an outside investigation, too. If she angled her gaze just right, she could make out the window handles on the inside of the room; if even one of them was just slightly off, it might be a sign that the killer had left through a window, and used some trick to avoid disturbing the snow. But they all appeared to be firmly locked, like the balcony door. And the only other door in the room was, as far as they could see, closed up on every edge with tape, though in any case the murderer could not have used this door without disturbing Carver's corpse.

The room was hermetically sealed. Not even air could escape. It truly was a perfect locked room, with only the corpses of the murdered inside.

Footsteps crunched again through the wet snow, in echo of the ones which had just left. Alex felt a lack of actual surprise to see Yva return empty-handed. "Weren't you going to get something to break the windows?" Alex asked, more or less rhetorically.

"I made Vi do it," Yva said. "Instead, I had my eye on this…"

With an unnecessarily dramatic flourish, she brandished a tiny, silvery key with a small hole for a keyring in its head – this being, of course, the enigmatic window key once again.

"No sense smashing the whole window in," she reasoned. "We'll simply knock a hole right next to the handle, reach in with the key, and unlock it from the inside."

Cornelia frowned at this. "Say, that resembles a standard locked-room solution, doesn't it? If there was an unknown duplicate key on the inside the whole time, the murderer could pretend to be using the key from the outside while actually turning the key that was left inside. Which could previously have been turned to *lock* the door from the outside using good old string."

"I agree," Yva nodded, "which is why *I'm* going to unlock the door, since neither of you can be trusted."

Alex sighed. Surely there had to be a way of checking everyone's actions… "It's a glass door. We can all check that there's no key in the lock *right now*," she pointed out. "And once we break the window we can all put our hands in through the hole, under everyone else's observation, to feel whether the door is properly locked or not, just in case the outside handle has been rigged."

"Truly sensible," nodded Cornelia. "Now you're starting to think like a detective. Only by observing everyone's interactions around a locked room can you prove it."

"Or disprove it," Alex said; surely it would be disproven. Adam Carver certainly wasn't the killer, and she couldn't imagine where Franny Smythe came into it. "If it's not a perfect locked room –"

"Oh, it won't be," Cornelia replied easily. "I'm sure of it. But it won't be so easy to prove, either…"

A figure scuffled out into the snow across the balcony, and began treading his way carefully through the footprints of his predecessors. Apparently Vi had stopped thinking about Victoria Carver and started thinking about his expensive shoes. "This should do," he said, adjusting one sleeve and slipping out from within it one of the slimmer maces. "I didn't want to alarm anyone," he whispered covertly.

"That was thoughtful," Yva said, as she lifted the mace from his hand and swung it with sudden violence at the balcony door. The crash of flinching glass was out of all proportion to the relatively small hole she had punched, and for good measure she tossed the mace in through the hole, crunching onto a pile of glass chunks. "Best leave it there for evidence," she explained.

"Good grief, Yva, some *warning* would have been polite," groaned Cornelia.

Vi nodded forcefully. "Indeed! I'd been planning to record that."

"So now the police will think we just made everything up and we're all the killers?" Alex asked. "Great. Let's just crack the case, rather than cracking any more glass." The pun wasn't as good as it had been in Alex's head, but she was still quite pleased with it. In such a treacherous situation, a little relief was hard to find.

As planned, the four of them took it in turns to watch each other reach through the hole in the glass and jiggle the door handle. It was locked, and then it wasn't, for under very careful watch they let Yva reach back in, insert and turn the key, and turn the door handle, both moving as smoothly as if oiled. The locked room had been broken open. Alex hoped it had been worth it.

She stepped into the room and brought the cold air with her. It was a room designed for warmth, whether from letting in the sunlight through the (bad luck, immovable) skylights or from hard work exercising, which Victoria Carver apparently took surprisingly seriously. But on this grey and dying day, icy winds shuddered through the room – and the links of the chain and the limbs of the hanged woman stirred horribly.

And then there was Adam Carver, ghoulishly stringing Franny aloft. The non-detective parts of Alex would have been quite happy never to have seen his dead face again; but for her companions, unless one of them was somehow the murderer, it was their first sight of him. Only Vi seemed visibly affected; Cornelia was too dispassionate, Yva too ruthless...

"I really hoped it somehow wasn't true," Vi said, in a quiet voice. "So many books, never to be written. With respect, Alex – I really hoped you were wrong."

"Buck up," Cornelia ordered him. "Dead authors are good for business, aren't they? But at the moment, we have work to do."

They did indeed have work to do, and nobody else to do it for them. Alex, spotting an opportunity to turn away from the bodies, went over each and every window handle, trying them all, ensuring they were locked. It seemed pointless against the evidence of the snow, but she was starting to understand these locked-room mysteries now. Give the murderer an inch, and they would take a mile; the slightest gap in the seal around the room could be exploited in any number of ways... But the windows were indeed all locked, and there was nothing unusual about any of them.

She reluctantly looked around. Yva had gone straight for the corpses, of course, and Cornelia also appeared to be investigating something around Adam Carver's body. Not keen, instinctively, to get any closer to the ghastly dead – from an irrational yet overriding fear that at any moment their hands might reach out and grab her – she instead walked over to Vi, who was peering at a heap of pieces on the floor.

"It's Franny's phone," he said, looking up as Alex approached. "Smashed exhaustively to bits; I can't imagine anything is recoverable."

It wasn't an interpretation Alex disagreed with. She could only just tell that the wreckage had been a phone at all. "I wonder why the killer did that," she said; thinking of Vi's own extensive phone use, she added, "Maybe Franny got a picture of the killer? Or even found them here doing something suspicious?"

"Maybe," Vi mused. "I was thinking maybe she found Mr. Carver here; he could have been here the whole time, and nobody would have known."

Alex took a quick survey of the room. The exercise machines could disguise nothing, but a row of mirrors along the walls gave every impression – which she proved, moments later, to be correct – of being floor-to-ceiling cupboards stuffed with yoga mats, spare parts, miscellaneous junk, and the occasional nothing.

"There's definitely space in here to hide a body," she reported, looking at one such empty cupboard, "especially the way Mr. Carver was tied up." For good measure, she cautiously went through all of them to disprove an unknown murderer hiding. One more possibility checked off; there was nowhere in the room an unidentified person could have hidden, and nor could one have escaped from the room after it had been broken open without being noticed by all present. Alex chewed her lip anxiously; the possibilities were being ruled out, one by one...

She turned back to find Vi casting an ugly, bewildered look towards the end of the room where Adam Carver's body lay, at the end of a pointing length of chain. "What were you thinking, Adam Carver?" he murmured to himself. "Just what were you playing at...?" His eyebrows rose as a rattle of chains echoed from Carver's direction. "Hey, and what are *you* playing at, too? Stop that!"

"Were you not there when I said we were past the point of non-interference?" Cornelia's voice called from beside the body, where her slender form was straightening up. "Four people have died, so we should really get stuck in." As she strode across the room towards Alex and Vi, her place beside the corpse being taken by Yva in full police-doctor mode, Alex saw that she was grasping a familiar rectangular object in colourful paper and ribbon, which she was carefully untying.

"I'm pleased to see that the killer used a reasonable amount of ribbon on this one. The last two were frankly wasteful, even in the circumstances," Cornelia said, gesturing at the gaudy loops as she pulled them free. Alex got the feeling that the old lady was making a strange kind of joke, but there really was merely an ordinary and fairly conservative quantity of ribbon holding the edges of paper together. Cornelia at last untangled the knot and drew the paper away with a flourish, and as anyone might have predicted she unveiled a copy of *Conspiracies of the Obscure Tribunal*, the *Castles in the Sky* finale, like a rabbit from a top hat.

"Same edit to the title page as usual?" Alex asked, more to remain in the conversation than anything else, as Cornelia was surely about to tell her anyway.

Cornelia flipped the book open to its beginning. "As it happens," she began, and then her eyebrows knotted curiously. "No." She showed them the open book. It had a perfectly ordinary and unmodified title page, with Adam Carver's credit unobliterated. "Maybe the murderer was in a hurry," she said.

"Or maybe it means something," Alex mused. She looked around the room at the strange and deranged scene around them – the bodies of Adam Carver and Franny Smythe, abandoned without ceremony. "Maybe something's different about this murder…"

"We do have two bodies this time," Vi pointed out. "Although – if we'd been slower, maybe there'd have been two last time, too…" His gaze turned across the room, to a point Alex was trying not to see. "Speaking of which, I'd better go and make sure she stays respectful."

He stormed over in the direction of Yva, who was contorting various parts of Carver's corpse dispassionately. Alex turned away with a shudder.

"Did you find anything useful – over there?" she asked, omitting to mention the dead man. "Any good news, for a change?"

"Other than this?" Cornelia asked, hefting the book and finally passing it to Alex, who obediently opened her backpack. It was getting quite heavy, and nobody was thanking her for carrying it – but as usual, the moment to say anything was already gone. "Carver's body fits your description," she continued. "That's useful, though it's neither good news nor bad news. The definite bad news is that the tape seal around the door is complete, without a break. As it is now, you can't get anything even through the cracks between door and frame." Her mood seemed to darken further as she spoke; Alex's likewise. "The murderer really knew what they were doing."

"How are we even supposed to start on that?" Alex complained. "A room *confirmed*, absolutely, to have no way out even for air, let alone a person – I thought just a locked door was hard enough."

"Indeed, more than hard enough for countless authors before now, who died not knowing it *could* be worse," Cornelia said, with a sigh. "You know, I kept it to myself before, but in most cases, taping every border of the door shut would be excessive. Your room, for instance, or the armoury... Even a single tiny strip of tape between door and wall is something which would be impossible to attach from the other side. Going over the whole door was just showmanship." She turned her gaze back – no, it was more that it was *drawn* back, as if by a magnetic force – to the taped door. "In this case, though, it's different," she muttered, her meaning obscure to Alex. "If there was only the slightest gap... a mere sliver..."

"So you could put some string through, or something like that?" Alex asked. Thinking about it, it was true that you might be able to pull off some clever trick if you could just manipulate the room from the wrong side of sealed doors, though she wasn't sure what. "Turning a key from the other side?" Her great-aunt had mooted this earlier, but the key had not been in this room.

"Just so," Cornelia nodded, "though it's not quite as easy as it sounds. In the books, they need a certain amount of clutter just to get the angles right." She looked over at the closed balcony door, through the hole in which an eerie wind whistled softly. "I wonder," she muttered. "It's a long shot, but..."

She bustled over to the door, and Alex followed her, curious. She was turning something in her hands, and for a moment Alex thought she had slashed open both palms – but it was only the crimson ribbon she had taken from the fourth birthday present.

Cornelia opened the door, and slung a length of ribbon across the threshold, so that it was both inside and outside the room. Then she shut the door again, and locked it for good measure.

"We can close the door on it, at least; that's a good start," she said, her voice suppressing hope. "Alex, could you pull on that ribbon, please? See if you can drag it through?"

Alex picked up the end of the ribbon, and pulled gently. The ribbon ran tight from where it was trapped between door and doorframe, and didn't budge. She pulled harder, but still – it would not move...

"Hard as you can," Cornelia instructed, and Alex put her whole weight on the ribbon. But it was no use. The seal on the door was too perfect.

"Damnation," Cornelia muttered, as Alex sat back gasping. "Too good to be true. It's completely airtight; there's the murderer's excuse for only taping the one door shut, of course. You couldn't get anything through that join. And the windows will be just the same…"

Disheartened, Cornelia reopened the door and began to reel in the tape, and Alex's own heart sank yet again. She hadn't even understood the gimmick, and yet still it would not work. But if you *could* get string into this room, what would you manipulate? What could you do that could create a seal inside from the outside?

"I see how it could have been done," Cornelia muttered. "Just one tiny gap – and I can see how…"

"I don't even see that," Alex sighed.

"The how is trivial. You two should be clever enough to understand that."

That wasn't Cornelia; Vi was striding back. He had the attitude of someone who regarded himself as taking charge, his back straight and his voice haughty. Even his head appeared to be tipping slightly backwards with the straightness of his spine, as if he might tumble over, so that he was looking down his nose at Alex – or perhaps trying to look at Cornelia eye-to-eye.

"Oh, you've figured out the howdunnit, have you?" Cornelia asked, with unrestrained cynicism. "Go on, then, tell us. What has a mystery expert missed that a layman can see?"

"The simple truth that's right in front of your eyes," came his riposte. "Mystery experts try to make a mystery out of the simplest things, but the only meaning of the tape on that door is a confession. A confession that the culprit is still in this room!"

Alex blinked at him. "But I already searched the room. There's nobody here – except Franny and Mr. Carver." Oh, right. "You think it's one of them," she realised.

He nodded firmly; also, somewhat patronisingly. "This is a perfect locked room," he insisted. "Nobody could have gotten out of it. Therefore, there are only two suspects – Franny, and Carver." He gestured to the balcony door. "That door can only be locked on the inside, and the balcony snow is untouched, so that's a double assurance that nobody went that way. At the same time –" He gestured to the taped-up door. "That door has been taped up from the inside. Furthermore, the hinges are also on our side, which means the door opens towards us. Even if the door hadn't been taped shut, how could the murderer have pulled the door closed behind them whilst leaving Carver's body with his back flat against it?"

"There are several ways –" Cornelia began, but Vi cut her off, as if he really knew better than she did.

"It's a double-lock," he concluded. "Both ways out of the room are double-locked. It's a quadruple-locked room. Nobody could have left – and that means that it can only have been Carver or Franny who locked it, and then killed themselves. There's no other way."

Cornelia glared at him and the double-locked doors in equal measure. "There nearly is another way," she said, very quietly. "So very nearly. If there was only the tiniest gap…"

"Well, there isn't," Vi concluded, and turned his back on them. "Yva," he called, striding over to her. "One of these two committed suicide. Which was it?"

"What? Oh, sure. I'll give you my report," Yva called back, standing up from Carver's body and brushing her hands. With a start, Alex noticed that they were shaking. "This is so much fun… Maybe I should become a forensic scientist as well as a famous author."

"Spare us, please," sighed Vi. "Just give us the facts."

Yva licked her lips. "The bare bones?" There was a strain in her voice that Alex couldn't identify – not with certainty; but it was either fear, or an immense degree of suppressed excitement. "Okay," Yva continued, in an almost sing-song voice, "but I can't guarantee that you'll like it…

"Let's start with Franny," she said, walking over to the hanging corpse. Alex forced herself, now, to take a good look, where before she had only glanced, and saw again the persistent tape that had sealed the reviewer's mouth and tied her at the wrists and ankles. "She's been dead a little while now, so saving her would've been impossible, if you're still worried about that. The noose is tethered to Mr. Carver's body over there, which is clearly a lot heavier than hers and so is holding her up. I guess you'd say that if she was murdered she was probably hoisted up and strangled, but if she committed suicide, she'd have tied the noose around her throat, climbed up to the top bar, and thrown herself off."

Vi nodded. "A reasonable conclusion," he said.

Alex raised her eyebrows in incredulity. "Reasonable?" she asked. "How did she climb up there with her wrists tied behind her back and her ankles stuck together?"

Vi inhaled deeply. "She could have climbed to the top first and then taped them up herself. But people are more flexible than you'd think, and there's a way of bringing tied wrists under your feet so they can be at the front or back of your body, so she needn't have had them behind her back until she was ready to jump. And I'm sure you can hop and clamber about a bit even with your wrists and ankles tied." He imitated, ludicrously, what this would look like, and quickly stopped as it was far beneath his and everyone else's dignity.

"There's only a short length of chain between the top bar and her neck," Cornelia pointed out. "She wouldn't have had much room to manoeuvre up there."

"So it would have looked awkward. That doesn't disprove anything," Vi argued, in uncomfortable echo of an earlier Yva theory.

"Isn't there a way of telling if someone was strangled or hanged?" Alex asked Yva, remembering having read this somewhere.

"Yeah – but just to be clear, she wouldn't have been strangled the way you mean, like by hand. It takes ten or even twenty minutes to be sure, you know?" Yva casually explained. "If it was a case of long-drop hanging versus just hoisting her up, it'd be easy as her neck *would* be broken. But if she dropped, it was a short drop, and I haven't studied enough to tell the difference between that and just hoisting her up. Either way, she chokes to death – and just as you'd expect, I can't find a broken neck in there."

Vi nodded in satisfaction. "Then there's every possibility she was the culprit," he concluded. "I didn't want to say, but I thought that might be the case. If she was last seen alone with Colin in the armoury, it makes total sense for her to have killed him and captured Victoria when she returned. Then she sealed off the armoury, escaped somehow, and having finished whatever mad campaign of violence she was intent on, sealed herself in here and ended her life."

"So your explanation for the howdunnit of this room requires that you *don't* have an explanation for the howdunnit of the armoury," Cornelia said, analysing his ideas in an instant and giving them short shrift.

Vi flushed angrily. "One explanation is better than none. Franny is the murderer!"

"Nope," said Yva.

Vi practically spun to stare at her. *"Nope?* What do you mean, nope?"

Faced with three pairs of eyes, Yva let out an abrupt giggle, as if she had just heard a hilarious joke. "It was just too much fun to watch you bicker," she sniggered. "Sorry, but I already knew that Franny wasn't the killer."

Vi's jaw dropped, along with the last of Alex's hope. "She isn't?" he stuttered. "But – explain yourself immediately!"

Yva rolled her eyes at him before continuing with a smirk. "We all know the killer's modus operandi by now, right? They get their victims alone, bash them over the head to stun, and then tie them up with tape before killing them." They all nodded in agreement. "So if you're arguing that Franny is the murderer, you're saying that she just gave herself a light tap over the head to give the right impression, and then got on with setting things up after she'd recovered."

"Absolutely," Vi nodded. "It's the only way."

"Except there's simply no way!" Yva exclaimed, clearly relishing his bewildered expression. "Because, you see, *this* time, the murderer struck Franny just a little too hard…"

Alex gasped. "You don't mean –"

"Oh, but I do mean!" she replied excitedly. "Check her yourself if you don't believe me! The murderer practically caved in the back of her skull! Irreparable brain damage! Even if technically alive, Franny had effectively been killed before she got hoisted off the ground!"

"B-but then – that means –" Vi spluttered, and his eyes flew across the room. "It really *was* Mr. Carver –"

Alex groaned out loud. It was far, far too late for that. The truth which she had known for twelve hours was about to be horribly confirmed...

"Guess again!" Yva rebuked him. "Pallor mortis, algor mortis, rigor mortis, livor mortis! This man has been dead since last night!"

The silence of the grave fell upon the room; churchyard silence where the cold wind may blow but no living voice speaks.

The only available killers – were dead.

"It's an insoluble problem," Yva murmured, and her eyes were alive with fire as they locked with Alex's own. "A perfectly, beautifully insoluble problem..."

Chapter Twenty
Hidden in Plain Sight

The murders were over. With four books and four bodies accounted for, and the remaining suspects with no inclination whatsoever to split up, that much was plain. But that was by no means the end of the investigation, of course. Even as the murders had ended, for those of the survivors who had only just started taking things seriously it was the investigation's beginning.

At the urgings of Quinn Shillerdyce and a grief-stricken Victoria Carver, and possibly also at the urgings of the potent Carver minibar, the six remaining instituted an exhaustive search of the mansion for a possible intruder, a hypothetical extra person who had struck down four people and squirreled themselves away. With the search party arranged as an impromptu panopticon in which every member was being constantly watched by another while a chain of witnesses observed the corridors and stairways, they went from floor to floor and room to room, scouring every cupboard and crevice for the slightest hint of an unknown guest who could have committed the murders – somehow.

But there was no extra person. The killer could not even have thrown themselves into the sea, with the windows all locked from the inside and no tracks in the snowy courtyard leading over the edge. The murderer was not a stranger, some eleventh unknown who had crept in from outside of Carver's Rest, killed to their heart's content, and slithered away again in outrageous defiance of locks and bolts and walls and tape – not unless they truly were a ghost of gleefully selective solidity. The murderer was hidden in human form and in plain sight among the known occupants of the mansion, and there was not even the hope of denying that fact.

Midday was approaching. The outside world was still ruled by shades of brutal grey, like prison walls no less concrete for being built of air and water, supplemented by actual walls no less effective. The party, no joyous assembly, had reconvened to slump in despair around Adam Carver's study, fresh from a detailed examination of the bodies conducted by Cornelia Crow, who had by popular request agreed to verify Yva Dysart's conclusions – not least by Yva herself, to whom accusations of waywardness were nothing more than another delicious opportunity to prove people wrong. The amateur pathologists' verdicts agreed in every particular. Adam Carver had died the previous night. Maria Bole had died sometime over breakfast. Colin West had died a little while before being discovered, and Franny Smythe had died around the same time. The causes of death were exactly what they appeared to be. There were no faked or staged deaths. Everything was real.

It was little comfort that midday brought the hope of signalling to the outside world, by the medium of their taxi rides coming to ask for them. The intercom and front gate control had been confirmed still to work, despite earlier anxieties of sabotage, and so all they had to do was wait; all they *could* do was wait. Victoria Carver curled in an armchair, her head tucked deep between her arms, turning in on herself like a turtle. Quinn Shillerdyce was staring moodily out of the windows whilst tossing back glasses of whatever alcohol he could find at more frequent intervals than his cool demeanour would dictate. Vi was hunched over his tablet, writing out his testimony and backing up his crime scene photographs and furiously crunching out plans and back-up plans and supplementary back-up plans for how the *Castles in the Sky* fandom could best weather this storm. Yva Dysart looked blissfully at ease, reclining in a chair and gazing into the middle distance, having told anyone who would listen that she felt privileged to have witnessed the footprints of a genius who could create such locked-room mysteries as even she could not solve. As for the one woman who truly *could* explain the impossible, she had occupied the desk of Adam Carver himself, where she was poring furiously over the mysterious birthday presents the killer had left behind.

And Alex? She was trying to think. To sort through everything she had seen, and use it to make the impossible possible.

Adam Carver, lying dead in her bedroom with the only exit sealed up from the inside, and yet minutes later both body and seal had vanished. How had it been done?

Maria Bole, impaled by the motion of a drawbridge while everyone who could have triggered it was locked in the house, with the only exit sealed up from the inside, and unbroken snow between the suspects and the crime scene. How had it been done?

Colin West, stabbed to death in an iron maiden in a room with the only exit sealed up from the inside, and the only other person in the room bound and gagged. How had it been done?

Franny Smythe, clubbed and hanged in a room with its exits sealed up or locked from the inside and barred with unbroken snow. How had it been done?

Or rather –

How could these have been done, and then made to *look* impossible?

That was the real question, and Alex turned it over and over, considering and discarding one theory after another. Take Maria's murder, for example; what if somebody had snuck outside, pulled the lever that sent her to her death, and snuck back in, taping the door shut behind them? That was a perfectly reasonable version of events. All you had to do was explain how they did it without touching the snow.

Well, what if they *had* used string, she reasoned? While it was still snowing, they had set up a length of string leading from the drawbridge lever to the front door. In the morning, when the snow had stopped, they pulled that string, reeled it in, and taped the door shut behind them. Again, that was perfectly feasible. All you had to do was explain how Quinn Shillerdyce had seen the door taped shut before going to breakfast, but Alex herself had seen the drawbridge still down some time later. Removing the tape and replacing it exactly over the old marks wasn't a realistic option. And Quinn had sounded very confident in his description of the airtight quality of the seal, so claiming that he had been simply mistaken was not enough...

But you didn't have to take people's word for it. Alex realised that, of course. It's a whodunnit; someone was a murderer, and that person was a liar – so check what happens if you assume someone was lying. Say that Quinn had lied about seeing the door taped shut before breakfast. However, he could not have left the breakfast table, triggered the drawbridge, and taped the door shut behind him in the time between Alex looking out of the window and her arriving at the bottom of the stairs; even if he had, somebody would have doubtless remarked on it, since it solved the problem. That would require Quinn to be an accomplice to one of the two people who either did leave the table or had never been there – Victoria Carver, or Cornelia Crow, who could have pulled the string and then taped the door shut themselves.

That theory… was technically possible, Alex admitted. So long as you proposed that idea, the impossible murder of Maria Bole was not impossible. At that point, you could then take your theory and try to apply it to the other murders – to create a unified theory to explain all of the deaths. The crimes were committed by either Victoria Carver or Cornelia Crow, most likely in alliance with Quinn Shillerdyce. How did that work?

Victoria Carver being the killer would trivialise Colin's murder in the armoury, of course. She had killed Colin and secured the iron maiden, taped the armoury door shut, faked an attack on herself, left behind several long strips of tape with which to tie herself up, and then thrown the roll of tape and the mace out of the window; had then simply locked the window with the window key (which she herself had taken) and put it in her pocket, after which she used the loose tape to tie herself up. All well and good. Two of the murders could be explained, in the loosest sense, with Victoria Carver as the killer.

Unfortunately, however, that was as far as it went. Victoria Carver as the culprit could not explain the howdunnit of the first and fourth murders – Adam Carver's and Franny Smythe's. Adam Carver's murder remained a perfect one, with only one way out of the room inarguably sealed from the inside and with absolutely no hiding-place between those four walls which Alex could not have detected; indeed, the layout of the room almost seemed arranged specifically to *prove* that nobody was hiding there. And then there was the matter of how Carver's corpse and the tape around the door had been whisked away. It was clear that the murderer could work at lightning speed. Could Victoria and Quinn have been hiding in the room across the corridor, and leapt out to clean up while Alex's back was turned? At a stretch, perhaps. But they could not have gotten out of the room in the first place, and nor could they have hidden inside. The same applied to Franny's murder; the seal on the room was perfect and everyone was accounted for at the time it was broken. No whodunnit theory could on its own merits explain the howdunnit of these two rooms…

But things got even worse once you arrived at the *why*dunnit, and that was where Alex was really stuck. She could accept a least likely *who* and an improbable *how*, but never an implausible *why*. What motive could Victoria Carver possibly have had for the four murders? And four murders had definitely been planned from the start, Alex was sure of that; the calling card of the signed books proved it. You couldn't argue, for instance, that Maria had witnessed something incriminating about Carver's murder, and then Colin about hers, and then Franny about his; nor could you claim that the murders had been committed by separate individuals for separate reasons. The murderer was a single individual involved in all the murders, and had anticipated from the very first that they would be killing four people. So where did that leave the Victoria Carver theory? You could invent any motive you liked for why she had killed her husband; say she had lied about loving him and killed him out of hatred or jealousy for an affair, or that she lied about being independently wealthy and killed him for the money. Where did everyone else come in? Nobody was going to commit murder simply as a bluff; it was ludicrous. If Victoria just wanted to kill Adam Carver and, to dig up that old slander, Maria Bole for having an affair, she could have simply arranged to be alone in the house with the two of them, knocked them on the head, and thrown them off the balcony. She could then tell the police they had gone out for a walk and never came back, and if their bodies were ever washed up, it would be impossible to tell that they hadn't just fallen off the cliffs. Why was it necessary to throw a grand party and kill two extra people? The whole thing made no sense.

Yva had dismissed the very idea of motive earlier. But as Alex pored over the possibilities for the truth behind the murders, she became increasingly certain that the murderer's motive was the key to the entire mystery.

A crackling sound across the room broke Alex out of her reverie. Cornelia had apparently finished with the presents, and was piling them into the backpack. Noticing Alex watching, her great-aunt said, "It's nearly twelve. Goodness knows if the roads are usable, but if anyone comes for us, I intend to be at the intercom for them."

"I'll go with you," Alex said, getting up. What she really wanted, though, was just to talk to Cornelia about the murders; to talk to someone rational and hash everything out. In this room full of suspects, she doubted there were any sensible conversations to be had.

Cornelia nodded, as if this was just what she had been expecting. "Very well," she said, before directing her next remarks to the room: "As for the rest of you, I'm sure you understand the importance of remaining under mutual observation…"

"Go ahead and do the busy-work," Yva yawned, while Vi nodded in agreement. Victoria and Quinn gave no sign of having heard, or of caring. Alex shouldered her backpack and she and Cornelia walked out of the room, the latter shutting the door as she left.

"Well," Cornelia grinned, as they stepped out of earshot, "everyone is now trying very hard not to accuse one another, aren't they?"

Alex nodded slowly as they walked. "I think it's because the possibilities ran out," she said. "We know the murderer has to be one of us – one of *them* – and the first three murders all have holes in them that let you imagine a possible solution… But the fourth murder was a perfect locked-room murder. We all guaranteed it."

"All we guaranteed was that the room was sealed in exactly the fashion it appeared to be," countered Cornelia, as they reached the bottom of one flight of stairs and turned around the landing to reach the other. "All that means is that there's no easy way out of it. The murderer came up with a method which allowed them to either get past those seals, or create them from outside the room. The detective just has to put the hard work in to replicate that method."

Easier said than done, Alex thought. "What about the other murders?" she asked. "Do you think the murderer used the same gimmick to get through all the doors?"

"Oh, goodness me, no," Cornelia replied, with a slight chuckle. "The other three taped rooms are superficially identical, but each required a completely unique approach."

The old lady continued to chuckle to herself, oblivious to Alex staring in shock. Cornelia's statement had been made with complete certainty – such certainty that she was almost *casual* about it, without even a hint of doubt or ambiguity. How could she be so certain? Why was she so certain – when there were only two ways a person could know the truth behind the impossible murders at Carver's Rest?

They reached the bottom of the second staircase. A long straight walk ahead of them was the door to the lobby, standing wide open; and beyond, the front door of Carver's Rest, tangled remnants of the tape that marked it still scattered about. Alex took a deep breath, trying to calm her mind before she spoke.

"Great-Aunt Cornelia," she said, slowly and firmly. "What makes you so certain about the way the murderer escaped from the taped rooms?"

Cornelia Crow looked down at Alex, her expression arch, her eyes unreadable. What she saw when she looked at Alex was unknowable. What she was thinking was unknowable. But there were only two answers to Alex's question.

Cornelia Crow was the killer.

Or...

"Why, Alex, dear, it's quite simple," she said, with a narrow smile. "I solved the mystery hours ago."

An alien sound made them both jump. Across the empty halls, the intercom was buzzing...! Alex hated to leave the conversation there, but she also wanted to leave this house one day, so she dashed into the lobby at once. A light flashed on the small panel installed next to the door. Darn darn darn, how do you work this thing? It was probably only a few seconds, but it felt as if it took her too long to work out which button opened a connection to the outside world.

"Hello? Is anyone there?" she asked the crackling void.

A crackly voice came back almost immediately. "Yeah, I'm here for an Alex Corby. Tell her I'm freezing my nose off out here, putting it politely, so if she could hurry up..."

Of all the taxi drivers in all the world, it just happened to be hers who was first back. "It's me; I'm Alex," she spoke urgently into the intercom. "Please – you have to get back in your car, and go and get the police. Something terrible has happened – there have been murders, and we're trapped in the house!"

"What? Oh, yeah, I'll bet," buzzed her interlocutor. "Look, girly, I don't have time for kids' games here. It's bad enough I was stranded at some godforsaken hole of a village while you took tea with Count Moneyrich, and you better thank your lucky stars I had plenty of time to get the car through the snow and here. And you're telling me to just turn around? I will at this rate!"

"It's not a joke!" Alex tried to impress upon him through his ranting. "Please listen! We can't get out of here, so you have to fetch the police…"

"Now look here!" burst in Cornelia Crow, leaning over Alex's shoulder and putting her mouth very near to the intercom. "I don't have time for games either, so hush up and listen! Four people have died in this house overnight and we've been stranded in the building for hours. This is an urgent criminal situation and if the police later found out that some fool held back the investigation because he went off in a huff, there might well be charges levelled! Now, instead of trying to guilt-trip a traumatised young lady, how about you do something useful and drive back to town, which you're going to do anyway because we have no way of getting out, and take one minute to put in a call to the police while you're there? Or is just that too much to ask?"

She scowled ferociously at the intercom, as if her bile could seep through to the other side. For a long moment there was only the crackling of the connection to fill the air.

"Will do," the voice replied. "But I'm calling the papers right afterwards."

There was the sound of a slamming door, and the groaning of an engine, and then there was only rustling silence again. Alex cut the connection.

"Now in a *really* good mystery," her great-aunt said, "*he* would be the killer."

Caught off-guard, Alex laughed. For just for a second, it was once again as if none of it was real, and the bodies in the bizarre locked rooms around the mansion were nothing but an author's whim. Alex hoped that nobody upstairs had heard that laugh. They might have gotten the wrong impression.

And besides, there was something more important on the cards than a mere joke.

"But seriously – have you really solved the murders?" Alex asked her great-aunt. "Do you know who the murderer is?"

"Oh, I pegged the murderer two deaths in," Cornelia shrugged. "At first I wasn't certain, and certainly had no proof, so I contrived to gather more information – and of course you know how that worked out. I tried to limit the danger by grouping people together, but everyone except you managed to sabotage my efforts, so really they just got what they deserved." She shook her head with too-shallow ruefulness. "But yes," she continued, "after investigating each scene I had a pretty good idea of how the murders were done."

Alex stared at her. And yet Cornelia deferred resuming her monologue. "*Well?!*" burst out Alex at last. "How were they done?"

Cornelia tilted her head slightly, staring at her great-niece. "But of course I can't just *tell* you. It would be dishonourable to give away the solution to a mystery, remember?" she explained, infuriatingly. "It's an old canard the detective always uses to avoid giving the game away early – but you have to be able to work it out for yourself. If you can't reproduce my conclusions, how will you know if they are reasonable? How will I?"

As Cornelia issued this so-reasonable explanation, Alex felt like a person whose detective novel has been snatched away a few chapters from the end. "Can you at least give me a clue?" she fumed.

"But you've had all the clues," Cornelia replied, almost surprised. "They were all there, right in front of you. You just have to be creative in how you approach them. Of course, the *real* mystery of the body in the bedroom was always how it was removed so quickly, and once you work that out then the murderer's escape route becomes quite obvious. As for the murder at the gates, the clue of the singed ribbon simply gives it away. The corpse in the armoury is unspeakably trivial once you ask why the murderer took a certain action, from which everything else follows naturally. And the sealed solarium was, as I should have seen at once, all about just how much you can manipulate if you only have a small gap in the seal, including – ah, but I'm getting ahead of myself."

"I'm getting nowhere," Alex admitted, despite an extra helping of hints. "Maybe it's obvious to you, but you've read more locked-room mysteries than I ever will. I don't know if I have the experience to see what you see."

Cornelia's face fell, and for the first time she looked actually saddened. Her eyes collapsed into their shrunken sockets, like empty windows on unseen depths. "Once there were locked rooms enough to fill a city," she murmured, her voice the wind in empty streets. "A metropolis, policed by brilliant detectives who specialised in such problems. Whose fault is it that those rooms have all been boarded up and forgotten, the detectives buried with their authors, and their tools rusted almost into nothing?" She sighed, and Alex sensed her disappointment; the disappointment of a reader whose favourite genre had all but disappeared. But she seemed to pull herself together. "Still, there's more to a mystery than just the howdunnit," she considered, brightening a little. "And in fairness, there were a few extra clues you didn't have – ones which only I had. Although I only discovered them after the murders were over, so I don't really like to count them." Her voice fell to a mumble. "But you know, maybe they count towards the one thing I'm still not certain about…"

"What are you talking about?" asked Alex, uneasily. They had not separated once since the murders had concluded; not even since the discovery of the second murder. How could Cornelia Crow have gathered some extra clues exclusive to herself?

Cornelia Crow snapped her fingers, as if coming to a decision. "Come with me, and I'll show you," she said, beckoning Alex down the corridor. "You're a sensible girl, and what's more, you're a good one. I think it's fair to play favourites just with you, before letting the others in on this catch. And speaking of fairness, I suppose there's Knox's 8th to consider…"

Ever more befuddled, Alex allowed herself to be led to a room at a remote corner of the ground floor – a sort of reading room, all armchairs and sofas and lamplit tables set in cosy nooks. The room made the best of the equivocal winter half-light, with great windows on two walls providing what an estate agent would for once without exaggeration call stunning views of the coast, black cliffs made white with foam and crumbling away into the distance. Cornelia settled herself at one end of a sofa with a wide and low table, and gestured for Alex to join her.

"Did I ever tell you that I came to Carver's Rest to solve a mystery?" she said, lifting the discarded backpack to the table. "The mystery of why the fourth and final volume of *Castles in the Sky*, *Conspiracies of the Obscure Tribunal*, was so lacklustre. I formulated a theory about that, of course, as I formulate theories about everything, and I wondered if the reason it was so bad is because *The Fourth Wall Crumbles* was so good. Myself, Yva, and

Colin – our masterpiece…" Thump, thump, thump – one by one she drew the murderer's autographed Carver books out of the backpack, and laid them out on the table in order. "Without having to bother with the extended publishing process, I wondered if we might have beaten Adam Carver to the punch with a fanfiction which anticipated the intended finale *too* correctly – that all the ideas, plot twists, and solutions we had projected were indeed correct and the very ones he had planned." She straightened each book in its own space so it could be opened without touching the next, and continued. "The result to Carver being that, to avoid accusations of plagiarising his own fans, he had to completely rewrite his own finale to differ from the intended one in every respect. Hence the long wait; hence the wildly off-beat ending." She laughed lightly to herself, suddenly, unexpectedly. "It all seems so silly now," she chuckled. "I never even got a word in. Although, you know, I have an idea that the mystery I'm solving right now might in fact be the same one."

"…Again, I'm not really sure what you're talking about," Alex said, looking between the books on the table and Cornelia Crow. Her great-aunt's easy manner was increasingly unsettling in this house of danger.

"You will if you read this," Cornelia said, tapping the cover of *Death in the Walls*, "and read it properly. We were so busy with the murders that we didn't take the time to read carefully enough. We looked at the beginning of the books, but the murderer must have been disappointed when we didn't notice what was at the *end*…"

Alex's eyes went very, very wide, and her shaking hands were already fluttering the pages of the first volume. "What is it? What's at the end?"

"The same thing that's at the end of many books," calmly said Cornelia Crow. "An author's note."

And on the very last page, opposite the concluding statement "END OF VOLUME ONE," there were more words, handwritten in a free and curving script.

"'Introduction, by the Author,'" Alex read, eyes taped to the page. "'Please excuse the late appearance of my introduction. Ordinarily, I would have placed it at the beginning of the book; but I was obliged to break with convention on this occasion. I hope you will understand…'" Her voice trailed off as her eyes skittered down the page – then back up it, and down again, for she could not quite believe and not quite take in exactly what she was reading. At last, her eyes turned upwards from the page, and met the gleaming sockets of Cornelia Crow. *"Really?"*

"Really," Cornelia replied, with characteristic understatement. She gestured towards the table. "There are more," she said, tapping the covers of the remaining volumes in turn. "The murderer's been leaving little clues for us all along, nicely gift-wrapped like the unasked-for presents they are. Make sure you read them all."

As if she could resist. Having read to the end of the bizarre introduction and invitation by the self-styled Author, Alex was already flipping to the back of *Hand at the Threshold* to find the next note. "Rules for the Author"… This was a more surreal experience. Alex could see the relevance of a few of the rules, but she didn't understand how the murderer hoped to avoid being caught by accident or luck, for instance. "These are those Knox rules you were talking about earlier," Alex remembered, frowning at them. "But you also mentioned a – Van Dine, I think? Who were they?"

"Mystery novelists," Cornelia replied, briefly. "Dead now, of course."

Of course. "Now I see these written down," Alex went on, frowning at the page, "I think I remember reading about them, in a Robin Stevens book." It was a breath of fresh air in that charnel house to name an author who was actually alive. "She didn't think much of some of the rules, but whoever wrote this says they changed them."

Cornelia mused on this one. "They aren't the only set of rules for detective fiction. But they're certainly the better-known." She looked as if something was bothering her, though. "I wonder if there was a reason why the murderer didn't use Van Dine's Twenty Rules instead. If perhaps they *couldn't*…"

Alex didn't linger. She skipped straight to the end of *A Coffin Nail Creaks*, a book she had reread often enough to know almost by heart, and there were the "Methods of the Author". Alex made a face at the page; these were even more obscure and academic than the Rules. And yet they weren't unhelpful; knowing that the murderer had limited themselves was another great clue. But why were they there? Why was the murderer helping them?

"Why is the murderer giving themselves away?" Alex asked, staring at the swirling signature of the killer of four people. "Are they mocking us?"

Cornelia Crow looked away, and declined to give a straight answer; but at length she said, "I think this may explain it." She was gazing at the final book – the unsigned book, *Conspiracies of the Obscure Tribunal*. "It's the Author's final word on the matter."

Their final word… Gingerly, as if turning the pages of a museum piece or the jaws of a mantrap, Alex began to leaf towards the end of the end. Page after unsatisfying and illogical page gave way as the climax drew in – and beyond it, she sensed something momentous awaiting her, a more wild and daring twist than any attempted in that book the Author disowned; something like an ending, or rather, a point of no return. "The Author's final word," Cornelia's voice repeated in the ear of her mind, as the page fell open and Alex saw what was written there.

The Author's challenge.

CHALLENGE
from the Author

Dear Reader,

My congratulations on making it this far. If you are reading this, then my work is finished. In case you were in any doubt, let me be, at the last, explicit: I am the criminal, the one you are searching for. I am the murderer. Assuming that all has gone according to my plan, I present to you four impossible murders, for your delectation.

But of course, nothing that truly happened can really be impossible. Surely you have attempted to devise a solution to the problem I pose? Well, dear Reader, now is the time. The story is over, the clues have all been presented, and further assistance, though possible, is unnecessary. To those observant enough, to those creative enough, to those ingenious enough: This is the point at which the mystery can be solved.

In the spirit of the game, and to eliminate answers which defy that spirit, I give to you four confessions. Thus, the case against me is complete.

1. I am one person, and my name is known to you. I am not part of an alliance or conspiracy, I used no accomplices, I confided in nobody what I intended to do.
2. The victims are truly dead. None of the deaths were faked, and nor were the bodies manipulated to disguise their time of death.
3. The victims were not chosen at random. I killed only those I had motive to kill, and never simply an inconvenient witness.
4. All four rooms were hermetically sealed. The seals on each were perfect and not even air could escape; nonetheless, I did.

No more needs to be said. As the Author, I hereby issue you a formal challenge: Solve the mystery. How did I do it? Why did I do it? And who am I?

Until we meet again.

The Author

Chapter Twenty-One
Final Hints

Alex looked up from the page. Breathed out, long and slow. "Wow," she concluded.

Cornelia nodded, with something almost approaching good-naturedness. "Quite," she at last agreed. "The murderer must have been rather frustrated that we didn't find these before. Reading them all along would have done wonders for the atmosphere."

Alex tried yet again to overlook Cornelia's blasé response to the violent murders of four people. "Is that really why the murderer wrote all these notes, though?" she asked. "Just for the atmosphere? To intimidate us?" She looked down at the finished book. "Or do you think this is sincere – I mean, that he, or she, really *wants* to be caught?"

"I'd say it's almost certain that they want to be caught," Cornelia nodded. "Indeed, they *will* be caught, even if we simply sit on this information and do nothing. I assumed that from the very beginning."

Alex frowned at her. "I know you're always one step ahead, but... Genuinely. How do you *know*?"

"Well, it's to do with the reason we were all sealed in here – which is the same reason why the best murder mysteries are set before this century," Cornelia declared: "Forensic science."

Alex leaned back in her chair, staring up at the ceiling. Of course. "DNA evidence," she murmured. "Microscopic analysis."

"Just so," Cornelia nodded. "Technology has finally outpaced the tricks of mystery. The age of closed-circle mysteries where all the suspects are shut up in one house is over; a hair, a flake of skin in the wrong place, and the police can instantly lay their hands on the culprit." Her lip curled in distaste. "That's why modern *crime novels* are all about gritty urban gunmen who shoot dead their targets and then vanish into the city streets never to be found."

That wasn't *entirely* fair, Alex thought – but there was a grain of truth in it, and certainly the police would bring every device at their disposal to bear on a multiple-murder case involving the death of a famous author. The killer had nowhere to hide. And yet they had tried to shut the police out anyway. "The killer knew they would be caught, but still tried to stall the police," Alex thought out loud. "It can't just have been about buying time to kill everyone, since they could have slipped a knife in anyone's back while nobody was looking. So they needed to buy time to kill everyone in an *impossible* way."

"I'm sure the murderer was buying time for the survivors, too," Cornelia interrupted, gesturing to the book in Alex's lap. "They want to be caught, but…"

"…they want to be caught the old-fashioned way," Alex understood. "They want us to deduce their identity, just like a classic mystery. Whoever it is must be a big fan."

"Ha. That hardly rules anyone out," Cornelia smiled mirthlessly. "But it would be well worth considering what the Author's notes give away." She glanced towards the open doorway for a moment. "We have plenty of time before the others start wondering where we are – so let's prise this case wide open. Even I could do with a little verification for my own theories; I don't always tumble to the *why*…"

Alex sat up straight again, and mentally cracked her knuckles. Right: They had a fresh batch of clues – indeed, they had *all* the clues. It was time to get to work.

"Let's start with the rules, then," Alex said, picking up *Hand at the Threshold*; they baffled her the most. "I'm not really sure how the murderer expected some of these to work in real life. How could the murderer stop us from solving the mystery by accident? Stop people from being racist or sexist, even? I mean, that would be nice."

"That's why they're really rules for *writing* murder mysteries rather than solving them; they aren't for us," Cornelia explained. "Still, a guarantee of no lengthy scientific explanations is always welcome, as there really are a lot of mysteries which need a chemist or mechanical engineer to solve. I would be more worried about the permission given for up to one secret passage – although I suppose it depends on what you call a secret passage, really."

When is a secret passage not a secret passage, Alex wondered. Perhaps when it's not always a secret? She set the idea aside for the moment. "What about those other rules for detective fiction you mentioned – Van Dine's, I think?" Alex recalled. "The murderer seems like a total mystery geek. If they didn't use those rules, it might be because they had to *break* them."

"Van Dine's Twenty Rules…" Cornelia squinted at some distant point as she concentrated. "There was some overlap with Knox's, I think, but most were less about fair play and more about particular clichés Van Dine didn't like. No secret societies or professional criminals allowed; accidental death or suicide out of the question; no locked-room murders committed only after the room is broken open…"

Alex's heart leapt at the mention of locked-room murders, but sadly this one didn't seem to apply. She'd opened Adam Carver's first locked room and Colin West's impromptu coffin herself and found the victims definitely already dead, while Maria Bole and Franny Smythe's deaths had been confirmed through the windows even before the doors had been opened. There was no shortcut to a locked-room solution here, sadly.

But on the other hand, the murderer had personally provided a giant set of clues about locked-room solutions.

"A murder that happens after the locked room is opened would be – Class A, where the murderer wasn't really in there when it was locked?" Alex reasoned. "Then there's Class B, where there wasn't really an inside lock, and Class C, where they're both legit and the murderer just never left. If the Author is telling the truth, we should have seen at least one of each."

"I think we can take the culprit at their word, since they were bold enough to surrender a handwriting sample," Cornelia suggested. "Four impossible deaths, and the murderer uncaptured – this is an individual with considerable confidence in their murder plan. Every detail of the locked rooms must have been plotted well in advance." That was a clue in itself, but Cornelia didn't labour the point. "Now," she said, nonchalantly, "I presume it is obvious to you by now which class each murder fits into."

Alex pursed her lips and looked away. Obvious how, exactly? Though now she thought about it, there were certain indications. "I guess *one* of them is obvious?" she attempted.

Cornelia sighed gently. "Think about the circumstances," she said, in a teacherly manner. "There are a number of clues in the arrangement of the rooms – the way you never *really* got to search the first crime scene, for instance, or the fact that the fourth crime scene had two different exits. Even if you can't see the solution at first, such details create a strong presumption in favour of a particular class. And from there, you can start to think about what a solution in that class would look like for your problem."

That was the kind of careful, evidence-based approach Alex could agree with. A lot of their attempted solutions, whether of *Castles in the Sky* or the Carver's Rest murders, seemed to involve throwing around pre-packaged theories or relying on flashes of ingenuity. But if instead you looked at every detail of the rooms and tested how reliable they really were, you might be able to work it out step by step.

On top of that, Alex realised, there were really two approaches here: Trying to prove a theory, as Cornelia suggested, or instead trying to disprove it. For instance, if she thought about Franny's murder, Alex had entered the room with everyone accounted for and had searched the room carefully without finding anyone hiding, which ruled out Class C. What about the other two classes, then? Class B would seem to imply that there was some way of either locking the balcony door or creating the seal of tape from the outside, while Class A would imply that Franny had done the locking before dying to some kind of devious trap. Which of those seemed more realistic? And beyond that, which of the three remaining murders, then, could have been a Class C?

Although this way of breaking down the crimes was helpful, Alex still felt uncertain. It seemed like several of the impossible murders, or rather the impossible escapes, would require physical tricks of the kind Cornelia and Yva had been throwing around in their discussions – arts-and-crafts gimmicks involving string and who knew what else. Clearly there were answers, and she was sure it was possible to reach them – but maybe she personally didn't need to figure out exactly what they were.

"What if I tried something different?" she said, just quietly enough that Cornelia wouldn't necessarily hear. She did, though, and raised her eyebrows, so Alex explained. "I just wondered if starting at the whydunnit might be easier than starting at the how."

Cornelia sniffed. "Unconventional," she said, with a hint of disapproval. But then she softened. "I prefer the howdunnit because it often gives away the whodunnit; but the whydunnit should do the same. It's simply a matter of narrowing down the motives. However…" She gestured helplessly. "There's a reason why motives are always revealed at the end of murder mysteries, you know; one is spoilt for choice. Adam Carver foolishly gave everyone a motive, and deducing which of those was most likely to be acted on or who was mad enough to go through with it is a hopeless task."

"Are you sure?" asked Alex – arguing from the front foot for a change. "You said yourself that the murders must all have been planned in advance. The killer can't have dreamt up all these plans on the spur of the moment, and I don't see them going rooting through Carver's cupboards for multiple kinds of tape." Accounting for everything the murderer had said and done, there was really only one conclusion which made sense, and she said it now. "Mr. Carver's threats last night have to be a red herring, and the real motive must be much older."

Cornelia blinked rapidly at Alex in surprise, and it was a few moments before she replied. "*Well.* When you put it that way, it all sounds so reasonable."

Alex couldn't really tell if her great-aunt was being ironic or not; but she had a good feeling about this approach, for once, and continued. "If someone was just intimidated by Adam Carver – I don't think they'd have written these," she said, tapping the nearest volume of *Castles in the Sky*. "The murderer obviously has a point to prove, and it's one they can only prove by playing murder mysteries with us. And the books also prove they must always have planned to kill four people – and none of the motives Adam Carver gave would also require getting rid of Maria, Colin, and Franny. So their motive must be bigger than just Carver." She thought back over the murders once again, about the ease with which the murderer had danced around them and constructed their mind-bending problems. "And they must know Carver's Rest," she concluded. "Especially if their ideas were unique and wouldn't work anywhere else."

"I'll guarantee that one," Cornelia interrupted. "If my solutions are correct, then – let me count… no, arguably not one of them could be applied to any generic room or door." She looked faintly surprised for a moment. "Yes, you're right. The murderer *did* have to know the house. Still, we were all given the tour yesterday, but…"

She shook her head, musing into her lap. "It would be quite the turnaround from first sight to coming up with an impossible gimmick. If there was just the one locked room, maybe – but four?"

"Exactly! It has to be someone who had *already been here*!" Alex exclaimed, feeling more and more excited. "The murderer must have visited before – so they must have known Adam Carver personally for longer than just one day!"

"Then how do you explain the other three victims, eh?" Cornelia asked, eyeballing her. "The murderer claimed not to be going after mere witnesses. So what links all four of them?"

Alex thought on this. "Well, the murderer appears to be really devoted to the idea of killing four people," she pointed out. "So long as they were committing murder already, then maybe they had stronger motives to kill some people than others. Sure, they said they wouldn't kill just to get rid of an inconvenient witness – but what if they had a potential motive to get rid of a witness anyway?"

Cornelia's expression became dubious. "That makes the motive sound rather like a red herring to me."

"I think the murderer must have been a very angry, very bitter, and very ill person at the limit of their sanity – and probably beyond it," Alex answered, firmly. "Even if they had the strongest reason to despise Adam Carver, maybe it wouldn't have taken much for another person to set them off." She paused as a thought occurred to her. "Looking at it that way," she said, "it's probably important that the first two victims were both professionals with real jobs, but not the second two."

"Franny was a sort of a professional, mind," Cornelia cautioned. "Certainly no fan!"

"True," Alex admitted. "She didn't even really care for *Castles in the Sky* – not the way Colin did, or we do."

"Her opinion was disagreeable – but revealing, yes, we can't forget that," Cornelia mumbled, and there was something suddenly faraway about her voice. "Indeed, I wonder if her murder might be the most illuminating of all…"

"Wait, what?" asked Alex, for whom this was all getting a bit cryptic again. "Do you think you've got it?"

"Well." Her great-aunt said it in that tone which suggested she could be wrong but was sure she wasn't. "Just thinking about the idea of people or objects which didn't fit the pattern, I was reminded of something we'd seen today – and it had some shade of relevance to my own theory about the order of events. Yes, if you think of the murders in terms of the odd ones out, everything starts to become rather clear."

"Which odd ones out? Do you mean, like, in the murders, or…" Alex's gaze fell on the covers of the four books in front of her. Four volumes of *Castles in the Sky*, signed by the Author. "Or in these? What did I miss?"

"Oh? Can't you work it out for yourself?" Cornelia asked, quite rhetorically. "I don't have any more clues than you do. In fact, some of the best clues came from you in the first place."

Alex scowled at her own stupid slow mind. Right, this wasn't a mystery book she was reading. She couldn't just coast to the end here and let the detective lay it out for her. This was her real life – and even though there was nonetheless a detective who knew the answers, *she* wouldn't just tell Alex, either. It was like the worst kind of mystery, an unfinished mystery without an author where you had no choice but to become the detective yourself. And she did indeed have to work it out for herself.

So, she did. She closed her eyes, and let herself forget about the questions for a moment. She ignored the distraction of everything she didn't know, and focussed instead on everything she did – and tried to let connections form. She looked back on everything she knew about these books, both her beloved *Castles in the Sky* and these specific annotated copies…

And she started to see. The murderer's motive – just a murky suggestion at first – but then it linked to one piece of evidence after another, to statements let slip and situations formerly strange, connecting and reconnecting into a web of truth in which everything held together.

And in the centre of that web, weaving and trapped by it – the least likely suspect.

"So that was it," she murmured to herself. She had quite forgotten Cornelia. From the motive, several of the mysteries posed by the Author were already disappearing – vanishing like that evil spirit she had so absurdly feared. She opened her eyes; everything was dazzling. "It was so obvious!" she breathed.

"Did you see it?" whispered Cornelia Crow, her excitement terrifying. "Did you have the Eureka moment which all puzzle-solvers live for?" She leaned in closer. "Do you *know*?"

"I – I think…" Alex began, her thoughts having run so far ahead of her that she hadn't even had time to check them – "Yes. I know. Not the how, not all of it – but the why. And from there, I think I do know *who*."

"And was it a fair mystery?" Cornelia demanded. "It's not just intuition, is it? Could any one person have worked out the motive from the clues?"

"Yes," Alex replied, unhesitating. "Definitely. It's barely hidden."

The murderer's motive, and *Castles in the Sky…* Yes, it was barely hidden, the truth that lay in the pages of the books she loved. The books, she thought, that in the end the murderer also loved – some of, at least. She would never look at them quite the same way again. So instead, she looked at the one other person who knew the truth, or at least part of it – Cornelia Crow.

"You really think you know how the murders were done?" she asked, meeting her great-aunt's eyes. "And who the murderer is?"

"I'm certain of it," Cornelia answered, with an assured nod. "The person I'm thinking of gave themselves away with a foolhardy lie; it was inevitable that somebody would find it out. But by the time I was sure, there was nothing more to be done." She looked sceptically at Alex – maybe a little apologetically, too. "And I did *have* to be sure. I didn't just let the murders continue because I wanted more mysteries to solve, if that's what you were thinking."

"Not seriously," Alex admitted – which was to say that it had, in fact, crossed her mind. Did Cornelia Crow care more about mysteries than people? Maybe. Perhaps even probably. But she had no reason to hide the truth, either. The more she cared about mysteries, the more she must want to know if she was right – and Alex, too, wanted to know if she was right.

"I have an idea," Alex said to her, abruptly. "I'm thinking of a name – the name of the person I think is the murderer. You think you know who the murderer is, too. So, let's check each other's answers."

A grin flashed onto Cornelia's face. "And about time, too. Shall we say on the count of three?"

Alex smiled, too. It would all be over soon; in a sense, at the moment they spoke. "Agreed. And then we'll know for sure."

Cornelia nodded her assent. "Then – three."

"Two," Alex said firmly.

"One!"

And in two voices they spoke a single name.

The name of the murderer.

CHAPTER TWENTY-TWO
DEATH OF A GHOST

"Ah, good. You're all still here," Cornelia said as she and Alex strolled casually back into Adam Carver's study, where the remaining four people were waiting and where Alex was glad also to see that no more outrageous or impossible events had occurred to muddy the waters in their absence. Cornelia was in an exceptionally flippant mood, one which Alex in part shared. It was a mood of triumph, mostly for Cornelia; and relief, mostly for Alex. Between the two of them, they knew everything.

"Don't see where else we'd be," groused Quinn. "The two of you were a while, though."

"Well?" Vi demanded. "Did you manage to signal to anyone, or not?"

"You don't need to worry about that," Alex quickly answered. "We got in contact with a taxi driver. He's gone to call the police."

"But more importantly," Cornelia interrupted, "the mystery has been solved, so there is really no urgency about fetching the authorities anymore."

Yva, who had been reclining blissfully in a chair, shot bolt upright as if on oiled hinges. "Wait, what?"

"It seems to me," said Victoria, her voice struggling to remain even, "that this mystery has been repeatedly 'solved' today by one mad theory or another – and to no good end."

Alex, who had been tasked with carrying the four hardcover volumes of *Castles in the Sky* back up the stairs, dropped them on Adam Carver's desk with a resounding *thump*. "That was before we had these – I mean, before we really looked properly at them." She spread out the books and opened them in turn to the Author's notes. "The murderer wanted to be caught, and these messages tell the whole story."

Even the non-fanatics were intrigued, though Yva was of course in pole position after shoving Vi aside. "Let me see!" she screeched, hoarding the books like a dragon. "Introduction – Rules – Methods – Challenge? Why wasn't I told I was being challenged?!" Her face swung up to look at Cornelia Crow, and it showed a rare expression for Yva Dysart, something pained like a seagull being teased with dangling chips. "You broke Knox's 8th!" she whined. "That's the only one that really matters!"

"I didn't withhold any clues. Look, I'm showing them to you right now," Cornelia said, waving airily at the books. "There you go, that's all the evidence, now whodunnit? Come on, chop chop!" She slammed *A Coffin Nail Creaks* shut practically on Yva's fingers. "Too late! Now, quietly sit there while I explain everything."

Yva roared in frustration, wrestling for the book like a small child with a toy. "Wait wait wait, give me more time, I'll definitely explain it any second now!"

Alex actually felt a little bit sorry for her. But only a very little bit. "You can keep reading if you like," she said, frowning forcefully at Cornelia as she did so. Cornelia removed her hand, and Yva, not giving the thanks that Alex didn't expect, returned to poring over the books. "But," Alex continued, "since everyone's gathered here, we're going to end this and explain everything."

"More silly games," muttered Quinn.

"More mystery clichés," Vi corrected.

Victoria just looked tired – more than tired, in fact; it was that disgusted weariness of somebody just *done* with everything. "You really think you know what happened, do you?" she said, her voice like a waiting knife. "After it's all said and done and nobody can change anything?"

"That's right," Cornelia crowed, completely overlooking Victoria's defeatist mood, and she was even in high enough spirits to hazard her own attempt at a catchphrase. "The truth has already been determined – by me."

Alex spoilt the moment a little by clearing her throat. "And me," she pointed out.

"And by you, of course," Cornelia amended. "I have no intention of downplaying your role in solving the mystery. In fact," she said, growing especially magnanimous, "why don't you begin? For the motive *is* the beginning, however late in the day it may appear – and in this case, the motive is particularly helpful in identifying the murderer."

Suddenly, everyone's eyes (with perhaps one exception) were on Alex again; a position she never envied, but which seemed to be happening more and more often. And yet it didn't feel so uncomfortable this time; the anxiety was still there, of course, the uneasiness about the people around her and what they might be thinking – but it had receded, and she felt she could speak freely. As was traditional for the parlour denouement, the audience had gathered around her in a semicircle, silent and expectant. And as was traditional, one of them also knew the truth – and that wasn't including Cornelia. What would happen once it all came out, Alex couldn't be sure. But there was no more need to put it off. It was time to explain it all.

"Let's just go over the basics," Alex began. "Ten people, fans and professionals alike, gathered in this house to celebrate the success of Adam Carver's *Castles in the Sky* tetralogy, and apparently to hear him announce a new book. Adam Carver planned to stage a murder mystery as part of the event, centring around himself; but instead, something went wrong, and he was murdered for real, followed by his agent Maria Bole, the fanartist Colin West, and the reviewer Franny Smythe. Each of them was killed in a way which made it seem impossible for the murderer to have been there, just like in *Castles in the Sky*, and at each crime scene, the murderer left behind a book which they had signed and written in." She paused, and looked around the semicircle. "Does everyone agree with what I've just said?"

There was silence for a moment; then Vi cleared his throat. "Well, obviously," he declared. "Why would we disagree with the things we all know?"

Alex really felt bad for him sometimes. "Because the thing is, you should have disagreed," she replied. "Two of the things I just said were wrong. One of them will have to wait, but let's start with the mistake that's really the key to the whole mystery." She looked over to the desk, where the four books still lay open. "Um, Yva, I'm going to need those."

Scowling bitterly, Yva stepped away from the desk, and the semicircle rearranged itself. One by one, Alex started to flip the pages back – from the very end, to the very beginning. "Volume One, *Death in the Walls*: Adam Carver's name has been crossed out from the title page, and replaced with the signature, 'The Author'. Volume Two, *Hand at the Threshold*, same. Volume Three, *A Coffin Nail Creaks*, same. Volume Four –"

She let the book rest on the title page, and let them see for themselves. The grand finale to the series, *Conspiracies of the Obscure Tribunal*, by Adam Carver – and the Author had not denied it. Although the murderer had added a detailed note to the endpapers, the title page had not been defaced with the others.

"Cornelia showed this to us when she found it, remember?" Alex asked a gawping Vi. "We didn't dwell on it at the time, but maybe we would have if we'd been paying attention to the Author's notes. The implication of their edits is pretty literal, really."

"What implication?" sniped Victoria.

"Surely," Vi cried, charging melodramatically to her aid, "you're not suggesting that Adam Carver did not write *Conspiracies of the Obscure Tribunal*? That's preposterous!"

Alex put her fingers to her temple. "No, Vi. Mr. Carver definitely wrote this book," she answered. "There's no question of it. Cornelia even verified that it resembles his earlier fiction." She paused to brace herself. "It's the rest of the series that he didn't write."

Alex had expected more of an explosion of incredulity. Vi tried his best, putting all his energy into a rallying cry of "*Outrageous!*" – but Quinn only growled something inaudible about conspiracy theories, while Victoria clutched her head wound. In retrospect, Alex would realise that Yva too had been curiously silent.

"I'm afraid it explains everything," she said, as apologetically as she really felt. The dream of Adam Carver, the great author and her idol, really was dead; vanished into the mere mist of which it was made. "Remember the way the final book was delayed for so long, and didn't live up to our hopes; didn't even solve the series's mysteries in a way we could accept? Adam Carver used a ghostwriter for the first three books – not someone hired for the purpose, I think, but somebody who'd given him their own story to look over. Somebody with a personal connection to Mr. Carver, which is why they came to him in the first place; but also somebody from whom he could take the credit, and probably a lot of the money, without them realising until three books in that they'd been given a raw deal."

"You're mad – and completely wrong!" interrupted Victoria, flaring up in anger. "Completely, *completely* –"

With difficulty, Alex spoke over her. "It's not too hard to imagine what must have happened then. Maybe Adam Carver had assured this person – 'the Author' – that he was just taking care of the publicity, that it meant more time and freedom to write without the burden of fame, maybe that an established name was needed to get the books out there in the first place. That's probably where Maria Bole came in; she'd worked as Mr. Carver's agent for years, and would've known they were onto a good thing and how to make a success out of it. To the author who'd been written out of their own story, Maria Bole must have seemed just as complicit as Adam Carver."

"This is slander," Victoria announced. "Absolute slander – and my lawyer will certainly hear about this. I'll ruin you before you can ruin my husband!"

"Steady on," murmured Quinn. Vi looked uneasily from Alex to Victoria, seeming unsure now as to whose side he should be on.

"Anyway, this con could never have lasted forever," Alex continued – fully committed to finishing her story without stopping to fight fires. "By three books in, it had to be very obvious to the Author how big a success the series was – and how overboard Mr. Carver had gone in selling himself as the genius responsible for it all. So when he came to the Author asking for the final volume in the series, the Author simply refused. They wanted a bigger piece of the pie. This was the true creator, after all, and their legacy was being stolen. They must have demanded some acknowledgement of authorship, and used the production of the final book as a bargaining chip. Until Adam Carver agreed to those terms, the final book would remain unwritten – and Carver's star would only sink. The Author intended that Carver would be exposed as a fraud either way; it was simply a matter of how much agency he had in the process. But from Adam Carver's perspective, that wasn't something he could allow. He enjoyed his fame and his fortune, and he wasn't about to give it up. So he did the only thing he could do in that situation –"

"Write the book himself," grunted Quinn. "Damn him, no wonder it missed so many deadlines!"

"That's right," Alex agreed. "The Author hasn't made any claim to have written *Conspiracies of the Obscure Tribunal*. It must have been Adam Carver's own idea of what the conclusion of the series would look like – one written without any idea of the answers to the mysteries, maybe without any idea of what we even *liked* about the books. It was just fanfiction, basically – for the series and for his own early work. And so whether because Carver was still haggling with the Author, or because it just took him that long to write something passable, the final volume in the series was massively late – and a huge let-down to the fans who'd been following the series. Of course, with a rave pre-review by Franny Smythe and *Humble Mom Reviews*, that didn't matter to the general public."

"Philistines," muttered Cornelia.

"So, assuming that this deduction is correct," Alex began –

"*Ab*duction," muttered Yva. "It's different."

Alex hurried on as Victoria too opened her mouth to object. "Where would this leave the Author? The rug had been pulled out from under them. Adam Carver had successfully fooled the world into thinking that he was the real author of *Castles in the Sky*, and he no longer needed his ghostwriter. The Author had been betrayed by the person they trusted to give them their break in fiction, and their creative legacy had been stolen and twisted; they were left with nothing, powerless to prove the injustice they'd suffered. For a truly dedicated artist, that must be a powerful motive for revenge."

"Can't say I disagree with you there," Quinn assented, his expression grim and frightening. "Don't know what I'd have done, if it had been me…"

"Maybe not – but we know what the Author did," Alex ventured. "They took their revenge on everyone they blamed for stealing *Castles in the Sky*, and they did it in a way which revealed how –"

"But, but, how did they arrange everything?" Vi interrupted. "If Mr. Carver had broken it off with this ghostwriter, how did they end up here with all these professionals and fans – all the people who had become this lunatic's enemy?"

Alex frowned at him for interrupting, but it was a reasonable question. "Simple," she shrugged. "By faking a reconciliation. They cooked up their murderous plans, and then they went to Adam Carver and said they were willing to let bygones be bygones. He'd won fair and square, and even proved he could write – but he hadn't found it easy. I'm guessing the Author suggested a return to their old arrangement, on more equal ground; the Author would write books, and Adam Carver would get them published. I really think Carver would have leapt at the chance. He always looked like he was loving fame; and if he didn't even have to do the writing, he'd just be getting paid for celebrity, his real passion. The Author claimed they were preparing a new book, and it might even have been true; Quinn, you said you saw some paper on Mr. Carver's desk, and we never found it, so perhaps that was a preview. And then, once the Author had Carver's trust again, the Author proposed this party. It would be a big celebration of Adam Carver personally, in which he'd star in a murder mystery and announce a new book. How could he resist? Of course he agreed – and to the Author helping out, too. The Author could claim the bedroom needed for their plan, run some experiments with string and tape – and when the time came, set the guest list and even prepare the invitations themselves…"

"Nobody has been living in this house except me and my husband!" hissed Victoria. "I wrote those invitations! The guest list came from Maria!"

Cornelia parried instantly. "We saw your handwriting on the calendar in your room, and it was scratchy and rough; completely different to the smooth hand on the invitations," she replied. "As for Maria, judging from comments she made to Vi and Alex yesterday, she knew nothing about the fandom and would have had no idea who to invite." Cornelia had been standing by the whole time, letting Alex explain her theory – but when it came to backing up that theory with evidence, she had always been ready.

Vi had baulked at Cornelia's rebuttal, and took a jerky step away from Victoria. "So, what – all this was a lie?" he asked, looking dazed. "This whole party, all of us – we were all just tools for someone's public revenge?"

Alex shook her head. "There's more to it," she said. "That's what I was trying to explain. The Author had another goal which they could achieve the same way. I think that, by getting their revenge, they were also proving the truth about *Castles in the Sky* and its authorship."

"Barking mad!" spat Victoria. "I don't have to listen to this." But though she turned her back on Alex and stormed away, she only made it a few steps before she had to lean on a chair for support. Or perhaps, no matter what she said, she *did* have to listen to it.

"The Author left us clues pointing to their motive. That's how we were able to work out this much," Alex went on. She was close to the end now; close to the real meaning behind the murders. "It wasn't just a matter of putting their signature to their books and scattering them around. Anyone could do that. Instead, when the depth of their grudge pushed them to murder – they made sure it very clearly echoed *Castles in the Sky*. The connection is obvious. Who better to come up with these impossible murders in a castle than someone who'd already written three books' worth of them? The Author was showing off. They wanted to tell a story – and for that they needed an audience. And more than that, they wanted somebody to catch them."

"Which is where I come in, of course," Cornelia could not help adding. "You don't just invite an expert at solving murder mysteries when you're planning on murdering a lot of people unless you really *want* to be caught."

"I'd say it's Alex who appears to have solved everything," Vi pointed out, giving Alex a smile she didn't quite care for.

"Patience, patience," Cornelia said, not quite refraining from rolling her eyes.

"Anyway," Alex resumed, a little flustered by an actual compliment, "with the killer's identity and motive revealed, their notoriety as a multiple-murderer who killed a famous author would see their story spread everywhere." She was winding down now, her contribution coming to a close. "Nobody who'd read or even heard of *Castles in the Sky* could fail to learn the truth. That was the Author's final goal – to take control." She paused, and thought of the person who she knew was behind all this. "No matter what the consequences."

She fell silent, giving her explanation time to sink in; giving herself time to soak it all in, too. This was probably the longest speech of her life, and much like giving a presentation at school, a task she always did her utmost to avoid, it was hard; it was truly hard, to put so much of herself out there, to expose herself and the way she thought to the world. Probably the Author had felt the same way once. Just writing a book was enough for them, and being put on display to the whole world was too much… and one way or another, they too had tried to find a way to avoid it. But in the end, the truth would always catch up with you – you had to ride the wave, or be washed away. Alex didn't know if she pitied or hated the person who had signed themselves as the Author, but she knew that she understood them.

"I deny it," Victoria Carver was mumbling, facing away from them. "I absolutely deny it all…"

"Deny it all you want, but it's solid as stone," Quinn growled in an undertone; louder, he said, "you're not leaving it there, though. You going to put a name to this person? A real name?"

"Yes," Vi exclaimed, looking lost again, "just who is this person? Who is the Author?"

Alex steeled herself. Ride the wave, or be washed away… "Well," she began, giving herself one last moment before embarking on the final revelation, "when you consider everything, there's really only one person –"

It was a blink-and-you'll-miss-it moment, and Alex blinked and she missed it. One moment, the semicircle was standing silent and tense around her; the next there was a sudden burst of movement and cries of surprise and four people were flooding out of the door too fast for Alex even to tell who was first. A man's cry of "Stop right there!" echoed down the hammering hallway…

"What just – ?" stuttered Alex, blinking after them in astonishment – and then Cornelia was next to her, seething.

"Blast! That fool!" Cornelia cursed, and with a thrust of her cane, "Get after them!"

Alex didn't need telling twice, not least as the second time would probably involve the cane jabbing her; she was hurling herself forwards and after them in a second, not knowing what had happened, dreading what *would* happen. She hadn't seen it, but somebody else must have run, too; somebody had tried to escape, and everyone else in that instant had put two and two together. And Alex hadn't seen it coming; for all the joy of suspense, the logical paving of the way, she and Cornelia really should have started with the *who*…

A cacophony of footsteps was smashing the stairs below her, and she caught the last trace of a smooth head vanishing down the stairwell; she wheeled around the banister, holding on tight and letting her own momentum carry her around, and then she was plunging back down into the depths of the house, the shapes of people flitting past in her peripheral vision as the chase surged along to the next flight of stairs; a female voice screamed in rage, and Alex was stumbling over the stairs and practically throwing herself over the banisters to be around the central stairwell and hurtling down to the ground floor, shapes in wild motion cutting the air ahead of her. They were heading for the front door –

No! They were *not* heading for the front door – they were stumbling that way, then adjusting their course, streaming off to the left – a door was banging somewhere nearby –

Alex jumped the last few steps and nearly collapsed at the foot of the stairs. As she twisted her body, she saw a figure throw himself through the nearest door on the left –

The armoury – !

Alex staggered through the door and clutched the frame as she stopped for gasping breath. She could afford to stop, for everyone else in the room had stopped as well. They were frozen in a kind of tableau, like the moment at the end of an act where the players hold their pose and the curtain descends.

Standing near the centre of the room, facing the windows at the back... was Quinn Shillerdyce. His arms and legs were spread, as if he had been about to try and grab someone, or else be ready to leap out of the way.

A little way over to the left of him... was Vi Malik. He was half-crouching, seemingly trying to turn on a dime, one hand resting on top of the open exhibit case he had been moving to circle around. Alex could see his expression in profile, and his eyes were wide with alarm.

Paused stalking around the right wall of the room, swaying on her feet but neither moving nor dropping... was Victoria Carver. Her fingers were twitching at her sides, and occasionally a tremor would cross her entire body, as if she was under some immense and easily-imagined strain.

And near the rear of the room, back flat up against the windows but standing firm... was Yva Dysart. She was the only one whose face Alex could fully see, and there was something about her expression both wild and yet terrifyingly certain and resigned; as if forced into a course of action she neither understood nor wanted to take, but to which she was now wholly committed and would never, ever abandon.

And she was the one holding the knife.

It wasn't a very long knife, but it was very sharp, and all the ornate designs in the world upon its hilt were not enough to make it merely ceremonial; and it had clearly been removed from the central exhibit case within the past few seconds. Yva was gripping the knife like she never meant to let go, and without moving its blade seemed to point first at one person and then another who might be foolish enough to approach her. Beneath her furiously furrowed brow her pupils were wide, her lips pressed thin. "Nobody move," she hissed. "Nobody move. Not one of you move…"

"Now, um, Yva," stammered Vi, a hesitant smile trembling on his face, "don't do anything you'll regret…"

"Oh, I won't," she hissed; the knife tilted in his direction, and he recoiled.

Alex tried to take a step further into the room, but found that she could not; her legs twitched and refused to move for her. Loath though she was to confess fear, it was what she felt at that moment. Yva Dysart was the one person left in Carver's Rest whom she thought might genuinely be dangerous. They should have expected this. But what on earth was she going to do? "For goodness' sake, Yva," she choked out, "put the knife down!"

"I refuse!" Yva screamed at her. "Of course I refuse! Do you really expect me to just sit here and accept this?!" Her eyes suddenly swept the room, crawled over it frantically searching for something she clearly could not find. "I need more evidence – no, I need more time, I need quiet, I need to *think*…"

"She's out of control," Quinn muttered to himself, and glanced sideways at Victoria. "We might be better stepping out of this room, actually…"

"Oh no you don't!" cried Yva, pointing the knife at him now. "Nobody leaves this room until I'm done! Especially not you, Corby!" Yva angled the knife across the room at Alex, and it wasn't worth the risk that she knew how to throw those things. How had it gone so wrong? "Your theory is nothing but slander!" Yva continued. "You have no proof! You can't prove what isn't true! And I'm not just going to sit there and shrug and demand to talk to my lawyer either! I won't let anyone tarnish my good name and bright future, no matter what I have to do!"

"You won't get away with this," stammered Victoria, who was now holding her hands out defensively. "You can't kill all of us."

"No, *you* won't get away with this!" Yva roared. "And we'll see how many people I can kill —"

"Best not finish that statement, Yva, in case somebody takes it the wrong way," a casual voice rolled from the doorway. "Or, worse yet, takes it the right way."

Alex risked taking her eyes off Yva and turned her head. There, strolling through the doorway as if she wasn't facing down a knife-wielding maniac, was Cornelia Crow. Unlike everyone else in the room, she seemed relaxed and at ease, and Alex sensed that she had probably walked her way there. She stopped beside Alex and looked at Yva appraisingly, as if surveying a child throwing a temper tantrum. "Now, what's all this in aid of?" she asked.

"Scapegoating me for the murders!" Yva exploded. "I'm not a puppy for you to sit there and kick! I'm the world's next great bestselling mystery novelist! You can't do this to me! You want to convince everyone of your crazy theory about me writing *Castles in the Sky* and killing everyone for revenge, but I won't let you get away with it!"

So *that* was it. "Yva, just listen," Alex exclaimed —

But Yva had paused her rant only to inhale as deeply as she could; and positively bellowed, "*Alex Corby and Cornelia Crow are the culprits!* With this theory I can explain all four murders —"

Cornelia arched an eyebrow, and said, "We weren't talking about you."

Yva froze mid-sentence. It was like somebody had simply pushed the pause button on her, knife held out, mouth held open, eyes practically taped to Cornelia. "What?" she said, quietly, in the next moment.

"We weren't talking about you," Cornelia repeated softly. "We don't think you're the Author. We don't think you're the murderer. Goodness, child, be sensible."

Yva fumbled the knife as she dropped her arms uselessly to her sides, and suddenly she was just an awkward teenager like Alex, looking as if she had no idea what to say or do next. Any one of the three people confronting her might have rushed in at that second, but they too were staring at Cornelia in open astonishment. "But of course you were," Yva said, her voice normal if a little nonplussed, as if she had merely been contradicted about the weather or the time. "Of course you thought I was the murderer. I mean, that's just obvious. You think it's someone who was the real writer of *Castles in the Sky*, and the only other person capable of that is me. How could you think it was anyone else?"

And just like that, Alex felt she at last understood Yva Dysart; saw through all her quixotic moods and unfeeling hardness to the one genuinely warm thing within her – the unassailable core of pride at her heart, pride so fierce it would even devour an accusation of murder as a tribute to her genius. A pride which would make even the truth of her innocence painful.

"There were a couple of indications," Cornelia declared, in response. "For instance, you couldn't be guilty of one of the murders, and wouldn't be guilty of another – and for all that amusing theorising then neither you nor Vi *really* had time to commit two impossible crimes without the other noticing. But the point that really matters is your writing style. I apologise, Yva – but most of us have read your fanfiction, and stylistically it doesn't measure up to the real thing. Character motivation, personality – *likability*, to be brutally honest – are all lacking. No, you couldn't possibly have written *Castles in the Sky*; and therefore you cannot be the Author."

Yva blinked in surprise, but that was her only outward reaction; inwards, it was difficult to be sure how a pride like hers would stand being so casually cut down. But if the truth did sting, then like everything else, it washed over her quickly enough, like water over stone. No single wave, no matter how enormous, would ever wear her down. "But that doesn't make any sense," she said. "If it's not me, then who *is* the murderer?"

"Yes, bloody say it already!" erupted Quinn. "We just had a dagger waved at us for no damn reason! This has gone on long enough!"

Vi swallowed, and nodded his agreement. Victoria likewise said nothing, but her hand nervously sought out the wound upon her scalp. Four pairs of eyes were watching the two at the doorway – Alex and Cornelia.

They were not the only people in the room who knew the truth, of course, but they were the only ones willing to advertise it. Perhaps indeed it *would* have been wiser to start with the who, rather than the why – and for that matter, Cornelia had planned to cover the how before they finally put a name to the murderer. The truth was something they had felt would be neither accepted nor understood without the support of a whydunnit and a howdunnit. So they had tried to put it off.

And besides… Alex did not like the answer to the whodunnit.

Even though the murderer was in the room, she did not want to point at that person. Although they had committed murder, although they had not truly been anything like as nice a person as she had thought, Alex still believed that that person had deserved better. She pitied the sad fate of the Author.

Cornelia sighed exaggeratedly. "You really haven't worked it out yet?" she asked. "The murderer is –" And she pointed directly at one of the seven in the room.

The witnesses spun to stare at the murderer. But although they met the killer's gaze, he did not truly look back. Nothing would ever be seen again through the cold, dead eyes of Colin West.

Chapter Twenty-Three
The Taped Mouth

"That is the worst and dumbest theory yet!" Yva pronounced, but not everyone's response was so readable. A dubious cringe marred Vi's face, while Quinn had marched to the windows to stare fixedly away; and Victoria was sagging against the wall, her face in her hands.

"It's actually pretty logical," Alex replied, not just for Yva's benefit; there could be no advantage to anyone in leaving lingering doubts. "Once you know the murderer's motive, it explains why Adam Carver, Maria, and Franny were targeted. But where does Colin fit in? He doesn't – and that's reason enough on its own to be suspicious."

"From there, there are several clues as to his involvement," Cornelia picked up from there. "Remember how DaVinciCorpse would always go on about artistic integrity on Besieging Heaven? Furthermore, certain remarks he made to Alex in this very room suggest he didn't regard himself as only an illustrator –"

"But you're seriously suggesting he wrote *Castles in the Sky*?" Yva demanded, pointing angrily at the corpse. "Him?! DaVinciCorpse, anime fanartist extraordinawful?"

"You know, we get so used to thinking of each other as mere stereotypes – fanartist, theorist, writer of fanfiction – that perhaps we forget that a person can have multiple talents," Cornelia mused. "Colin chipped in with some very useful ideas while we were planning *The Fourth Wall Crumbles*, as I'm sure you recall. Did you ever wonder what he might be like as an author rather than an artist? I did."

"He couldn't give away his true identity on Besieging Heaven, obviously," Alex pointed out, "but he could try his hand at other ways of expressing his love for the work he authored. And speaking of his work, he *did* try to give us a push towards looking in the back of the books, back when Great-Aunt Cornelia picked up the one by Maria's body. Things would have been very different if we'd only listened."

"And of course, on that same occasion he tried to quite literally *cover up* a murder – throwing a sheet over Maria's corpse so that

Quinn and Victoria wouldn't realise their little game had gone awry…" Cornelia reflected.

Quinn's head jerked back. "I remember!" he gasped. "I couldn't see a thing, so I thought – and then later I figured he was the only one here with an ounce of *respect* –"

"But hold on, aren't you forgetting something very important?" Vi interrupted, looking little more convinced as he stared down at Colin's remains. "Would Colin not have been locked in a room, locked in an iron maiden, *dead*, while Franny was being murdered? I don't see how he can have committed the fourth murder."

"Oh? Who says Franny was the fourth?" Cornelia asked, and Vi paused to let a frown cloud his face. "Was it just because we found them in that order? Because the murderer left his books in that order? You believed what you were meant to believe. It was a good red herring – but Yva, surely you knew better…?"

"*No!*" Yva exclaimed, not in reply but in horror of her own ignorance. "Why didn't I see it?! The times of death – they were about the same, but strangulation takes *longer*. Franny's death had to be set up first!"

Victoria had blanched yet paler than she already was. "Colin –" she stammered, "Colin killed himself? After all that, he committed suicide?"

Quinn came slouching back to tower over everyone else. His shoulders were sagging, and he looked exhausted. "I just want this over with," he muttered, bleakly. "Can you prove that it was him? Is there a smoking gun?"

"*Yes*," Cornelia answered, simple and straight to the point, "and it involves a mug of water, if you must know. But there's more to it than just that."

"We can show that Colin committed suicide – and explain how," Alex cut in, "and for that matter, Cornelia can explain how he committed *all* the murders. We think he might even have hidden a confession somewhere, just to make sure – that missing sheet of paper from Mr. Carver's desk…"

"Alternatively," Cornelia added, "we can simply ask the one person who *knew* that he was the murderer." She looked across the room. "Can't we, Victoria?"

The glare of accusation whipped back across the room and struck Victoria. But she seemed immune to outrage; she might not even have heard. No, with her hands covering her face, she could see no evil, hear no evil, and speak no evil...

"There's no point denying it anymore," Cornelia cautioned her. "Once the police become involved, it won't take long to prove that you lied for him. All it will take is to compare the invitations we all received to a sample of his handwriting – the signatures on his illustrations, for instance – and there are bound to be other ways of showing that he's been up here for days."

"Don't think we don't understand," Alex interrupted, not wanting to put the woman in the stocks; Victoria hadn't known there had even *been* any murders until the murderer was already dead. "We know why you didn't tell us the truth. It was for your husband's sake... and for your brother's sake."

"Her *brother*?" hissed Vi, and it was this remark that made Victoria finally drag her hands away from her eyes, and turn her tear-tracked face towards Alex.

"How did you know?" she croaked. "How could you possibly have known?"

"Well, it was just a guess." Alex looked away. "Until you said that, anyway."

"When we were talking to you in your room, you mentioned a rich brother a little out of the blue," Cornelia explained. "I did wonder if you'd unconsciously let something slip – perhaps because he was in the house, perhaps because you wanted to assure yourself that he had nothing to complain about. There were other links, too; the way he freely used your first name but was shy about anyone else's..."

"When we were working out the motive, we thought that the murderer was probably a sibling or another close relative of yours or Mr. Carver's," Alex added. "That was the sort of link that made sense, if the murderer thought he might be their gateway to getting published."

Slowly, deliberately, Victoria Carver reached a trembling hand into one of her pockets and pulled out a diminutive handkerchief. She turned away from them, so that nobody could see her face as she wiped her eyes that would not stay dry – and remained turned away, perhaps avoiding her brother's eyes, which stared with the illusion of an accusation – until very quietly she said, "I didn't *know* he was the murderer."

A plunge in the icy sea could scarcely produce a sharper intake of breath. "So it's true!" gasped Vi, who then let out an awful sigh. "This is going to be *terrible* for the fandom."

"Do shut up," Cornelia advised him. "Now, Victoria. Very well, you may not have *known* – but you must have suspected, surely. You of all people would have known how strong Colin's motive was – and once you realised that people were actually dying, you did conveniently leave out the fact that he had been up here for days helping with the arrangements."

"Well, of course I had to protect him – I always have… and he was past harming anyone by then," Victoria admitted. "He was my brother – and I knew how he had suffered. But Adam was my husband, too, and I believed the best of him. No, I *still* believe the best of him. It *was* a good deal. The two just – didn't see eye to eye…"

"Did you try to help?" Alex asked. "Colin, or Adam – did you take sides?"

"I tried not to," she sighed. "I tried so hard to smooth it over. And then when things broke off after so long trying to make peace between them, and Adam started writing his own last book… I said nothing, because I thought it was better that way. The scandal would have ruined them both if it had been known; Maria convinced me of that."

"Ah, so she *was* involved," Cornelia nodded.

"Yes," Victoria admitted. "From the start. She knew Adam would sell books better than Colin. That was Adam's strength, the way writing was Colin's. My brother had always been writing and illustrating his own stories, even when we were children, but he was too shy to show them to anyone but me… until at last he asked me to show them to Adam." Another tear slipped down her cheek, and she dabbed the handkerchief at her eye in frustration. "And that makes it my fault, too. I was so *stupid*…"

"So these two got it all right," Quinn said, jerking his head in Alex and Cornelia's direction. "Right? Adam and Maria screwed

Colin over, and then he came back saying all was forgiven and set up this whole shebang."

Victoria sniffed. "Yes, that's right. It was all true. I can't believe I didn't see it sooner – when I heard that Maria had supposedly been killed, or even when I couldn't find Adam where he was supposed to be found." She shook her head, looking back on her mistakes. "But we were alone when he told me about Maria's death – and he whispered to me that it was all part of the game, that Adam had revised things last night and hadn't had time to tell me, and I just had to play along…" She began to sag, as if her regrets were weights hanging off her. "But I didn't understand why he killed the Smythe girl. I'm still not sure why he didn't kill *me*."

"We did consider that," Alex explained. "We think he had other possible targets, if he could only be sure they deserved it. Quinn, for instance – when Colin showed you his portfolio of *Castles in the Sky* illustrations, we thought maybe they'd been in his original manuscript. Perhaps he was trying to see if you recognised them, to find out if you were part of the conspiracy against him."

Quinn looked shaken, his fiery personality doused. "Dodged a bullet there," he murmured.

"And as for Franny," Alex went on, "her reviews were a huge boost to the popularity of the series, and especially the last book, which really shouldn't have been reviewed as well as it was. But that wasn't all; if it had been, Colin could probably have looked past it – but Franny also said something really stupid right in here, and we should have been more interested in just who heard it. It was something nobody should admit in front of a group of fans."

"She'd never even read the last book!" Cornelia exclaimed. She still looked angry about it. "She just had her assistant dash off a puff piece on the assumption that the quality was the same! She even claimed that she'd never been a fan of the series!"

Vi and even Yva looked shocked. Quinn didn't appear to understand what the fuss was about.

"…Yeah," Alex resumed. "For the real author of the series to hear that Franny's dishonest reviewing had made Carver's usurper book a hit – I think that made him furious. It was probably only a few minutes later that he killed her. Choosing her specifically as his remaining victim was a spur-of-the-moment decision."

"What a piece of garbage," Yva remarked. Alex wasn't sure whether she meant Colin or Franny, but had a dark suspicion that it was the latter.

"And so," Victoria said, looking at the floor, "that only left me."

Alex nodded. "Right. Colin only wanted there to be four victims, but because of what he wanted to achieve, the last victim had to be himself."

"That's where reading classic mysteries will get you," said Yva. "The killers scarcely ever go to trial in those. Why would they?"

"Recognition and affirmation are all very well," Cornelia agreed, "but I don't imagine Colin would have enjoyed prison. There was no way for him to get what he wanted and live to enjoy it. It was a trap with no way out, but at least it could be on his terms."

Victoria was staring at Colin's body still – with a kind of horror. "Such hate," she whispered. "Such hate, and such despair. Had I but known…"

"You tried, at least," Alex said, trying in turn to comfort Victoria. "He can't have seen you in a totally negative light."

"So he attacked me – but he didn't kill me," Victoria said. "I wonder if that was the only form of kindness he had left, at the end."

"Perhaps," Cornelia shrugged. "Or perhaps you just happened to be in the way."

Alex sighed. "He'd chosen the armoury for one of his impossible murders because of the iron maiden," she said. "He'd thought up a trick that used it. But then, it must have been right after he got back from dealing with Franny – you showed up before he had time to do anything. And I think he probably saw an opportunity to make you suffer the way he thought you deserved. It wasn't just that he attacked you – he also made you into an obvious suspect in his own death. I'm sorry, but even if he couldn't kill you, he probably wanted you to be accused."

Vi chose this moment to butt in. "Of course, I wasn't about to stand for that," he interrupted, puffing up his chest like a proud bird. "I rescued you from that fate."

"Yes, by making yourself prime suspect instead with your blundering," Cornelia sniped.

Victoria spoke over their bickering. She seemed lost in a memory. "It was when I started to come around that I realised just how seriously wrong things had gone… I was terrified. I couldn't say, because it would mean explaining why – but my first assumption, when I realised that I'd been attacked and taken prisoner, was that it was Colin; that he had gone completely mad and taken revenge. But then he was dead, and I didn't see how. He was the only other person left in the room when you broke in, and that made me suspect him more – even the way he had been stabbed in the back was clearly a message for me, I see that now – but at the same time I couldn't imagine how he had arranged it." She again shook her head, this time as if trying to stay awake, to ward off oblivion. "I don't see how any of those deaths could possibly have happened."

"Well, that's the elephant in the room, isn't it?" said Quinn. "How *were* they all done, anyway? All those murders."

"I have to confess, I'm still stumped," Vi said, apologetically. "Colin being the murderer… I don't see how it makes any of the crimes any easier to solve."

"Then you aren't thinking hard enough," Yva retorted. She seemed to be regaining her old spirits. "There are a couple of important points involving him that suddenly look much more interesting."

"Well, that's just too bad," Cornelia smirked, "because it's not your turn. It's mine. And everyone else has to listen up. That's right," she announced, projecting her voice to fill the room, "it's time for the best part of any locked-room mystery. You've had the why, you've had the who – and now I'll tell the lot of you *how* Colin West committed all four impossible murders."

CHAPTER TWENTY-FOUR
BREAKING THE SEALS

"You know," Cornelia remarked, as she and Alex led the group through the halls of Carver's Rest, "it's a funny thing, but a few of the wrong solutions people have been throwing out for the locked-room murders were actually quite close to the truth."

"Were any of them mine?" Yva demanded.

"Yes," Alex admitted, a little reluctantly. She hoped that being nearly right but still wrong would not boost Yva's ego.

Yva just smiled with something like contentment. "I can live with that," she said. "No shame in losing to the master. In half a century, I'll be as good as you are."

"In half a century, I'll be dead and won't care," Cornelia returned. "Now, we've almost reached our destination, the place where we can show you the solution to the first mystery..." She paused, leaning heavily on her cane, as they reached the window overlooking the wild sea at the head of the middle-floor stairs. "There's just a little background to fill in first regarding Colin West's stage-managing."

"Yeah, because if you ask me, he got pretty darn lucky," Yva brooded. "Alex seeing Carver's body in her room, for instance – that only worked because she read her invitation wrong and took all day to get here."

"Luck had nothing to do with it," interrupted Alex. This was, understandably, a sore point. "Colin wrote the invitations himself for a reason. He *deliberately* made his handwriting ambiguous so that someone would end up arriving in the evening."

Cornelia cleared her throat. "Yes, we took the liberty of comparing our invitations," she said, and produced a pair of familiar card squares. "Notice how the tail of the 'a' in '10am' is elongated a little too far. Doubtless there is variation among all the invitations. The aim would have been to lead at least one person to read it as 'pm', but with plausible deniability when their error was revealed. Any one of us might have fallen for it."

"It just happened to be me," Alex said, bitterly. Knowing that she had been tricked rather than being stupid didn't make her feel enormously better.

Not everyone was content with this explanation. "Still seems like luck," grumbled Quinn.

"Well, there is an element of truth to that," Cornelia admitted, Alex's pride not being her own. "Very likely Colin had reserve plans – for not everything went his way, after all. Carver was killed in his office, judging from the bloodstains left there, and *that* surely was not part of the plan; moving the body so soon after the curfew was risky, especially after Quinn Shillerdyce had barged in just before. Colin must have been there even then; probably threw himself behind the desk the instant he heard a knock at the door, and of course Carver couldn't risk exposing his ghostwriter."

"Colin probably meant to lure him to the guest room first – but Mr. Carver must have been stubborn," Alex speculated. "Perhaps he realised that something was wrong… I guess we'll never know for sure. Either way, Colin attacked him there in his office, using one of the maces from the armoury; taped him up, and probably explained his grievance and whole plan while Mr. Carver could do nothing to resist. And then Colin killed him."

"That was a bad moment for him, though," Cornelia resumed. "Not only did he have to move the body, but he had to leave Carver to bleed out first to minimise the risk of bloodstains. Time was getting tight! But part of the point of the curfew and general lights-out – his idea, of course – was to limit any threat of discovery. So far as moving Carver into position is concerned, Colin hefted a heavy mace right in front of Alex earlier; a quite literal show of strength, though naturally it's far easier to drag a body *down*stairs than *up*. It was also fortunate for him that poor roads and poor driving had kept poor Alex even later than planned – but it wouldn't have felt fortunate; he must have had some dark thoughts wondering if she would even get here. Of course, Colin was also responsible for Maria staying up late for reasons she clearly wanted to keep secret; a replacement dupe, perhaps?"

"Shall we move on with the, um, practical demonstration?" Alex asked her. She hadn't learned much about Cornelia from their few family gatherings over the years, but she *had* learned that her great-aunt would talk about mysteries all day if nobody stopped her.

"Oh, yes." Cornelia gave every impression of genuinely needing the reminder. "Alex and I decided that this locked-room illusion would particularly benefit from example, so we –"

"Mainly me," Alex mumbled.

"– arranged one or two things in order to show you what happened," Cornelia continued speaking. "For instance." She brandished an object in front of the group. It was a roll of tape.

Alex took the tape from Cornelia – she was the one who would be using it – and Cornelia, beckoning with a wizened finger, led them down the corridor. "Remember," Alex explained, "that it was the middle of the night; the windows were dark, and the lights were off. I couldn't see anything in the corridor except for the glint of metal on the last remaining key." In daylight, however, it was easy to distinguish the second door on the right in the north wing. Alex put a hand on the door. "I'm going to recreate the locked room I found," she said. "When I go in, I'll put a bit of tape on the inside of the door, and then I'll do what Colin did to disappear."

Alex was aware that she had more or less promised to perform magic right in front of them. The tape was just for show; the real seal *this* time was the fact that five people were going to watch her walk into the room, and then not find her inside it. How could it be done?

Cornelia had figured it out, and after a few hints pointing to certain of the day's activities, Alex had gotten the gist, too. It just remained to be proven – but it was an eerie and sinister feeling, stepping into the murderer's footsteps. Alex took a deep breath, and in a single swift movement slipped through the door.

The door slammed behind her, leaving her alone in the room. It looked exactly as it had when Alex had entered the previous night; she and Cornelia had already staged it just right, clearing away any tell-tale objects and opening the wardrobe so that it would be obvious there were no hiding-places. There were just two things Alex had to do. First, she unpeeled a length of tape from the roll and tore it off, sticking it across the doorframe and door to join the two together – and covering the keyhole in the process, just in case Yva was cheating and looking through it. And second... she moved, with difficulty, the object she had prepared earlier.

A minute later, with a sound of unpeeling tape, the door was shoved open. "Ready or not!" called Yva's unmistakeable voice, slightly muffled, and a rumble of footsteps rolled into the room.

Alex couldn't see any of them. Fortunately, they couldn't see her, either, as was clear from the way the footsteps began to thump around the room while confused voices reached her.

"The hell...?" came an indistinct grumble that could only be Quinn. "Where is she? Forget the tape, we all saw her walk in!"

"This is bizarre," she heard Vi breathe, close by. "No, she's not behind the door – but there's nowhere to hide."

"Then she must be – *here*!" an overexcited voice cried, followed by a faint but hurried rustling and creaking. Well, it wasn't a terrible idea, dismantling the bed, but it was still the wrong idea; Alex was nowhere near it. "Not even in the mattress?" Yva's obvious disappointment filtered through a few moments later.

Cornelia tutted loudly. "Don't be silly. How would she get inside that thing – or out, without leaving obvious traces?"

"Then where –" Footsteps spun around the room. "But the room's empty! What's the trick?"

"And I have another question," Vi joined in. "Why are we doing this *here*? I thought this was Maria's room."

A beat, as the implications sank in, and then it was Victoria who said, "Yes, I saw it immediately. I don't know how you did it, but she must be behind..."

"Well done," murmured Cornelia. "Of course, you had a number of advantages which Alex lacked, in the circumstances. You can come out now, Alex."

Alex didn't need telling twice; it was dark and not a little creepy in her hiding-place. Carefully, she reached forward and pushed a little, far enough to let a little light in, far enough to let her fingers out, and then she grasped the edge of the panelling and moved it aside.

To the people watching, mouths agape, it must have been like a nightmare, or a scene in *Castles in the Sky*. With a groan of wood, a section of the wall behind the door seemed to shift, tilt forwards, revealing a dark hollow behind it – and from that abyss, a hand reached out...

In moments, the illusion resolved itself into reality; Alex, gasping, shoved the tall sheet of wood-panelling to one side, leaning it against the corner so it would not fall. Behind her, the square passage that opened into the ensuite bathroom had one bare wall where the panelling had been removed.

"Attention, please," Cornelia announced. "Everyone take note, this is *not* a secret passage; it is an ordinary feature of six of the ten bedrooms of the house which everyone standing here has encountered. It may arguably have been transformed *into* a secret passage, Knox's 3rd allowing us one, but it is not by nature –"

"No, no, Victoria, it's alright," Vi interrupted, seeing Victoria staring at the dismembered wall panelling. "We tested this, they screw on and off like fun!" Victoria fixed him with a pained stare. "We were – we were sent to search for secret passages by Cornelia…?" he pleaded, dishonourably passing the buck.

"Oh, I never expected you to find any secret passages," Cornelia said, wryly. "That was just an excuse, I'm afraid. I sent you to see how easy it was to remove the panelling."

Yva turned on Cornelia, eyebrows aloft. "Then – you already *knew*? That it was Class C?"

"It followed logically from the premises," Cornelia said, as if to imply it was obvious. "Alex's experience presented two problems: The murderer's absence from a room sealed from the inside, and the disappearance from that room of the body and the door tape. I realised immediately that the second problem could be explained if the room Alex returned to was not, in fact, the same as the one she left. In a pitch-black corridor with a long line of doors, it's not difficult to say how the confusion could have been created."

"How did I know I'd come back to the same room? I'd left the door open, my backpack in the doorway, and the light on," Alex pointed out. "But while nobody could have removed the tape and Adam Carver's body in the minute I was away, they *could* open up the next door along, turn on the light, and move my bag across, and the gift-wrapped book, too – switching off this light and closing the door as they left. The door to the second room was never locked, but I never noticed it as there was no key in it – because its key was actually in *this* door, where it couldn't turn because of the tape stuffed into the lock. So long as I didn't notice that it was a shorter distance back to the room the second time – and under the circumstances, why would I? – then everything else would look convincing."

"And that's why Colin was hanging around in the corridors!" Yva realised. "He switched the rooms around in seconds, dashed across the landing, and then acted like he'd only just shown up."

"And by being there, he could show you that the body had vanished and prevent you from raising the alarm," Vi added.

"Yep," Alex admitted. "Right from the start, he was tricking me."

"Don't be too hard on yourself. You'd had a bad shock, and it was a clever trick," Cornelia said. "But you see why, in the cold light of day, I had an immediate suspicion that the rooms had been swapped. So what else, I asked myself, was possible with two different rooms? And the answer, as I knew from my own rather comfortable bedroom, was that some of the rooms had ensuite bathrooms."

Alex glanced over at the square space she had emerged from, which led into the ensuite. "The entrance is kind of hidden behind the door anyway. If you just unscrew the panelling at the end and push it forward from behind – and Colin had plenty of time to practice – then it just looks like a continuation of the wall." Alex glared at the nook; the simple answer seemed to be mocking her. "I'm not ashamed of being tricked," she reflected. "I was so panicked, and the light was so dim... But I should have figured it out when we found Vi and Yva taking the panels off earlier – in *this room*, even."

"I'd like to remind everyone that I was commanded, by the detective herself, to go on a wild goose chase for secret passages we all knew we wouldn't find," Yva scowled. "A fine way to treat your protégé."

"Stop calling yourself that. And I couldn't risk showing my hand to the murderer; just by his being on the scene, I had reason to suspect Colin," Cornelia sighed. "Of course, it's on the very same subject that he gave himself away with what was, in retrospect, a rather silly lie. I'll always wonder whether or not it was a deliberate clue."

"What did he say?" Victoria asked, in a small voice.

"He implied," Alex said, "that he'd left his room to get a drink of water. He even spilled it in front of me, so that I'd know." She paused. "But later, we learnt that Colin's room had an ensuite bathroom. Why didn't he just fill it from the tap?"

There's your smoking gun.

"Because not everyone drinks tap water? There are some places where people only drink it bottled," Yva objected, but they ignored her.

"But…" Victoria turned to Alex and Cornelia. "How did Colin convince Maria to let him use her room? This *was* hers, you said?"

"I said," mumbled Vi.

"He didn't convince her," Alex explained. "I guess he'd been staying in the south wing the past few days, next to you, Victoria?" She nodded. "But before everyone else arrived, he would have swapped to one of these rooms and taken both keys so nobody else could claim them and mess up his plan. He could have given his original room key to Maria – trying to look kind – and then when he attacked her overnight, he simply took back that key and swapped rooms again. It was all stage management."

Cornelia clapped her hands. "Which rather brings us to the second murder – the murder of Maria Bole. No practical demonstrations this time, but as what happened is really quite obvious, I don't anticipate objections. Shall we take the weight off our feet?"

The scene switched to the sitting room downstairs, a room Alex had seen but never set foot in. With the tension dissipating, they could rest, if not happily, then at least easily. As they took their seats, Alex let her eyes rest on Victoria Carver. She could tell that it would probably be a long time before Victoria was truly happy again, but as the truth came out bit by bit she seemed to be regaining some sense of self – with no more secrets and mysteries, she could slowly come to terms with the truth. That, Alex thought, might be another reason to solve mysteries; so that people could move on from tragedy.

Cornelia was ruling the roost from the spindly-legged chair she had mentioned, which turned out to be very old and very tall and very ornate, something like an ivy-clad gravestone. Alex had found a rather humbler and, she thought, comfier chair that got the job done without putting on a show. Of course, certain detectives really enjoy putting on a show.

"The flippant among you would say that the first locked room had a secret passage as its solution," Cornelia began, staring archly across the room of twisted light, the shape of clear and stained-glass windows shifting across faces in arcane patterns. "Would you like to know what the flippant explanation for the second locked room is?"

"I can't think of anything I would like more in the world!" Yva declared, scarcely bothering to conceal her flattery. She bounced back quickly.

"Well, why don't you set the scene, first," Cornelia suggested, receding into the shadows of her throne. "This is one of the ones where you were very nearly right, so you may as well have one last stab at it."

Alex rolled her eyes. If Yva was ever going to learn from her mistakes, it was a kindness to throw her a bone from time to time. But the way the fanfiction writer was rubbing her hands together in ghoulish pleasure still gave the impression that it was more than she deserved.

"It began at midnight – the witching hour, last boundary between dead yesterday and today born mewling," Yva intoned, and she was in storytelling mode again; her voice richer, deeper, projected as if over an open fire. It drew them all in despite themselves, and in the stained-glass shade, flames seemed to flicker across her face. "Colin West, the ruthless and impenitent murderer, quickly changed into outdoor clothes and left the room where he had carelessly abandoned the corpse of his victim, Adam Carver – in no hurry to hide his actions, for he felt neither shame nor fear, knowing that he was untouchable so long as night's velvet shades wreathed his actions like a shroud. Below, lured to a midnight rendezvous where none could penetrate their mysterious communication – the blameless Maria Bole, who merely saw an opportunity and took it, as we all would. But though West had doubtless invited her under the guise of secret negotiations and reconciliation, in fact his heart was set only on brutal and bloody murder from the start."

Alex restrained an interruption for the sake of getting this over with.

"The meeting was settled for the gatehouse," Yva continued, on perhaps less shaky ground, "for which reason Maria was lingering in the lobby at past eleven o'clock when she retrieved Alex, subsequently committing herself to the cold to avoid scrutiny. West arrived soon after; their footprints were quickly obscured by winter's treasure." (Somebody quickly stifled a laugh into a cough.) "And once there – it required only for Maria to be duped into turning her back for a second, and then a mace slipped from a museum exhibit and into a pocket knocked her to the ground in a trice. Instantly, West drew forth a roll of tape, and stopped up her mouth so she could not scream when she awoke – and then, with the brute strength concealed within his heavy frame, he dragged her out onto the snowy drawbridge, to a point he had doubtless previously established by careful measurements. He hurried away for a few seconds to retrieve a length of chain and a pair of padlocks from the tower storeroom – supplies he had previously determined existed, and likely prepared so as to be extracted within a moment – at which point he looped one end around Maria's wrist and padlocked it tight, fed the chain through the anchors at the drawbridge's upper corners, and then drew the remaining end to Maria's other wrist and padlocked it tightly there too, ensuring the chain was pulled taut in a triangle such that Maria could not move and would be, when the drawbridge was raised, suspended in the air. Following this –"

"Following this," Cornelia interrupted, "is when I imagine he rifled Maria's pockets for her room key and stole back to the house to switch their luggage around. I expect that's also when he hauled Carver's body back upstairs and hid it in the solarium; past midnight and with most of the lights off, he would be relatively secure from detection."

"I bet he took the sword from the house on the same trip," Alex added. "One mace missing would probably go unnoticed unless anyone took a really good look at the armoury, but the sword was a different story and would have been hard to smuggle out in daytime."

"Yes, *thank you*, kindly remember who's telling this story," huffed Yva. Not being allowed to show off seemed to bother her almost as much as being wrong. "*If* I may be allowed to continue without further rude interruptions: Following this, Colin did all that stuff you just heard, only I would've narrated it better. He then returned outside, dragging menacingly the broadsword, sheltering the hilt from the falling snow. This was the critical point – the minute where, if at all, it was most likely he would be overheard and discovered: When he lowered the portcullis. Would its echoing crash against the ground draw forth suspicious guests? It was possible, which was why he hadn't lowered the portcullis before returning inside – so he had to work quickly, steeling himself against all nerves. Leaving the broadsword momentarily in the gateway, he ran up the tower stairway to the controls, and lowered the portcullis. Almost falling over himself in his haste, he plunged back down – and, with the portcullis fallen, he then hefted the great broadsword and passed its blade through one of the holes in the grating, doubtless preselected based on calculations performed on the previous days. Pushed in to the hilt, which could not fit through, the weight of the blade held the sword in balance – making it a comparatively simple process, employing layers and layers of heavy-duty adhesive tape, to secure it in place. The stage was set; all that was now required to execute Maria in the most gruesome fashion was to pull the lever that would cause the drawbridge to rise. Certain, now, that nobody was coming to confront him, West returned to the gatehouse above, where he sabotaged the portcullis switch and set in process the plan of hideous ingenuity which would, in accordance with Carr-Rawson Class A locked-room murders, destroy his hated foe while he calmly sat down to breakfast, blood pudding on his plate! (Not literally.)"

With this underwhelming denouement, Yva's narrative lapsed. It was some moments before those not privy to the secret of the second murder realised that she wasn't going to continue. "Well?" demanded Quinn, exasperated. "What did he do, then?"

"I don't know," Yva shrugged. "I've been told I was nearly right, but nearly right is, annoyingly, still wrong. As I said, Colin must have set up some clever system, because he was there all through breakfast giving himself a perfect alibi. Classic Class A – automatic murder by a diabolical machine. It even explains why the front door was taped shut; it's easy enough to tape a door shut from the inside if you're *already* inside, which is exactly what he did, but it also makes it nicely impossible for the murderer to be hiding outside – since Colin couldn't have known it would snow that night and add an extra layer of proof that nobody had crossed to the gatehouse that morning. *Ergo*, the murder was really set in motion last night, it just didn't take effect until morning." She looked across to Cornelia again, irritation setting in. "Well?" she demanded, this time. "What *is* the flippant explanation for this one?"

Cornelia grinned just a little too widely, as if about to tell a joke she had been holding back for some time. "A self-removing machine which left no evidence –"

The explosion which followed was so predictable that Alex had already shuffled her chair back a bit. "That was *my* idea!" Yva screamed at Cornelia with a banshee's fury. "That was my idea and you spat on it! You stole from me!"

It came uneasily to Alex that, whether you were a socially anxious innocent or a terrible person who couldn't be trusted by anyone, it must be a killing blow to be betrayed by the only person you trust. Whether or not Cornelia even realised it, Yva's trust, or admiration, or at the very least *envy* was something that redeemed her, if only just the tiniest bit. For Yva's sake, then, Alex spoke up and said, "Cornelia didn't steal your idea. Hers is different."

Yva also had a disorientating way of drawing up short at times, of interrupting her own moods no matter how deeply they seemed to run. "What? How is it different?" she quick-draw replied, very suddenly controlled and comparatively calm again, and Alex wondered if her feelings were even really capable of running deep.

"You'd know already, if you had only let me finish my sentence," Cornelia scolded her. "To repeat what I had attempted to say," she resumed, with a glare that demanded silence, "Maria's murder was caused by a self-*removing* machine which left no evidence *in the gatehouse* – not a self-*destroying* machine which left no evidence at all. In other words, this theory is backed by actual, physical evidence – and you've all seen it."

"You sure about that?" Quinn quizzed her. "I haven't been outside all day; Victoria neither."

"Thank goodness," Alex heard Victoria mutter to herself.

"So," Quinn continued, "I don't see how we'd've seen any evidence out there."

"That's hardly an objection," Cornelia scoffed. "After all, I brought the evidence inside myself."

And she drew forth a hardback volume from *Castles in the Sky*, slightly battered. Volume Two, *Hand at the Threshold*…

"Now there's irony for you, Yva," Cornelia grinned. "One of the books she stole was the very instrument of Maria Bole's doom. Poetic justice, don't you think?"

Light seemed to be dawning on Yva, who looked ready to kick herself, but everyone else remained baffled. "Well, it's not just the book that's important," Alex pointed out. "There's also the packaging it came in – particularly all those loose loops of ribbon."

"True," Cornelia admitted. "But the book is the lynchpin, the one part of the mechanism which couldn't be replaced or done away with; and the rest, anyone could have gone and looked at the remainder of and understood, if they'd only asked the right question. And it was fairly apparent at a glance; you did notice the blackened ribbon-end, didn't you?"

Alex nodded. "I thought maybe it was dirt, but then later you told me it had been singed. And that really does make it pretty obvious just what sort of thing happened this morning."

"It's a straightforward deduction," Cornelia agreed. "How did the ribbon get burned? By the candles in the gatehouse, the only flames nearby. How did the gift leave the gatehouse? Well, considering that we found it in a battered state at the foot of the portcullis, it must have fallen down the portcullis shaft. And how did it come to fall? At this point it's natural to connect the burnt ribbon, the deliberate placement of candles in the gatehouse by the murderer, and the fact that he needed some way of pulling a lever downwards without being there in person…"

Yva was grinning now. "It's an arts-and-crafts solution," she said. "I should've adapted my string theory to use the ribbon that was already there – and candles only ever do one thing in a locked-room mystery. You wrap the book around with ribbon, leaving two very long loose ends. Tie one end into a loose loop and hang it over the top of the drawbridge lever, balance the book on the opposite end of the portcullis shaft near the door, and hold it up with the remaining end of ribbon. Then you slip out of the control room and bolt the gate, bringing your end of ribbon through the bars, and loop it around the bars and knot it to itself directly above the bolt. Using a thick roll of tape, tape over the bolt again and again –"

"I checked at the time, and the end of the tape was on the outside and pointing upwards, confirming that the bolt had been taped from that side," Cornelia supplemented. "The bars were too tight to reach through, but once the tape was anchored to the bolt you could roll it through the gap and it would swing down underneath, where you could retrieve it and repeat the process."

Yva nodded at her. "Anyway, all that tape doesn't just keep the room locked up, it gives you a broad enough base to stick a candle on – you could even gouge a hole for it – and all the candles will have been those multi-hour candles, so you can predict exactly where the flame will be at a certain time. You cut a notch in the candle at that point, pass the ribbon loop through it to touch the wick, and when the wick has reached that level then the ribbon will burn – and snap."

Alex resumed for the finishing touches. "The book's support fails and it falls down the shaft, which puts its weight on the ribbon around the lever and pulls *that* down, and once it's down then the last loop pulls off the lever and the whole thing falls to the bottom of the portcullis – where we found it," she concluded. "And meanwhile, the drawbridge is rising, bringing Maria towards the point of the sword..."

She didn't want to think about that aspect any more. The rest was enough.

"So, the top suspects were actually the ones at breakfast the whole time," Quinn nodded.

"And Colin did come down early," Victoria admitted. "Before we understood, he must have wanted to be seen."

"And he must have been pleased when people arrived late," Alex said, thinking of herself and Vi, "or left early, or never came at all."

"It certainly widened the pool of suspects and possibilities, though I was confident right away about what had really happened," Cornelia shrugged. "If you were only paying attention, it was quite obvious."

How well this went down with everyone else in the room was also quite obvious.

"Gloating is only fun when you get to do it yourself," Yva sniffed. "Move on already. There are still two mysteries left."

"But only one true murder," Alex pointed out. "Franny Smythe – though Colin didn't decide until this morning who it was going to be. But he knew *where* it would be; a remote part of the house where nobody would find a body until after his own death. He wanted us to think that the last victim was the murderer, who committed suicide – because that was actually *true*, it was just Franny who was a big red herring. It didn't make sense unless you understood the motive."

"For that reason, the last lines of the Author's notes hinted at the true order," Cornelia observed. "What were they, now – 'Let the game begin', 'Shall we continue?', 'I must interrupt you no more,' 'Until we meet again.' In retrospect, the third is obviously the last; and what more fitting than for the false fourth book to be a red herring?"

"But how could he have convinced Franny to follow him up there, though?" Victoria asked, waving a hand upwards. "My brother was never particularly... sociable. But he must have managed to lure her away almost as soon as I left the armoury with you two."

"Understandably, you never came into the solarium," Alex began, "so you didn't see Franny's phone, smashed up on the floor. That was a hint. Our theory is that Colin left a minute for the coast to clear, and then pretended to suddenly have the idea that the highest room in the house might get mobile reception. Franny took the bait and rushed upstairs, with Colin right behind her – and once they entered the room, well... she still had her back turned."

"And he didn't have to worry about being disturbed up there, either," Yva inserted herself. "I bet that was important. Setting up that locked room must have been complicated."

"A quadruple-locked room," Vi brooded. "Impossible in four ways. Colin couldn't have used either door."

"In a way, he used both," Cornelia could not resist throwing in. "Though I suppose you might say it was half-and-half..."

"Oh, come on!" Vi groaned, incredulous.

Cornelia, who apparently never tired of being cryptic even to the very moment of truth, merely grinned. "Alex, if you'd care to review the problem for us?"

Alex felt vaguely like a detective's secretary, as if she should be looking at a clipboard. "Inside the solarium, Franny was found hanged from the neck by a chain tethered to the arm of the late Mr. Carver, himself propped against the corridor door. That door was sealed airtight with tape stuck over the cracks, applied from inside the room, and the already airtight balcony door was locked, which can also only be done from the inside; the balcony itself was covered in an unbroken layer of snow, with no snow having fallen since nightfall," she recited. "Also, the balcony key was found in Victoria's pocket, put there while she was tied up in the armoury."

"Of course, while this appeared to take the balcony key out of the equation for Franny's murder, once you understand hers was really the *third* murder then the key comes back into play," Cornelia pointed out. "It was Colin who had smashed the jewellery box and stolen the balcony key, when he returned to the house after we discovered Maria's murder. He had it in his pocket the whole time, up until he found the chance, and the desire, to lure Franny up to the solarium and knock her down while she was distracted. Regardless of how badly she'd been injured, his first step was nonetheless to retrieve a roll of tape from whatever corner he'd hidden it in, and tie her up like all the other victims; then he hurried back to the corridor door and taped over the cracks – but, and this is the crucial element, the bottom edge he would have left only *half*-stuck, attached to the door but folded away from the floor. That didn't stop him from dragging Carver's body from the cupboard and propping it against the door, at which point it was practically locked, with no way for a human, at least, to pass through it without disturbing the seals."

"After that," Alex said, "he arranged the set-up which would slowly but surely kill Franny – putting a chain around her neck, hoisting her over the bars and tethering the chain tight to Mr. Carver's arm... Thankfully, she wouldn't have been conscious for any of it." It wasn't a nice thought regardless. The murders Colin had committed were particularly vindictive. But even so – "Maybe it was a relief to Colin that she was unconscious, too," she added. "Maybe it's wishful thinking, but I hope this wasn't the real him; that he had to really force himself."

Victoria nodded sadly along, but Yva spoilt the mood by rolling her eyes. "So naïve."

Alex glared at her. "Well, we'll never know," she reluctantly conceded. "Either way, afterwards Colin unlocked the balcony door

– but before he opened it, he'd have spent a few minutes setting up the way he'd *re*lock the door, which I'll let Great-Aunt Cornelia describe; he'd probably been testing it in secret for days. Today, though, he also had to deal with the unexpected snow on the balcony – but he improvised. Vi, could we see your crime scene photos for a second?"

Vi started, having resigned himself to being an audience member only, and quickly pulled out his phone to swipe his way to the balcony photographs. Once in her hands, Alex held up a picture of the snow-covered balcony, and pointed – to what *surrounded* the balcony.

"Colin left through the balcony door," she said, "but he didn't have to step onto the balcony itself. He put his feet on the railing."

Alex was glad nobody but her great-aunt had seen her own cry of self-reproach, after being nudged towards the explanation earlier. The railing, as had been observed at the time, was extremely ornate and naturally had any number of footholds – and was quite clear of snow.

"Yes, by putting your feet through the railings and holding onto the upper rail, it's possible for an agile person to move along the balcony without ever touching the ground," Cornelia explained. "The answer was literally in front of your eyes, but the illusion was seductive. The Author had done so many seemingly impossible things that another was accepted without question. Of course, that was not the full extent of his trickery in the solarium."

"When Colin left by the balcony, he left the key in the lock on the inside and closed the door, turning the handle behind him," Alex went on. "He re-entered through one of the other two balcony doors, which he'd have unlocked earlier in preparation and would relock after he was done, and then he returned to the corridor door of the solarium for his masterstroke. You'll probably get the idea if I say that it's to do with string."

"Oh, here we go!" Yva enthused. "With all that exercise junk in there, it'd be easy to tie the string to the key and loop it around enough stuff to lock the balcony just by pulling the end. And that's why he needed the open gap under the door!"

"Just so," Cornelia replied. "Though more likely Colin used ribbon, since he evidently had reels of the stuff. He would have threaded the key onto a length a bit longer than twice that of the room, with the key hanging from the middle and both ribbon-ends ultimately passing under the corridor door. On their way, one end could be twisted around a window handle, under the gym equipment, and finally under the door, to create a lever system which would turn the key when pulled; the other end of the ribbon would instead lead straight out from the key before being wound around a bar or some such and then again under the door. When Colin got back to the corridor door, the two ends of ribbon were waiting for him; he held both, pulled one to turn the key and lock the balcony, and he pulled the other to pull the key out of the balcony door altogether, hauling the whole arrangement of key and ribbon out under the corridor door to join him. At that point, the other balcony doors on the floor could be locked for good measure, and that left us with the locked room as we discovered it – with the exception of the untaped gap under the door. At that point, Colin only needed a way of folding down that last strip of tape so that it would stick against the floor, sealing the room entirely."

"But how could he do it?" repeated Quinn. "You went into the room and found it all stuck down. Only a person inside the room could do that."

"Well… not exactly," Alex said, tentatively. "This only works for the gap underneath a door – on most doors, the other three edges are overlapped by the doorframe – but it turns out that there is actually a way of taping over that gap from the other side of the door, if it's just wide enough. There's something else you can move with a piece of ribbon slipped under the door."

"Well, what is it?" urged Vi. "Is it an electric fan or someth–"

"The tape itself," Cornelia said simply.

Vi choked mid-sentence.

"It's quite straightforward when you try it for yourself," she continued. "As I explained, Colin ran a length of tape across the bottom of the door, wide enough that if pressed down it would stick to the floor, but folded upwards to leave the gap open. After that, he pressed a piece of ribbon across the entire length of the tape, with some extra at one end, and slipped that under the door with the ribbon-ends from the key (he could have just used one of those, if he was careful). Once on the other side of the door and with the balcony key retrieved, all that remained was to pull that additional ribbon to draw down the edge of the tape against the floor, with the rest of the strip following as the ribbon slowly unpeeled its way along. By the time the ribbon pulled entirely free, the final strip of tape would have stuck across the entire gap, even a little tucked in as if somebody had pushed it with their fingers from the inside – but really, it was *pulled* in from the outside." Cornelia leaned back in her chair complacently. "It's a perfect example of a Class B locked-room mystery, where the murderer was in the room to commit the crime and departed while making the door appear to have been locked from the inside."

"Colin even went one better and locked *two* doors from the wrong side," Alex said, "but only because he needed two doors for the trick to work at all. He couldn't leave through the taped door, and he couldn't retrieve the key through the locked door; it had to be both. Beating the snow was just a bonus; if he hadn't thought of a way to get across that, he'd probably just have swept the whole balcony."

It was clever, Alex admitted to herself. Taking a step back, looking at the locked room as if it had been a work of fiction – she was impressed. But was it right to feel that way about a real-life murderer? It was not easy to reconcile a stroke of genius with vengeful violence.

It was no real surprise who did reconcile it, though. "Fair play to him," Yva commented, as if they were still talking books; "that really is a solution worthy of the author of *Castles in the Sky*." She leaned back, her expression grudgingly respectful. "Maybe I *should* have given him more credit as a mystery creator."

"High praise, from you," Cornelia remarked. "Yes – it would have been perfectly acceptable had he only written his plans down rather than carrying them out."

Vi cleared his throat loudly. "Yes, can we please not forget that this man killed three people?" he reprimanded them. "Let's get some perspective here. Yes, we are mystery fans. Yes, Colin wrote our favourite books. Yes, he's a *murderer*. When this gets out, the fandom is over."

"That's your idea of perspective?" interrupted Victoria, and startling Vi who had for once quite forgotten her. "Your *fandom* is over? My *life* is over."

But it was Cornelia who shook her head. "Only the lives of the dead are over."

Alex, gladdened to see Cornelia express a little sympathy, also spoke up. "Victoria – I can't appreciate what you've lost, but please don't let what happened ruin your life; or ruin your memories of Colin, or Adam, or Maria and Franny either. It wouldn't be right only to remember what went wrong." She sought out Victoria's eyes, which only reluctantly met hers. "Don't give up. That was Colin's mistake."

Vi and Quinn nodded their agreement. But there were still uncomfortable questions left.

"So… how did he do it, though?" Quinn asked, looking back and forth between Alex and Cornelia. "Colin didn't want to face the music, I get that much – but how?"

Alex stood up. "We'll show you," she said. "This was Colin's last act, and I'm sure he thought it wouldn't hurt anyone else. Let's mourn that, at least."

Cornelia glanced across the room, at a clock too ornate to comfortably read. "Yes, it's time to wrap this up. The police will surely be here soon, and I want to hand them the solution giftwrapped with a bow."

Victoria flashed a look of dread upon the door to the corridor – knowing there was only one place left. "Do we have to?" she asked, quickly. "Will it change anything?"

Creaking like an old floorboard, Cornelia pushed herself up from her throne. "So long as you always have questions, it'll never truly be over," she said. "Decide for yourself if that's something you want."

She swept out of the room ahead of Alex, who followed. One by one, she heard footsteps join behind her; four sets of footsteps. Soon, it would indeed be over.

Nothing had changed in the armoury; the only thing that could change was how they felt about what had happened. Colin's body still lay uncovered on the floor. Alex found it harder to meet his gaze dead than alive. She did not know what to see in that cold and grim visage.

Looking back, she saw that one person *was* meeting Colin's dead eyes, at last. What did Victoria see there? Perhaps what she wanted to see. "What is there left, then?" she asked, her voice fluttering. "Colin had – finished – upstairs; he must have only just beaten me back to the room; must have watched me, through the very hinge of the door…"

"And struck the moment your back was turned," Cornelia supplied. "He couldn't risk you advertising that he and Franny had left the armoury; it would have been too much of a giveaway later. But he wanted to leave you in suspense as to who the murderer was, too, so he couldn't meet you face to face."

A bitter smile crossed Victoria's face. "He only ever disagreed with me in writing," she said. "Never in person."

"No wonder he took to Besieging Heaven," said Vi. "The real DaVinciCorpse was not what I imagined."

Yva shrugged. "Some people have weird problems speaking their mind. I wonder what kind of a face he wore when he was committing murder?"

"We almost found out," Alex said, and was not sure if she would have wanted to. "We were probably only a few seconds short of catching him with Victoria…" Even though no murder had happened in that room, in the end, she still felt guilty for not having been able to stop something that had happened just a few walls away, just metres away, had she but known it.

"Don't beat yourself up about it," Yva, of all people, said. "Fortune favours the bold, and murderers have the luck of the devil." She paused. "And it would've been pretty rubbish if we'd just caught him red-handed before he could get to the last impossibility."

There was nothing like Yva's insensitivity to get Alex explaining again. "Well, anyway, what happened right after that isn't difficult to imagine," she said. "Colin tied up Victoria with tape so she couldn't move or tell what was happening, and then he taped the door shut, too. There's no trick there now that we know Colin was the murderer; he just sealed up the door himself and then never left the room. It's what follows that's more complicated."

"Like how he came to be tied up and stabbed in the back, and then shoved in an iron maiden which was itself tied up," Quinn pointed out, his expression dour as ever. "If you can explain *that*, I'll believe in magic."

"Please," Cornelia scowled petulantly. "It's not magic. It's just taking advantage of a lack of imagination about what's physically possible. And as for the iron maiden being tied shut – that was immediately suspicious. Why was the ribbon there? To prove that Colin could not have killed himself? And yet fastening things on the wrong side of doors was the murderer's forte. It wasn't proof of anything. Rather, it was another impossible challenge."

Alex had been standing expectantly beside Cornelia until the vital moment, and reached into her backpack to draw forth one last book – Colin's last, *A Coffin Nail Creaks*. Suppressing a little queasiness, Alex carried the book across the room, in the direction of the iron maiden and the body on the floor.

Cornelia was continuing her explanation while Alex worked. "Just to tie up a few loose ends, I should note that we never did find a roll of tape in this room, or in any other suspicious place," she was saying. "But why would Colin leave free evidence just lying around when he had a bottomless pit to throw it all in? Consider that there are marks on the side of this cabinet showing that a couple of strips of tape have been *removed*. Colin could have peeled off two last lengths, stuck them down for when he needed them – and then used the balcony key to unlock one of these windows and throw the tape roll into the sea, along with all that string from the solarium and the absent mace, too. Then he could lock up the window and place the key inside Victoria's pocket, and nobody would be any the wiser. At that point, he could loosely bind his own ankles with the first strip of tape, just enough that he could still comfortably hop or shuffle about. But he had something important to do before he could tape his own wrists together."

"And what was that?" asked Vi.

"Stab himself in the back," Cornelia said.

Alex stepped back from the iron maiden, contemplating her handiwork. Yes, she hadn't had as much chance as Colin would have to practice it, but if it was just a matter of reconstructing what he had done, it wasn't so difficult. This seemed to eliminate the final problem; which just left eliminating the penultimate problem, and Cornelia's solution was earning her no end of complaints.

"People can't just stab themselves in the back!" Quinn was roaring. "And even if they did they wouldn't just go walking about afterwards!"

"If somebody has been stabbed in the back, there needs to be someone else to play backstabber," Vi declared. "I've never heard of any murder mystery written so sloppily- as to claim otherwise."

"Then you haven't read widely enough," snapped Cornelia. "Anthony Boucher debunked this myth in –"

"You really can stab yourself in the back, though," Alex said, arriving back in time to prevent a retro spoiler. "You said it yourself earlier, Vi – people are more flexible than you'd think. It just depends where you're aiming for."

"Some angles are, in fairness, impossible for normal people with no hypermobility," Cornelia grumbled, "and even more for people whose joints aren't what they used to be. But it's definitely possible. Remember the angle you said Colin had been stabbed from, Yva – a right-handed upwards strike? Did you never wonder why the attacker didn't simply stab him straight rather than choosing such a finicky angle?"

The trick is not to go over your shoulder. Alex traced her right thumb across her waist and, passing her arm behind her back, drew a line upwards until her thumb was pointing up through the back of her ribcage, just left of her spine, towards her heart. "It's definitely awkward," she admitted. "Nobody would do it unless they wanted to fake an attempted murder – or a real one. But that's exactly what Colin was going for."

There was a certain begrudging assent to this argument, but Quinn scratched his head. "Haven't you just killed him, though? He still has to tape his own wrists and tie himself into the iron maiden. Good luck doing that with a knife in your back."

"He didn't need luck," Alex said. "And" – she sighed – "Yva already covered this earlier, and she was right. Colin was pretty heavy-set. It was possible for him to stab himself deep enough for the dagger to lodge, without actually piercing his heart."

Victoria made a sharp noise and looked away. Vi and Quinn went rather pale. "He didn't go any easier on himself than anyone else," Vi murmured, and shook his head. "Why didn't he just *tell* someone?"

"We wouldn't have believed him," Alex sighed. "Or at least –
he wouldn't have believed that we'd believe him."

"And his obsession with murder mysteries suggested another
way," Cornelia mused. "A way which, for a man like him, might
even have seemed easier than taking the risk of opening up to another
person."

Alex reflected sadly on what felt like her failure as a friend, even
to a friend she'd never really had until today. She had not known
Colin – or rather, DaVinciCorpse – particularly well; she doubted
anyone had known him particularly well. Most friendships on
Besieging Heaven were more casual than that; a few people had
formed closer and more intense relationships, but just a handful. If
even the most respected person on the site had claimed to be the true
author of the series, would anyone have taken that seriously?

"So are you going to finish this explanation ever?" Yva
impatiently barged in. "Colin just taped his own wrists afterwards;
totally possible, probably easier with tape than with anything else.
And then he just had to get in the iron maiden, pull the door shut –"

"Yva, we were *there*," interrupted Alex. "Just try and be
sensitive for one minute, okay?" She sighed, and reasserted control;
she would never have thought it would come so naturally. "But
you're right. Once in the iron maiden, it was easy; in fact, it's
because the iron maiden is a fake that he had room to manoeuvre.
The magic trick was essential to his plan."

"And that's why all the blood was in the iron maiden regardless,"
Yva said, snapping her fingers. "That just leaves tying the iron
maiden shut, and it'll be case closed!"

Victoria glared at her with a searing hatred which seemed to wash
off Yva like water. Nothing was going to change her, and Alex saw
now why Cornelia didn't even try. For Yva to learn and grow as a
person seemed no more likely than it was for Colin or even Adam
Carver to have overcome their own flaws. You have to recognise
them as flaws first.

Cornelia coughed gently. "Time to close the lid on this, I think,"
she declared. "Just a little longer, Victoria. Colin's final moments
were not his final move…"

She was right. It was time to finish this.

Alex stepped away from Yva, whose grin faded into a milder and slightly flattering interest as she saw what had been prepared across the room, around the iron maiden. Alex had rewrapped *A Coffin Nail Creaks* and hooped the many extra loops of ribbon over the top of the metal coffin so it resembled a hellish Christmas tree – but she had left the door to the chamber wide open, and the repackaged book itself was balanced atop the door, not unlike a bucket of water left atop a doorframe to soak people. The aim here, though, was slightly different.

"I'm not actually going to climb in there, obviously," Alex pointed out. "But I'm sure you understand what happened. Colin had set up the iron maiden like this before he stabbed and bound himself. Then he shuffled his way inside... and because his hands were taped in front of him, he could reach forwards" – she took a deep breath – "and pull the door shut."

Alex gave the door a swift shove, and everything fell into place.

Dislodged, the dead man's present slipped down the front of the iron maiden, pulling its loose loops of ribbon with it. But as the surface of the iron maiden widened, sheer and round when closed, the loops pulled tight – until at last they were drawn taut around the coffin, and could fall no farther. The result was just as they'd found it: The iron maiden now had rings of ribbon tying it shut, sealing the door closed. And it could be done even if the person who had set it up was inside…

Alex looked at the perverse sight, the gruesome icon of torture with the cheerful ribbon and birthday present wrapped around it, and felt a sense of deep weariness settle over her. It was like a portrait of Carver's Rest. "After that," she said, "he only had to lean back, and it was all over."

And it was all over. The mystery had been solved, and the murderer lay dead at Alex's feet. Who he was, how he had done it, and why he wanted to – all had been answered. Alex felt her legs start to sag beneath her, and put a hand out to the wall to steady herself; with the urgency of explaining the murders now resolved, it was as if the terrible strain of the past twelve hours, nausea, sleeplessness and hunger were catching up with her all at once, having politely waited their turn. The crimes of Carver's Rest, so ghastly and unreal, had been locked away as the coffin drew shut –

all mysteries and impossible murders drifting back into the realm of fiction, where some would say they belonged. The proud but slightly mournful smile upon the time-worn face of Cornelia Crow suggested that not everyone would agree.

Alex had set out to avenge Adam Carver's death, but now she was no longer sure who had been avenged. With Colin West dead as well, she was no longer sure who had suffered the most. What mattered was that the suffering which had claimed four lives had now ended – and she and Cornelia Crow had shown why; and so that chain of suffering would add no further links. However prurient it might have felt to be a detective, who could say what would have happened if the mystery had gone unsolved? Forensic science could have cracked the case, but would the police have really understood?

Similar thoughts had evidently been passing through the mind of someone else. Standing beside Cornelia, Alex was surprised when the two of them were approached, breaking the stillness and the silence, by Victoria Carver.

"One day, I will want to thank you for this," Victoria said; and it seemed to cost her a lot to admit it. "I have to believe that I will want that. Right now, everything is – so raw. Having to hear what my brother, and my husband, did… But I think one day I will be happier for having heard it this way. Not just what happened, but why it happened." And she bowed her head.

Relieved though she was at having solved the mystery, Alex had no idea how to respond to anything resembling praise. She didn't feel as if she had done most of the work – but she might have to get used to being important. "There's really no need…" she began.

"All in a day's work," Cornelia said affably. Although she had spent the day seeming thrilled, determined, moved in a way Alex had never seen her before when she only sat in her dark home reading mystery novels – now that it was all over, she seemed so very much at ease that it was as if nothing had happened at all. It had all come so naturally to her.

Alex thought it would be some time before she herself was able to move on, though – and she was sure the same must be true of Victoria Carver. "What will you do next?" she asked her. "After everything is sorted out?"

Victoria gave an exhausted sigh, looking as tired as anyone must after being dragged to their lowest and out again. "I don't really know," she admitted. "I'll need time to grieve – for Adam and for Colin – and then I suppose I'll have to do some hard thinking about what to do about their legacy. This terrible ending was all because their work meant so much to them, and I don't want it just to be buried in ignominy."

"I'd be happy to help," Vi piped up. "Nobody knows more about the *Castles in the Sky* fandom than me. I'm sure we can figure out a way to steer the course, and create a legacy which people can still admire."

"If that's your choice, count me in," Quinn said abruptly. "*Castles in the Sky* did a lot of good for me, and though I don't make a song and dance of it, I've always been proud of my work. No matter what happened behind the scenes, I'm not going to put it behind me."

Yva's eyes were shining with self-assurance once again. "I'm proud of *my* work, too – since it's pretty much official now that, with a little help, I wrote the real last book in the series," she bragged. "But next time, I'll write something better, all on my own. Colin gave us a wonderful mystery here – and it makes me want to cook up my own taped room, with a solution nobody else has ever thought of..."

Alex looked at them all. She had not expected such a truce; and it gladdened her. "Well, if it's okay to think this, then – I'm proud too," she said at last. "I'm sad about everything, and nothing's going to be the same, but I'm glad that I could figure out the truth."

Cornelia smiled at her, and Alex felt that, yes, perhaps the old lady was proud of something, too – or someone. "There is much to be said for not letting one's talent lie fallow," she grinned.

"Perhaps we should call that the moral to this story," Vi suggested, and looked disappointed by the groans. Infamously, every volume of *Castles in the Sky* ended with the narrator delivering an increasingly ridiculous moral. There was considerable debate as to whether to take them seriously.

Alex, for her part, had always been on the fence about the morals. "I hope this story has a better moral than that."

"I hate morals," Yva said, and nobody doubted it. "I do have one last question, though."

Alex sighed – something she felt she had been doing a lot lately, and would be doing a lot more in future. "Go on."

Yva cocked her head. "I know it doesn't matter, because we had all three before this – but what class of locked room covers suicide?"

It was at this point that Victoria and Quinn turned around and left the room, while Vi shook his head in exasperation. But Cornelia seemed intrigued, and gave the question the time of day. "Suicide should normally fall under Class A, where the lock is genuine but the murder is disguised – the idea being that there was no murder, and therefore no murderer in the room," she lectured. "I do wonder if there's a case for Class C, though – where the murderer is still hiding in the room. There's an argument that that's true."

Alex was surprised to find that the problem had caught her imagination – and her heart. "I guess it depends on your point of view," she said. "Did Colin make the ultimate escape from a perfect locked room? Or is he still trapped here, and can never leave?"

The four of them cast one final look upon him – upon their fallen friend and enemy, Colin West; both a fellow fan and the very object of their admiration, a companion in detection and the shadowy author of the mystery. Was he in the room with them, even now? Or was the real Colin West somewhere they had never seen?

This, at least, was an insoluble problem – a question put to rest only by distraction. All the living and dead occupants of the house were disturbed, if not by a noise, then by a force – a juddering, chopping vibration that set a tremor through the walls of the house, passing through glass and stone as freely as through empty space. They did not realise the clouds had parted until a shape approaching through the air scattered the sunlight.

"Finally," Alex said, and she crossed to the window and looked up into the sky. "The police have arrived."

"If they want me," replied Cornelia, turning for the door, "I'll be reading."

AUTHOR'S NOTE

Dear Reader,

There is an evil spirit which is driving me to kill.

It has always been with us and haunted others before me; and those who read its victims' confessions, it possesses with an irresistible compulsion.

As long as somebody is reading this, that spirit is sure to kill again.

Regards,

The Author

www.ingramcontent.com/pod-product-compliance
Lightning Source LLC
Chambersburg PA
CBHW051440050726
47593CB00005B/1868